'May I present myself? I am Matthew Nchembe. But you must know that . . . I will shake your hand.'

Each had a serious glint in his eyes. It was the first time Brian had ever shaken an African by the hand.

'Now we are friends,' Brian stated with determination, 'and I trust you.'

It was, he believed, the best way in which he could return the other's similar compliment and, as he spoke, a strange feeling of kinship washed over him, an emotion he had never before experienced. He realised quite suddenly he very much liked this African, this terrorist, this enemy . . .

'We shall meet again,' Nchembe predicted. 'If you pass Wamumu again, maybe the inspector will allow you to visit me.'

'I'd like that.'

'Be a good *mzungu*,' Nchembe said suddenly, his single hand tightening. 'Remember we will need people like you in the new Africa, the black Africa.'

Also in Arrow by Martin Booth

HIROSHIMA JOE
THE JADE PAVILION

BLACK CHAMELEON

Martin Booth

for Bill.

a bit of Africana

[signature]

ARROW BOOKS

Arrow Books Limited
20 Vauxhall Bridge Road, London SW1V 2SA

An imprint of Random Century Group

London Melbourne Sydney Auckland
Johannesburg and agencies throughout
the world

First published in Great Britain by Hutchinson 1988
Arrow edition 1989

© Martin Booth 1988

This book is sold subject to the condition that it shall not,
by way of trade or otherwise, be lent, re-sold, hired out
or otherwise circulated without the publisher's prior
consent in any form of binding or cover other than that
in which it is published and without a similar condition
including this condition being imposed upon the
subsequent purchaser

Printed and bound in Great Britain by
Courier International Ltd, Tiptree, Essex

ISBN 0 09 960360 8

Kenya: 1956

1

Brian lay on his back in the grass, watching a locust climb the thick stem by his head. It was a large insect, twice the size of his thumb, its body emerald green with ochreous dots haphazardly decorating its horny thorax. From the shine on its body, it might have been varnished. It had three needle-sharp spines on its scissored hind leg – it had only one leg as the result of a skirmish with a black-and-white shrike, which Brian had observed.

The sunlight was brilliant, already hot; in the segment of sky over his head, Brian could see not even a hint of cloud. He had removed his pullover before stepping into the bush, partly because he was too warm and partly to avoid burrs hooking the wool: to remove them usually unravelled the knitting and infuriated his mother. What was more, this particular pullover was a prized possession sent out to him by his grandmother in Devizes who had knitted it specifically to his own requirements – khaki, tight-fitting with sleeves which reached only as far as his biceps, and with brown denim patches sewn onto the shoulders so that the butt of a rifle should not wear the wool thin. Already, in just the months since Christmas, the patches had become besmirched with oil.

This locust was not one of the common locusts, buff-brown with olive markings and half its size. It might, he thought, be a kind of giant grasshopper. Not only was it brilliant green but, when it flew, its wings were carmine and made a rustling louder even than the biggest of the dragonflies which inhabited the Loriam Swamp and the banks of the Tana River.

Gradually, it made its way higher up the stem. A warm breeze riffled through the grass; the locust clung on with its forelegs, swaying unsteadily from side to side. It was then that Brian noticed it had lost not only a long jumping leg when the

3

bird had swooped at it but also a large section of one wing-case.

'Titch!'

He sat up but the grass was too tall for him to be seen.

'Titch! Titchner!' the voice repeated with a sharp and worried edge. 'Where are you?'

Brian made no immediate reply, savouring Chopping's concern.

There was a hustling sound as a stone rattled through the dry grass-stalks to thud against an ant hill beneath a stunted wait-a-bit thorn bush.

'Don't pillock about.' The anxious voice had risen a semitone with fear.

'I am a member of the Fuckawi tribe,' Brian called in a low voice with what he hoped was a spooky accent. There was a silence from the direction of the road then another stone thumped against the ant hill.

'Never heard of them,' replied Chopping, frustratedly reiterating, 'Where are you?'

Brian stood, brushing the tall grass aside with his hands, walking as if wading through the cover.

'That first rock nearly hit me. What do you want to start chucking rocks for?'

'I thought the Micks —' Chopping began, but Brian's sardonic snort cut him off.

'The Micks! The Micks!' he teased derisively. 'The Micky Mouses! The Mau-Mickey-Mau-Mouses.... You thought I'd been caught. For God's sake! If I'd been captured ten yards off the road do you think they'd have left you standing there shouting your head off? Anyway, most of the Mau-Mau are in detention or deep in the Aberdare Forest...'

Brian gained the murram road and sat on the bumper of the broken-down Land Rover. It was, he reasoned optimistically, still nine hours till evening, and the boy was sure to be back with assistance by then. He smacked at a fly which had landed on his thigh just below the hem of his very short shorts. It fell dead in the dust and he picked it up and placed it on his palm, looking closely at it.

'Don't you get tired of creepy-crawlies?' Chopping asked. 'No wonder they call you "Bugger" at school.'

'No, I don't.'

The fly was not a dreaded tsetse but a sort of bluebottle. Its abdomen was covered with black bristles and glinted azure in the sun. In death, its sucker-tipped proboscis projected beneath bulbous, glossy eyes.

Hanging from the front nut of the spare wheel-mounting on the bonnet was a canvas water bag. Brian flicked the fly off his hand and, pulling the bung and tipping the bag, rinsed his hands and face.

Chopping was watching the bush with a nervous eye. Something spooked a flock of weaver birds in a nearby umbrella thorn acacia, and he spun his head as they rose in a yellowish haze, alarming each other.

'Why are those weavers taking fright?' Chopping asked.

Brian squinted against the glare of the sun.

'There're ten Micks crouching in the shade, waiting to shoot them down with Patchetts,' he reported. A cicada scratched its metallic noise briefly from a rotting stump. 'Hear that? They're loading their magazines.'

'That's not funny.'

'Then why ask such a damn-fool question. How should I know? Maybe there's a snake in the tree. Maybe that shrike's about. Maybe there's a *chui* underneath waiting to leap into the branches.'

Chopping reached into the Land Rover and pulled his rifle out from under the crumpled heap which was their tent.

'Is that for the Micks or the *chui*?'

Chopping made no reply.

'You'll not drop a full-grown leopard with a two-two at this range unless you can get him in the head.' Brian scanned the tree once more. 'There! Third big bough up on the left. See it?'

'No,' said Chopping.

'There!' Brian said again, his voice dropping. 'Just coming into the sun...'

'No,' then, 'Yes! What is it?'

5

'Schnook of some sort. Want to go and see? Could get him with a close shot...'

Chopping hesitated, then lowered his rifle.

'I don't think so. The last one I shot I had made into a wallet after I'd cured it. But it still ponged like hell. Of saltpetre as much as dead snake.'

Brian sat down again on the bumper and leaned forward. His back was in the shade of the bonnet and radiator but the sun on the nape of his neck seared into him.

'Let's put the roof on. It's getting hotter.'

As they struggled with the tarpaulin, hauling it over the framework of iron rods and pressing the studs against the steel nipples over the windscreen, Chopping said, 'What was that tribe?'

'What tribe? Oh! You mean the Fuckawi. They're a tribe living up near Lake Rudolf,' Brian explained solemnly. 'They live in long grass over eight feet tall and they are only four feet high so when they run through the grass from village to village, or on their way to their *shambas*, they have to jump up and down every now and then to see over the top. And when they jump, so everyone knows they're coming and they don't think it's a Masai raiding party, they shout, "We're the Fuckawi! We're the Fuckawi!"' And he jumped up and down, ramrod straight like a Masai moran.

'It's all desert up by Lake Rudolf. I flew over there in a Locust Survey Cessna with my father...'

'Oh! Come on!' Brian exclaimed, his humour giving way to mild exasperation as he considered that he was to spend the next six days in Chopping's company. 'Where the fuck are we? Where the fuck are we? It's a joke!'

Finally, Chopping understood and laughed. Brian gave him a comradely but painful punch on the arm as he climbed into the driver's seat.

As the sun rose higher, Chopping grew increasingly apprehensive. He fidgeted, walked around the Land Rover, kicked the wheels despondently and weighed the canvas water bag in his hands at least twice every hour as if they were stranded in a parched landscape far from human succour. He kept his .22 on one of the side-benches in the back of the

6

vehicle, a bullet in the breach. He drank little but often had to relieve himself. He did not then seek the privacy of the roadside cover, preferring instead to stand in the open facing a lantana bush covered with red murram dust.

The few Africans who passed by on foot or occasionally on their bicycles drew suspicious glances from him and he did not, as Brian did, respond to their cheerful greetings.

'You really are a bit of a prick,' Brian said at last, breaking a fifteen minute silence during which Chopping had patrolled the vehicle twice and strolled vigilantly down the road for thirty yards in either direction.

'Why?' he asked belligerently.

'Because there's nothing to get het up about. The boy'll be back with a repair man from Fort Hall. That's only twelve miles or so. There's no point getting worked into a lather ...'

'And what if ...' Chopping began.

'What if! If he can't get one he'll either 'phone my father or go on to Thika. There's a garage there. We drove past it. A Stanvac one.'

'And they do Land Rovers, do they?'

There was a sarcastic edge to Chopping's question which Brian chose to ignore. His companion was getting on his nerves.

'Let's eat,' he said matter-of-factly. 'Oudu's packed some boiled eggs and there's some lettuce and bread in the tin ...'

As Brian sliced the eggs on the lid of the tin with his sheath knife, a small African boy appeared from the tall grass. He came without any sound, startling Chopping, causing him to reach for his gun.

'Scared of a *toto*?' Brian asked.

'He shouldn't creep up like that.'

Brian smiled at the boy and said, '*Jambo.*'

'*Jambo, bwana,*' he answered shyly but made no attempt to approach the Land Rover. He had seen Chopping move and had caught sight of the rifle. Both made him wary. Guns in anybody's hands meant but one thing to him.

'*Habari? Njoo hapa,*' Brian invited, beckoning to the child; yet as soon as he raised his arm, the boy turned and ran off through the grass from which he had materialized, the

7

progress of his departure announced by birds as he flushed them from the foliage.

'Why'd he run off like that?' said Chopping.

With an air of finality, Brian put his knife down on the seat and looked Chopping straight in the eye.

'Now look; let's get things in the open. We're going to be out here for a week. I want to get some shooting in and so do you. Where we're going it'll be remote, possibly lonely and distinctly dangerous at times. The area's apparently crawling with leopard, got a good lion population and not a great deal of human habitation. I don't want to waste my game licence, and I don't suppose you want to waste yours.'

'Meaning?'

'Meaning if you're so skittish here, on a road and near a village, then what the hell are you going to be like under canvas in the bush?'

In the distance, from the direction of Embu, a dust cloud was appearing which could only signal the approach of another vehicle, the first they would have seen since leaving the main road and breaking down. Chopping looked at the dust cloud. He assessed it would be another five minutes before the vehicle causing it reached them.

'I'm merely being cautious,' he defended himself. 'This was a bloody dangerous place in the Emergency.'

'It isn't now...'

'Who says?' Chopping interrupted. 'Just because thousands of Mau Mau are in the clink doesn't mean some aren't still on the loose. They haven't caught Kimathi yet. He's their damn general...'

'Don't you read the papers?'

'No. Most of it's propaganda these days,' Chopping stated.

Brian was getting impatient: he was regretting having agreed to take Chopping along, but his father had made it a pre-condition of his borrowing the Land Rover.

Chopping's parents had recently divorced, his mother leaving for Mauritius with her lover, and Brian's father had suggested that Chopping go shooting with his son to take his mind off domestic matters. To that end, Brian said to himself, the trip was already successful. Chopping was no longer

8

concerned with his parents' separation. Instead, he was more worried about having his throat cut by a Mau Mau terrorist.

'Last week's *East African Standard*. The police reported Kimathi and his gang penned in to a small area of the Aberdares thirty-five miles west of Nyeri. We're forty miles south-east of Nyeri. You're the Maths genius in our year. You work out the length of the third side of the triangle...'

The cloud was now less a smudge on the horizon and more a definite plume of murram dust.

'There are no Micks here,' Brian continued with determination. 'They've never been where we're going, beyond Tharaka. And Kimathi, if he has it in for you personally, will have to climb over Mount Kenya and get down the other side before he can get you in his sights.'

The drumming of heavy-duty tyres drew closer, and another Land Rover came into sight down the long line of the road, set against a backdrop of billows of dust folding outwards from its wheels. As it came closer it began to slow and the dust behind swept forward to engulf it. When it halted in front of the boys' broken-down vehicle, the dust surged over them, causing Brian and Timothy Chopping to hold their breath, purse their lips and screw their eyes up tight.

'So!' called a voice from the centre of the dust. 'Which of you is Master Titchner?'

'I am,' Brian announced, squinting through slit eyes to ensure the worst of the dust was passed.

'I'm Inspector Broomhall. Now, what's up?'

Brian opened his eyes to see a police officer standing before him. His khaki socks were dusted with red grit and he wore a revolver in a holster with a leather flap folded over the butt.

'The drive shaft's cracked, sir,' Brian said.

'Reverse the *gari*,' Broomhall ordered his African driver, 'and back up to the front of this *bwana*'s *gari*. Then you pair of beauties,' he indicated two bare-footed Africans seated in the rear of his vehicle and both dressed in khaki shorts and white vests, 'get a rope round the bumper. '*Pesi*, '*pesi*!'

'*Ndio, bwana*,' the driver replied and, jarring the gearbox into first, drove off to turn.

9

'Got a call from your father,' the inspector explained. 'Your boy couldn't get anyone at Fort Hall so he 'phoned Nairobi and your dad rang me. We're in the club together...'

Brian expressed his thanks as the police vehicle backed and the two Africans leaped out to fasten the tow-rope.

'The universal joint's gone, too,' Broomhall commented, bending down and looking beneath the Land Rover.

'It happened as we went into that *donga*.' Brian pointed to a dried-up river bed a hundred yards down the road. 'I don't think we bottomed on it. The shaft just went.'

'It happens,' the inspector said laconically, straightening up. 'If you get in and steer...' he suggested.

'Where are we going, sir?' Chopping asked. 'Are you taking us to Embu?'

'Nope. We'll give you a tow to Wamumu. There we can certainly replace your U J and maybe do something about the drive shaft. See how bad the damage is. By the way, your boy's returned to Nairobi. Your father wants him back. You,' he addressed Chopping, 'riding with us?'

Chopping nodded and clambered into the rear of the police Land Rover with the two Africans. Brian was pleased to see his hunting companion had chosen to travel apart.

The drive was slow. They had to cross more than a dozen *dongas*, and the road, being little used, had been ungraded since the rains. The sides of each *donga* were steep and the towing vehicle had not only to get itself up each bank but also hoist up Brian's Land Rover. The rope had, at all costs, to be kept clear of the ground. If it rubbed on the abrasive earth it would fray. In the bottom of several of the *dongas* the deep, soft sand was an added hazard; the tow-rope had to be untied and the disabled Land Rover pulled through by means of the winch mounted on the police vehicle. It was a long process and although they had less than ten miles to go, it took the better part of the afternoon. By the time they reached Wamumu the sun was well down, the evening birds beginning to call in the surrounding bush.

They halted before a large enclosure surrounded by a barbed-wire fence ten feet high and supported on stout wooden poles. Along the fence-top as well as on the ground to either side of it were rolls of barbed-wire, the latter staked to the stony earth by strong metal rods.

As the tow-rope was unhitched and stowed in the tool compartment of the police Land Rover, Brian thanked the inspector for his help.

'We'll see what we can do for your buggy in the morning. You're on a hunting trip, aren't you?'

'We were hoping to be. Only for six days – five really: we've to be back on the sixth. We were hoping to shoot near Grand Falls – or between Tharaka and Dami – if the crossing point over the Tana's still okay.'

'Just as well you broke down here then,' the policeman commented. 'Out there you'd be stuck for days on end. Tonight,' he gazed about, 'you'd best pitch your tent about a quarter of a mile down that-a-way.'

He pointed in the direction of a drop in the land and a clump of acacia trees on to the branches of which the lowering sun was shining, picking out the silverish bark.

'Is there water down there?' Chopping asked.

'Water! About here, at this time of year? Not a chance. I'll see a trusty brings a *dhebi* full down pronto.'

'A trusty?' Chopping enquired.

'Wamumu's a detention centre,' Broomhall explained. 'We've got six hundred of Jomo's lot locked up here. Still, nothing to worry about. They're as near as dammit rehabilitated by now – and most were pretty reluctant oath-takers in the first place. The tough nuts are up near Marsabit. Northern Frontier Province. All we've got here are those who were coerced in or went in out of some misplaced ideal. Or because it offered an alternative to digging the *shamba*.'

'Can't they cut their way out? Or tunnel?' asked Brian.

'They probably could, but most don't want to. The food's regular and they don't have to work hard at anything much. For many, as I say, it beats sweating in the *shambas*, though they do grow some crops here about the place, inside and outside the wire. Just mealies and so on. We let some of them wander about during the day. They come back in at night. Still, as a precaution, can you please give me the bolts from your guns? And your ammo. I must take them to the office

11

and lock them up. Nothing to concern yourselves about: you can have it all back in the daytime.'

Brian cheerfully surrendered his bolt and ammunition but it was not without a show of reluctance that Chopping disabled his firearm.

Broomhall bade them good night, then called to one of the police askaris at the gate.

'*Moja dhebi ya maji.*'

Before they had even erected the main poles of their tent, an African in his late thirties arrived with a square tin kerosene container full of water. He placed it by the nearest acacia, covering it with the sopping cloth which had hung over the rim as he had carried it by a makeshift wooden handle. The sides of the container were blackened with woodsmoke.

'*Asante sana,*' Brian said as the African walked off through the scrub in the direction of the detention centre. He waved an acknowledgement lazily with one hand but did not bother to turn around.

'Do you think he was a Mick?' Chopping mused with morbid curiosity.

'Probably,' Brian answered as stoically as he could muster. 'I expect he's raped more nurses and nuns than you've dreamed of having it away with heifers from Kenya Girls' High School. Now can we get the flysheet on?'

In a sulking silence, Chopping helped to hoist the flysheet over the tent, pegging it down and knocking the stakes home with a mallet. The tent put up, Chopping started to unload the Land Rover and carry their equipment to the campsite. It was safest, Brian reminded him, to bring everything down so they would lose nothing from pilfering. It was not that the Africans inherently were thieves but simply that they did not have the European code of ownership – and they were innately curious. Often they would remove objects for which they had no use and which they could not hope to re-sell. All they ever really stole for gain was food, which they kept for themselves; Brian had long since learnt, on safari, it wasn't the guns and ammunition you necessarily kept under lock and key but the tea, sugar and cooking oil.

12

While Chopping arranged the tent, constructed the metal frames of the camp-beds and stowed away the two metal trunks in which they kept their clothes and food supplies safe from the predation of ants, Brian wandered down the gentle slope from the acacias towards a *donga*. There were no stones of any size around their campsite and he needed to find a few sizeable specimens with which to construct a hearth.

The orange sun was just touching the horizon and the bush was washed in a warm, eerie light which Brian knew would last for only a few minutes. The dried grass and the sparse, thorny scrub glowed strangely. The shadows darkened even as he watched them. The transition from day to night was a magical, mysterious time, one Brian savoured, although he kept his emotion to himself. At school, the others would have jibed at him for being so poncing. It wasn't done for an eighteen-year-old pupil at The Duke of York School to harbour such poetic thoughts.

He quickly gathered some large stones, heaving them on to the bank of the *donga* at the point where a game track dropped to the sandy bed. In the loose soil he noted a number of tracks – several Thompson's gazelles and a dik-dik had passed that way. In the centre of the *donga* were some pellets of dung which he picked up and rubbed between his fingers. Had they been fresh they would have been sticky but, instead, they powdered and drifted away on the evening breeze.

As there was still a little time before the daylight went totally, he ranged down the *donga* in search of other tracks. He had covered a hundred yards before he found any marks other than those made by the dik-dik – the trotter marks of a warthog leading to a hollow in the bank where a boar had rooted. The gouges made by the beast's savage tusks showed as deep curved scars in the earth.

Returning to the stones, he piled them in his arms and staggered back up the rise. Arranging them in a square on the ground beneath the sparse mantle of the acacias, he gathered some fallen twigs and branches, lighting them with the aid of grass tufts. Everything was tinder dry and, in less than a quarter of an hour, they had a blazing fire at which Brian set about preparing the first food of their safari.

13

It was a simple meal. Balanced on the stones around the perimeter were two saucepans, one of tinned stew and the other of water from the *dhebi*. In the ashes nestled four large sweet potatoes.

'Did you see anything when you went for the stones?' Chopping enquired, his mouth full of stew.

'Some spoor. Tommies and an *mgingi*. Further down an *ngiri*'s been grubbing about. None fresh.'

'What's an *mgingi* and an *ngiri*?' Chopping criticised, annoyance in his voice. 'I do wish, Titch, you'd use English names instead of kaffir ones.'

Brian made no answer. He preferred to think of the animals by their native names. After all, he reasoned, they were African creatures. And he didn't like Chopping referring to them as kaffir names. It was the word 'kaffir' to which he objected, more than the criticism. Once, he knew, it had meant specifically a Bantu tribesman or a negro in general, but the South African Boers had twisted it into a derogatory term like 'wog' or 'nigger', and he didn't like it. Yet, as with his thoughts on the beauty of the African sunset, he kept his preferences to himself. If his 'liberal' opinions were discovered in school he would not merely be ragged – he would be ostracized.

The grey smoke from their fire wafted into the branches of the acacias, and the yellow flames reflected off the trunks. From some distance a hyena chuckled once and was answered by another in its pack.

'It's getting a bit chilly,' Chopping observed as he scraped bits of gristle off his plate and into the fire where they hizzled and spat; the hyena called again. 'Do you think we'll have that hyena round the camp? If we do, we ought to keep the fire going, don't you think?'

For a moment, Brian considered the animal, waiting for it to call again, but it did not.

'Maybe: he's probably planning to skulk round the compound dump.'

Later that night, before he raised the tent flap, Brian stood quite still by the camp hearth. The thin smoke was fragrant, the charcoal and ash crackling quietly and warming his bare

14

legs. A night bird he could not identify whistled briefly some way off and, from the direction of the *donga*, he heard the cackle of the hyena, and he saw a vague form furtively slip behind the trunk of the tree furthest from the fire. He caught a glimpse of its spotted flank in the glare of a flame flaring up as the remains of a log slipped into the embers. Above him, partly damped out by the light of the moon, was a sheet of stars.

2

In the weak half-light hanging over the bush before sunrise Brian dressed, left the recumbent Chopping curled in his sleeping-bag and made his way down to the *donga*, following the spoor of the hyena. It had not returned, having instead joined a small pack of others with which it had – as Brian had deduced – foraged the refuse dump on the far side of the camp. He followed the tracks as far as a line of bushes beside the dump and stopped there, crouching low. Although they were ungainly animals, with a loping gait and a reputation as scavengers only marginally less repulsive than the vultures, he admired them. They survived against the odds and he knew, despite their predilection for strewing the contents of dustbins all over the lawns and driveways of Nairobi, and eating offal from the bins at the Athi river abattoir, they were also adroit hunters, operating in an organized pack much as do wild dogs.

The dump was not large. Despite holding the rubbish of a large population, it covered no more than a quarter of an acre. There was little trash because the Africans were so skilled at recycling. An old car tyre could be fashioned into sturdy sandals, paper could seal cracks in the walls of houses or be used as fuel. Waste food was fed to chickens or consumed by the pi-dogs which wandered around every African settlement. Plastic, tin or wood were used as fuel or building materials. There were few pickings remaining for the hyenas.

At first Brian did not see them. A new, deep pit had been dug and the hyenas were in it, scouring the garbage at the bottom. He did not hear them either for they were comparatively silent in the dawn and the noise of their excavations and turnings-over were muffled by the ground. He drew a little nearer and caught a glimpse of the top of one of their heads, the shaggy mane rough against the outline of the round, bear-like ears.

16

Withdrawing to the cover of the bushes, he lay low and waited. As soon as the sun came up, they would be off.

From the detention centre drifted the sound of a length of steel rail being hit with a hammer – the usual reveille for many an African settlement. As soon as the ringing ceased, Brian heard a door open and slam shut; then a shouting voice drifted across the scrub.

Four hyenas materialized out of the pit to stand on the edge, their heads hung low and facing in the direction of the human voice. One raised his head, his shoulders sagging to accommodate the move, and snuffled.

One after another, the creatures turned quickly and loped off towards the *donga*, heading away from Brian's campsite. He watched them go and wished he had his father's camera. The hyena group standing on the alert would have made an impressive photo: they were barely twenty feet from him.

Chopping had collected some kindling and was boiling the remains of the water in the *dhebi*. He had cleaned out the saucepan from the night before with a mixture of ash from their hearth, water and sand from the *donga*.

'Morning!' he greeted Brian. 'I saw your footprints. Been after the hyena?'

Brian nodded and commenced collecting larger sticks for the fire. It was Chopping's turn to cook the meal; they had agreed he would make the breakfasts and Brian the evening meals. This suited both, for Brian enjoyed preparing what they had shot during the day and Chopping hated cooking.

'I suppose we'd better see what they can do with the Land Rover,' Brian commented as he ate rashers of tinned bacon with his fingers. The smoke had given the crisp meat an earthy, dense taste and a powdering of ash stuck to the rind and fat.

'I don't expect very much,' Chopping said pessimistically. 'We'll just have to scratch the trip and get a bus back from Embu. Or maybe the police'll give us a lift.'

'We might get some shooting in around here,' Brian replied. 'I don't know if it's a Kikuyu reserve but there can't be any harm in asking.'

When he had cleaned their frying pan and drunk the

17

remainder of his coffee, Brian left Chopping reading *Moonraker*; in school, they were forbidden to read Ian Fleming's novels on the grounds that they were morally corrupting. The punishment for being caught in possession was a caning laid on with a religious zeal appropriate to a boy's boarding school of high Christian principles. Brian had been paddied, as they called a caning, for the offence when in the fifth form.

Brian noticed, as he crossed the worn dirt area by the gate, that the Land Rover had been pushed into the camp and the rear of its chassis raised on wooden blocks. In the guard-house, he asked when Inspector Broomhall would be in.

'Inspector Broomhall coming late morning,' the askari on duty reported. He was a sergeant and the three chevrons on his uniform had been laundered so often they were fraying at the edges. 'But Inspector Lewis coming in one quarter hour. He want to see you.'

Brian thanked the sergeant and sat on a bench outside the door to await the officer. Under the far end of the bench lay a pi-dog, snoring quietly, dreaming and twitching its paws.

The sun was well up but the sky, unlike the day before, was covered with hazy cloud which Brian knew would dissipate by midday. A platoon of askaris marched by, their bare feet kicking up the dust, their rifles sloped. As they passed, the tassle on each fez swung in unison with the others. Only the leading corporal's was out of time. As they turned about to be inspected by the sergeant who had left the guardhouse, the pi-dog started barking at them. The sergeant ignored it. It lay down with its muzzle on its paws and went back to dozing.

As the platoon was dismissed, Inspector Lewis arrived on foot, much to Brian's surprise. He had expected a vehicle to drive in, and the officer's sudden greeting startled him.

'Been taking the parade?' he asked.

'Watching it, sir,' Brian replied. 'They're very smart.'

'These boys do well. It's not a happy job having to guard your own kind, but they all get on. By and large. There's a great deal of give and take. We only occasionally have a set-to and then it's over a woman rather than tribal loyalties or politics. Now,' he entered the guardhouse, returning the

18

sergeant's salute, 'to sort out your *gari*. I've had a word with Inspector Broomhall and he's put a couple of the detainees on to it. They're good at the job, so we should have you set up in a day or two. They'll do the drive shaft today and your father's sending out a UJ. Until it's done, you're welcome to stay here.'

The officer noticed Brian's crestfallen look and reached inside his pocket for the key to the steel cabinet. 'How much ammo do you need for today?'

Brian was taken aback. He had expected them to have to sit about their tent for two days, kicking their heels.

'Can we shoot around here?'

'Not exactly,' Lewis replied. 'But if you push off about five miles south-east you should be all right. Not too many *shambas*. Bush opens out a good bit, too – into open savannah. Couple of river tributaries with a bit of water left in them as well. But no shooting over water, and remember how far a slug can travel.'

'Yes, sir,' Brian said eagerly.

'So! How many?'

'Thirty rounds of each calibre, please,' Brian requested.

'Let's say forty. Just in case.'

Inspector Lewis counted eighty rounds out of the boxes, dropping them into a manila envelope with the bolts.

'What's your gun?' he asked as he dealt out the .275 cartridges.

'A Rigby, sir.'

'Rigby, eh? Fine guns – you're a lucky lad – best sporting rifles in the world. Mauser actions. The Queen shoots with a Rigby.'

He folded the envelope flap and rolled an elastic band around it.

'By the way,' he continued, 'any rounds you don't use must go back in the box at the end of the day. Okay? And don't leave empty cases about in the bush: they can be recharged, after a fashion. If they're not made into jewellery first.'

'Okay, sir,' Brian agreed.

'Before you go off, could you just drop in to the camp? The

boys who're fixing your *gari* might want a word and it's polite...'

'I was going to ask you if I could...'

'Good. I thought you might. Pick up your ammo and bits from the sergeant here when you're done with the *gari*-fixers.'

It was strange entering a detention camp. Though it did not resemble the usual concept of a prison, in that it had no high walls or clanging iron gates, Brian felt distinctly uncomfortable. The askari in the gate sentry-box was armed and could shoot if he was ordered.

The panelling on the sides of the Land Rover was already warm from the sun, and the bonnet as hot as if the engine had been running. Projecting from beneath the vehicle were two pairs of black legs, the feet braced against the ground to give the hidden bodies a purchase. Both were barefoot but one had a buff-coloured scar around the ankle just above the bone. For a moment, it reminded Brian of the sort of marks left by slave manacles, which he had seen illustrated in a history textbook. A sound of metal grinding against metal issued from the direction of the gearbox housing, intermingled with heavy breathing.

'*Jambo*,' Brian greeted the legs. The grinding noise ceased and the feet relaxed their grip on the earth. He continued, '*Nafikiri kuna kitu kilichoharibika katika jointi ya gurundumu.*'

'*Ndio, bwana,*' came a reply muffled by the bodywork. The voice was breathless with effort. '*Na shafti ... ina ufa...*'

The pair of feet with the scar scrabbled on the gravelly dirt to haul their owner clear; the other pair thrust to push theirs through. The one pair disappearing and the other lengthening caused Brian to smile wryly. It was just like Africa as his father often described it – a continual exhibition of opposites.

The first to emerge was the man of the disappearing legs. He stood up on the far side of the Land Rover and looked straight into Brian's face with wide, staring eyes. He was in his late twenties, shorter than Brian and with an uncharacteristically narrow nose. Brian wondered if he was part Masai – the Kikuyu homelands had been raided for centuries by

20

Masai seeking to expand their cattle herds and adjust the balance of womanhood in their *bomas*. His hair was the usual tight mass of curls but was longer than was common and had been teased out. It was with a feeling of mild trepidation that Brian returned the stare: Dedan Kimathi and General China were said to wear their hair long and matted. Perhaps the action of rehabilitation was not as complete with the inmates as Broomhall had led him to suppose.

'*Jambo,*' Brian repeated. '*Habari?*'

'*Zuri,*' the man replied morosely.

The other African rose beside Brian and chuckled.

'Ndegwa wants to know how much you will be paying us to repair your Land Rover. I told him "*Shilingi moja*" but he does not laugh because he has no sense of laughing.'

This other African was of Brian's height, of similar build and probably not much older. His hair, unlike his partner's, was cut short, but he was also different from his fellow in that he had the majestic bearing of a true-born Kikuyu. The most handsome of the East African tribes, the Kikuyu had finely shaped faces and well proportioned bodies. The attributes which might make some tribes appear less good-looking to the European – wider lips and nostrils or larger ears – were absent in them; and the African standing next to Brian was an example of the Kikuyu at their finest. Whenever Brian read the stories of Rider Haggard, it was the Kukes of whom he thought when the author described a kingly chief or a brave warrior.

'We shall pay you both something,' Brian promised, only to become aware immediately that he was being patronizing, and regretting it. 'Do you think you can repair it?'

'It will not be hard,' came the reply. Evidently the Kikuyu was not as affected by Brian's words as he had feared. 'The joint is finished but another will come. The shaft is crack – cracked – but we can weld it.'

'How long will it take you?'

'Two days maybe. Not more. Tomorrow night – *isha kabisha*!'

An insect settled on the African's chest and he raised his

left arm to swat it away. The arm had been amputated just below the elbow.

Brian looked away, embarrassed and shocked by the deformity. He always felt queasy in the company of cripples and mental defectives. Flying out from long leave the year before, he had sat in the BOAC Argonaut next to an Egyptian who had lost all but one of the fingers from his right hand. He had asked Brian to unscrew the top on his miniature bottle of whisky for him. Brian was relieved when the man disembarked at Rome, even though the old lady who took the Egyptian's place smelt strongly of garlic and sweat.

'Is there a *duka* near here?' Brian enquired. An idea had formed in his mind to try to compensate for patronizing the two Africans: his father had told him it was his position as a white to rule – to rule fairly and justly, not patronizingly – and to be humane in his dealings with Africans. They were, he said, like children who had to be looked after but disciplined when necessary.

'If you go down through the buildings, you will find one. The stock is not good.'

'I'll come back later,' Brian said, 'in the afternoon.'

'That is good. We shall see you,' said the one-armed African and he spoke rapidly to his fellow prisoner in Kikuyu.

The camp buildings were constructed in rows. Some were square buildings with sloping roofs, some A-frames like tents, some merely one-roomed structures and others much larger. Water taps were situated at corners and the pathways between the buildings had been swept clean and sprayed with water to lay the dust. On a few empty sites, vegetables were growing in small allotments. Few of the buildings had windows and all, regardless of their shape or size, were made of corrugated iron sheeting from which the sun reflected brilliantly.

At some of the open doorways, Africans squatted or leaned. One or two were filling *dhebis* with water from the stand-pipes to irrigate their vegetables. A few were reading books or newspapers, but most were smoking and chatting at their ease. None stared at Brian or even hinted he appeared out of place; but none greeted him, either.

The camp store was in one of the A-frames. It was unlit

within but the sunlight flooding in through the open door gave more than sufficient illumination. There was no counter but shelves, arranged with a minimal supply of staples, and a table behind which sat an elderly African with drooping ear lobes. He was looking vaguely out of the door and smoking.

'*Nataka mbili pakti ya sigara*,' Brian ordered, adding, '"Crown Bird".'

The old man reached for a carton on a shelf to his side, his lobes swinging against his neck as he turned.

'*Asante*,' Brian said and gave the man four shillings. He opened a golden State Express 555 tobacco tin and removed seventy cents change, counting the coins carefully and piling Brian's four shillings onto a stack of other shillings, placing them all with the lion's side upwards, the Queen's or King's head downwards.

The cigarette packets had a crown stork printed on them, the proud bird erect with the halo of thin feathers around its cranium. Under the sunlit cellophane they seemed to glisten as if coming alive.

The legs were protruding once more from the Land Rover as Brian walked up to it. From beneath came a hammering and much grunting. He went down on his haunches, waving the two packets of cigarettes under the chassis.

'These are for you while you're working,' he said loudly to combat the din.

The hammering stopped with a thud and Brian saw the front end of the drive shaft drop to the dirt. A right hand reached out to the packets.

'Thank you very much. I do not smoke but Ndegwa does.'

A sentence of Kikuyu was spoken followed by Ndegwa saying '*Asante sana*,' in a less morose voice than before.

'We see you later. Today we can fix the drive shaft.'

As Brian walked off, he could hear the hammering recommence by the differential. It sounded not unlike the reveille bell.

Handing over the envelope of bolts and bullets, the sergeant also gave Brian a note. To it was attached a key on a large paper-clip. The note read:

Parked around the back. Full tank. Bring back by six at latest. Watch out for dongas! Happy hunting – Lewis.

'It was damn good of that Lewis, don't you think?' Chopping asked as Brian drove the short-wheelbase Jeep through the scrub and on to a track little more than two tyre ruts winding through the bush.

'Very decent indeed. And it's tanked-up, too. We'd better give him something towards the petrol.'

The Jeep was an ancient, left-hand-drive model of American manufacture. It rattled and squeaked, bounced and jolted, the shock-absorbers clouting the mountings on even quite minor bumps. The steering was loose and the clutch had to be depressed right to the floor before it would engage. Second gear screamed menacingly. The passenger seat upon which Chopping had positioned himself was only partially bolted to the floor and, until he grew accustomed to the vagaries of the vehicle, he had an awkward time keeping himself upright and the guns, which lay across his lap, unharmed.

They drove for four or five miles along the track. At first, small villages appeared frequently, the round, reddish wattle-and-daub thatched huts invariably surrounded by *shambas* of maize plants shimmering in the heat haze. A cow or a few scrawny goats were tethered to stakes in the ground or to scantily-leafed trees. Pi-dogs cursorily barked at the Jeep; children and women gazed at it; wiry chickens scattered under the wheels. Occasionally they came across a man on a black bicycle pedalling slowly towards them. He would dismount and pull his machine to the side of the track to let them pass. Brian shouted out '*Asante*' to each one but none replied or waved.

After a few miles, the villages became infrequent, the track even less visible than before. Game paths meandered through the bush, the trees becoming more gaunt and spread apart, the undergrowth thinner. Despite all the game paths, however, they saw no animal life except one gazelle in the distance and a brown snake which whipped across in front of them.

24

Then, as they drove over a stony rise, the landscape changed suddenly and quite dramatically. From being scrub and semi-arid tree cover, it broke into rolling savannah with clumps of trees and patches of dense thorn or kai-apple bushes. Everything more than fifty yards ahead was liquid with heat.

'This'll do,' Chopping said approvingly.

Brian swung the vehicle under a low white thorn acacia and switched off the engine.

After the drumming, creaking and whining of the Jeep, the silence of the bush was profound. It took a moment for Brian's ears to become accustomed to the lack of noise. Gradually, then, he could discern the new sounds – the soft wind in the grassland, the crying of a bird unseen against the starkly blue sky, and the crackle of his boots as he stepped to the ground.

Before they left the Jeep, they drank their fill and topped up their canteens which clipped onto their belts. With the bullets divided equally between them and their rifles loaded, they walked into the grassland.

They did not move together but about fifty yards apart, maintaining a low profile when they came to a rise in the ground. The heat bore down on their bush hats. Tracks and spoor marks were everywhere: obviously the area was well stocked with game. Brian came upon the pug-marks of two lions but they were at least a day old. He found where they had lain in the midday heat under a thorn bush, small craters in the dust caused by saliva dripping from their panting mouths.

Their plan was to try and bag a bushbuck for its skin and, if they saw one with a fine head, a Thompson's gazelle or an impala. A dik-dik or two would not go amiss either: Brian had only to shoot five more to complete the dik-dik rug he was sewing for his bedroom. If chance brought them something else, so much the better. Chopping had been asked by his younger brother at boarding school in England for porcupine quills with which to make fishing floats and he wanted too a small crocodile or monitor lizard skin.

They had gone about a mile from the Jeep when, in an open

area surrounded by thorn bushes, they came upon a mixed herd of Tommies and impala, some grazing and some browsing on bushes.

Creeping carefully as close as they dare, and keeping a fallen tree-trunk between themselves and the leisurely moving herd, the two boys studied the animals, trying to assess the best spread of horns or the least marked skin. The wind was not in their favour and they had to move parallel to the antelope to get more fully downwind.

Twice they thought they had been spotted by the leading bucks. The herd – as one – stopped feeding and faced in their direction, ears alert and noses testing the breeze. Calves cavorted to their mothers' flanks and a few of the antelope stamped the ground but, seeing no definite threat, they soon resumed their inexorable search for food.

After twenty minutes, Brian and Chopping agreed who should have which animal. Brian had chosen an impala buck with a perfectly symmetrical spread of horns; Chopping was going for a Tommy doe with a clean pelt.

Very slowly, Brian raised himself behind a dead, leaning tree; on the trunk by his hand were several old marks from elephants' tusks. Chopping lay on a termite mound, his head and rifle projecting around the side. Both levelled their sights on their allotted targets.

It was Brian to fire first. As soon as the report rang out, the antelope would be away, leaping and springing through the grass, weaving and ducking. Chopping would have to shoot almost simultaneously.

His foresight settled just behind and below the shoulder of his impala, Brian took in the slack on the trigger, held his breath and squeezed gently with his finger.

The rifle jarred slightly. Chopping fired a split second later.

Brian's impala fell on the spot where it had been grazing. Chopping's gazelle staggered several yards, its neck outstretched and its head tossing, disappearing below the line of the brown grass. The remainder of the herd was gone from sight within twenty seconds, the last animal leaping ten feet in

26

the air to clear a thicket. The grace of its jump took Brian's breath away.

'Got 'em!' Chopping exclaimed with quiet satisfaction, snapping back the bolt.

Together, they approached their kills. Brian's animal was dead, lying in the long grass as if pole-axed. A red hole in its shoulder showed he had hit it spot on target. Its glazed eyes were open, its tongue hanging loose from its mouth. Already a fly had found it and alighted on the teeth, a blot against the creamy enamel. A false hornet was hovering over the cavity of the ear. As Brian had guessed, the horns were exceptional, both in length and in the way in which they turned upward, the surfaces smoothly spiralling. From the impala's anus had oozed a number of pellets of dung and, as he lifted its head to study the horns more closely, it kicked violently with its hind legs, the body's electricity running down.

Chopping's Thompson's gazelle was also stone dead but had slipped partly down an ant-bear's burrow in which its hindquarters had become lodged.

'Titch! Can you give me a hand?' he called. 'Mine thinks it's a porcupine and has gone to ground.' He laughed with the delight of having killed.

With care, they dragged the two carcasses towards some bushes and tucked them under the shade, covering them with thorn branches to keep off any scavengers that might smell the kill. Jackals and hyenas were not a problem in the heat of the day, but vigilant vultures would be.

At four o'clock, they drove the Jeep round the sites of their kills. In addition to the Tommy and the impala, they had succeeded in bagging three guinea fowl, two dik-dik and Chopping's much sought-after monitor lizard.

It had taken the two of them to kill the reptile. When Chopping had first spotted it lying on the floor of a *donga* in the shade of a thorn bush, he had stopped, signalled to Brian some yards away that he had seen something, and then stalked to within twenty yards of the creature. It was a large specimen, at least six feet long. He aimed at its ear but was so excited the shot went wide and hit the lizard on its back. Far from penetrating the skin, the bullet merely ricochetted off,

27

whining and spurting up a whiff of dust from the bank above. The monitor lizard took umbrage, flicking itself around to face the direction of the threat, moving as easily as if it was a three-inch-long gecko.

Chopping stood his ground, ejecting the spent case and pushing another into the breach. The click of the bolt alerted the keen lizard which started to run towards its antagonist. Although its jerky movements were clumsy in the way of reptiles, it was fleet of foot and quickly closed on Chopping, its red mouth gaping and hissing. He fired again. Brian, from along the bank, also fired. The first bullet hit the lizard in its open, spitting mouth; the second struck it in the side of the head between the eye and the ear. It stopped, half turned and commenced thrashing the sandy floor of the *donga*. For ten minutes it raised a cloud giving it an adequate smokescreen. Finally, however, its struggling and beating about slowed. Chopping took the opportunity of placing a final bullet at close range into the lizard's skull. He was delighted and spent thirty minutes skinning the lizard with his sheath knife while Brian sat on the top of the bank and watched several vultures arrive in a nearby baobab.

The drive back to Wamumu took them longer than the journey out. The gazelle and dik-dik hides and the already-stiffening skin of the monitor lizard were folded on the floor of the Jeep but the impala carcass was dumped across the back, the head lolling out one side and the hindquarters the other, both protected from wearing on the metal sides by handfuls of grass woven together with strips of bark. They had decided to skin the impala at their camp and offer the meat to the two Africans repairing the Land Rover.

Brian was forced to drive slowly to avoid the impala slithering about, damaging the horns. Twice the trophy snagged in bushes by the track but – luckily – on neither occasion were the twigs thorny, so the muzzle and face were not scarred or scratched.

'That's a damn good bag!' Inspector Lewis exclaimed as Brian returned the ignition keys to him with the rifle bolts and the ammunition. 'And you've not wasted many slugs either.'

Reaching into the space beneath the impala, Brian lifted out one of the guinea fowl and offered it to Lewis.

'We wondered if you'd like this as a small thank-you, sir. And we'd like to pay for the petrol.'

Lewis was both surprised and pleased.

'That's very generous of you both. But I think you might offer the bird to the boys who're fixing your buggy. As for the petrol – came out of the prison officers' pump. Ask no questions!'

'I'm going to give the boys the impala. I only really want the trophy and we thought...'

'Jolly good idea! They'll soon make a good supply of biltong out of it. And flog a good bit to their fellow prisoners, no doubt.' He studied his watch. 'Tell you what: you can go over to the camp now and see how they're getting on. Should be nearly through. You can drive in,' he gave the Jeep keys back to Brian. 'The sergeant here'll come with you. Save you lugging the meat in. They'll skin it for you in there and take the head off. How's that? Leave your guns here, of course. And I gratefully accept my Sunday lunch.'

Brian readily agreed and he, Chopping and the sergeant drove through the barbed-wire gates.

The Land Rover stood where Brian had last seen it, still mounted on wooden blocks. There was no sign of the two detainees.

Chopping showed distinct signs of nervous tension as the sergeant said, '*Pinda kulia!*' and Brian turned right at the main gate to follow the road around the inside of the perimeter fence.

'You want to get off here?' Brian enquired.

'Yes,' Chopping answered. 'I most certainly do.'

'In that case, can you get the fire lit and water on? I'll not be long...'

'I'll even prepare the guinea fowl,' Chopping volunteered. 'Roast?'

Brian nodded as Chopping jumped out of the rear of the Jeep, the brace of guinea fowl swinging from his hand by their necks.

'Watch after my skins,' he called as Brian pressed the clutch pedal down to the floor and rammed the gearstick forward.

The road followed the wire which consisted, once they had turned the first corner of the rectangular camp, of two fences with a guard-walk between them: the rolls of barbed-wire were more dense here than at the front.

A workshop had been installed in one of the larger A-frames half-way down the camp and from the doorway came the explosive flickering of an electric arc flame. Even though the afternoon sun was still strong, it could not combat the momentary flares which cast the shadows of a group of curious children onto the wall of the square building opposite. As Brian walked through the crowd of *totos*, they gave way to him, stepping aside to stare at him, chattering to each other and calling to him.

The workshop smelled of hot steel, flux and oil. By the wall was a thick-gauge metal tool chest with a heavy-duty hasp and a padlock hanging free from the lid. On a three-legged stool beside the chest squatted an askari. He was unarmed and watchful, his duty being to ensure that only approved items were manufactured.

Across an anvil, balancing between it and a wooden vegetable crate, was the drive shift. Leaning over the red-hot metal was the one-armed detainee. In his hand he grasped the metal welding rod, while the other electrical connection was pressed to the end of the shaft by Ndegwa. The welder's visor was held in place against his face by the stub of his arm. He was sweating profusely, drops of perspiration falling from beneath the mask to hiss and evaporate on the shaft. He did not see Brian enter.

'*Maji!*' he ordered.

Ndegwa let go of the contact, threw a switch on a makeshift wall panel and slopped a dipper full of water over the drive shaft. A cloud of steam engulfed the welder. As it thinned, he put down the welding rod and removed the visor to see Brian standing there.

'It is finished!' he said triumphantly. 'Only some buffing to do.'

Brian studied the weld. It was, he could tell from having

30

taken a course in metalwork at school, a good one which
would hold firm for a long while.

'You can now go over as many *dongas* as you like. Even
fast,' the Kikuyu said humorously, then, turning to the
guard, asked, '*Saa ngapi?*'

'*Saa kumi na mbili u robo,*' answered the askari, tapping at
his battered wristwatch.

'Good!' He spoke as much to Ndegwa and the askari as he
did to Brian. 'I think we can put the drive shaft back into place
now and fix the universal joint in the morning. But it will be
dark soon.' He looked at Brian. 'Will you hold the lamp for
us?'

'Anything I can do,' Brian offered, quite amazed by the
African's ease when talking with him, not up to him or, as
Kikuyus could do, down to him. Never before had a native
faced him almost as an equal.

Ndegwa ran a grinding-wheel over the weld, smoothing
the metal scar and showering sparks on the earth floor; then
the two detainees left, carrying the drive shaft between them,
Brian driving slowly behind in the Jeep. On reaching the
Land Rover, Ndegwa went to the guard on duty at the gate
and was given a long flex, on the end of which was a light bulb
in a cracked Bakelite holder screwed into the end of what had
once been the top portion of a wooden standard lamp. He
handed this to Brian and scrambled under the broken-down
vehicle. There followed twenty minutes of groaning
interspersed with curt comments in Kikuyu as the day
merged into twilight and then darkness.

Throughout the replacement of the drive-shaft, Brian sat
cross-legged on the ground holding the bulb under the Land
Rover. Occasionally, beetles clumsily flew in after the light
but Brian swatted them down with his free hand. Moths also
congregated in a halo around the bulb but none were of the
large forest varieties and they caused no trouble.

At last, the shaft was fixed at one end and propped up with
stones at the other awaiting the arrival of the new universal
joint. Ndegwa collected the tools and surrendered them to the
sergeant as the other detainee swung out from under the Land

Rover, hoisting himself up with his stump of arm, the round end thrusting into the gritty soil.

'We are finished for tonight,' he announced. 'Tomorrow we shall fit the *jointi ya gurundumu*. It will arrive with the bus from Fort Hall.'

Brian stood, brushing the dirt off his legs and shorts as he handed the light to Ndegwa and pointed to the Jeep.

'I was wondering if you would like this *swela* for meat. I would like just the head as a trophy.'

'That is most kind of you. Yes!' acknowledged the detainee, rubbing his stump against his shorts to remove the gravel adhering to it. 'I should like it very much and we shall all share it. Good meat is not common in the camp.' He felt the animal's haunch with his oily hand, leaving a smear of grey grease and dust on the buff-coloured hair. 'May I keep the skin also? It will make a good covering for the floor of my room.'

'Of course.'

The African called to Ndegwa, '*Nataka kisu!*'

He grabbed the two front hooves in his one hand, his fingers tight as wires round the thin ankles. He was so strong he could lift the front quarters of the impala single-handed. Ndegwa used both hands on the hind legs.

'We shall see you in the morning. Or maybe later. The Land Rover will be finished by noon if the bus is early.'

'Before you go . . .' Brian began hesitantly. He was not sure how he should address a Mau Mau prisoner. Until now, their conversation had been somehow impersonal, always referring to the broken-down vehicle or matters relating to it.

'Yes?'

The detainees lowered the buck carefully to the ground, making sure the horns did not scrape on the dirt.

'I wonder . . .' Brian began again, 'if you would give me your name.'

It sounded so terribly patronizing. He was afraid the detainee would think he wanted it in order to report to Lewis or Broomhall how good he had been over the Land Rover, and he could hear himself saying, as if he was Chopping, 'That boy who fixed my *gari* was a competent fellow.'

32

'My name?'

The African appeared momentarily startled.

Somewhere in the centre of the camp the steel rail was being hit by a hammer, a signal it was only a few minutes to lock-up.

'My name is Matthew Nchembe,' he said. 'I shall see you tomorrow.'

3

'What's Nchembe like?' Broomhall echoed Brian's words as he unlocked the cabinet. 'Well, he's a Kuke, of course, and a convicted terrorist. You can't get away from the fact he was nicked by the security forces. But, if you accept those bounds, he's a nice enough boy. Better educated than most as you'll have gathered. Speaks good English, helpful about the camp. Bit of a spokesman when one's needed but without being a barrack-room lawyer. God knows! There're enough of them in some of the camps.'

Brian gazed out of the door in the direction of the main gate beyond which stood the Land Rover. The vehicle lay in the long shadow of the first prison building. The guard was changing under the supervision of the askari sergeant.

Broomhall tipped the box, one hand holding back most of the contents. The released bullets rattled on to the glass covering of the desk top beneath which were various sheets of government notepaper – a list of official telephone numbers, a guard rota and a photograph of a wrecked car and a dead rhino on the Nairobi-Mombasa road.

'Here are your bolts,' Broomhall said, handing them to Brian. 'Forty rounds each again? Trust that's enough for you to pluck me and my wife a brace of guinea fowl out of the *bundu*!'

Brian laughed and replied, 'We take orders. Anything else you'd like, sir?'

'Don't think so. What are you two after today?'

'I want a few more dik-dik. Chopping isn't bothered. He's cock-a-hoop with the monitor.' Brian watched the relieved guard march out of sight past the door. 'I've still got a leopard on my licence but the chances in broad daylight aren't good. I don't suppose...'

'Not a chance!' Broomhall interrupted, forestalling the request. 'Back by six and not because we need the clapped-out old *gari* you're borrowing. If it conks out, I don't want to have to go and find you in the dark.'

'Very well, sir,' Brian acquiesced.

As Broomhall counted out the ammunition for the day, he asked, 'What so interests you about Master Nchembe?'

Brian toyed with the bullets on the desk, dividing them into groups of five and standing them on end.

'I've never seen a real ...' he began.

'Mick?' the inspector asked.

'Yes.' He paused, unsure if he should go on. 'What more do you know about him?'

'Quite a lot,' Broomhall answered. 'A deal more than we know about most of them. He claims he's about nineteen years old – and the medico agrees it's a fair guess. Calls himself Matthew Nchembe having dropped his given name, whatever it was. We don't know it and I doubt he does now. A good number of them keep their names from us in any case. They've their own system of identification – make their own ID bracelets out of the aluminium cladding of the quarters so they know each other and can avoid using their real names.'

'And his family?'

'No record of his father. We've reason to believe he was an askari in the King's African Rifles and got it in the war. His mother's still around, or so he tells us. Want another envelope?'

Brian shook his head and Broomhall closed the stationery drawer. In the sunlight streaming through a slit in the window shutters, Brian noticed that the photo of the dead rhino was yellowing and cracking at the edges.

'I'll put them in my pocket,' he said, scooping the bullets off the desk and into his bush jacket.

'Born in the Aberdares some place,' the policeman continued. 'Lived in or near Gilgil as a child where the family had a *shamba*. They moved after a bit to near Rumuruti where the mother got a job on a farm – general house servant to a farmer up there.'

'Any brothers and sisters?'

'A sister, perhaps. I seem to recall she disappeared from the scene when Nchembe was still a bit of a *toto*. Anyway, he got to go to a mission school around Rumuruti and that's where he flourished.'

The sergeant entered and smartly saluted his superior officer; to Brian, he said, '*Jambo, bwana.*' Brian returned the greeting.

The sergeant's arrival caused Broomhall to hold his peace about Nchembe.

The officer followed Brian outside to the Jeep and, as he hoisted himself into the driving seat, Broomhall asked, 'Aren't you interested in how chummy got into the Mau Mau?'

'I suppose I am,' Brian admitted. 'More curious, really. How do any of them get in?'

'They're coerced, most of them. Join up or your mother-sister-father gets it. Enlist or we burn your *shamba* and your *rondavel*, rape your grandmother, kill your grandfather. Do as you're told or we'll cut your cock off and feed it to the hyenas...

'Of course, once they're in they don't necessarily join the forest armies. They might be undercover agents – fifth columnists, of a sort. They needn't fire guns. They can coerce others instead – approach domestic servants in Nairobi and blackmail them into poisoning their employers, demand food for those in the bush, steal guns or money from their *bwanas*. That sort of thing. They are an army but they're really very disorganized. Not like the EOKA in Cyprus or the Communists in Malaya, for example. Maybe that's why we call them Micks. Mickey Mouse army.'

'I don't suppose Nchembe was much good as a fighter with just one arm,' Brian suggested.

'Now that's where you're wrong,' Broomhall corrected him. 'He was one of the very few real fighters. When he was sixteen. If you've got five minutes, I'll tell you his story. Know it well because he's the only one of his sort we've got here.'

Across the bare circle of earth before the main gate, the pi-dog was wandering in an aimless, half-hearted fashion. When it reached the very centre of the circle it lay down in the sun, dropping as if exhausted, its back legs splayed behind it and

36

its forepaws pushed out in a luxurious stretch. It was a dog of a nondescript buff colour and its hackles were rough: somewhere in its parentage there had been an Afrikaner's Ridgeback.

'When Nchembe was captured – in a sweep near Lake Naivasha – he was dying. A number of his buddies had bought it and he was minus the lower portion of his left arm. Well, not exactly minus it. He still had a bit of it hanging from the upper part. He had suffered a fairly common Mick fate.'

Broomhall paused to see if Brian understood the implication. It was plain he did not.

'Happened to a number of them in the bush. With the shortage of firearms they took to making their own. These were crude affairs, to put it mildly. Some were made with fragments of captured or stolen weapons glued together with spit and a prayer. Some were constructed out of anything which looked gun-like. To the African, who hasn't really grasped the ins and outs of the manufacturing process, if a thing looks right, it is right. Hence the barrels were made of water piping, the bolts of bolts – of the nut-and-bolt variety – and the sights were nails or screws drilled into the front of the barrel.'

'They sound like children's toys.'

'They were! Like the sort my five-year-old knocks up in the garage of a Saturday afternoon, to play soldiers with. Anway,' Broomhall went on, 'Nchembe had done himself a gun. To be fair, he did a passable job on it. The piping was a fair fit for the shotgun cartridge it was made to fire. The stock was wooden and carved. The breach was steel and fairly well tooled and the thing didn't have a bolt. It seems to have fired rather like a flintlock: a nail came forward on a powerful spring and clouted the detonator.... Much of all this he spilled at his first interview. It's in his file.'

'He had his gun with him when he was caught, then?' Brian enquired.

'In a manner of speaking: he was holding the remnants of it.'

'What do you mean?'

'These Mickey Mouse guns weren't exactly effective. They

might have fired a few times but more often they simply exploded in their owners' faces. Nchembe was lucky. His blew up after he had lowered it from his shoulder. Apparently it had misfired and he was about to check it when it went off. Otherwise he'd have lost his head.'

'That's horrible!' Brian exclaimed. His hands were sweating where they gripped the steering wheel.

'Not nice, I agree.'

The pi-dog dragged itself to its feet, took a dozen steps and lay down again. An off-duty askari swerved his bicycle to avoid the dog.

'After he was captured, they considered Nchembe was hard-core – one of the real nutters, the dead-keen johnnies. And, in a way, he was. Started off in a detention camp way up north but his subsequent interviews set him apart from most of the others.'

'How?'

'After their initiation – and that's a gruesome business, I can tell you – the majority don't know why they're in. Their immediate concern is next week, not next month or next year. The average bush African doesn't think ahead. Precious few know why they are fighting. Again, they're not like the EOKA and that crazy priest of theirs, Makarios, set on independence. Now there's an aim for you. The Mau Mau – bar a possible handful, and Kenyatta himself, of course – simply fight an enemy because they're told to. Stands to reason they don't have any direction – far more Kukes have been killed by the Micks than Europeans or Asians. It's just that when a white settler is butchered, it makes the headlines.'

Brian thought of the Rucks. The farmer, his wife and their six-year-old son had been betrayed by their farm workers and hacked to death with *pangas*. The uproar had been intense, culminating in a near-riot of whites on the lawns of Government House, demanding action, protection and revenge from a Governor who was himself regarded as being pro-African.

From within the guardhouse came the jangle of the telephone bell.

'Nchembe, though,' Broomhall continued, 'he's different.

38

He joined in to get his country free of colonial rule. Readily admitted it at the grilling sessions. Realized, after a while of being a Mau Mau, they weren't the ones to get it and this wasn't the way. Violence, it appears, is now out where he's concerned but quite what he does intend to do next is anyone's guess...'

The inspector brushed from his arm the dust which had stuck to his skin from pressing on the mudguard. Where he had leaned was a damp oval. He patted the bonnet. 'Take care of Jessie the Jeep, won't you? Have a good day's hunting.'

'Hope so,' Brian replied. He pulled the choke knob out to its fullest extent, starting the Jeep with the first press of the button.

'Don't forget the guinea-fowl,' Broomhall called from the door of the guardhouse. Brian waved his confirmation.

The Jeep skidded around the pi-dog which made no attempt to shift itself out of the way. It did not even raise its head as the wheels showered it with grit: it merely closed its eyes and, after the dust had settled, half-heartedly scratched itself.

Going down the track to the tent, Brian heard the asthmatic wheeze of the horn of a country bus. It would, he thought, be the one Nchembe was hoping would deliver the spare part.

Driving the Jeep along the same track they had taken the previous day, Brian told his companion the story of Matthew Nchembe. Chopping was dismissive.

'Serves the kaffir right! He asked for it. Joining the Micks, threatening the loyal Kukes, making his own gun ... I mean – making his own gun! Most of them can't sharpen their own *pangas*. Our gardener attempted to sharpen his when we had a bit of brush to clear behind the servants' quarters. Got the knife and tried sharpening it on the grindstone in our neighbour's workshop. Hell of a noise! Everyone rushed over to see – he was trying to sharpen it with the blade at right angles to the wheel. Pitted the blade – all three foot of it. If that's what they do to a *panga* ...'

The Jeep bucked over a *donga*. Chopping ceased talking to

hold on and protect the rifles and his knees from banging on the dashboard. Once out of the river bed, he continued, always at his most verbose when discussing the African.

'You know what Churchill told the Yanks in the war? When they weren't in it? "Give us the tools and we'll finish the job." With the kaffirs, it's different. With them it's "Give us the job and we'll finish the tools." Do you get it?'

He laughed loudly.

'It's a bit corny,' stated Brian, but Chopping liked the joke and laughed again.

They left the Jeep at the same spot they had the day before but decided this morning not to shoot together. Brian specifically wanted dik-dik whereas Chopping was out to shoot what he could. They agreed to split up, meeting back at the Jeep at two-thirty. By then, the majority of the animals would be hiding from the heat, and Brian wanted to get back to Wamumu before the afternoon was gone.

He had two reasons for an early return. The first was that he wanted to see if the universal joint had arrived on the bus: if it had not, he and Chopping would have to return to Nairobi in a similar form of public transport. The buses were slow, uncomfortable in the extreme and potentially dangerous. Their rifles and camping equipment would have to remain at Wamumu for collection later.

The second reason was that he wanted time to talk to Matthew Nchembe.

'Half past two then,' confirmed Chopping, looking at the sky to judge the time.

There were no clouds in sight except two small cumuli far to the west and, because it had been chilly during the night, the air was clean and sharp. To the north they could see the snow-covered pinnacles of Mount Kenya rising through the first of the day's heat haze. To the left of the mountain rose the low outline of the White Highlands. Brian followed Chopping's gaze.

'The Kikuyu call it *Kirinyaga*,' he said. 'It's where *N'gai* – God – is said to live.'

'Godless bloody lot, if you ask me,' Chopping announced.

With his B S A resting along his shoulder, his hand around

40

the foresight, Chopping set off southwards. Brian, his Rigby tucked under his armpit and resting on his forearm, headed east.

For the first mile, he walked without regard to silence but he kept a cautious eye open for animals. Not far from the Jeep he found some fresh buffalo dung and decided to watch out for the great, grey beasts. Though only a form of wild cattle, even if armed with a massive pair of horns forming a thick plate across their brows, they were more dangerous than any domestic bull could be, utterly unpredictable and relentless in their efforts to gore an enemy. Even lions were cautious of them. Their trail headed southwards but they could double back.

After thirty minutes, Brian arrived at a *donga* in the bottom of which the sand was not as desiccated as might be expected at that time of the dry season. He knew from such a sign that if he was to work his way down the *donga* he could possibly find water – and where there was water there would be game. With this in mind, yet conscious it was not sporting to kill directly over water, he stood still and spent a moment – as he always did when hunting alone – concentrating his attention. Then, with his nerves primed, he set off carefully, alert to anything he might sense.

The sand over which he was walking was a rich pattern of tracks, some fresh and some days old. Impala, baboon, porcupine, mongoose, gazelle, warthog, snake and a variety of bird tracks intermingled and over-printed each other. Droppings littered the ground, and on a dead tree bough projecting from the floor of the *donga* were piled the heap faeces of a civet. Brian nudged the pile with his foot and knelt to study the contents. Knowing it was an omnivorous feeder, he recognised dung-beetle wing-cases, fruit pips and the teeth of a small rodent. From the other end of the bough wafted the noxious smell with which civets mark out their territories.

In the sand by the side of the bough were two sets of dik-dik prints and scattered droppings. They were very fresh, the nap on the sand still raised where the tiny pointed hooves had fallen. The few pellets of dik-dik dung, when Brian rolled them between his finger and thumb, were moist.

41

The Rigby was loaded, a bullet in the breach, the bolt pressed forward with the safety catch on. Brian was ready for the first dik-dik to appear.

He remained quite still and listened. With the experience of years of hunting, he filtered from his brain the bird calls whistling or piping in the bush. He was concentrating on other sounds.

In the long grass on the bank of the *donga*, level with his head, there was a distinct rustle. It stopped, started, stopped again. He registered it as the noise of a skink running through the leaf litter and ignored it. Nothing else came to him.

The Rigby now held in both hands, Brian edged forwards. Thirty feet ahead, the *donga* went into a gradual curve and, in order to use this to his advantage, he crossed the sand to keep to the longer bank. The sand gave him almost total silence underfoot.

The sun was hot, the shadows short and deep. He was half-way around the bend when a guinea fowl caught his eye. It was in the centre of the *donga* and he immediately thought of his promise to Broomhall, yet he did not raise the rifle and fire. Rather than scratching at the earth in search of seeds, the bird was standing erect, head up and bobbing slightly. It was not looking in Brian's direction but at a point on the shorter bank yet to come into vision.

Quite obviously, the bird was intently watching something. Brian froze and studied it. It had not seen him and he hoped it would not; if he alarmed it and it flew or ran off then whatever it was watching would understand the signal and vanish. Similarly, if it took fright but not at his presence he would know for certain there was something around the corner still ignorant of him.

As he watched, the guinea fowl thrashed its stubby wings and took to the air, alarming shrilly. Four or five others in the brush did likewise, their round, un-aerodynamic bodies crashing through low branches as they made good their escape.

Brian wondered if it was the civet. This was unlikely as the creature was primarily nocturnal but the droppings and scent

42

sprayings had been extremely fresh. He could hope: he had never shot one.

He was deciding whether to remain where he was and let the civet show itself when he heard from out of sight round the bend a sliding of earth followed by a gentle thud. Very smoothly, he raised the Rigby to his shoulder, easing off the safety catch.

For fully half a minute nothing happened and Brian was just starting to think that whatever it was that had driven off the guinea fowl had gone when – as if by some conjuring trick – there appeared in the very centre of the *donga*, in the middle of his field of vision, a male leopard.

It was not looking in Brian's direction but had its head turned away even though it was standing broadside on to him. Its ears were pricked, listening for the guinea fowl.

It was a young leopard in the finest possible coat, the rosette markings on its hindquarters so dark as to be almost black. The general colouring was a rich golden brown and the white underside of its belly was clean; as its tail flicked, Brian could see the white lower surface flash.

He aligned his sights on the leopard's shoulder, just in front of the bone, and squeezed the trigger. The report from the rifle was amplified by the sides of the *donga*.

The leopard spun round to face him. It moved so quickly he did not see so much as a blur – one moment it was side on, the next facing him. As a reflex, he pulled back the bolt and thrust another bullet into the breach, all the while keeping the sights on the leopard's head. Yet a second shot was not required: the first had, as Brian aimed, penetrated the lungs.

It was obvious the animal was not going to spring. It remained standing for perhaps a minute then swayed, its hind legs giving way before its front. Gradually, it lowered its belly to the sand and its head to its paws. It shivered once and its head fell to one side, the whiskers resting on one foreleg. Had he not just shot it, Brian might have thought it was asleep.

Keeping the rifle loaded and with the safety catch off, he bent his knees, picked up a stone the size of a tennis ball from the *donga* wall and threw it at the leopard. The missile hit the ground and bounced on to the animal's neck. It did not move.

43

Brian's legs grew weak. He sat on the sand, leaned against the bank and put the safety catch on. His hands were shaking now. Looking at the kill, he just could not believe it. He had set out to complete a dik-dik rug and ended up with a leopard, his first big cat.

At the sound of his gun, everything had fallen silent. The bird calls and the scrabbling of lizards had ceased. Now the sounds of the bush returned: birds sang, insects sawed and clicked, the skink on the bank showed itself opposite Brian, its inquisitive reptile's snout dodging from side to side, the thick black tongue oozing in and out, testing the air and tasting the presence of human. It darted back into the grass.

Brian walked over to the leopard. It was so beautiful he could find no thoughts in his head to describe it. He was a tangle of emotions – triumph, pride, exuberance, sorrow...

Slowly, savouring the moment, he knelt by the leopard and touched it. It was warm from the sunlight. As his hand rested on it, the fur twitched under his palm. The whiskers were coarse and stiff; the claws, when he touched them, sharp and thick with dried matter. The leopard had recently killed and eaten. The tail flicked once more against the sand.

'For the rest of my life, I shall remember this.' He spoke aloud. Then, '*Chui*!' he exclaimed jubilantly and set about the logistics of getting his kill to the Jeep. He did not want to skin it where it lay in the *donga*. Firstly, he was doubtful if his knife was sharp enough for the task – withdrawing it from its sheath and testing it with his thumb reinforced his doubts – and, secondly and more importantly, he wanted to show it off to Chopping. He grinned self-indulgently at the thought of Chopping's envy.

The leopard was heavy. Brian hauled it to the top of the bank, taking great care with the pelt, then hoisted it upon his shoulders, the feet hanging down on either side of his chest, the belly fur pressed to his neck. There was no blood on the pelt: as he knew, the skin of cats was so loose the chances of the bullet hole in the skin coinciding with the wound in the tissue were slight. Any bleeding would be subcutaneous. The rifle was an added burden but this was a once-in-a-lifetime opportunity and Brian was not going to lose it.

It took him over an hour and a half to reach the Jeep. He dared not put the leopard down as he was not sure he would be able to lift it again, so when he needed to rest, at increasingly short intervals, he leaned against a tree, the leopard pressing into the bark and providing him with a musky pillow. By the time he caught sight of the vehicle parked in narrow, midday shade every muscle in his shoulders and arms ached, his back was sore and his legs nearly giving way. He lowered the leopard into the rear of the Jeep, covering it with the canvas roof to keep the flies and hornets off.

It was, he reckoned, about one o'clock. He sat in the shadow of a nearby bush until his spine could take it no longer then lay back and arched his legs. Through the twigs, the sun sparkled and the blue of the sky hazed with heat.

He did not doze: that would be the ultimate foolishness. It was not from a fear of predators or the Mau Mau that he stayed alert but from a terror of cobras and puff adders. After an hour, he heard the distant cheeping of guinea fowl and, somewhat rested, set off after them.

As he arrived back at the Jeep, a brace of birds swinging from his hand, Chopping appeared out of the bush.

'That all you've got?' he said disparagingly.

Brian made no immediate reply. He dropped the two birds on top of the canvas.

'How about you?'

Chopping had been planning his surprise.

'Come and see this!' he demanded excitedly.

Brian followed him for half a mile to a clearing in the centre of which was a dead buffalo. It was a large bull with a wide spread of horns, flecks of foam dried around its mouth and wide, black nostrils. It had clearly been in a lather of rage just before its death.

'Good shot!'

Brian praised Chopping lavishly: it had been a finely placed bullet which had shattered the huge animal's spine and it was no mean feat to bring down such a beast with such a small calibre rifle. From the angle of the shot, Brian guessed Chopping had had some elevation.

'Treed you?'

'Yes,' Chopping answered sheepishly, jerking his thumb over his shoulder. 'That one over there.'

It was a medium-sized pod mahogany, the first ten feet of its trunk completely devoid of branches or even knots.

'I don't know what deserves the greater praise,' Brian joked, 'the shot or getting into the tree.'

'Both!' Chopping said with no pretence at modesty.

Brian punched the buffalo on its flank. It was like striking a leather-clad punch-bag full of damp sand.

'What do you want to do next?'

'Keep that head! Isn't it fine? I'll get it mounted at Rowland Ward. The vultures can have the rest.' A heavy flapping behind a bush announced the arrival of one of the scavengers. A maribou stork circled high overhead, riding a thermal. 'Been keeping them at bay. Can you give me a hand?'

Brian was a little worried his leopard might not be safe under the canvas but he had to agree to Chopping's request. So long as he had the cat skinned within eight hours, it should be unspoiled.

As they hacked at the neck muscles, slicing and splitting the flesh and sawing between the topmost vertebrae, the gathering of vultures shifted to the mahogany, to be joined there by the stork. A few alighted on the ground but kept a wary thirty yards from the carcass. Every now and then, Chopping threw a handful of dirt at them and they rose on huge, slow wingbeats to settle back in the branches. When the head was finally severed, the two boys wiped their knives, hands and knees with bundles of grass and carried the trophy back to the Jeep by the horns.

At the vehicle, Chopping was about to swing the buffalo head into the back when Brian stopped him.

'Hold on a minute. I've got my bag under there.'

'So you did get some dik-dik,' Chopping said. 'I thought a brace of guineas was a bit slight for the likes of you.'

Brian reached over and flung back the canvas.

'Christ! You got a leopard!'

Brian made no comment as Chopping ran first his eye and

then his hand over it. He lifted one paw and tested the claws with his finger.

'You lucky bugger! You lucky, bloody bugger! Where did you get it? I didn't hear a shot.'

'A couple of miles east. I was in a *donga*. I didn't hear your shot either.'

Chopping pushed at the leopard's head. The tissues were just beginning to stiffen. He felt under the animal's shoulder for the bullet hole.

'Textbook hit,' he commented. 'How the hell did you get it back here?'

'Carried it across my shoulders.'

Brian flexed his arms to ease the muscles. They were aching again with the effort of cutting the buffalo.

As they slowly drove along the track, Brian related his killing of the leopard, deliberately calling the animal a *chui* all the while.

It was still the middle of the afternoon when the two boys arrived in Wamumu, parking the Jeep in the shade of the guardhouse. As soon as Brian stopped the engine, there was the usual clicking as the exhaust pipe cooled and contracted.

In the guardhouse, Broomhall was seated at the desk with Lewis at his side. They were leafing through report sheets in manila folders, passing quiet comments on the contents. The askari on duty was absent.

Brian knocked on the open door. As Broomhall looked up he closed the folder, laying it face down on the desk top so the cover was hidden. It took him a moment to recognize Brian standing against the glare of the sun on the murram ground outside.

'Ah! It's you, Brian. You're early. What time is it?'

'Yes, sir. About three.'

'Well, come on in. Shove the door to, will you? Jim: stick the fan on.'

Lewis leaned back in his chair, pressing the switch of an antiquated official-issue fan which began to spin inside a black wire cage. It ruffled the papers and raised a small blizzard from the ashtray. Lewis re-adjusted the head with a butterfly knob on the side. As soon as he had tightened it

47

again, the head swung round to the original position, so he removed the ashtray instead.

'Public Works Department!' he said scathingly. 'You can tell anything from the PWD – it doesn't work or it's past it. Dim as NAAFI candles, that lot.'

'I don't want to interrupt your work,' Brian said, 'but I've got the promised guinea fowl...'

He held up the brace of birds and Broomhall tipped his chair back, slapping his hands to his stomach.

'Wonderful! That's most kind of you. My turn today, Jim!'

'With wife and encumbrance, your need's greater than mine,' Lewis replied.

'Get your dik-dik?'

'Not exactly,' Brian admitted.

Broomhall was too shrewd an interrogator to miss hidden emotion in a voice; usually he picked up guilt or cunning but now he sensed suppressed excitement.

'Let's see it, then. We're not doing anything that important here.'

When they set eyes on Chopping holding his buffalo head, balancing it on the side of the Jeep, both men offered their congratulations. Chopping accepted their praise but without the pleasure he had anticipated when he shot the animal.

'The real trophy's in there,' he said grudgingly, glancing into the Jeep.

Brian's leopard was lying across the well between the rear seats. The sun was not shining on it and the colours seemed all the richer for being in the shade.

'My word! That is a fine one,' Broomhall complimented Brian, turning the leopard's front paw and spreading the pads apart to run his index finger in the fur between them. 'Drop him in one shot?'

'Yes, sir. In the shoulder.'

Broomhall felt along the pelt until his finger came upon the bullet-hole.

'Right on the mark! You must be very proud. It's an exceptional trophy. You two've certainly had one hell of a day!'

'That's one of the best leopards I've seen taken around these parts,' Lewis commented. 'Jolly well done.'

Brian again related the incident and Broomhall made a note of where the animal was shot. A number of goats and dogs had been taken by a leopard from the furthest *shambas* along the track and he had been asked by the locals to stop the carnage; he wondered if this was the culprit stretched out before him.

'You two've got a lot to do now. Get that head emptied out a bit and skin the leopard. Done one before?'

Brian had not, and admitted that, during his long haul of the dead leopard through the bush, his chief anxiety had been that after the thrill of the hunt he might make a mess of the trophy.

'Tell you what, then,' Broomhall suggested. 'Get Nchembe, our resident one-armed bandit, to do it for you. He's fixed your *gari*, by the way – and that impala's finished. He knows what he's doing. Did a lion for me a year back, just after he got here. A damn fine job he made of it, too. I don't know where he picked up the knack but he has it. Treated the pelt, as well. Supple as anything now.'

Broomhall's suggestion was readily accepted and, the unspent ammunition replaced in the safety of the cabinet, Chopping took the Jeep down to the tent with his buffalo head, while Brian, following an askari, entered the camp, the leopard across his shoulders once more.

The Land Rover had been lowered from its blocks and turned around. As they walked past it, Brian could see from the tyre marks in the dirt that the vehicle had been driven round and round at full steering lock, to test the shaft and joint.

The *totos* gawked at him as he passed the corrugated iron buildings, the sun striking so hotly from the surfaces that it was like stepping beside the open door of a furnace. The prisoners watched him pass, whispering and murmuring amongst themselves. Only one spoke to him: it was Ndegwa.

'*Mzuri sana, bwana – kidogo!*'

The African stressed his last word with a sneer and Brian realized the addition of *kidogo* was a deliberate insult but he ignored it.

'*Asante*,' he replied, smiling. '*Chui si kidogo!*'

Ndegwa did not answer: the leopard was indeed not small, and the irony turned back on the detainee.

Nchembe's hut was close to the perimeter wire. From the doorway, he could look through the barbed-wire in the direction of the boys' tent. As Brian approached with the askari, Nchembe was squatting on the step. He stood up.

'That is a very fine *chui*,' he complimented Brian. 'I had been told you had shot one. Was it a dangerous time?'

'Not really,' Brian admitted. 'He did not see me. He was looking the other way.'

'That does not matter. Maybe he saw you in his dreams,' Nchembe reasoned. 'Today was his day to die so he did not mind. Maybe he wanted to look away like the man about to be executed closes his eyes.'

Brian felt a wave of sadness come over him; the exhilaration of having killed the leopard diminished somewhat.

'I hadn't thought of it like that,' he said.

'That too does not matter. It is the nature of things to live and die.'

Brian lowered the leopard to the ground and Nchembe rubbed his only hand across the leopard's head.

'So now you would like me to remove the skin? As I did for the *bwana* inspector's lion? I will do so gladly but I must ask a payment of you for it.'

'Of course,' Brian tried not to sound offended. 'As with the *gari*, I insist on paying you something. In fact, I was going to ask you how much we owe you for doing the repairs.'

'You have paid for the *gari* with meat,' Nchembe answered, 'and I have the head for you to take to Nairobi to the ... *duka ya....*' He was lost for the correct phrase.

'Taxidermist,' Brian said.

Nchembe laughed and repeated the word, adding, 'That I must remember for my notebook.'

'So what can I pay you for doing the leopard? I have some shillings with me or – if you will trust me – I will have some money sent for you.'

'I do not want shillings. If you will let me, I would like some of the teeth of the leopard.'

50

Brian could hardly refuse such a reasonable offer.

'Of course,' he said. 'I only want one for myself. One of the incisors. The pointed ones.'

'Yes, I know that. The sharp ones for holding prey.'

From the darkness of his quarters, Nchembe brought a cut-throat razor and a strop. He fastened it by a length of cord to the staple in the wall which held the door open, tying the knot skilfully, one-handed. To keep the strop taut, he held the loose end to the ground with his foot. Wetting the leather from water in a nearby bucket, he set about sharpening the blade which was already well worn and slightly sickled. The askari, noting the prisoner and the *mzungu* seemed not to need his presence, wandered off in the direction of the camp *duka*. In the afternoon, the men tended to congregate there to smoke and talk.

Brian sat cross-legged on the ground, watching in silence as Nchembe squatted, rolled the leopard onto its back and pulled its legs outwards.

'You will help me?' the African asked.

Shifting forwards, Brian took hold of the hind quarters and held them spread. *Rigor mortis* was setting in, the flesh stiff and unyielding. Nchembe sat astride the leopard's chest and nicked the soft skin between the hind legs, his stump of arm pressing the flesh flat, the razor moving very close to the amputation. Brian felt a quiver of nerves lift the hair on his neck. He thought of Broomhall's comment – the Mau Mau cut off the penises of their enemies ... The razor was near to the fly on his tight shorts.

Very carefully, Nchembe moved the blade down the central line of the leopard's belly from its genital area to the start of its throat.

'I keep the underfur,' he commented, his voice quiet with concentration. 'If you do not like it you can cut it away later. I think it best to keep it. The softness is good to touch.'

'Who taught you this?'

'No one. I just know how to do it. Perhaps I have seen the *wazee* doing this and learnt when I was a *toto*. I cannot know of this.'

'Perhaps it is instinctive,' Brian suggested. 'Just as it is easy for Europeans to do some things, so it is for Africans to do things from their own world.'

Nchembe grunted, moving the razor along the underneath of the leopard's skin, his stump adeptly folding back the ever-increasing rolls of skin. Brian marvelled at how the African was doing with one hand what he would find difficult with two.

After some minutes of silence, and just as Nchembe completed the belly, removing the skin from the lining of greyish fat and slimy layers of subcutaneous tissue, Brian asked, 'What does your name mean?'

'Mean?'

'I thought common names were based on patronymics...'

Nchembe looked up from where he was starting on one of the forelegs: he had not understood.

'On one's father's name,' Brian went on, searching for an example. 'Like Njeroge *wa* Kamau – Njeroge son of Kamau...'

'That can be the case but not so for me. I have my own name. You will know I was called Matthew when I went to school. And I was nicknamed '*na jembe*' because I was good at digging in the school *shamba*. Do you know what that means?'

'It means "with a *jembe*" – a digging implement.'

'You know many Swahili words...'

'Not many,' Brian conceded. 'Only enough for everyday talking.'

Gripping the leopard's foreleg under his half-arm, Nchembe concentrated on cutting round the paw so it should come free and be able to flatten out, the pads and claws *in situ*.

'I changed it to Nchembe. It is a better name...'

The foreleg done, the African turned his attention to the hind leg on the same side. Brian shifted to allow him to grasp the leg under his arm again.

'Now I work around the animal and roll it over as it is cut. The head is last. This one is to have a flat head.'

He had made the decision; he had not asked Brian.

'You are strange for a young *mzungu*,' Nchembe stated, the

52

hind leg finished and his razor starting to slice carefully along the line of the leopard's back, Brian rolling the animal over.

'Why do you say that?'

His hands were slipping on the cold flesh and, by the shoulder, there was a mass of black, semi-clotted blood under the pelt which was making his hands a sticky maroon.

'Why are you interested in me?' Nchembe asked. 'We seldom have Europeans in the camp – except for the officers, of course, and some visiting politicians from London last month.' He looked up thoughtfully for an instant. 'They too were interested in me...'

Brian was lost for words. He could not come straight out with the fact of his curiosity nor could he immediately admit to liking the African. The former would have been patronizing and most likely have had Nchembe stop his task and walk away. The latter would have made him cautious and on edge. Yet both were true and valid reasons: he was curious to be in the company of what his kind viewed as the enemy in a bloody war, and he did like the African. It was not something he could assess logically. Just as he had found an immediate affinity for some people at school – or an instant hatred of others – so he had a sudden and firm response to this African of more or less his own age.

Nchembe accurately interpreted his silence.

'You are wondering about me as a Mau Mau soldier?'

'No, not really ...' Brian began but decided truth was the best course to follow. 'Well, yes, I am, in a way. I have not met a ...' he was not sure how the word would sound '... terrorist before.'

'I am not a Mau Mau. I was one but that was before. Now I know it was wrong.'

'They do evil things,' Brian said.

'Yes, they do. I have done this. But that is not what I mean in wrong. I mean they are wrong. They are not doing it right.'

He was silent then and Brian made no reply. The razor was beginning on the second hind leg and he rolled the leopard further over. It looked ugly and lewdly naked without its spotted, luxurious skin.

'What are they not doing right?'

Nchembe stopped cutting, dipped the razor in the bucket and began to sharpen it again on the leather strop.

'You will not understand. This is for Africans.'

'Tell me.'

Working the razor back and forth, Nchembe looked out through the detention centre fence. The sun was casting the shadow of the building through the barbed-wire and across the earth on the far side.

'Are you worried I will report what you say to the inspectors?'

Still Nchembe said nothing. He ceased his slapping of the blade on the wet strop and tested its sharpness on the door frame. It cleanly sliced a thin sliver of wood.

'Perhaps you will. But then, they know my thoughts so I will tell you. Even though you are a European. But first, you hold the leopard for me to cut. My arm,' he moved his stump in a short circle in the air, 'is tired. The joint on your *gari* was very hard to fit.'

Brian held the last of the leopard's legs vertical while Nchembe skinned it.

'Now I will tell you. What they are doing wrong is fighting with the gun and the *panga*, the bomb and the grenade ... And they are killing our own people more than the British or the Asians. This is not the way. What we want is our freedom from colonial rule, but what is the use if we kill our own kind to get this? We must instead use the same weapons as the Europeans ...'

He did not take his eyes from the delicate cutting around the paw. One slip of the razor here could ruin the pelt: cutting was difficult where there was little flesh and the skin was near the bone.

'Those weapons,' he went on, 'are not the gun and spear. Not threats and blows. They are propaganda, politics, education of the masses to rise not in an armed struggle but in one of ideology and belief. Once we believe in freedom, we will be free. We can kill, of course. But for every dead man ...'

He hesitated, then went on, 'A man is only a small part; we must strike at the whole body. Think what would happen if all Africans refused to buy from Asian stores. That,' he said

54

triumphantly as the skin, pad and claws came free in one piece, 'is power for the masses.'

'I can understand you wanting to be free,' Brian said. 'Not all Europeans are against this...'

'Most are. The farmers, the settlers, the South Africans who came here many years ago, the businessmen... When we are free, there will be a place for them here. We shall still need them to prosper. They will not be the rulers. Yet they will not be the small people either.'

With Brian holding the head still, Nchembe started making small, deft incisions to the skin covering the skull. This was perhaps the most difficult part of the operation and, although it required close concentration, Nchembe did not stop talking.

'The time will come,' he prophesied with assurance. 'One day, Kenya will be for Kenyans. Then we shall have one country of the people, for the people, by the people. White men can live here and prosper with us. But they shall know they are in our land.'

He lowered his head close to the leopard's, watching carefully where his blade was working. Brian felt the African's breath blowing across his hand. Every now and then, as he progressed across the animal's cranium, Nchembe pushed Brian's fingers along with the back of the razor.

'That is the way it should be,' Brian said. 'A land must belong to those who are its natural inhabitants. As the game reserves belong to the animals.'

Nchembe stopped cutting. His eyes flashed as he turned his face upwards.

'This is not for preservation!' he said quietly. 'This is for progress.'

'I didn't mean it to sound like that,' Brian said defensively. He thought for a moment and, knowing the Africans' love of parables, went on, 'Africa perhaps should be like a zebra – a mixture of black and white – evenly distributed – running as a herd in harmony.'

Nchembe laughed and replied, 'That is funny. Do you know why the zebra is so brightly striped? It is not to hide himself. It is to confuse those that hunt him. If Africa was so,

55

it would confuse many people! They would not know which way Africa would run. The South Africans ...' He grew serious. 'No. Perhaps it would be better if Africa was like the kudu bull.'

'How?'

'The kudu is strong and beautiful. Its horns curl towards the sky. And it is grey, a complete mixture of black and white. But there is a problem. Across the shoulders of the kudu are thin white lines: those are the Afrikaners. Do you see how the kudu often stands in the shade under a tree and rubs his shoulders on the bark? He is not scratching at ticks in his fur: the tickbirds rid him of those things. No. He is trying to erase the Afrikaners...'

Nchembe cut along the black lips of the leopard's mouth; the skin was thin here and parted easily. The art was to prevent it ripping.

'Where do you go to school?' Nchembe asked suddenly.

'The Duke of York School. On the Ngong Road, towards Karen.'

'I know of it.'

He was parting the cheeks from the side of the mouth, each cut less than a quarter of an inch long. Already the whiskers were free.

'What would happen if you said this in your school?'

'I should not be popular.'

'Would your fellow pupils beat you?'

'Probably.'

'But you are strong.'

Brian smiled and replied. 'But they are many!'

Nchembe stood up.

'Roll the *chui* over.'

As Brian rolled the skinned cat, the earth stuck to its stringy, fatted tissues; Nchembe was holding the pelt in one piece, the skin from over the skull hanging like a loose cap.

'Now you know how it feels to be an African!' he exclaimed. 'We think the Europeans – the *mzungus* – are many and we are afraid of them. But it is not so. It is we who are the many. That is why we shall win without killing.'

From within his quarter, Nchembe produced a cloth bag of

saltpetre and, spreading the skin on the ground fur side downwards, sprinkled the chemical liberally over the surface of the trophy, rubbing it in with his fingers.

'I trust you. Yet I do not know your name. You are just *Mzungu*.'

'*Jina langu ni* Brian Titchner.'

Nchembe laughed loudly at the Swahili.

'May I present myself? I am Matthew Nchembe. But you know that.' He put the razor on the doorstep. 'I will shake your hand.'

Brian's palm was tacky with congealed blood and Nchembe's was glutinous with strands of fat and skin tissue, grainy with chemical crystals. As they gripped each other's fist there wept out from between their fingers an ooze of greyish matter.

Each had a serious glint in his eyes. It was the first time Brian had ever shaken an African by the hand.

'Now we are friends,' Brian stated with determination, 'and I trust you.'

It was, he believed, the best way in which he could return the other's similar compliment and, as he spoke, a strange feeling of kinship washed over him, an emotion he had never before experienced. He realised quite suddenly he very much liked this African, this terrorist, this enemy.

'But your trust is worth more than mine,' the African commented, interrupting his thoughts and holding up the bag of saltpetre, 'because with this I can make gunpowder.'

Placing the rolled-up skin gingerly in the rear of the Land Rover, Brian said, 'Thank you for fixing the *gari*.'

Nchembe shrugged.

'You will let me give you some money? For you and Ndegwa?'

'Ndegwa will not take it. He is more a Mau Mau – he does not like white men. And I have been paid in meat.'

Brian did not press the matter, instead starting the Land Rover.

'I will come back tomorrow, before I leave,' he promised.

'That I know. For I will have the leopard's tooth for you.'

As the vehicle bumped over the ground towards the tent,

Brian looked up the slope to the camp but was unable to decide which of the corrugated buildings was Nchembe's home.

4

The new moon rose late and was only in the bottom branches of the acacias by the time Chopping and Brian kicked over the fire, seeing the last of the rubbish burning in the embers. With the clear sky, it was chilly; the flames dead, there was little to keep them out of their tent, the warmth of their sleeping bags and blankets.

There was insufficient room inside for the two of them to go through the cramped struggle out of their clothes and into their bags so they were obliged to undress one by one. Chopping entered the tent first: he did this every night. Brian was annoyed at Chopping's selfishness but said nothing. In some ways, it was a relief to be able to stand in the bush alone, watch the stars or the moon, listen to the callings of the animals, the only hint of Chopping's presence being an ill-defined, scrabbling shadow moving haphazardly under the tent canvas.

An owl hooted distantly as Brian moved to the far side of the acacias where there was no undergrowth except thin, bent grass. Here the moon was unscarred by boughs and the cold air lent it a faint halo. He had once seen wide, dense rings round a full moon when on leave with his parents in Britain, a country they usually avoided on their vacations, preferring to go to the Seychelles or Mauritius, where his father indulged himself in his passion for painting birds and his mother could swim or snorkel to her heart's content.

That year, they had flown to the United Kingdom for Christmas to stay with his Uncle Phillip, his parents wanting him to see a British winter and experience snow – he had only ever seen it in the distance on Mount Kenya, Mount Kilimanjaro, the Drakensberg or the Ruwenzori Mountains, and the Mountains of the Moon to the west of Uganda where the forest gorillas lived. They also wanted him to meet his aunt, Phillip's wife Ada, who was dying of cancer in a discreet nursing-home on the seafront at Eastbourne.

The trip, for all its sorrow and tension, had been an interesting one. Brian had not expected to see palm-trees growing on the British seashore, albeit straggled examples with the tips of their fronds browned by the sea and the frost. And they bore no vestige of nuts. He had been taken to the Tower of London and shown the Crown Jewels but was unimpressed by them: they were too gaudy to be anything more than glass. To Brian a diamond was the small, quartzite-looking chip projecting from the matrix of a pebble which he had picked up – by vast good fortune and to the never-ending jealousy of his school friends – from the ground on a holiday in South Africa. He had also seen Buckingham Palace – where the King was dying of the same disease as was killing his aunt; the Houses of Parliament; the British Museum and the Elgin Marbles, and the Natural History Museum in South Kensington which had depressed his spirit to the lowest ebb of the whole stay in Britain. In glass cases or on pedestals surrounded by dusty ropes stood stuffed lions, tigers, leopards. Even a stuffed elephant stood in the foyer to the museum. Other creatures he usually gave no more than a moment's attention to – hyrax, impala, gazelle, dik-dik, various lizards and snakes – were being gazed at by knots of animated schoolchildren, boys in long shorts and dark blazers, girls in bottle-green or navy-blue skirts which projected from beneath their overcoats. Each child, like the creatures mounted in the cabinets, seemed lifeless, drab. Brian left the museum with an unease boiling in him which he could not understand.

There were two highlights to his holiday. The first was being taken to Oxford where he was shown around the university town and given lunch, with the dean, in his father's old college.

Brian wanted from that moment to follow in his father's footsteps, to wear a gown and dine with deans and professors.

The dean enthralled him: an old man who smoked a pipe with a loose bowl which periodically twisted on to its side as he talked and deposited glowing tobacco on the front of his gown, whereupon the conversation would be interrupted by a hurried flapping of the gown and stamping-out of tobacco on the much-scorched carpet. He was an internationally respected apiologist. For the first ten minutes of their meeting Brian had been under the impression that the man was an expert on apes, yet his talk kept returning to attempts to persuade Brian's father to obtain a hive of African killer bees. No such creatures existed in Kenya, so far as Brian knew.

To keep Brian occupied after lunch, as he and Brian's father shared a bottle of the college's port, the dean had given Brian access to a cupboard at the rear of his 'rooms', as he called his one-roomed office-cum-sitting room.

In the cupboard was an assortment of boxes. Some contained beetles or parts of beetles, some butterfly wings in cellophane envelopes, some an assortment of crickets. All were desiccated, mounted on card or cork, their legs missing or their antennae absent. Some had been neatly sliced in two, longitudinally, by a very sharp blade which had made easy work of even the thick beetle carapaces. The dean, catching sight of Brian looking bemusedly into the boxes, directed him to one on the middle shelf and labelled *Papilionidae – mostly demodocus.*'

'You take extreme care with those, boy!' the dean had cautioned, as if speaking to a servant.

Brian opened the box. Laid out with scientific precision, packed in cotton wood, in layers divided by strengthened corrugated cardboard, were over one hundred immaculately painted toy soldiers.

The other highlight of the holiday had been provided by his dying aunt. On Brian's last visit to Eastbourne, his parents put on a brave face, for his mother, Aunt Ada's younger sister, knew they would not meet again. Uncle Phillip asked him to leave his aunt's room for a few minutes. Brian stood in the corridor, the odour of disinfectant and medicine tickling his throat, gazing out at the sleet-swept promenade. The piles of the pier which he had longed to visit (only it was 'shut for the season') loomed like a recumbent skeleton in the cold mist, reminding him of the dead dinosaurs in the museum.

When he was called back into the room Brian saw his aunt had had her pillows puffed up and was sitting more erectly than he had seen her do before. Across her lap, seeming to dent not only the blankets and the quilt but even her legs, lay a long package tied in twine and wrapped in brown paper.

Brian's uncle said, 'Your aunt would like you to accept this gift.'

His aunt smiled wanly in agreement. She was unable to talk for long and then only in a whisper.

Brian expressed his thanks quietly. Being in the nursing home was like being in church – no one spoke loudly.

'It is only a small gift, but your aunt wants you to have something you will treasure for the rest of your life and which will remind you of her.'

Brian heard his mother sniff behind his back and catch her breath.

'Thank you very much,' he repeated, this time a little louder. Without being bidden, for he thought it best, he leaned over the edge of the bed, kissing his aunt on the side of her mouth. Her claw-like fingers shakily rose from the bed to brush his cheek.

'Undo it, then,' his uncle murmured.

Under the brown paper was a polished wooden box with brass clips. He snapped them out and lifted the lid. Within, in felt sections and wrapped in baize cloths, was the Rigby.

A rustle over his head announced the arrival of an owl in the acacia. Brian saw the dark blot of the bird outlined against the moon's halo; it stretched its wings and coughed, a pellet falling through the twigs and sparse leaves to land gently in the dust by the trunk. A night bird which had been singing mournfully in a thorn bush thirty yards away abruptly ceased its calling. From the far ridge across the *donga* came the grunt of a lion followed by the sharp yap of a jackal.

Turning towards the tent, Brian watched as the circle of moths and midges gyrated around the area of canvas directly above Chopping's lantern. Although the batteries were going flat, there was still enough of a glimmer to attract them. A flicker of shadow through the cloud disturbed its chaotic order for a moment: Brian wondered what species of bat it was.

'I'm done,' Chopping called. His silhouette lay down on the shadow of his camp bed.

Brian did not answer and Chopping extinguished his lantern. The switch had a loud click to which the owl responded with a similar noise.

There was an ill-defined mystery about the bush under moonlight. Shadows seemed slight but were in fact dense. The browns, buffs and ochres of the sunlit hours were drained of colour until the entire landscape appeared as an under-exposed black and white photograph. In this eerie world of greys and blacks, Brian customarily felt a deep sense of satisfying fear.

He enjoyed being afraid. It took only a quick shock to unsettle him. He hated being taken by sudden surprise, a fact some of his peers in school capitalised upon when they sought to hurt or rag him. Yet the gradual accumulation of rationalised fear was something in which he revelled, to which he looked forward. If it grew upon him slowly he could savour it, test himself against it and relate to it. For this reason, he enjoyed standing in the moonlight, surveying the shadows and listening to the night sounds of insects and small rodents, night birds and hunting, nocturnal predators. There was nothing of which to be truly afraid. He could identify every sound he heard, whether it was the far-off lion grunting or the owl flexing its wings.

At last, satisfied with the night, he walked round the acacia to the tent, pulled the flap aside and entered, tying the laces across in loose bows behind him.

He undressed to his underpants, pulled on a vest and wormed his way into his sleeping bag. Before lying down, he quickly cast the weak beam of his torch over the interior of the tent. From the ridge pole hung Chopping's shoes – safe, he hoped, from the intrusion of snakes or scorpions. Just beside them was splayed on the canvas a threatening but harmless spider, fully four inches in legspan. On the ground by Brian's metal trunk a thin column of ants was patrolling the earth on the off-chance of discovering a hole or some spillage of food.

A moth appeared from the folds of the canvas and alighted on the torch glass. Brian flicked it with his finger. It fell twitching to the ground where its movements attracted the ants; by morning, it and they would be gone with no trace remaining except, perhaps, a thin path beaten by their minuscule legs.

Brian extinguished the torch and turned over, pulling the sleeping bag up to his head. Like an African, he slept with almost his entire head under the covers.

He was woken by a gentle but insistent shaking of his shoulder. Rolling onto his side, he peered through the darkness, discerning nothing but a vague human form leaning over him.

'What ...' he began dazedly.

A hand clamped over his mouth so fiercely that it pressed his lips against his teeth and he tasted a thin smear of his own blood. He tried to sit up but the same hand, forced against his mouth, prevented him.

'Ptts!'

Lips rubbed against his ear.

Brian was terrified: this was the sudden fear he abhorred. A single thought coursed through his mind – Ndegwa, who would not accept a European's money. Yet the odour coming from the body was not the earthy, catching scent of an African. It was more a warm, cloying smell. Underlying it was a honey-ish, meaty, sour stink like that of rotten flesh smeared with treacle.

'It's me!' the mouth hissed into his ear, a fine spray of spittle wetting his skin. 'Chopping!' it added unnecessarily.

His eyes now adjusted to the gloom. Brian recognised Chopping's outline. Above his head, the ridge of the tent was vibrating gently as if under the influence of a minor earth tremor.

'There's something – or someone – outside!' Chopping murmured. 'Don't make a noise.'

He removed his hand and Brian gulped a deep breath.

As if gripped by a dustdevil, the tent lurched violently. The poles, bamboo dowelling fixed to each other by brass screw joints, creaked and bent.

64

Brian brought his knees to his chin, silently slipped out of his sleeping bag and reached under his bed for his sheath knife. He eased it from its leather scabbard, grasping the antler handle firmly.

'Torch!' he muttered.

With considerable trepidation but mounting excitement, his heart pounding and his breath coming in short, inaudible gasps, he raised the side of the tent where the low canvas wall, below the bottom of the pitched roof, hung vertically. Chopping snapped on the torch.

At that moment, the sloping tent roof bulged inwards. One of the upright poles bent and splintered.

There, right against the canvas and in the torch beam, was the plate-sized front paw of a lion.

'Christ!' Chopping yelled, his presence of mind lost. 'It's a bloody *simba*!'

The lion was even more afraid. With a throaty snort which echoed in the tent, it fled, only to become entangled as it tried to escape in the ropes and fly-sheet. There were a few seconds of thrashing, scratching pandemonium, accompanied by terrified growls and a strangled scream from Chopping, then the ropes broke free either of the pegs or the canvas and the end of the tent collapsed. The fly-sheet tore from the roof and was whipped away.

The sounds of the lion, enmeshed in the fly-sheet, faded somewhat then returned as the creature rampaged through the grassy patch beyond the acacia, trying desperately to rid itself of its temporary coat. At last, with a loud half-roar, it shed the covering and charged off through the moonlit bush.

Brian unlaced the tent flap and stepped outside, his knife in his hand. The moon was low and weak. He guessed it was not long until dawn. Chopping emerged from the wreck of their tent, holding his rifle by the barrel.

'Going to club it to death?' Brian asked, unable to disguise the laughter behind his words.

'You stab it, I'll club it,' Chopping replied.

Brian sat on the fallen log by their now-dead fire and started to laugh. Chopping sat next to him and joined in.

'By the way,' Brian said, in friendly mockery, 'I do wish you'd use the English words.'

'What do you mean?' Chopping asked, his laughter falling.

'You said "Bloody *simba*" when you saw the pug.'

Chopping, for a brief moment, took on the years and voice of his father.

'Mere aberration,' he excused himself. 'Heat of the moment...'

There was little point in returning to bed so they dressed, retrieved their box of matches from the ruin of the tent and lit a fire. With pullovers on under their bush jackets, they sat close to the flames, boiled a pan of water and made themselves sweet, black coffee. As the dawn broke, they surveyed the damage.

The lion had somehow inveigled itself into the space between the tent and fly-sheet. Brian guessed it was rubbing at an itch, had gone too far under the canvas and then lost its temper at the moment they had so startled it. A hundred yards away they found the remains of the fly-sheet, shredded and hanging in strips on a wait-a-bit thorn bush.

After the morning ringing of the steel rail had sounded from within the camp, Brian left Chopping to break camp and walked up to the guardhouse. From the platform on top of one of the timber trellis-work guard towers, an askari waved down to him and called out. His words were indistinct. Obviously, the hullabaloo of their pre-dawn escapade had been heard by askaris on night duty. Inspector Lewis was in the office, counting out the contents of the petty-cash box.

'Hello!' he exclaimed, as Brian knocked on the door. 'Hear you had a spot of bother in the night.'

'After a fashion, sir,' Brian allowed.

'One of us came down to see you were okay. Saw you both building a fire so decided not to disturb you. It's always fun facing the aftermath alone. Without the interference of us adults.'

He laughed then, his hand spilling a neat stack of shillings which dominoed into his other carefully ordered piles of coins, knocking them down.

'Damn!' he swore, adding, 'Had a visitor, I believe?'

'A lion got caught up in the guy ropes. I'm afraid he got a bit stroppy with the fly-sheet.'

He related the sequence of events to Lewis who grew increasingly amused as the narrative unfolded. When Brian reached the climax, Lewis's laughter was exceeded only by Broomhall's; the latter had come in behind Brian and eavesdropped on the conversation.

'It was just as well you didn't have your bolts,' Broomhall observed, patting Brian on the shoulder.

'Why's that, sir?'

'If you had had them your instinct would have been to shoot the lion. Aiming through the tent, you'd hardly have been sure of an instant dropping shot. And you've seen what wounded lions can do ... I once saw one utterly demolish a lantana bush in his anger at having been wounded. He spun around and around so fast there was not a chance to draw a bead on him. Only a Patchett could have brought him down. We just had to wait until he was exhausted.'

'I hadn't thought of that,' Brian admitted as he realized that because of the detention camp rules, his life – and Chopping's – had probably been saved: he would certainly have fired had he had the chance.

After a pause, Lewis recommenced counting out the petty cash.

'We'll be on our way this morning,' Brian said.

'No need to ask if you've had a good time,' Broomhall replied. 'One monitor, a damn fine *chui* and a few passably good trophies isn't a bad bag for a few days in an area you expected to give only a couple of brace of birds – for which, thank you very much! Had them roasted and covered with cream sauce. One of the few dishes our cookboy's taken to with relish.' He grimaced. 'Pardon the pun.'

'I wondered if I might go into the camp once more?' Brian requested.

'See chum Nchembe? Yes, go ahead.'

Brian fidgeted and Broomhall sensed there was something else on his mind.

'Has he been...' Brian began hesitantly. 'I mean, is he ... rehabilitated?'

Broomhall rubbed his chin. He had missed shaving one spot of his neck. His fingers rasped on the roughened skin.

'I suppose, in a way, he is. He's not a Kimathi-ite now. More a Kenyatta-ite. He's for peace and stability with majority rule. I think his denunciation of the oath is genuine. Not just following Kenyatta's 1952 curse on all things Mick. What do you think, Jim?'

Lewis completed his counting of a pile of fifty shillings and looked up.

'I'd agree with that. I think he's educated enough, intelligent enough if you will, to see the best way forward's not to go and massacre his fellow Kukes.'

'Will he be released soon?' Brian asked.

'That's doubtful. Not many are let go. Not yet. Some of them in there are still very nasty characters ...'

Brian, taking his leave of the two officers, made his way across the dirt patch of the parade ground and stood by the main gate as it was opened by the askari on sentry duty.

Within the camp the prisoners were just stirring. Crowded around standpipes, they were filling their *dhebis* with water, washing themselves or drinking. At a store shed, there was a long line awaiting the issue of tools: every day a work party was marched out of the camp, chivvied into lorries and driven off to work on road-building or repairing in the direction of Embu. Nchembe, Brian guessed, would not be required for such labour.

He found Matthew Nchembe's quarters without any difficulty; Nchembe was sitting on the step soaping himself. As Brian approached, he tipped a dibber of water down his front, disregarding his tattered shorts which were soaked and clung to his thighs. In the morning sunlight, he looked handsome and proud, his ebony body shining as if oiled.

'*Jambo*! Good morning,' Brian greeted him.

Nchembe smiled.

'So you keep your word; you have returned. To say goodbye to me. And to get your tooth, no doubt.'

He looked over his shoulder and spoke into the darkness of the A-frame. A voice replied and he entered the building. Brian, curious, stepped to the door and crossed the threshold.

The air within was thick with the stink of sleeping bodies, cheap tobacco smoke and *posho* porridge. Around the walls were low beds and, against the far end, a double tier of metal-framed bunks. In the centre was a table with orange boxes for chairs. From the roof hung strips of the antelope meat drying into biltong. A column of aluminium food bowls stood next to an oil lamp with a heavily sooted glass.

'*Jambo*,' Brian said to the three Africans sitting on the edges of the beds. They made no reply but glowered at him, the whites of their eyes stark in the light searing in through the doorway.

Nchembe, rummaging in a box beneath one of the bunks, said without glancing over his shoulder, 'It is best for you to wait outside. These fellows ...' His words faded but their meaning was plain.

Brian stepped back and left the closeness of the room, thinking how the atmosphere was not just thick with stale air but also with a tension of animosity.

'Here is your due,' Nchembe said, closing the door behind him and stepping into the sunlight. From within came a grumble of low voices.

'I'm sorry ...' Brian began, darting a look at the door over the African's shoulder.

'There is no need for you to do this. They are not clever men. They will not make trouble for me, either. This is not your Duke of York School.'

He held out his fist and opened it, palm upwards. Resting on the lighter, brown skin of his hand were two leopard's teeth – an incisor and a molar. Both were cleaned of flesh, shining as white as had the detainees' eyes in the semi-darkness of the A-frame.

'For you.'

Brian took the teeth and rolled them from side to side in his own hand.

'I have kept the same two teeth,' Nchembe said. 'The remainder I have sold. This one,' he pointed to the molar, 'I will give to a friend. It is the sharp tooth I shall keep.'

'Then I shall give my molar to my friend, too,' Brian replied, wondering as he did so if Chopping would accept it.

He gazed through the wire of the detention camp boundary. From down the slope came the sound of the Land Rover starting. Chopping had loaded their equipment.

'I should like to keep in touch and write to you,' Brian ventured, transferring the teeth to his left hand.

'That would not be good. It is not usual to receive letters.'

The African spoke quietly, his rejection of the idea firm, yet Brian believed that he too was reluctant to sever their relationship.

Nchembe offered his hand and Brian took it in his.

'Thank you for fixing the *gari*, and skinning the *chui*. And for talking.'

'We shall meet again,' Nchembe predicted. 'If you pass Wamumu again, maybe the inspector will allow you to visit me.'

'I'd like that.'

'Be a good *mzungu*,' Nchembe said suddenly, his single hand tightening. 'Remember we will need people like you in the new Africa, the black Africa.'

He spoke with such power, such pride and assurance that Brian could find no suitable reply.

'I shall certainly come back to see you,' he promised and, as he walked away, felt a lump rise in his throat.

At the corner of the camp, as he turned to follow the perimeter wire to the main gate, he looked back. Nchembe was standing by the wire, speaking to a sentry positioned between the two fences. He faced in Brian's direction and waved the stump of his arm.

5

Oudu, dressed in his best white *kanzu* and with a red fez balanced upon his tight curls, entered the sitting room carrying a mahogany tray of glasses which chimed against each other as his bare feet slapped on the parquet floor. He slid the tray onto the bar, flicking at the polished surface around it with a duster.

'*Saa ngapi mabwana wanafika?*' asked Brian.

'*Saa kumi na mbili, bwana kidogo,*' the houseboy replied.

'Six o'clock.'

Though Brian was now eighteen, the servants still called him 'Little Master'.

Brian looked at the gold Eternamatic watch on his wrist: though he seldom wore a watch in the bush, he always did at home or at school. There, time was of the essence whereas in the bush it was of little import. One woke with the sun and slept when it lowered.

'Are you ready, Brian dear?'

His mother entered behind the servant. She, too, was carrying a tray upon which were bowls of cashews, sultanas and Bombay mix with several plates of chipolata sausages, cubes of cheese and fresh pineapple on cocktail sticks. She lowered her tray to a coffee table and cast her eyes rapidly over her son.

'Oh, Brian!' she exclaimed with resigned parental exasperation. 'You're filthy. What have you been doing?'

'Diana,' he answered enigmatically, 'and her daughters.'

'I hope you've finished.'

'Not quite. I came in to get a pair of pliers. The wire's still loose.'

'Well, do leave her and get changed. The first guests'll be here any minute. One would have thought,' she added sharply, gazing obviously at his new watch, 'that buying you a two-thousand-shilling gold watch for your birthday might

71

encourage you to some semblance of punctuality. I daren't think what you're like at school ...'

'It's the holidays now,' he replied in defence.

'That's as may be.' His mother gave him a stern look. 'Get changed. And washed. Anyone'd think you still needed an ayah.'

'I can't,' he pleaded. 'If I leave the wire loose they'll escape ...'

'Very well,' his mother surrendered herself to his procrastinations. 'But if you're still out there when the guests arrive, you come in through the kitchen. And don't be seen looking as if you've only just come in from the *shambas*.'

Collecting the pliers from the tool kit in the pantry, Brian went out through the kitchen, grinning at Oudu as he passed by.

'*Nyoka mbaya sana*,' the servant grimaced.

'It's not a snake,' Brian said in English. 'It's a chameleon. *Ni* "kam-ee-lee-on".'

'*Mbaya sana!*' Oudu repeated, puckering his nose, and shaking his head vigorously.

The African hatred of certain harmless animals both amused and fascinated Brian. Some creatures that were dangerous they accepted with stoicism whilst others drove them to paroxysms of disgust.

In the garden, on the bank which dropped away to the boundary fence not only of the Titchners' property but also of the city of Nairobi, there stood an ornamental bush with thick foliage and drooping yellow blossoms. The afternoon sun fell upon the bush and the blooms attracted a wide variety of insects. It was an ideal home for Brian's chameleons.

Brian usually owned only one of the reptiles at a time. His best and latest specimen had been caught in Langata Forest whilst he had ostensibly been taking part in a house cross-country trial run. This was an especially large Jackson's chameleon, the species with three horns, two projecting from the creature's forehead and a third rising on its nose like a rhino's. He had placed the chameleon inside his singlet and walked on, limping convincingly as he neared the finish line. That evening, he had ridden home for the holidays on his bicycle, battling against the wind along the Ngong Road, the chameleon inside his shirt. Its rough hide against the skin on his belly irritated him but he was quite determined to reach home safely with the reptile unharmed if a little short-tempered.

In the security of his bedroom, he had measured it and, when the servants were absent from the kitchen, weighed it on the flour scales by the water purifier. It was exactly a foot long with its tail almost uncurled and it weighed ten ounces. Assuming it to be male, he had named it Charlie. For several weeks, it lived in his bedroom during the day, eating any flies which ventured in through the window. The servants kept clear of the room and all would have been well had not Charlie decided to quit the ceiling and step ponderously, in the way of chameleons, on to an Airfix model of an Avro Lancaster suspended from the criss-cross of strings and sticks which ran from side to side of the room.

It had taken Brian over a month to construct the model kit his grandmother had posted out from England with a batch of *Eagle* comics. Not only had he gone to infinite lengths to ensure the glue had not smeared and scarred the fuselage but he had painstakingly painted the model in the colours of similar aircraft he had seen flying low over Nairobi on their way to bomb the Mau Mau in the Aberdare Forests.

Charlie, with the slow agility unique to a chameleon, had somehow lowered himself down the thin twine holding the model in mid-air and settled on the body of the aircraft. Either the twine loosened or broke, for when Brian returned one afternoon the model was smashed on the chair by his bed and the chameleon was ineffectually trying to clamber up the cupboard door.

A cage was then made for Charlie with a deep sandy floor in which was set a saucer of water. As insects did not enter it, Brian had to pass an hour every evening, as the sun went down, fly-hunting with the chameleon. The garage doors faced west, the woodwork scorching in the afternoon. After five, a large number of fat, glossy bluebottles and green-backed flies congregated on the door. Brian would stand

73

before the doors with Charlie ranged along the side of his hand, his split-toed front feet gripping his index finger.

Carefully, Brian selected a fly and aimed Charlie at it. With a slow deliberation, the chameleon's eyes wandered independently of each other until it finally saw the target. Both eyes then swung forward under their conical lids and concentrated, and the grey-brown reptile's mouth opened, just a fraction, revealing the saurian pink interior. Its long tongue would then flash out and fix on the fly. Quicker than Brian's eye could follow it, the tongue would be out and back again, the blunt jaws of the chameleon chewing on the insect before swallowing it, the lumpy bulk going down the striated throat. On the woodwork where the fly had been would remain a damp, slightly sticky blot.

The cage was a timely innovation. Within days of taking up residence, Charlie had laid eleven off-white, leathery eggs in the sand and undergone a re-christening: he became Diana.

Diana's eggs hatched but the cage almost became her coffin. One day, near the beginning of the rainy season, the cage became the centre of attention for a safari ant column. They were marching through a corner of the wire and sensed the chameleon's movement. In next to no time, the ants diverted from their path and attacked the chameleon, already weak from dehydration and laying the eggs. Brian arrived just in time to flick the ants off, being stung badly himself in the process. The cage was moved, the eggs placed in warm sand in the airing cupboard – without the servants' knowledge – and another cage constructed of large-meshed wire on the ornamental bush.

This was a perfect pen for the chameleon. The framework did not touch the ground but encased only the foliage. The young chameleons, not an inch long, joined their mother yet had the freedom to leave the bush if they wished. Whilst they grew, they were safe behind the mesh from birds. The holes kept Diana in but allowed insects to visit the flowers and be eaten by her. It was ideal except that a neighbour's cat had tried on a number of occasions to get through the bottom of the cage. It was this marauder's attacks upon the cage which Brian was so anxious to repair.

74

As he twisted the wire with the pliers, he heard a car grinding down the murram driveway from Lockinge Road. It stopped before the garage, two doors opened and closed, his father's voice drifted around the side of the house.

'Bernard! Josie! How are you both? Haven't seen you since you got back from leave. How was Venice ...?'

The voices faded into the house and Brian quickly finished his task. If he got to the cocktail party too late, his parents would be furious.

In his bedroom, Brian quickly tugged off his shorts and shirt, washing his face and arms in the basin by the window. Through the grid of supposedly burglar- and grenade-proof wire bars across the window he watched another two vehicles swing into the driveway. One was a large, black Ford with an African chauffeur, the other a pale blue Austin saloon with a spotlight mounted on the side of the windscreen, reminding him of the rally cars in the Coronation Safari which took place every Easter.

As he entered the large drawing room, the sun slanted in through the picture window overlooking the Kikuyu reserve the other side of the garden fence. It was warm and caught the crystal of the glasses lined up on the bar behind which Oudu was pouring drinks.

Cocktail parties were not events towards which Brian looked with enthusiasm. He was usually the only person present under twenty-five. His father sympathised for he understood Brian's position: he was neither a man, and therefore one of the gathering, nor a boy who could be excused. People – by which his father meant civil servants, businessmen, lawyers and doctors – expected to see Brian present at such get-togethers. Besides, his father reasoned, it was the best way to learn the social graces.

There were times when both his parents despaired of Brian, lamenting his bush habits and his *bundu* ways. Attendance at sundowner and dinner parties acquainted their son with a more civilised way of life. It was one thing to be conscious of the animal world, to appreciate and understand it, but few people, his father regularly reminded him, made a living out of the bush.

75

Brian walked around the edge of the room towards the bar, Oudu noticing his coming and prising the top off a bottle of lager. He knew the young *bwana* was allowed two beers on such an evening.

The room, despite its size, was quite crowded, the cool evening breeze flowing in through the french windows and along the polished parquet floor. Some of the drinkers, mostly the men, had gone outside to stand on the terrace. A year before they would not have dared, but they were more relaxed about the Mau Mau Emergency now that the security forces were so successful in rounding up the terrorists. Nevertheless, as Brian walked out of the sitting room, he noticed one of the guests was wearing a revolver in a holster beneath his sports jacket.

His father was sitting on the wrought-iron railing below which the terrace dropped ten feet to a bed of tea roses and a moonflower bush, the latter already attracting insects as the pallid trumpet blossoms unfurled and put out their scent, undetectable by humans but a drug to any moth. A mile distant, across the plain of close-cropped grass and against the scar of orange on the western horizon, Brian could just discern the plumes of smoke rising from the Kikuyu village.

'Ah! There you are! Come over here.'

His father beckoned to him and Brian transferred his beer from his right hand to his left, surreptitiously wiping his right palm on the seat of his trousers.

'I don't think you've met my son. Brian, this is Bruce Roscoe.'

'How do you do,' Brian said, offering his hand which was grasped in a firm, almost painful grip; he responded by tightening his own fingers.

'I'm very well, thank you,' Roscoe replied in a terse South African accent. 'How are you enjoying your holidays? I reckon you think they're a bit short, eh?'

Before he could reply with an expected pleasantry, Mr Titchner said, 'Brian's not wasted his short vacation. He's been out hunting with Bill Chopping's boy.'

'Really!' Roscoe glanced at Brian. 'I was out with Bill just yesterday. We were looking over some elephant damage down in Tsavo. Between Kenani and Kyulu.'

The mention of the Tsavo Royal National Park caught Brian's attention. Cocktail party conversation was not his metier but if it turned to a subject in which he was knowledgeable – which was restricted, outside his school-work, to hunting and game stalking – he was quick to exploit the opening. That was a technique his father had taught him: never be a silent witness, always speak up for yourself. People remembered those who impressed themselves politely on a discussion.

'Do you work for the Game Department, sir?' he enquired.

'Me? No, not bloody likely! I don't want to be a nursemaid to a lot of wild animals.' He sipped at a large scotch. 'Bad enough running an army of kaffir labourers without having to look after the rest of the fauna.' He grinned expansively. 'No. I work for EAR&H. Inspection.'

Roscoe spoke the initials as one word. Brian learned much from it, and wondered how the man had come to be invited to his father's party. The European line inspectors with East African Railways & Harbours were not the type to mix with the likes of the Titchners. They were usually poorer, lived in suburbs of Nairobi closer to the town centre, and were considered only a cut above the Asians.

'What was the elephant damage?' Brian's father asked.

'Nothing really. The line was undermined in the rains by a bridge over a *donga*. We had a load of gravel and stone delivered but the bloody *nugus* were pinching it and running off into the bush with it. Found some used ten miles away as the base of a *banda*. Claimed they'd found it in the bush – cut stone! They must think we're as stupid as they are. Anyway, to protect the stuff we had a stout fence put in around the site by Bill's company. Stuck a couple of askaris in there to keep an eye on things. Second night, a herd of elephant came down the *donga*. It's wide just there and from the spoor I'd reckon there were upward of fifty. Well, you know what it's like when they get to a road or the railway – they get scared and edgy. Right by the slip they were spooked – probably one of the askaris, windy as hell, fired his rifle in the air or something. Result was the tuskers stampeded. Down went the fence, the gravel gets kicked about, the newly-cemented blocks – still wet – were pushed over. Hell of a mess. Lucky the rails themselves were unharmed ... Except for the usual liberal deposits of elephant dung.'

'Have you worked where the man-eaters of Tsavo operated?' Brian asked.

'On the very spot. Last year in the rainy season. The line runs through a swampy area and occasionally we get problems with culverts. Don't get the problems with the *simbas*, though. Maybe that's a pity – a few lions might trim the kaffir population down a bit. Bloody sight more efficient than the security forces, if you ask me...'

A dark-haired man joined them. He was wearing a blue striped white blazer which might have been more appropriate to a yachting regatta on the Isle of Wight than a cocktail party in Africa. The navy blue tie he wore over his light blue shirt bore a crest repeated in a diagonal pattern the length of the material.

'Hello, Titch! How are you keeping?' he greeted Brian's father, Brian turning his head – it was confusing sharing the same nickname with his father.

'Greg! Good of you to come and at such short notice. Didn't see you arrive.'

Oudu approached with a tray of drinks, Roscoe helping himself before the houseboy reached the newcomer. That the glass he took was intended for another did not occur to him and Brian noticed his father's disguised displeasure at the South African's boorishness.

A Queen's Counsel, Gregory Holborn had only the day before returned from his long leave in Europe. Unlike most government officers, he seldom returned to Britain. His wife was Italian, and he usually spent his six months of vacation in the mountains of central Italy.

'Sorry I'm late. Got a puncture on Hurlingham Road. Someone's been trimming their hedge and the thorns're all over the place. Damn great things like nails! You forget such little niceties when you return from civilization.'

78

'Gia here?' Mr Titchner asked, craning his neck to look past Roscoe who was well into his second scotch.

As if to provide him with an answer there came from inside the drawing room a lilting laugh followed by the loud giggling of Brian's mother and the strident guffaw of old Mrs Mordant.

As his father introduced Roscoe to Gregory Holborn, Brian seized the chance to slip away. Although he should have liked to discuss the Tsavo lions with the Afrikaner, he sensed he would not have had much of an opportunity to get a word in. Roscoe was what his father termed 'a tufter', a man more intent on talking than listening.

The women had congregated around the bar, either sitting on stools or standing against the marble slab of the counter. Only old Mrs Mordant was sitting in one of the armchairs, her glass of pink gin balancing on the wooden arm.

The division of the sexes – those men not on the terrace were grouped in twos and threes around the drawing room – reminded Brian of dances for senior boys at The Duke of York. On those occasions, girls were transported over – rather as prime heifers in the bloodstock sections of the annual Royal Show – from either Loretto Convent or the Kenya Girls' High School. Once in the school hall, they waited in knots for a boy to approach one of them from similar knots of boys across the expanse of the dance floor. The first of these encounters were conducted either by the very brave, the most charismatic, or the head-boy under instructions from members of staff determined to get things going.

It was with amusement that Brian attended the termly dances. Occasionally, music was provided by a band of soldiers from the security forces or of the boys themselves, but at the last dance Brian had attended the music came from a gramophone in a mahogany cabinet and two unwieldy speakers perched upon the footlights to the stage. The records provided were invariably cut by big bands in the immediate pre-war years and belonged to one of the masters who, in collaboration with a mistress from the High School, ran an inter-schools Scottish dancing team. Only towards the end of the evening was a boy allowed to put onto his own gramophone – the school machine did not operate at 45 rpm – one of the new singles considered by and large by the staff, and especially by the headmaster, as cacophonous at least and morally corrupting at worst. The last quarter of an hour of the dancing was therefore devoted to jiving to the beat of Bill Haley and his Comets, Tennessee Ernie Ford, or a new singer whom Brian liked and whose record had only recently been brought to the school by a fifth former returning from holiday in the United Kingdom: Lonnie Donegan and his record 'Rock Island Line'.

When the sexes split apart at the dances, Brian noticed, the staff used either sarcasm or cajolery to get them together. Had any of his teachers been at the cocktail party, what might they have done? But of course he knew. They would have segregated themselves. Adults were still a mystery to him.

He edged towards the end of the bar to ask Oudu for his second beer.

'My word!' Gia Holborn exclaimed, breaking into Brian's reverie by putting her arm around his waist and squeezing him. 'You are growing more handsome by the week. Dotty! Your son will kill ladies sooner than we think ...' She tickled his lowest rib through his shirt and added in a stage whisper, 'Maybe I should be your first conquest, yes?'

Brian liked Holborn's wife. She was vivacious, lively and had a wicked sense of humour which he appreciated. In many ways, she was unlike any of his parents' other female friends. She was without airs, and frank, often to the point of being acutely embarrassing, especially, he often thought, to him.

'Training him to be a true Kenyan are you, Gia?' Mrs Mordant asked loudly.

'What do you mean?' Brian asked, smiling awkwardly and hoping that, by speaking, he would persuade Gia to let him go.

'Shame on you, boy!' the old woman remonstrated. 'You should know your own heritage.' She addressed the other women, her head turning from one to the other so the loose skin on her neck folded over the high collar of her blouse.

'Don't tease so, Peggy,' chided a woman in a khaki skirt and shirt which resembled an army officer's battle blouse more than an article of feminine attire.

'Tease! Me, tease!' Mrs Mordant softened a little. 'Maybe I do a bit. But that's not the point.' She rallied to her former self. 'In the old days, before the war and all this Mau Mau nonsense, a young whippersnapper like Brian would have been out and about by his age. Not listening to this infernal rock and roll shindig and playing with himself in the bathroom.'

Her coarse comment drew no approbation, just a tutting sound from Gia Holborn.

'You should not be so cruel, Peggy. Not to a poor, defenceless boy. He cannot fight back at you.'

'In the old days,' Mrs Mordant repeated, picking up the strain of her monologue, 'as a number of us know very well,' she looked keenly about the room, casting her eye over the men 'boys of eighteen were ... Think of the parties. At Naivasha. "Clouds" – Now I remember quite clearly 1926 at "Clouds"! Those were *real* parties.'

Once she had begun, it was quite difficult to stop Peggy Mordant; few wanted to. She was an old Africa hand and her anecdotes, full of gossip and laced with scandal, were both entertaining and lessons in history.

'Have you read *Vertical Land*?' she enquired of Brian, still held embarrassingly by Gia Holborn's arm.

'No, Mrs Mordant. Is it a novel?'

'Mrs Mordant! There, you see!' She looked from one woman to the next seeking understanding. 'Mrs Mordant! In the old days, I was Peggy to any male over sixteen. Pegs to those over twenty-one. And, no,' she looked straight into Brian's eyes, 'it's not a novel. Well – yes and no. There's a bit of fiction in it. Freddie de Janze wrote it – Count Frederic, if you look in the lists of the nobility. He described Happy Valley as "the habitat of the wild and free". He was so right!'

She took a swig of pink gin from her glass and guffawed once more, a rough, almost masculine noise which was gauche yet curiously infectious. Brian could feel Gia Holborn's arm vibrating with suppressed laughter.

'What has become of manhood?' the old woman lamented,

shaking her empty glass in the direction of Oudu. 'When I was a younger woman, there was none of this ...' She briefly waved her hand dismissively in Brian's direction, her heavy gold charm bracelet rattling as it slid down her wrist.

'They still seem fine to me!' Gia retorted and gave Brian's waist a barely perceptible squeeze.

'Maybe,' Mrs Mordant answered dubiously as Oudu took her empty glass in exchange for a full one. 'But where are the Raymond de Traffords, the Michael Lafones, the Jock Broughtons? I ask you ... and poor Josslyn.'

'Don't be so morbid, Peggy,' said a woman who had joined the group from the direction of the passage leading to the bedrooms and bathroom. She stood next to Brian and he could smell newly-applied perfume.

'Who was Josslyn?' Brian enquired innocently, his question meeting momentary silence before Mrs Mordant spoke.

'You really are remarkably ill-tutored,' she criticised; there was no ring of humour in her words as there had been at first. 'Josslyn Hay, the Twenty-second Earl of Errol. He was the founder of Happy Valley.'

Gazing into her glass, she fell silent. No one else spoke. The woman next to Brian, in her early middle age, fidgeted her foot along the crack between two of the parquet floor tiles. The men were jovially chattering on the terrace.

'What happened to him?' Brian asked.

His mother cast a stern look in his direction but she was too late. Mrs Mordant beckoned to him but Gia Holborn tightened her grip on his waist and he heard her breathe, 'No.'

'He was shot,' Mrs Mordant replied matter-of-factly, a catch in her voice. 'Not far from your little school. In the earhole.'

It sounded quite obscene stated that way.

Brian was about to ask how or why, assuming the Mau Mau had had something to do with it earlier on in the Emergency, but his mother succeeded in silencing him with a grimace. Mrs Mordant was not to be so easily quietened.

'Don't you want to know why? Are you utterly lacking in

82

insatiable curiosity? Unlike the Elephant's Child? I suppose you've read Kipling ...'

Brian nodded.

'At least one bit of our crumbling Empire's entered your head then.' Her charm bracelet rattled as she transferred her pink gin from one hand to the other, by way of her lips. 'Joss was murdered because he was too good at rogering.'

'That's enough!' Gia Holborn said half-seriously, trying to defuse what was becoming an awkward situation. 'Leave it alone.'

'By Jock,' Mrs Mordant continued unheeding. 'Who admitted it to Juanita – or so the rumour goes. I believe it.'

Oudu entered with a tray of fresh pineapple cubes and cheese, olives stuffed with pimentos and anchovy butter spread on small square crackers. Mrs Mordant was the first person to whom he offered the tray and she scooped a handful of olives from the bowl as if they were peanuts, the juice dripping onto the polished floor where it remained in tiny droplets, like water blisters under the skin.

'I bet he doesn't even know what rogering means,' she said disparagingly, her words a little slurred as she looked Brian in the face. 'Do you know, Brian?'

'Agreeing?'

He hazarded the guess, basing his reply on his only knowledge of the word other than as a name – that RAF pilots said 'Roger and out!' at the end of radio messages.

'Not quite,' she replied brusquely. 'It means fucking.'

She closed her eyes, her head lolling slightly to one side as if she were instantly asleep.

'Enough of this!' Gia Holborn said loudly, then, lowering her voice, told Brian, 'She's DD ...'

'DD?'

'Disgustingly drunk. Forgive her. She's an old lady and, you know, old people live inside their lives. Even the Mau Mau aren't as important to her as the past.'

She released Brian who, used to the pressure of the woman by his side, leaned away from her.

'Are you married, or do you live in Kenya?'

Mrs Mordant spoke suddenly yet her eyes remained

closed. Her body was shaking so much the charms on the bracelet banged and thudded against the wooden arm of her chair. Whether from laughter or sorrow Brian could not tell for her face was smiling but tears were welling from beneath her closed lids.

'Brian, come out here a moment.'

It was his father's voice; through the window Mr Titchner was beckoning to him. Brian welcomed his intrusion for it gave him the opportunity to leave the women. He had been somehow afraid of both Mrs Mordant and Gia Holborn. Unable to decide what it was that made him uneasy, he had felt threatened both by the former's drunk sarcasm and the latter's sexuality, which had confused him. Brian liked girls, enjoyed their company and the thrill of sex he felt dancing with them but he had not discovered, until this evening, the same feeling in the presence of a woman who was some years older than himself.

Standing with his father was a tall man whom Brian had not previously met. He was sandy-haired with sharp, hazel eyes, his arms tanned and leanly muscular.

'Brian, meet Keith Collis.'

'Hello, Brian.' The man's voice was quiet, his handshake fierce yet not as arrogant as Roscoe's had seemed; Brian sensed it was testing as much as greeting him. 'I've heard a lot about your recent exploits out towards Embu. Understand you shot a good head of impala. Also got your first leopard, your father tells me.'

'Yes, sir. A male. Sixty-nine inches over the curves.'

'Good specimen! I hear he's got a virtually unmarked coat, too. Where did you hit him?'

Brian related briefly his shooting of the cat, all the while Collis listening intently, occasionally nodding his head with approval or understanding.

'Got the pelt back yet?'

'Yesterday, sir. My father collected it from Rowland Ward.'

'I'd like very much to see it, if I may,' Collis requested, adding, 'and you don't need to call me sir. I'm not a schoolmaster or a civil servant. Not exactly.'

Brian led the way through the sitting room and along the passage. The house was constructed on an L-plan, one wing containing the sleeping, the other the living quarters. In the angle of the building was a large bougainvillaea bush beneath which geckos rustled in the leaf litter. Opening the door of his room, Brian ushered Collis and his father in, closing the door behind them.

On his bed was spread the leopard skin. He switched on the bedroom light and closed the window, his fingers deftly slipping the catch shut through the wire grid. As Brian drew the curtains, Collis knelt by the bed to examine the trophy.

'A very fine beast,' he complimented Brian. 'About two and a half years old. Maybe three. Male as you say.' He felt for the bullet hole with his finger. 'An excellent shot, too. Bang on target. You must be very pleased.'

Brian grinned appreciatively.

Rising to his feet, Collis asked, 'Did you skin it yourself?'

By the careful manipulation of previous conversations with his parents, Brian had succeeded in avoiding telling them exactly how he had had the carcass skinned. Caution being the better part of valour where his father was concerned, he had held back the details, simply saying that Broomhall had arranged for it to be done for him. He repeated this half-lie to Collis.

'Pity!' he remarked. 'Nothing so satisfying as doing your own.'

'I did help,' Brian said. No sooner had he spoken than he knew he should have kept silent.

'I wasn't aware of that,' his father commented. 'Who did the skinning then?'

Brian could no longer hide the truth. To lie in front of a stranger would annoy his father, he suspected, more than admitting he had entered a detention centre – albeit with permission – and collaborated in the task with a former terrorist.

'One of the detainees did it. I stood by and gave a hand.' He added, defensively, 'It was okay by Inspector Broomhall.'

His father made no reply, nor gave an intimation of his thoughts, but Collis said, 'Those boys from the bush know a thing or two. I've a few in my unit working out of Narok. What they don't now about gamecraft isn't worth knowing.'

To turn attention from himself, Brian asked, 'Are you a hunter, Mr Collis?'

'That's one up on "sir". Try Keith next time ... And no, I'm not a hunter in the sense you're thinking. I'm with the Game Department. Field research on the Loita Plains – giraffe. A bit of liaison over the border with Tanganyika: migration of wildebeest through to Serengeti. And back again, of course!'

As they returned to join the party, Collis said, 'If you'd like to come out with me on a survey next school holidays, you'd be welcome. That all right with you, Titch?'

Brian's father agreed, adding, 'It'll be a nice farewell for the lad. Won't it, Brian?'

It was then that Brian remembered, the coming June, he would be sitting the last of his school examinations, hoping to follow in his father's footsteps to Oxford, the city of dreaming spires, legless beetles and pristine toy soldiers.

As Oudu cleared away the empty glasses, tipped the contents of the ash-trays into the dustpan and wiped clean the polished floor where Mrs Mordant had sat, Dorothy Titchner leaned back in an armchair and stretched her hands in front of her. Her husband sat on a bar stool swilling a lump of ice around his tumbler.

'Peggy got tight again, I see,' he observed, raising the glass to his lips and sucking at the meltwater. 'Poor old Harry must live a dog's life.'

'The fate of the man who marries more than thrice,' his wife retorted. 'She has more memories of her own in which to dwell than a sheik who's gone through all one thousand-and-one Arabian Nights. Her language this evening was a bit ripe, too. It grows redder the paler her pink gin gets.'

Her husband laughed and said, 'Perhaps blue-er might be a more appropriate colouring. I think her memory is primed by angostura bitters much as a diesel engine can be set running with a squirt of commercial Sure-fire. One burst and a twist on memory's key and she's up and running.'

'And who, dearest,' Dorothy Titchner enquired, 'was that awful little man from the railways?'

Brian could tell his mother was irked by the mere memory of the South African: she only called his father dearest when she was annoyed.

'Bruce Roscoe,' her husband told her. 'He's a friend of Harry's. Quite how, I've no idea.'

'Do you remember that atrocious busybody at the Muthaiga Country Club two Christmasses ago?' she continued. 'An ex-Colonel in the KAR, or so he claimed. Saw the war through guarding Italian PoWs building the road to Nakuru.'

'Don't think I do,' his father replied. 'Fair number of them about these days. Even in the club.'

Brian recalled the man well. It had been the first occasion on which he had attended a formal ball and his mother had spilled a Bloody Mary all down the man's dinner jacket. She never drank vodka and it only occurred to Brian the following day that she had ordered the drink specifically for that purpose.

'His name ...' his mother tapped her fingers against the ball of her thumb to try to jolt her memory. 'I hate it when I can't remember names.' Her fingers stopped. 'I've got it – Colonel Cedric Trivalyen.'

'Ah, him!' exclaimed Mr Titchner with feeling. 'The man with Wandering Hand Trouble.'

'Too right! A bad case of WHT, that one. Do you remember, after the dance I had more little bruises on my bum than I got that time out by Magadi when I went for a pee behind a bush and bumped up against those *siafu*?'

'Bum-ped! I like that, Dotty.'

They laughed at the memory of Brian's mother indelicately picking, swiping and flicking vicious safari ants off her posterior. That had been the first – and only – occasion on which Brian had seen any grown woman naked except in the American magazines which circulated through the dormitory underground network at The Duke of York.

'Barf ready, mem'sahib,' Oudu announced.

'Thank you, Oudu. And thank you also for very good

service this evening.' She glanced at her watch and looked up to Mr Titchner. 'It's after ten, darling.'

'Right!'

He tugged his wallet from the hip pocket of his trousers, removing a ten shilling note which he folded and gave to the servant. The arrangement was that Oudu was paid a bonus if he had to remain up after ten o'clock and had worked satisfactorily.

'*Asante sana, bwana,*' the African answered and left the room, his white *kanzu* brushing against the doorpost.

Brian's father followed their servant and saw him out through the back door, locking and bolting it behind him. He then patrolled the whole house, testing the doors and windows and drawing the curtains, before returning to the sitting room with an automatic pistol in his hand. Releasing the magazine from the end of the butt, he checked the rounds and snapped it back in place.

'Another beer, Brian?'

'I've had my two,' Brian replied, dropping on to the bar the copy of that day's *East African Standard* which he had been cursorily reading.

'Have another. We've got to get you ready for the old college wine cellar. And the port. In fact ...' his father reached under the bar, '... let's try a glass now.'

From the bathroom came the faint strains of Brian's mother singing to herself.

The bottle his father produced had not been opened and, as he stood it carefully on its base, Brian noticed the cream-coloured label with maroon printing upon it. Beneath an engraving of an heraldic badge was printed 'Merton College, Oxford'.

'Not my alma mater,' his father observed, pulling the cork. 'More a college for poets and artists – Blunden, Keith Douglas and that inscrutably boring and obscure Eliot – and so not for me. But their port ...' He poured out two glasses, handed one to his son, and raised his own. 'Here's to your exams. I know you'll do your best.'

Though a scientist by training and an administrator by profession, Brian's father never ceased to surprise his son. He was widely read and knew of poets and painters, jazz musicians, film stars and actors as well as the erosion problems in the Kikuyu homelands, the failure of the Groundnut Scheme in Tanganyika and the complexities of the Tana River Project.

Neither father nor son spoke after their toast. The former was savouring the smoothness of the port and the latter was catching his breath.

'Sip it,' his father advised. 'It's not lager or gin and tonic.'

The distant singing ceased and Mrs Titchner called, 'I'm out, dear. Running yours.' Her last words were drowned by the splash of water.

'Mr Kitchener rang me the other day,' Brian's father said pointedly.

Related to the famous lord, Mr Kitchener was Brian's favourite master, a tall, thin and angular man who wore round, tortoiseshell-framed glasses and taught English. He was also the master in charge of day boys and liaison with the parents of Sixth Form boys over academic matters. News that a schoolmaster had contacted his father, however, was not welcome; such communication was rare outside the writing of reports and meetings at social or sporting functions.

'You needn't look quite so disconcerted, Brian. It wasn't bad news but simply to say that the staff have confidence in you and think you'll do well enough to get through to Oxford. Your likely grades look promising. They were just worried you'd run out of steam or get blasé about it. You've got to keep the pressure up to the very end.'

'I know that,' Brian confirmed.

'I know you do, too. But it's easy to lose your momentum. Just ... just keep it up, that's all.'

The taps were turned off and Brian's mother came in wearing a black cotton dressing-gown embroidered with red and gold dragons, a memento from a holiday spent in Singapore. She was barefoot, her painted toe-nails matching the scarlet of the dragon's tail where it reached to the hem of the gown above her ankle.

'Time for bed, boys,' she said in a brisk, matronly manner,

giving her husband a quick wink which did not escape her son's attention.

'You go ahead, dear,' Mr Titchner said. 'I'll be along shortly.'

She kissed Brian on his cheek and said, 'You behaved very well in that awful situation. It's not easy knowing what to do when your elders and betters prove themselves only to be your elders. But do,' she added with a hint of exasperation, 'watch me next time.'

'Quick question before I plunge into thirty-per-cent chlorine,' his father said, setting his glass of port on the bar and studying his fingernails as if deciding whether or not to scrub them.

The action was a warning to Brian. The real intention behind his father's offering him a port was about to show itself. Whenever his father looked at his fingers, he was about to drop a bombshell.

'Yes?' Brian replied, feigning innocence. He had an inkling of an idea what was coming next.

'Just curious,' his father began, waiting for his wife to leave the room before going on. 'How did you get the leopard skinned?'

'Inspector Broomhall shot a lion last year and one of the detainees whom he trusts skinned it for him. I was worried about the leopard skin because I'd no idea what to do so the inspector let the Mick do it.'

He thought it wise to use the derogatory term: his father might infer from the dismissive remark a lack of concern.

'How did they let him out? I thought Wamumu was one of the more closed camps.'

'They didn't – though some of the detainees do come out on work parties and things.'

'So you took the leopard in?'

'Yes.'

'And you stayed there and helped with the skinning?'

Brian hesitated. His father took it as an affirmative.

'Do you think that was wise? I assume Broomhall wasn't with you.'

'I had an askari. And I'm sure it was safe otherwise the inspector wouldn't have allowed it ...'

'True,' his father agreed thoughtfully; there was evidently something on his mind.

He raised his glass and Brian did likewise. The second swallow of port was not as tart as the first. He almost liked it.

'How did you find your Swahili stood up to it?'

'The detainee spoke English well. He was the one who fixed the Land Rover, with another one who spoke no English and was a bit nasty. He was quite friendly ...'

He had avoided looking at his father as he spoke and, when he did face him, he saw his father was not looking like a man well pleased with his son.

'What – what was his name? – did you think of him?' Mr Titchner enquired casually, twirling his glass between his forefinger and thumb, holding it against the glow from a table lamp across the room. The bulb was dimmed so it should cast no shadows upon the curtains. Shadows provided targets.

'Matthew was ...'

'I see. You got on to first-name terms with him.'

There was an ironic edge to Mr Titchner's words and Brian realised he had been inveigled into giving away more than he had intended.

'It wasn't quite like that,' Brian began defensively but his father raised his hand to silence him.

'I'm not criticising you, Brian. Meeting even a Mau Mau terrorist can give you much in your life ... After all, it's an experience. But I want to warn you. These people – especially the hedjumacated –' he stressed the word with the pronunciation an African might have used but he gave it a comic and mocking intonation, 'are very clever. They know the armed struggle won't get them what they want so they are turning into skilful politicos. Having failed with the *panga* they're turning to propaganda. Words and ideologies. A good number of them are Communists. Don't forget that.'

Brian opened his mouth to speak but his father interrupted.

'Let me finish.' He drained his glass. 'You know from history lessons the way to get to the heart of a nation is through its youth. Hitler knew that only too well when he set up the Nazi youth organisations. He had them so well indoctrinated they ratted to the Gestapo on their own parents.

'Now these new African types have got the same message. The Kenya African Union have learnt as much already. The KAU suffered a terrible setback in 1953 with the massacre at Lari – ninety-four killed, children crucified, old Chief Luka burned to death ... Now they've seen the error of their ways and they're trying to right matters. To do that they're re-writing history. A bit. And to do that you need a new history to take its place. The new past has to be in the minds of the young.'

Brian's mother called from the bedroom, 'I'm putting the light out now. Don't be long.'

'Just coming!' Mr Titchner answered, then continued, 'What better than to get a few young and impressionable white minds on their side, eh? Think about it. I don't want to restrict your movements and I don't intend to lay down the law. But if you go back to Wamumu on your way to a day's shooting, and you meet this man again, bear in mind what I've said. Moderation. Think about it.'

'He's not really a man,' Brian said as his father placed the bottle on a shelf under the bar. 'He's only a year older than I am.'

Brian finished his port and put his glass next to his father's on a small wooden tray.

'And something else,' he went on. 'He said they had failed with violence and had now to find a peaceful solution.'

Mr Titchner gazed up at his son from where he was bending over the bar.

'Did he?' he remarked thoughtfully. 'Did he, indeed. Well, you must definitely remember what I've said ...'

6

The steel span of the railway bridge was hung with an iron casting of a silver rose, the emblem of the school, a representation of the white rose of the royal house of the Dukes of York. Beneath it was scrolled the school motto – *Nihil Praeter Optimum*.

As he sped past the two hockey pitches and under it, Brian noticed that someone had painted the metal. At the end of the previous term, it had been besmirched with lines of rust from the railway girders.

Each Foundation Day, January 28, the boys were encouraged to sport in their lapels white roses obtained either from a florist who visited the school the day before or from their homes. It was a vain attempt at supporting the ancient heraldic arms as the buttonholes invariably wilted well before midday, January being the height of the Kenyan summer.

As he freewheeled in neutral through the shadow of the bridge, the exhaust of his light-blue Vespa scooter put-putting gently, Brian recalled his first Foundation Day with pangs of tormented embarrassment. Someone, out of either malice or devilment, had told him that those with connections with the House of Lancaster were permitted to wear red roses. As his father's family hailed from Preston, Brian had cut, from one of his mother's best tea roses, a deep red blossom still curled in the bud. He had been at home on an exeat the weekend before Foundation Day Monday and had stood the flower in a thin vase in his bedroom overnight where it partially opened, filling the room with perfume by morning.

At school, he thrust it through the buttonhole in his lapel and held it in place with a safety pin. As a result, he had been ragged, bullied or teased continuously until lunchtime when he had surreptitiously tugged the dying flower out of his jacket and flushed it down the junior boys' lavatory at the back of the hall.

A narrow tarmacked road joined the school drive on his right and, instinctively, Brian glanced up it towards the buildings of Speke and Lugard, the boarding houses situated most distantly from the main school block. A small, fat boy was running helter-skelter down the slope, a leather briefcase clutched to his chest with one hand and a satchel swinging from the other. He was, Brian assessed, a second-year, plainly someone's fag for the week; the briefcase clearly belonged to his prefect.

It was strange going to school on the scooter. Brian had been a boarder in Lugard House since the end of his first year but now, in his final term, his father had arranged for him to be a day boy and live at home where the atmosphere was more conducive to study. Staying in Lugard would involve the responsibilities of dormitory duties, discipline and supervision of junior boys, and much of his now-precious time would be taken up with sport and the necessities of daily living. It was better he lived at home with all his creature comforts catered for. His housemaster, Mr Hesketh – whom the seniors referred to behind his back as 'Duke', because his initials were 'HRH' – had not approved of the move but had come to terms with it. Brian was not Head of House and had agreed to maintain his fair share of house duties and chores.

There was a screech of pain from behind him. Brian braked hard, the back wheel of the Vespa skidding on gravel. He struggled to keep the machine upright, the handlebars horizontal.

Looking back, he saw the fat boy had tripped and fallen to his knees; the flap of his satchel had unfastened and his books were strewn across the road. Brian turned the Vespa around and, twisting the throttle grip, rode up to the boy who was frantically scrabbling to collect his folders and textbooks in between dabbing at his skinned knees with a dirty handkerchief. A forest breeze, blowing under the bridge, started to drift loose sheets of paper down the hill.

Brian hoisted the Vespa onto its stand, not bothering to stop the motor, and helped the boy. He was near to tears, fighting them back with choking gasps of breath. He thrust his work into his satchel and rubbed his finger along a deep graze in the leather of the briefcase.

'Oh, Christ! Oh, Christ!' he muttered. 'I'll get tackied for this . . .'

'It was an accident,' Brian said.

'Look what I've done to his briefcase. And I'm late. I'm sure to get tackied. By him. And detention. And I'm in the . . .'

The boy looked up at Brian as if only now realizing he was not talking to himself. Over his face slipped a look of respectful apprehension.

'You're Titchner. Lugard. You came second in the Peatling Bowl.'

There was a sense of awe in his voice. The Peatling Bowl was awarded for the best individual inter-house shot and junior boys tended to look up to the competitors.

'You're not a Lugard boy,' Brian observed. 'What's your name?'

'No, sir. Speke, sir. Penney, sir.'

Brian did not ask him why he was late. He could guess. The boy had been last in the shower, last to breakfast, delayed by having to polish his prefect's shoes, or collect his books, or make his toast.

'I'll give you a lift up to the main block,' Brian offered, tweaking the Vespa throttle to keep it idling. 'I didn't come second for the Bowl, I came third. Mouton came second. And you don't have to call me sir, either.'

Brian placed the briefcase next to his own on the footboard of the Vespa, jammed the satchel behind them and instructed the junior boy to hang on. Then, with the engine burbling loudly, he drove down to the stream, past the turning to the armoury and the swimming pool, up the hill below the school sanatorium and halted by the day-boy bicycle racks behind the school hall. The junior jumped off the pillion seat, thanking Brian profusely, taking his baggage and sprinting clumsily through the corridor and round the corner by the school prefects' common-room. Brian waited for the inevitable. It came. A voice shouted loudly and the junior was caught for running.

The Chemistry master had not yet arrived in the laboratory. The senior boys were sitting chatting in their places. Brian sat on a stool to one side of the room and looked out of the window. The breeze was stronger now, tossing the crescent-shaped leaves of the young eucalyptus trees planted along the kerb of Brooklands, the oval road encircling the main school buildings. The leaves flashed silver, olive-green and silver again.

Brian unclasped his briefcase and removed the two textbooks and the foolscap folder he would require for the morning's lesson in organic chemistry.

A practical lesson was listed on the timetable. Upon the teacher's demonstration bench was erected a fractionating tower, the glass retorts and tubes shining in the reflected morning sunlight. The Bunsen burner was alight, the yellow flame wavering almost invisibly and, across the desk top, a row of brown glass jars of chemicals and glass-stoppered bottles of acids stood together in a group, the labels colour-coded.

The boy beside Brian had spread his textbook out at the appointed page for the day's lesson. Brian reached across, revolving the book so he could see the page.

'Thanks, Glanmer,' he said. 'Benzene? I thought we did that last term. Hardly any point in revising it so soon.'

'We did,' Glanmer confirmed, 'but you know how he likes to revise. Big pracs. first. I'd like to do hydrocarbon bonding myself. Still don't get it. Not really ... Anyway, Titch, what were your hols like? We went for a week to Jo'burg.'

'They were okay. I did a bit of shooting ...'

'So they say. Chopping's told everyone about it. You got a big male leopard.'

'Not very big,' Brian admitted modestly.

A figure in an academic gown walked briskly along the corridor and the boys, seeing it, stopped talking and ruffled their books or folders in a business-like manner. The door opened and the master entered, dropped his file of notes on the very edge of the demonstration desk and bade them all a good morning.

The odour of the benzene was sweet and pleasant, not

unlike oil of almonds, addictive and poisonous. By the time the double period ended, Brian felt light-headed and thirsty for a cup of tea.

His books packed, he left the classroom and walked over the lawns of the quadrangle. He was allowed to walk over the grass, a privilege afforded only to the most senior prefects.

As part of the conditions of his becoming a day boy, Brian had agreed to do duty in Junior House. Here, first formers from all the houses were mixed from their initial year, each of the houses seconding one or two prefects there for their supervision. Brian accepted day duties and, once a week, an evening duty from which he returned home after lights out.

As a Junior House placement, he could go to the house dining hall for his tea. As he leaned against a low tree outside the door, drinking his tea from the school-issue enamel mug and controlling the dwindling queue of juniors, Brian saw Chopping walking along Brooklands.

'Slade.'

The junior whom he addressed was just finishing his tea and pouring the remains of it onto the ground under a small bush.

'Go and ask that prefect to have a word with me.'

'Yes, sir.'

Slade thrust his mug into another's hand and raced up the steps and out of sight to return, a moment later, with Chopping strolling behind him.

'Thank you, Slade,' Brian said, dismissing the junior who scurried off to be with a knot of his friends.

'Hello, Titch,' Chopping greeted him. 'Haven't seen you since the beginning of term. How's it going?'

'It's okay. The revision's a bugger. I'll be almost glad when the exams start.'

'I won't.' Chopping looked briefly at his timetable. 'I've got "Peg-leg" next ...'

As they climbed the steps from the Junior dining block, Brian said, 'I wish they wouldn't call Spencer "Peg-leg". He's a damn good teacher. *N'est-ce-pas?*'

Dominic Spencer was the French master, his wife the Junior Mathematics teacher: it was she who had fired Brian's

97

interest in maths in the second form and her husband whose accomplished teaching of foreign languages went beyond the bounds of academic study to a love of words and France. His lessons were strict, never banal and often entertaining.

'"*Vouloir* – to vish, to vant and to be villing",' Chopping quoted the master. 'But I don't see why not. He's got a metal leg.'

Brian thought of Penney and answered, 'I don't think it's right to take a rise out of someone's misfortunes. It's not ...' he searched for the correct phrase ... 'natural justice. Anyway,' he went on, 'I really wanted to ask you not to tell people about our safari.'

'Why on earth not?'

Brian could not justify his request in terms which Chopping would either understand or appreciate. He preferred to keep things to himself, to have a private life which was never brought into the life of the school. Chopping would not appreciate this: since his mother had left, he had become more and more school-orientated in his thinking, had turned to the school for companionship and support. School was a constant, an environment in which he knew his place, knew the routine, knew the rules. His home life, once so stable, was now an unknown quantity. Brian accepted Chopping's feelings but didn't want to be drawn into them.

'I just don't, that's all. I don't want my private life bandied about ...'

'But you shot that leopard!'

'So what? I'm told that boy who's just been made drum major of the CCF band shot his own leopard for his drum uniform. It's nothing special ...'

The school bell rang in the distance.

'Okay. Better get going,' Chopping advised.

At lunchtime, Brian rode his Vespa up to Lugard and ate with the boys in his house after which, his own books tucked under his arm, he supervised the common-room where some boys were frantically working on prep they had failed to complete the night before. There was little discipline to keep, for those in his charge were too concerned with their own affairs to cause trouble. Brian was able to concentrate on the benzene revision lesson and read swiftly through his notes on osmosis. The late afternoon lesson was biology.

At a quarter to two, the common-room cleared and Brian, with everyone else in his house, changed for an afternoon of games. The notice pinned on the board by the door of the Head of House's room announced rugger practice for the school 'A' XV and the house junior team with the remainder taking part in a house cross-country run, everyone to assemble at the start on Stirlings, the playing fields to the west of the main school.

In his old room, which was now occupied by a house prefect called Moorham – nicknamed 'Murram': when he exerted himself, his face went the colour of red earth so his moniker was not merely a convenient pun on his surname – Brian changed into his games kit, a dark green vest over a pair of cotton shorts. He wore no socks but only tackies, white plimsoles stained with black cotton soil. As he was no longer a boarder, he no longer qualified for a place on the fag rota and his shoes had not been blancoed.

'You know, Titch,' Murram said, 'you can borrow my fag. He's sure to be about. A funny little tick but quite good at shoes. And CCF kit. Awful at morning tea – makes it with lukewarm water. I think he's afraid of the boiling kettle. I tell him about it but he doesn't make the effort. I can hardly punish him for a crappy cup of tea.'

Murram had only recently entered the Duke of York, coming from a boarding school in Southern Rhodesia. He spoke like a South African but seemed, to Brian, not to be as coarse or cruel as most of the Afrikaners.

'It's okay,' Brian replied, tying the laces of his tackies tight.

The run was around the perimeter of the school grounds, a distance of three and a half miles or so, and he was well aware that some of it would pass through boggy ground. The first of the rains had come at last and the *donga* which ran through the school valley was running with water once more. The mornings were sometimes misty and cool and the afternoons, if it had rained before noon, were close in the damp sunshine. He thought of the *donga* near Wamumu where he had shot the

99

leopard. That would be running with water now and the brown bush would be greening rapidly.

'Titchner!'

Brian put his head round the door of Murram's room.

'Here ...'

It was the Head of House's voice.

'Can you get to the half-way point and check them through? Give me a list of the slackers ...'

'Okay. Are we running the full course?'

'Yes,' came the curt answer. 'You're dead right we are.'

Brian rode up to the school, Murram on the pillion. They arrived on Stirlings to see the school rugger XV practising passing, the team – with the reserves – spread out in a long line, jogging down the pitch and throwing the ball from one to the other. The master who coached them was marching along the touchline shouting instructions, encouragement and occasional criticism. Delamere House were also gathering for a cross-country run, their red vests, many faded with excessive laundering, clashing with the new green on the bushes at the side of the field.

Gradually, Lugard boys began to arrive and congregate in a bunch. The Head of House pedalled over on his bicycle.

'If you'd like to get on ahead,' the Head of House told Brian, handing him a clipboard with a list of names from which dangled a pencil on a length of string, 'we'll give you five minutes and then be after you.'

'Better give me a bit more,' Brian requested. 'I'm not as fit as the rest of you.'

The Head of House scanned the gathering of Lugard boarders and made a quick count. From across the field he could see a few stragglers appearing. They walked until they saw him facing in their direction then broke into a steady trot.

'They're not all here yet. You go off and we'll give you a bit more. I'll go counter-clockwise to the house and see no-one cuts across through the forest.'

The pencil fastened under the clip, Brian set off. He was not going to push himself and he was sure he had ample time to reach the half-way point with minutes to spare. He ran around the rugger pitch and through a few yards of brush onto Fosdicks, another rugger pitch on his right. Kirk House prefects were organizing a practice game there, most of the boys standing on the touchline in their games kit, watching. To Brian's left was a row of trees and a plain the other side of which, in the distance, was a Kikuyu settlement on a slight rise.

He entered the edge of the forest at the far end of Fosdicks, keeping to a path following the perimeter fence. The sun, which had been lurking behind high cumuli, came out and bathed the trees in clear light, deepening the shadows. Drops of water from the pre-noon shower clicked into the undergrowth.

After a mile or so, he came to a clearing and slowed to a brisk walk. Butterflies flitted over the grass and collected at newly-formed pools by the path. They stood in sunlight, sucking moisture from the damp earth or even the rim of the pools. They opened and shut their blue and black wings.

'*Graphium leonidas leonidas*,' Brian commented to himself, identifying them.

Near them flew some brilliant orange *Acraeidae* and, somewhere above his head, Brian could hear the rustle of a *Charaxes*. Scanning the forest canopy as he went, Brian spotted it; the butterfly flashed brown and white and he recognized it as the Pearl *Charaxes*. It was, he thought, a shame that soon these beautiful insects drinking at their pool would be scattered into panic by two hundred sweating, puffing, splashing, muddy boys.

The half-way point was at a place where the path turned through a forty-five degree angle to the right. On the corner was a large bush behind which was a trampled square of grass: all the houses secreted their prefects there on such occasions.

The rain had weighed down a branch over the hiding place and Brian raised his hand to brush it aside, taking care that there was no snake in it. Something had flashed liquid green in the dappled light and he was being wary.

There was no snake, only a large, brilliant emerald tree frog, its toes ending in little bulbous suckers. It clung to a broad leaf and, as Brian thrust the bough aside, wedging it behind another stouter one, it leapt away into the shade. He heard the 'splot!' of its body landing on a leaf.

As he waited for the first boys to arrive, he watched the butterflies drifting up and down the edge of the forest. Through the brush along the fence he could see a herd of cows grazing six hundred yards across the plain, two *totos* guarding them with a pi-dog. The sounds of the forest continued to be dominated by dripping water and the occasional call of an unseen bird. The only one to show itself was a black and white shrike flying in and out of the edge of the trees, hunting for grasshoppers on the plain. Every foray was successful, providing some insects so large that Brian wondered if perhaps there were a few locusts present.

Distantly one shout, muffled by the trees, announced the approach of the first runners. They would be the juniors who were always sent off first.

Along the path, out of sight around the bend, came a swishing of leaves. Brian slipped the pencil out of the clip and smoothed the stencilled list.

Suddenly, only a few feet in front of him on the path, there appeared a dik-dik. It was no bigger than a medium-sized dog, its tiny, Bambi-like horns sticking straight up from its head and its tiny hooves hardly denting the path. Its greyish fur shone with water and the minute white flecks in its coat gleamed where a beam of sunlight struck it.

Brian froze but the miniature deer had seen him, smelled him, heard him. It darted into the cover. The lowest branches twitched and shook for a brief moment.

Then came the first laboured footfalls of a boy.

When he appeared, he was wearing a red vest and, like Brian, was carrying a clipboard. As he ran, the shadows slipped over his face and Brian did not recognise him until he was almost at his side. It was Rudi Stadden.

'I see we're both doing bug-counting,' Stadden observed in his Afrikaans accent.

'It would appear so,' Brian answered coolly.

Ever since they had been in the first form, Brian had hated Stadden. He had been large for his age when only eleven and quickly earned himself a reputation as a bully. With his cronies, he had ruled the Junior House, when the prefects were absent, teasing smaller boys and demanding their tuck, provoking those he found had strong tempers but weak muscles. As the years passed, the other boys grew but still held Stadden in cautious awe. He was notorious for his dirty fighting, enhanced by his having taken judo lessons one August when on holiday in Durban.

Not only did Stadden's peers grow in size over the years. They also grew in intellect, in academic achievement and maturity whereas he remained behind, always in the lower sets or teaching groups, good only at sport and keeping discipline, which he did with a liberal use of the tacky.

Yet it was not for his bullying and strutting arrogance that Brian hated him most, but for his his blatant racial hatred of what he variously called niggers, coons, *nugus*, kaffirs, wogs and black bastards.

Many of the boys had racist attitudes. It was understandable and, in part, excusable. They inherited them from their parents – even their grandparents – from their position as the ruling race, their fear of Mau Mau and their misunderstanding of the African mentality. They were racially isolated. Few, if any, knew Africans as equals or came upon them in a social context. For the huge majority, the African was a farm worker, a domestic servant, a bus driver, a gardener, a tribesman in the *bundu*, a tiller of maize *shambas*, a herder of cows or a carver of souvenir statues on sale at the airport or the car park at the top of the Rift Valley Escarpment.

Stadden, however, was of a different breed. He did not, as most of the boys did, regard the Africans with disdain or dismissive disregard. He actively hated them. He swore at them, shouted at them, made no allowance for their ignorance, ill education, poor standards of clothing. To him they were barely as high in the natural order as baboons – he would refer to them as *nyani* then qualify it by saying they had hardly left the trees – and should be treated as such. He had recently boasted that he had shot two kaffirs on his uncle's farm near Solai but most put this down to fantasy. The African school staff, Brian had heard, referred to him behind his back as *Mbuzi-kuu* – 'The Great Goat'. It was a suitably vicious label, for Stadden's forehead was prominent and might have been made for butting.

'We sent them all off together.'

'What?' Brian asked. He had been thinking of Stadden, not the approaching hoard of mostly reluctant runners.

'The runts. We sent them all off together. They'll be here just now.' He scored through a name on his list. 'And this one's skiving.'

'How do you know?' Brian replied, knowing the answer he would receive.

'Chroist! What a fucking stupid thing to ask! He's skiving because I don't like the little runt.'

The shouts drew nearer. Stadden waited until the first boy was just beyond the corner bush when he jumped out in front of him and yelled.

'You're supposed to be running, you little *nugu*! It's not a bloody cocktail party at your snooty parents' place.'

The boy, in a red Delamere vest, was a first-former with long legs. He was evidently good at cross-country for he was at least fifty yards ahead of the next runner, who was shouting to him.

He started with surprise and fear. Juniors believed gangs of Micks – not to mention ghosts, ghouls, bogeymen and leopard – lived in the forest. Of those, only the last were true inhabitants, with the occasional visit from a forest lion.

'What's your name?' Stadden demanded.

'I wasn't shouting,' the boy protested, running on the spot to avoid getting a stitch.

To support his claim of innocence, a voice down the path called, 'Dick? Dick!'

'I know you. You're Tanton. Richard Tanton. A right little dick! You see me back at the house.'

'Why?' Tanton protested again.

'Don't get stroppy with me, you little dick. Now fuck off!'

The boy disappeared down the path. Stadden put a cross by his name on the list.

'That's not exactly the way to promote house spirit, is it?'

Brian asked. 'That boy's plainly one for your house cross-country team.'

'When I want your opinion, I'll ask for it. No wonder Lugard's got such a lot of wets in it...'

The boy who had been shouting was similarly caught and threatened by Stadden who was also critical of the next two boys to pass the bush. All four of the front runners were in red vests and Stadden was quick to point this out.

'For all your milk of human kindness, you don't have any real talent in Lugard. You need to get tough with them. Don't treat them like girls.'

'Perhaps you think we should shoot a few to teach them their place?' Brian enquired, his voice deliberately mild.

Stadden made no immediate reply: it took him a while to appreciate the irony in Brian's question.

A knot of five Lugard boys passed by. Brian crossed them off his house list. They were followed by a large bunch of mixed Lugard and Delamere runners which had both Brian and Stadden busy with their pencils, Stadden having difficulty keeping track. They were too quick for him. Then there was a lull.

'I heard from Chopping you got a leopard,' Stadden said.

'Yes. I did.'

'I also heard that you made friends with a one-armed kaffir.'

Brian did not answer. Instead, he watched the shrike fly in from the plain with a large dung-beetle in its beak.

'No answer? I figured it would be true. You're a typical kaffir-lover.'

Stadden spat, his spittle adhering to a leaf on the bush.

So, Brian thought, Chopping had opened his mouth even wider regardless of his request.

'This crippled kaffir of yours. Does he have a sister?'

'Why?'

'I thought perhaps you might have been screwing her. If you can't manage one of your own kind, why not try a *bibi* from the bush.'

'You're a foul-minded bastard,' Brian retorted.

'That's your opinion. And I've told you already when I

want your opinion, I'll ask for it. Anyway,' he leered at Brian, 'I'd rather have a foul mind than a fouled cock.'

'We're not in Lower Junior now,' Brian reminded Stadden.

'Meaning what?'

'Meaning I'd keep my mouth shut if I were you. If I choose to talk to an African it's my affair.'

'I hear your kaffir's a Mick, too. In a camp someplace. That about sums you up, Titchner. A fucking kaffir-lover. They ought to do you for consuming with the enemy.'

'Consorting,' Brian corrected him. 'Consorting with the enemy. Consuming's eating. I've not actually had dinner with him.'

'Yet!'

The runners were more spread-out now. Two seniors went by, one from each house. The first, from Lugard, was 'Murram' Moorham. He winked at Brian, tipping his head slightly in Stadden's direction.

'Don't you two do anything I wouldn't do,' he joked through gasps of breath.

'Your problem,' Stadden continued after a group of Delamere boys had gone past, berated by him, 'is you don't belong in Kenya. You're not right here. There's no room for people with your ideas.'

It was pointless to attempt to reason with Stadden. He was too narrow-minded, too blinkered to see beyond his own argument.

'If you say so.'

Brian's refusal to be drawn by Stadden was causing the bully to lose his temper.

'I do say so. So do a lot of the others. You're not popular, Titchner. You're just a piece of *pongo* shit.'

'If you say so.'

He was enjoying irritating Stadden. Now two carefully timed insults would be sufficient to set him off.

'What makes you think you're so good, eh?' Stadden went on. 'Off to university in Pongo? You're just a piece of *pongo* shit.'

'Perhaps. But it's better than being a *yarpy* turd.'

Stadden went white in the face. Despite his tan, he blanched, his eyes narrowing to thin slits. Brian now drove home his second insult.

'I wonder,' he mused out loud, 'how long it'll be before they have black engineers on EAR&H ...'

Stadden's father was a locomotive driver, mainly on the Nairobi–Mombasa line. He was touchy about the subject.

'They won't!' Stadden answered through gritted teeth. 'No kaffir could do the job.'

'I saw a goods train go up the line past Lugard last week,' Brian said. He spun the tale out. 'I was on line-patrol by the cutting because some of our second-formers have been flattening pennies on the rails. Was standing by the fence when a train went by. They go quite slowly up the incline. The driver was definitely an African. You can ask Pullford. He was with me and commented on the fact. Not a white face in the cab.'

Stadden's temper snapped. He flung the clipboard down and aimed a kick at Brian's groin. Ready for this, Brian dodged sideways. The kick, not meeting its intended target, put Stadden off his balance. Brian, twisting his own foot round, kicked Stadden on the thigh and he fell to the ground.

'You fucking bastard!' Stadden muttered and stood up. His left side was smeared with mud and dead leaves.

He hurled himself at Brian who, rather than grapple with his opponent, quickly raised his knee. It caught Stadden on the pelvis and deflected his lunge sideways. With his fist, Brian hit him hard on the side of the head. Stadden stumbled but did not fall.

By the bush lay a broken branch. Along its upper surface were thin, black mud tunnels made by termites. Brian saw the branch almost as soon as Stadden did.

Gripping the wood, Stadden swung it at Brian's head. He ducked but Stadden brought the branch round rapidly and the return swing caught Brian on the shoulder. The mud of the tunnels shattered and splattered like grapeshot over the side of his head, some entering his ear.

Brian grabbed the branch and tugged at it. Stadden, holding furiously on to his weapon, was pulled towards Brian who, this time, slapped rather than punched Stadden's face. Then he thrust his knee into Stadden's stomach. It winded him and he half doubled up, dropping the branch which Brian knocked away with his foot.

With his antagonist bent over before him, Brian thought their fight was over but he reckoned without Stadden's sly cunning. Suddenly, the Afrikaner bent down, scooped up a handful of the termites milling about where their branch had been and threw them into Brian's face. Instinctively, Brian closed his eyes and, as he did so, Stadden rabbit-punched his neck.

The pain was intense and Brian tumbled sideways. Stadden followed home his punch with another kick to the crutch but again he missed.

Brian – one eye closed against a termite – grabbed Stadden's leg and pushed at it. He fell backwards into the bush. Brian scrambled to his feet and, grabbing Stadden by his vest, half hauled him from the bush and slapped at his face, to and fro, first his palm and then his knuckles hitting Stadden's cheeks and brow. He then dropped his opponent into the bush and brushed the termites off himself. Most of them had fallen free in the scuffle.

Turning away from the prone Stadden, who was heaving breathlessly, Brian found himself face to face with a silent crowd of Delamere and Lugard runners.

'Right! Show's over! On your way,' he ordered.

'Good old Titchner!' exclaimed a boy at the back.

Another called out, ''Bout time Stadden got it.'

Two or three others muttered agreement but, Brian noticed, none of the vociferous ones stood at the front of the crowd where Stadden could note who they were.

As the boys set off to complete the cross-country course, Brian joined them.

'I'm not staying here with you, Stadden,' he said quietly as he left. 'I'd rather be in the company of real people.'

'You wait!' Stadden said to Brian's back. His teeth were clenched, his words forming behind them. 'I'll get even with you, you upstart kaffir-fucker.'

7

Once the examinations were under way, day-boy candidates were not obliged to attend school every day. Brian took advantage of this relaxation of the rules to stay at home and revise. Oudu provided him with coffee and biscuits whenever he requested them and all the servants were under strict orders to be quiet during the day.

Most of the while, Brian remained closeted in his bedroom, watched over by two new chameleons – named Romeo and Juliet, although he was uncertain of their sexes – which he had discovered in the Langata forest during further cross-country practices. Occasionally, he sat on a deck chair under the shade of the banana trees, overlooking the Kikuyu reserve and the far-off Ngong Hills. There he read and re-read his notes, learning what he felt would be vital for success.

The first exams he had to sit were the practicals. The Physics turned out to be not as difficult as he had feared. There was a light experiment and two on the subject of electricity. He found the hardest task set concerned the properties of liquids. The Chemistry paper included a titration, a chromatography question and the extraction of benzene. It was as if their master had had a sneak preview of the questions, though Brian knew it was simply the result of years of experienced examination-watching. The Biology paper, the last of the practicals, consisted of the dissection of the nervous system of 'a named small mammal' and the preparation and illustration of a series of microscope slides of various types of plant tissue. Each of the candidates had a different small mammal corpse upon which to work. Brian was luckiest, with a vervet monkey. Glanmer was the least fortunate for he was presented with a somewhat putrid rock hyrax in a jar of preserving fluid.

'God! I feel ill,' Glanmer confided to Brian as they walked together down the open corridor from the laboratory. The remainder of the school were still in lessons and from the other side of the quad came the rhythmic chanting of one of Mr Spencer's French classes.

'... *elle n'a pas, nous n'avons pas, vous n'avez pas, ils n'ont pas* ...'

'*Elles n'ont pas*,' Brian chorused, then said, 'so do I. I do wish they'd use xylol. Formaldehyde's utterly foul. Especially on a hot day.'

Almost with a reflex action, he tightened the knot of his loosened tie.

'It's not the formalin,' Glanmer answered. 'I'm sure I made a cock-up of the hyrax. What an animal! It must have been shot a month ago and left hanging in the bush. Most of the spine was so far gone it was spongey. The cartilage between the vertebrae was completely rotted away in places.'

'So long as you indicated the missing material properly in the diagrams, it doesn't matter. Remember the tilapia I had to do in the Lower VI exams? That was so rotten the scales had come off and I could find none of the afferent blood system. Not one single vessel. But I still passed.'

'How do they decide who gets what?' Glanmer pondered. 'You had the best specimen of all. A monkey! How jammy could you get!'

'I asked. They do it by numbered lots. Like a raffle.'

'I've never won a raffle. Not even one of those multi-prize affairs at the Royal Show ...'

Between the final practical and the first written paper, there was a twelve day gap. Brian worked hard at home, only riding into school on the Vespa when he discovered he was really still uncertain of a particular topic. The teacher would then give him a private quarter-of-an-hour session and help him with his problems.

By the eighth day, he was worn out. His mother had seen him growing more and more tired. He was up before she and his father left for work, was working after they had gone to bed. She only realized how late he was studying when she arrived back just after one in the morning from a dinner party at Thika to discover her son still poring over his books.

'You've got to have a day or two off, Brian,' his father

advised him. 'You'll be shattered for the papers when they come. And, let's face it, what you don't know now you never will ...'

'I just feel I can't let it go,' Brian replied.

'You must. You need to be fresh on the day. Peak of performance. Like an athlete,' his mother said.

'So ... you'll take two days off. That's an order. When I was up at Oxford,' his father had a brief nostalgic gleam in his eyes, 'I went sailing on the Hamble for two days before my finals. Got a first ...'

'Very well,' Brian succumbed. 'I'll just read a novel.'

'So we've got the Land Rover filled with petrol,' his father went on, 'I've bought you a box of copper-noses and you're off. I've rung Broomhall. Thought you'd like to go back seeing as you got your leopard there. He's expecting you this afternoon. And we hope to see you on Saturday morning. Oudu's aired the tent, as well, though you'll not have noticed. He did it behind the garage.'

'It seems I have no choice,' Brian said and surrendered to his parents' plans.

'What will you go for?' his father enquired as he shuffled documents into his briefcase and drank the last of his coffee.

'I don't really know. I've not had the chance to give it much thought.'

'Lion?'

'Not on my licence,' Brian said.

'Two on mine,' his father informed him. 'Have one of those ... We'll fix it up later. I'm sure I can square a transfer with Collis.'

By noon, Brian was well out on the road to Fort Hall. The sun was hot but not scorching. There had been no rain for three days. It seemed as if the rainy season was over, shorter than usual.

The farther Brian drove, the more distance he felt he was putting between himself and his studies and, by the time he turned right towards Wamumu, he was in full agreement with his parents. This was exactly what he needed.

Inspector Broomhall greeted him by the office, stepping

out and slapping his hand on the mudguard of the Land Rover as Brian switched off the engine.

'Drive shaft okay?'

'I kept to the real roads this time, sir,' Brian replied.

'Are there any real roads in Kenya?' the policeman rejoined. 'I think if we were to return in a thousand years the rule would still be to drive on the smooth side. The corrugations are getting worse – or my back is getting less supple.'

A work party of detainees was being marched up the hill from the camp rubbish tip. Some of them were carrying galvanised steel pails and others picks or shovels. Broomhall called to one of the askaris and two prisoners stepped out of the detail and approached him.

'You've brought your tent, I suppose?'

Brian nodded and jerked his thumb in the direction of the Land Rover.

'A new tent. The lion made a bit of a mess of the last one ...'

Broomhall laughed and looked the two prisoners up and down.

'I'll have these two johnnies set it up for you. Same place do you?'

'That would be perfect,' Brian said. 'But I'd like a bit of a thorn *boma* round it, if that's possible. If I'm on my own, I don't want to meet that lion again.'

'No sooner said than done!' The inspector issued some orders to the prisoners and then turned back to Brian. 'And, I'm afraid, I must ask you for the bolt and ammunition again.'

Reaching into the back of the Land Rover, Brian removed the bolt from his Rigby and gave it to Broomhall with the buff-coloured cardboard box of ammunition.

'Another guinea fowl this time?'

'I'll check with the mem'sahib. Even prison governors can't make an important social move without domestic approval.' He winked. 'Worse than Government House and the Colonial Office all rolled into one ...'

Within an hour, the tent had been erected, a *dhebi* of water delivered, a fire lit in a stone hearth and a supply of kindling stored by the side of the tent. Behind a bush, the prisoners

112

had dug a temporary latrine and the whole camp was surrounded by a *boma* of cut thorn bushes. There was only one way in, protected by a staggered entrance. To the side, there was a cleared patch of bush near the acacias where the Land Rover could be parked.

Once he had established his camp, Brian walked back up the hill to the office. Broomhall was seated at the desk, listening to a Duke Ellington concert on the BBC World Service. Every so often, the signal deteriorated into a whine and he had to readjust the tuning. He was attempting to improve the reception as Brian knocked on the doorpost.

'Come on in.' The inspector flicked the button on the radio and the music died out. 'Poor old London. Obviously something in the stratosphere between here and the Aldwych. When I was posted to Nyeri, we got much better reception. But down here ... I think Mount Kenya gets in the way a bit. Take a pew.' He indicated the corner of the desk. 'Sorry we're short on chairs. *Chai*?'

He held up a dainty cup and saucer Brian had not seen behind a tall pile of buff government folders.

'Yes, please.' He indicated the cup. 'I see you make some concessions to civilization out here ...'

He sat on the edge of the inspector's desk as Broomhall looked askance at the cup and saucer.

'My wife,' he explained. He shrugged his shoulders good-humouredly and called out, '*Tunaweza kupata moja kikombe ya chai.*'

'*Ndio, bwana,*' came a voice in reply.

'I wanted to ask a favour of you,' Brian said.

'Fire away!'

'Well, first – if you say no I'll quite understand. It is a bit of a big favour.'

'If you don't get on and ask it, I can't refuse it.'

An African manservant, wearing a pair of ex-British army shorts several sizes too big for him and a khaki vest, entered with a second cup of tea on a tray and gave it to Brian. He then handed him, separately, the saucer.

'*Chai-ingine, bwana?*' the man enquired, lifting Broomhall's cup but leaving the saucer on the glass table top.

'*Ndio. Na sahani ya biskuti.*'

When the African had gone, Brian continued, 'I'd like your permission to go into the camp and talk to Matthew Nchembe. I realise it might not be possible. I've no real need to go in ... No bust *gari*, no *chui* to skin.'

'Your father told me you'd make that request. He was a bit uneasy about it but I reassured him. Nchembe's no hard-core detainee. And I've no qualms about you going into the camp, so long as I know you're in there or the guard at the gate notes your going in and coming out.'

The servant returned with Broomhall's cup refilled and a plate of Nice biscuits. He put the plate on the table but did not place the cup on the saucer.

'He's new,' Broomhall explained, lifting his cup to its correct position on the saucer. 'Can't get the hang of saucers ...'

He sipped his tea, but it was too hot and he lowered the cup.

'Since you were here last, we've had a shuffle. Some of the hard-liners have been moved to another centre – your surly acquaintance Ndegwa with them – and we are gradually allowing out those deemed to be rehabilitated. Matthew Nchembe is likely to be amongst them, but not for a few months yet.

'So, you see, I think it's all right. I was in the camp this morning and told him you were coming. He said he'd like to see you ...'

Broomhall picked up the plate, offering Brian a biscuit. He accepted one and bit into it. It was damp and had lost its crispness, the sugar-crystal coating softened.

'In that case ...' Brian began. The idea was only then forming in his mind and he paused as he wondered if he should risk such an audacious request.

'What's that? Spit it out.'

'I was wondering if Nchembe could come out shooting with me.'

Broomhall leaned back in his chair and rubbed his hands along his belt.

'Now that is a tall order. I'll think about it. And I can't promise a thing.'

'Does he go out on work parties?'

'Sometimes. It's not that he's not trustworthy. He is. I *think*. I just wouldn't want to put temptation in his way. On the other hand, he'll be out soon...'

A car halted outside, the swirl of dust eddying into the office.

'I've a bit of business to see to, Brian. Why don't you come up to my quarter this evening for a bite to eat? I'm sure Cynthia would like to meet you. About seven? In the meantime, nip into the camp and see your Mick chum ...'

The car which had arrived was an official black saloon with a uniformed driver. Broomhall packed his papers into a case and was driven up the low hill towards the main road.

The camp gate was shut but the askari on duty, seeing Brian approach, opened it a few feet and once more he entered Wamumu. Remembering the route to Nchembe's hut, he kept to the well-worn path by the wire. As he walked, he fingered the leopard's tooth hanging by a silver chain around his neck.

There seemed to be fewer inmates in Wamumu. The steps to the buildings were not crowded and those prisoners who did appear, strolling through the camp on errands or chores, or sitting about smoking, did not glare at him. Some ignored his presence as if it was nothing out of the ordinary. *Toto*s still ran between some of the buildings, chasing a ball made out of a bundle of rags, yet they gave Brian no more than a cursory glance before continuing with their game. By a few of the huts slept tawny or brindled pi-dogs. They had been absent on his last visit and lent a sort of homeliness to the prison. Brian wondered if their admittance was part of an official policy of reducing the institutional feel of the place. More likely, he thought, they indicated a hole in the wire somewhere.

Matthew Nchembe was sitting on the step of his hut just as he had been when Brian had asked him to skin the leopard. He was rinsing out several tatty vests. From a line strung between a nail in the hut wall and an adjoining electricity pole hung two pairs of shorts, the water dripping from them cratering the dust beneath.

'*Jambo*, Matthew. *Habari*?'

The African had not seen Brian coming and looked up startled as he spoke.

'*Jambo. Vizuri. Vizuri sana. Na wewe*?'

''*zuri*!' Brian answered.

Nchembe pointed to a wooden box by the electricity pole and Brian pulled it over.

'Are you here with your friend?' Nchembe asked as Brian sat down.

'No. I have come on my own.'

'And your vehicle has not broken itself on the bad road?'

Brian laughed and replied. 'No! I kept to the main road from Thika. There are no deep *dongas* that way.'

Nchembe gazed through the wire in the direction of Brian's camp but could not see the tent because of the new green cover on the bushes.

'The rains have been good this year,' he observed. 'There will be much harvest.'

'I hope so,' Brian said. 'When there is food in the belly, there is peace in the heart.'

It was an old saying. Where he had first heard it, he could not remember: perhaps a servant had told it to him. Perhaps his ayah. He did not know if it was a Kikuyu proverb or a Luo one, or a Kamba.

'When the heart is at peace, the mind has time to dream. Do you know of that?' Nchembe asked.

Nchembe pressed the water out of his vest by gripping the material against the side of the bucket. It was not a successful way of wringing the laundry and Brian, without thinking, leaned forward and, taking the vests, screwed them up with both hands, squeezing the water out.

'*Ngai* must have intended for all those with clothes to clean to have two hands,' Nchembe said.

'Or a mangle,' Brian replied.

'That is another word I do not know. You bring me words...'

'You can put it in your book. It is a machine with a wheel

116

and three rollers. As you turn the wheel – with one hand – the clothes slide down a board and are forced between the rollers which squeeze the water out.' He looked up at the shorts draped over the cord. 'Would you like me to do those?'

Nchembe gazed at Brian. It was plain he was at a loss as to how to deal with this *mzungu*. He arrived unannounced – although Nchembe knew he had come to Wamumu, for the word had reached him almost as soon as the Land Rover stopped – and then, like a *mtumishi*, helped him with his washing.

With the shorts done and the vests hanging by them, Brian sat down on the box again. From inside his open neck shirt he pulled the leopard's tooth suspended from the thin silver chain.

'I have this.'

Nchembe reached inside the vest he was wearing and Brian saw he had one of the canine teeth dangling from a length of greased twine.

'It was a good leopard,' Nchembe commented. 'How is the skin?'

'It is good. I have it in my home.'

'Do you have it on the floor?'

'No. It hangs on the wall.'

'That is good. It is not right to use the skin of the *chui* as a carpet. It is to insult the spirit which lived inside the skin.'

Two *toto*s ran between them. Nchembe shouted in Kikuyu at them. They instantly stopped running and came back to him, staring at the ground and looking uneasy. When he had briefly chastised them, they left solemnly.

'There is no respect in the children.'

Nchembe spoke as if he were a village elder rather than a boy only recently become a man.

A silence fell between them. Brian had been looking forward to meeting Matthew Nchembe again, had been anticipating their meeting since just after his scuffle with Rudi Stadden.

Perhaps it was true he was a kaffir-lover, as Stadden had put it. He had never considered it before but he realised now that if someone who respected an African's dignity and human right to be himself was a kaffir-lover, then he was one.

As with all such categorisations, it was partially inaccurate, for he did not love all Africans. He could not like the dreaded Dedan Kimathi, General China and the other leaders of Mau Mau. He could not in any way condone their butchery – of only a handful of whites, but of hundreds, if not thousands, of blacks – their maiming of pet dogs, ham-stringing of domestic cattle and their implanting into the simple African mind the terrors of black magical reprisal. He also found it hard to like the Indian traders in Nairobi who as often as not treated the Africans with as much disdain, discourtesy and cruelty as did the Europeans. He had seen an Indian shopkeeper in a *duka* in Stewart Street once quite literally kick an African out of his premises for stacking soft bread beneath heavier tins of stewed fruit and jars of jam.

'Now it is better for him to be away from my shop,' the Indian had exclaimed. 'He is an ignorant and stupid black buggah.'

At the time, Brian had laughed in chorus with the other customers in the shop – and the Indian's Asian staff – but he had felt shame for his reaction afterwards.

Not only did he find a hatred in his heart for the terrorists hiding in the Aberdares, preparing for their last-ditch stand against the security forces, and for some of the Indians, but he had a hatred for the South Africans, too.

Stadden. He was a bastard, he thought. A narrow-minded, bigoted son-of-a-bitch. He hated Stadden, certainly. And yet he had to admit to himself: hatred was a funny thing. It was so complex and ungovernable.

What were the rules of liking and hating? At what point, he wondered, did one reach the fulcrum of decision, where hatred turned into love or vice versa? After all, he knew people whom he hated – or thought he did – but whose deaths would leave him with a sense of loss. His great-aunt on his mother's side always slobbered over him with kisses, told everyone within earshot – and a good few who would normally be beyond it – he had been a 'charming, curly-headed little monkey of a creature' when he was eleven, gave him a half-crown as if he were still a child and tut-tutted loudly if she saw him drinking a glass of beer, 'just like his great-uncle Sam – early to pay the penance to the second worst of men's evils'. He had often pondered on what she considered the worst. He hated Great-Aunt Dashwood, was forever attempting to disentangle himself from her bosomy embraces; yet, when her husband had died at the wheel of their clumsy and rusting Triumph saloon, and she had suffered a shattered pelvis in the ensuing crash, he had felt miserable for days.

'You are speaking very little,' Nchembe said, breaking their silence.

'I was thinking,' Brian said non-committally.

'Perhaps you are thinking of the bruise on your leg,' Nchembe suggested, pointing to the mottled skin with his stump of arm.

Brian rubbed it. It still pained him.

'You have been fighting?'

'Yes,' Brian admitted.

'You have been fighting, perhaps, because the boy who was with you here has told your white school-fellows you have been speaking with a terrorist.'

'No!' Brian replied quickly, perhaps too quickly.

He did not want to have to justify his peers, justify his race, admit he had been involved in a punching match with Stadden over his friendship with an African and an ex-Mick to boot.

Nchembe made no immediate answer but turned and emptied the bucket of dirty laundry water onto the ground where it spread quickly through the dust, pushing a barrier of dirt ahead of itself before suddenly dissolving into the ground.

'Why do you lie?' he asked.

'I don't know. And I'm sorry. And – yes: I had a fight with a boy who didn't like me talking to you.'

'Or being friends with me.'

'Yes.'

'So how do you feel about this?'

Brian had not considered his own emotions and, now

realizing this, he was surprised. He had thought over the philosophy and cause of hating but not of his own attitude.

'I feel indignant,' he admitted after a pause. 'I feel annoyed that someone who should be understanding is not. I feel cross that someone who is a ruler should be so insensitive to those he rules ...'

For a moment, he thought Nchembe was going to be angry himself.

'Do you rule us?'

'Yes. I think we do,' Brian said. 'We have made the laws and you have to obey them. Africans are our servants in our houses, not the other way around. We...

'You are wrong,' Nchembe corrected him. 'You think you rule but you do not.'

The *toto*s appeared again, preceded round the corner of the hut by their rag ball. As soon as they set eyes on Nchembe they halted. He stood up and kicked their ball towards them.

'*Ondoka*!' he commanded and they fled.

'How can you say we are not colonial rulers?' Brian questioned him. 'You even ride your bicycles on the side of the road we dictate you should ...'

'You are colonials, that is true. And you bring us your rules. That, too, is true. But you do not rule us. We rule ourselves, for we do not submit. Only those who submit – with their souls, not merely with their bodies – are ruled. We obey but that is not to say we are ruled. After all,' he added, 'how often do you see us keeping to the left of the road on our bicycles? All Africans are pragmatists – they waver from side to side as they will.'

He laughed and Brian marvelled at his vocabulary. He had never heard an African use such words.

'Where did you learn such good English?'

'From some of those so-called rulers – the missionaries. And I have read many books. Even here, in Wamumu, I can obtain books. Inspector Broomhall has brought me some and so I not only learn many things but I also improve my English. Now, tell me,' he said, squatting down once more, 'where did you learn Swahili?'

'From our servants.' Brian felt a pang as he admitted he had African servants.

'Which in particular?'

'My ayah, who looked after me, our houseboy. I learnt a lot from the *shamba* boy ...'

'And you say you rule us! You even entrust your *toto*s to us.'

Once more, the two of them fell silent.

This was not the conversation Brian had expected to have with Nchembe. He had thought to have talked about shooting, about the leopard skin and how many people admired it, about the bush and the animals and their ways.

'Did you beat the boy who fought you about me?' Nchembe asked suddenly.

'Yes.'

As he spoke, Brian realized he was proud of himself. It was not merely that he had successfully fought with Stadden who was, he now considered, a well-built and muscular boy with more than the average knowledge of what could be regarded as street-fighting technique, but that he had fought for a reason. And the reason, he now knew, was his defence of an African, one whom he believed to be his friend.

'That is good,' Nchembe smiled. 'It is always good to win in a fight.'

'Do you not feel bad you have lost your fight?'

Brian was not sure what had prompted him to ask such a blatant question. It must, he suddenly realised, have been a great blow for Matthew Nchembe, the terrorist, suddenly to find himself a captive – a prisoner-of-war, even. A prisoner of conscience.

'I'm sorry ...' he said rapidly, hoping to retrieve his tactlessness.

'There is no need to apologize. I have only lost one battle and, as I told you when you were here last, it is a futile war as it is being fought now. But in the end, I shall win. Africa will win. But the victory will not be over colonial rule or black skins over white skins. It will be a victory for sanity over insanity. Acceptance over rejection. Maybe even love over hate.'

Gradually, Brian understood what Nchembe had said. Hatred was not based on class or race. It could not be. Hatred had to be based upon individual relationships. Him and Stadden. Not him and the whole of Afrikanerdom. And love had to be based upon similar criteria.

'We are talking like two *mzee* around a camp fire. Let the old ones talk. We are young and must shape the future – that is our work.' Nchembe looked Brian squarely in the face. 'Now, tell me. Why have you returned to Wamumu? I am sure not just to talk with me.'

'I have come to hunt once more. I was lucky the last time. I shot my first leopard.'

'And you want another?'

'I have a lion on my licence. But I also wanted to see you, Matthew.'

'I am not sorry you have come, Brian.'

Apart from the servants, it was the first time Brian could think of an African addressing him by his Christian name. Usually, he was '*bwana*', or '*bwana kidogo*' – the little master.

Brian decided not to tell Nchembe he had asked permission for him to accompany him on his hunt.

'I am only here for two days – tomorrow night, I must leave. I have my A-levels ...'

He expected Nchembe to enquire as to what A Levels were but he did not. Instead, the African asked, 'When you have them, will you go to a university?'

'I hope so.'

'Where?'

'In England. I want to go to the university my father attended.'

'I should like to go to such a place,' Nchembe said, adding wistfully, 'but there is no such place in East Africa.'

'There is Makerere College,' Brian commented.

Nchembe frowned.

'I do not want to study agriculture,' he said, somewhat disdainfully.

Brian laughed loudly and Nchembe looked hurt.

'Why do you laugh?'

'Because that is all I want to study!' he explained.

Nchembe cast a quick glance in the direction of the barbed-wire fences and a patrolling askari, then asked, 'Will you go hunting this evening? For several nights, there has been a lion calling a mile away near a joining of two *dongas*. And, three days ago, a buffalo was killed in the direction of the place where you shot your leopard. It was only one lion ... A bachelor.' He smiled. 'Like me.'

'No. I am going to visit the inspector this evening. I'm going into the bush tomorrow,' Brian replied, wondering if Nchembe meant he was a loner rather than an unmarried man and his English vocabulary had, for once, let him down.

As soon as he left the camp, Brian drove to Sagana. There was, he knew, an Indian *duka* there which stocked European foodstuffs as well as paraffin, *dhebis*, cheap scissors and knives, string, maize seed and all the other paraphernalia of an African country store. From the Indian proprietor, he purchased a box of Cadbury's milk chocolates which, he was assured, were not melted 'at all. Not at all.'

Broomhall lived in a bungalow a little over a mile from the camp, across the main road from Fort Hall to Embu. It was a simple quarter with a large sitting room, a cramped dining room, a wide and deep verandah and a row of servants' quarters beyond a vegetable *shamba*. As Brian arrived, the last of the day's watering was being carried out by two *toto*s with a metal watering-can suspended from poles balanced across their shoulders.

A bedraggled flowerbed before the verandah contained a low border of crown-of-thorn plants behind which several clumps of salvia dropped their red blossoms towards the earth. All the plants were pock-marked with mud where rainwater, falling from the eaves, had splashed off the ground and dirtied them. A row of nasturtiums were the only healthy-looking flowers. They had climbed one of the roof pillars and their bright orange and yellow trumpets were still, even though the sun was very low, being visited by bees.

The inspector came down the steps from the verandah as Brian grated the ratchet of the Land Rover handbrake.

'My wife's keener on those you can eat,' Broomhall said, surveying the sorry floral display.

'You can eat nasturtiums,' Brian said. 'The seed-pods make pickled capers.'

'So I've heard, but I think we'll give them a miss. C'mon in and have a drink. G-and-T? Scotch and soda?'

'I'd like a beer, please, sir,' Brian requested as they sat in leather and wooden rourkee chairs lined with cushions. In front of the chairs were spread two zebra skins for rugs.

The houseboy came on to the verandah and took the orders. His white *kanzu*, at the lower hem where it brushed his feet, was soiled with the red earth. His sandals, fashioned from sole-shaped ovals of worn car tyre bound over with straps of webbing, sucked on the polished wooden floorboards.

'My wife'll be out in a moment,' Broomhall explained. 'She's tucking the kicker into his bed. Though he'll be out of it and want to see you before he nods off. Curious about visitors. As you can imagine, we don't get a lot out here. Do most of our socializing in Nairobi or Nyeri and then – as ever – it's other rozzers and we all talk shop and the Micks.'

The houseboy brought out the drinks. Broomhall removed a whisky from the tray and set a tumbler of gin and tonic on the bamboo coffee table. The African handed Brian a large glass mug of lager, the sides dripping with condensation.

'Oh, and one other thing,' Broomhall said. 'I'm grateful to you for calling me "sir" down at the camp but up here it's Terry. And Cynthia ...'

A door at the far end of the verandah opened and a pretty blonde woman came out holding a small, fair-haired boy by the hand.

She was obviously much younger than her husband and Brian guessed – as was so often the case – she was not a Kenyan white but a girl Broomhall had met on long leave in the UK, who had been bowled over by and subsequently married this tanned and muscular man, entranced by the thought of going to live in darkest Africa. That sort of wife always turned out in one of two ways. They either took Africa to their hearts or they were divorced and flying back to

124

London a year or two later by BOAC. The proof that Cynthia Broomhall fitted the former category stood by her side.

'You must be Brian,' she said, stepping forward and detaching her hand from the boy's. 'Welcome to Wamumu. For the second time. I do trust you don't have quite such an exciting stay.'

They shook hands: hers was cool and soft.

'I brought you these,' Brian said, instantly taking a liking to her and offering her the chocolates from Sagana. 'I do hope they haven't gone. One can never tell. And I'm sorry they're not wrapped.'

'That's most kind of you,' she said. 'I'm sure even "gone" chocs are edible!'

'I hope he does find a *bit* of excitement!' her husband exclaimed. 'Got his first leopard last trip. Maybe your first lion this?' He raised his glass. 'I was thinking of a *simba* in the *bundu* rather than the tent.'

'That was more embarrassing than scaring,' Brian said. 'Certainly looking back on it ...'

'Did you really have a lion in your tent, Brian?' the little boy asked, his voice bright and loud.

'You call all our visitors "sir",' remonstrated his father, lifting his hand to quell Brian's request that the child do otherwise. 'You have to show respect, son.'

'Did you really have a lion in your tent, sir?' the lad repeated.

'Not really; it was caught up in the fly-sheet. And it ran away and tore the canvas up.'

'Now! Bed!' commanded Cynthia Broomhall. 'Say goodnight.'

'Goodnight-father-goodnight-mother-goodnight-sir-goodnight-all-the-creatures-of-the-bush,' the child said, all in one breath, then he scampered off to his bedroom, the door banging behind him.

'I hope you like fish?' Cynthia Broomhall said, sitting in a third rourkee chair. 'One of the boys returned from a visit home – down near Mwingi – with some huge tilapia.'

125

'I like tilapia,' Brian said. 'I used to fish on the Tana when I was younger. We used to roast them over a fire on the bank.'

'Do you still fish?' Broomhall enquired.

'Prefer to shoot, si — Terry!'

'Always with a gun?' asked the inspector's wife.

Brian was a little confused by her question and said, 'I'm not sure what you mean, Mrs Broomhall.'

'Not Mrs Broomhall, please! Call me Cy. Not Cyn!' She smiled. 'That has a lot of connotations and was what the nuns called me in the convent. I dare say I gave them reason ... What I mean is, shoot only with a gun. Do you never use a camera?'

'I've not got the eye for pictures,' Brian replied. 'Art was never my strong subject.'

'You should try it! It's great fun. Terry bought me a camera for my birthday a few years ago. Just after we were married. I've got quite hooked on it. Always thought of it as just for snapshots of the family to send home –'

'But then she met old Corbett. Up in Nyeri, just before he died,' Broomhall cut in. 'Come along, Brian: drink up. Plenty more where that came from ... Juma!'

The houseboy promptly appeared on the verandah and Broomhall circled his finger over the glasses.

'Same again, Juma!'

'*Ndio, bwana!*'

'Who's Corbett?' Brian asked.

'Never read *Man-Eaters of Kumaon*, Brian?' Cynthia Broomhall clicked her tongue in mock disapproval. 'Oh! You should! Corbett was a hunter in India who shot tigers and leopards and all sorts. Then he saw it was wrong and stopped hunting for sport – but he did carry on shooting man-eaters. He's written a few books. Super, they are! You really must read them. And, after he stopped shooting, he started taking photos. And ciné film, too. He used to live in the Outspan Hotel, up in Nyeri. Knew the Sherbrooke-what's-their-names who own the place – Lady Betty ... He used to guide people at Treetops ... His old sister lives there still, I believe. She's got Baden-Powell's *banda* at the hotel.'

'Spent a fabulous evening with the old codger once,'

126

Broomhall added. 'If you could talk him into it, he'd show you his pictures. Took some fine ones out here, too, not just in India. We were fortunate enough to be at one of his lectures ... But his tigers! Took a stunning ciné of tigers – seven of the beggars all together at once ...'

'I thought they were solitary, like leopards,' Brian said.

'He called them up.' There was a tone of awe in Cynthia Broomhall's voice. 'All seven of them. One was a white tiger. They're very rare.'

'Astounding old boy. In his seventies, but he imitated a number of the wild Indian jungle animals for us. He could still roar like a tiger. Bit weak, he said, because of his bronchitis – but, I tell you, it raised the hairs on my neck. And that was in the bar at the Outspan!'

Juma returned with more drinks and said, '*Chakula tayari, mem'sahib.*'

'Grand!' Broomhall stood. 'Grub's up. Bring your beer through with you, Brian.'

Brian discovered he was hungry. The tilapia had been steamed and smothered with a saffron cream sauce. The boiled potatoes served with the fish were small and firm and the broad beans cooked with mint. Brian complimented his hostess: the following night, he assured her, would be hard tack and biltong by comparison.

'All from our own *shamba*,' Cynthia said with pride as they left the table and went back out to the verandah. 'Including the passion-fruit.'

By now it was dark, the moon not due to rise until after midnight.

As they returned to the rourkee chairs and Juma poured strong Kenyan coffee into bone china cups, Cynthia Broomhall said, 'You should take up photography, Brian. You really must.'

'She's evangelizing,' Broomhall warned. 'Does it to everyone. Mind you, she might have a point...'

'I don't mind,' Brian admitted good humouredly.

'Can I show you some of my photos? I promise not many. Nothing worse than having to go through peering at someone else's album.'

Brian could hardly refuse and, as Cynthia Broomhall went for her album, her husband said, 'She's taken this very much to heart. Wants to see all Africa divided into vast areas of wildlife park with the odd *shamba* here and there. It's a magnificent dream. I can't knock it, or her enthusiasm. But both you and I – I think? – know it's impossible. Once they get independence, it'll be coast-to-coast bloody *shamba*s with the odd clump of bushes housing a skinny gecko or a hungry boomslang. Even the rats'll live in little shacks with shiny tin roofs.'

He opened the box of chocolates and, having offered one to Brian, studied the key on the lid and helped himself to a nougat.

'Can't resist 'em!' he said. 'Not a little partial to those ones with a crystalised cherry in them ...'

The album Cynthia Broomhall was carrying when she returned to the verandah was thick and bound in black leather. She lowered it carefully to the coffee table, Brian and the inspector moving the cups and coffee pot to one side. The bamboo frame of the table creaked as the book rested upon it.

'I only want to show you a few,' she began and opened the album at a page bearing an eight-by-ten-inch colour print of a lioness. She was lying on her back in the shade of a thorn bush, her hind legs wide open and her white belly fur ruffled. A cub, barely hours old, was attempting to claw its way on to her chest while another lay alongside its mother and gazed directly into the lens.

Brian leaned over. It was a superb photograph and he said so.

'Oh, you wait a minute!'

Cynthia Brownhall turned over five or six pages and pulled aside the leaf of tissue paper, embossed with a pattern of spiders' webs, which separated the facing photographs.

The second photograph was of a Nile crocodile. It was a big brute – Brian estimated it must be a fifteen-footer judging by the egret perching on its back – running for the water. Unusually, its mouth was open and the yellowish-pink interior shone with blood, its wicked teeth festooned with scraps of flesh. The picture had been given a title, written on a square of white card in a neat hand and with a very thin nib. It read 'Croc. and Jockey'.

'That is fantastic!' Brian exclaimed. He put his head closer to the photo. 'You can even see the sand being thrown up by its feet.'

'They do move quickly,' she agreed. 'The first time I saw a croc go, it terrified me. That one was ...' she unfastened the picture from the adhesive mounts holding it in place and turned it over, '... a five-hundredth at 2.8. It was evening. On the Athi River near where the road crosses it to Ikutha.'

The other photographs she showed Brian were almost as good: a portrait of a giraffe, its prehensile black tongue twisting around a bunch of acacia twigs; a rear view of an escaping warthog, its tail erect with the hairy tuft on the tip blowing back; a head-and-shoulders close-up of a black rhino, a tick-bird balancing on the very point of its horn.

'I'm sure you could sell some of these photos to magazines,' Brian said. 'They are as good as any you see in *The National Geographic* ...'

'They're not for sale,' Cynthia Broomhall replied. 'It's only a hobby. But I'd like to have them shown where they might affect people's ideas. Make them think of saving Africa.'

'Been thinking of a book,' Broomhall added, 'but it would cost a lot to do. Even in black and white. Cy insists, if they appear at all, they should do so in colour. Looking at those, you can see why!'

'Yes, indeed I can,' Brian agreed.

'Do you know what Corbett said at his lecture?' she asked rhetorically. 'He said his motto was "Take nothing but photographs, leave nothing but footprints".'

She shut the album and helped herself to a chocolate. Some of them had indeed gone off-colour and were more beige than brown. The taste was unaffected.

'I think,' she declared through a hazelnut cluster, 'that is profound good sense.'

As Brian walked to his Land Rover, Cynthia Broomhall was on the verandah helping Juma to clear away the coffee cups and the cellophane wrappers of the chocolates. Her husband accompanied him.

129

'I've reached my decision, Brian,' he announced. 'You can take Nchembe with you tomorrow. I've fixed his pass and he's been told to be at the gate at dawn. Not told him why. Thought you'd like to surprise him.'

Brian's heart raced.

'But,' the inspector continued, 'I want him back by five at the latest. Don't let him carry your gun for you and don't load it until you need to. I don't for one minute think he'll try anything at all, but it's best ... He knows, by the way, that he's to be released, but he doesn't know when. I do. And it's soon. But that's very strictly *entre nous*.'

'Of course. I understand. And I'm very grateful, sir.'

'In the office – "sir" in the office!'

'Sorry! Terry ...'

'I'll not be about in the morning and Jim Lewis's been posted to Nyeri. Support role. They think they'll soon bring in Kimathi. When he's in the bag, the whole bloody affair will be over, in my opinion.'

'Thank you for a super evening,' Brian said as he sat in the Land Rover.

'Thank you for coming, Brian.'

As the engine came to life, Brian said, 'Do tell your wife I'll give photography a positive thought. When I can afford her equipment.'

'You needn't wait. She's only got a thirty-five mil. camera – a second-hand Leica.'

'The telephoto lens is what would hit my pocket,' Brian replied. 'I've got a camera now.'

Broomhall chuckled and confided, 'She hasn't got one. Nor does she enlarge them much. Those were all shot by stalking the subject. Why do you think the croc was running away?'

As he drove towards the detention centre, Brian could not get over what he had been told – that Cynthia Broomhall had taken herself so close to such dangerous game and without, presumably, a guard for company, or a firearm. Only a camera.

Brian woke early to the first wraiths of daylight on the eastern

130

horizon. He stirred the embers of his camp fire, finding they still contained a spark. Tugging dry twigs from the thorn fence – one of the advantages of a *boma*, he thought, was the ready supply of kindling it provided – he soon had a blaze going and quickly boiled a pan of water, some for his tea and some for a quick shave. This done, he drove up to the camp office to collect the bolt for the Rigby and thirty-five rounds of ammunition.

The askari sergeant on duty, who was expecting him, informed him that Nchembe was coming to the office at seven o'clock. It was advisable Brian did not enter the camp at such an early hour. As for Nchembe, it was better for him that his fellow detainees did not become aware of his leaving the camp to go hunting, alone, with the *mzungu*.

At seven o'clock, Matthew Nchembe arrived at the office in the company of an askari. He stood before the desk and was informed by the duty sergeant that he was being let out for the day. He was given a short warning on the foolishness of attempted escape and reminded of his possible forthcoming release on parole. The sergeant then scribbled in his day-book, peered out of the door at the first long shadows of sunlight and wrote the time of departure in the column on the right of the page.

'You are in the charge of the *bwana*. You can go!' he exclaimed authoritatively in English.

Brian, who was standing to one side of the desk, smiled at Nchembe who gave him a slightly perplexed glance. Then, bracing his shoulders, Nchembe turned about as if he was a private in an army and the duty askari his commanding officer.

Brian climbed into the Land Rover but Matthew Nchembe just stood by the passenger side and made no attempt to get into the vehicle. Until now, they had not spoken.

'Let's go!' Brian said. 'We've all day – well, until five o'clock.'

'Why is this?' Nchembe asked. 'I do not understand ...'

It had not occurred to Brian that Nchembe might not want to go hunting with him. He had simply assumed from their conversations in the camp that he would appreciate a day out of the confines of the barbed-wire and guard posts of Wamumu.

'I am going hunting,' Brian explained, aware he had supposed too much, 'and I asked Inspector Broomhall if he would allow you to accompany me. He agreed. I thought,' he paused, knowing he was blushing, 'you would like it ...'

Nchembe made no move for a moment. Brian wondered if he was suspicious and if the whole plan had not been somewhat ill-conceived. He was being the patronising white. But then Nchembe's face broke into a grin.

'I should like it,' he said and climbed into the Land Rover, his right hand gripping the back of the seat and his left stump touching the black windscreen mounting knob to aid his balance. Brian had lowered the windscreen before setting off. There was no need for it in the bush.

As they drove up the hill from the camp, Nchembe said, 'This is a surprise for me. If something is going to happen, I know of it. Usually.'

'It was only decided last night.'

'But you had made a plan for this?'

'Not really. I just thought it would be good for us to go out together. I did not expect Inspector Broomhall to give us permission.'

'To give you permission, surely.'

'No,' Brian said, 'us. It is the two of us who are doing this. Not just me.'

Nchembe fell silent as Brian steered the Land Rover along the track he and Chopping had taken a few months before. The villages and *shamba*s they passed appeared quite different now, with green leaves hanging on the bushes and the cultivated patches covered with rows of foot-high maize plants. The villagers glanced at them as they passed but were too preoccupied with their morning chores to do anything other than give a cursory look. The few *toto*s they saw did not run out and wave.

Eventually, they stopped at a *donga*. On his previous visit, Brian had been able to drive across it but the rains had re-cut the banks and no one had yet bothered to build a slope for vehicles.

'We can walk from here,' Brian said, reversing the Land Rover between two clumps of heavy cover.

From the rear well of the vehicle, he lifted out his rifle, a large aluminium water bottle and a small canvas satchel in which he had packed some bread, cheese and four passion-fruit. From under one of the bench seats, he pulled a second bush jacket.

Nchembe was wearing what he usually wore in the camp: a vest – on this occasion a dark blue one – a pair of khaki shorts and nothing else. His feet were bare and his head uncovered. Brian, on the other hand, was wearing a stout pair of shoes, knee-high socks, khaki shorts and shirt, a khaki bush jacket and, around his waist, a belt from which his sheath knife hung.

He offered the second coat to Nchembe.

'Thank you,' he said as he accepted it. 'My blue shirt is not good in the bush. The animals will see it.'

Brian went to put the satchel and water bottle over his shoulder, but Nchembe took them.

'I will carry these, for you will want to be free to shoot.'

'I can manage them,' Brian assured him.

'It is no trouble.'

With them slung from his left shoulder, his stump of an arm holding the straps in to his side, they set off southwards.

As they clambered up the far bank of the *donga*, Nchembe asked what Brian hoped to shoot.

'*Simba*,' Brian replied.

They walked in silence for about an hour, seeing nothing but a herd of gazelle and some wildebeest. Once or twice warthog or dik-dik ran through the cover and, in the distance, they saw the head and neck of a giraffe. Always alert for the spoor of lion, they found none fresh.

Arriving at a wide clearing in an area of thick brush, they halted and sat on a fallen tree trunk. The bark had been stripped off the wood and lay in tattered flags by the torn roots.

'*Tembo*!' Nchembe declared.

133

On the trunk beside Brian were indeed the gouge-marks of an elephant's tusk. The boughs too were devoid of leaves which had either been stripped by elephant or browsed by antelope.

Brian unscrewed the water bottle and took a swig, swallowing hard. He was already thirsty despite the fact that the sun was not yet as hot as he knew it would be.

He handed the water bottle to Nchembe who took only a little, swilled the liquid round his mouth and squirted it out.

'If you want to keep from being thirsty,' the African advised, 'do not swallow the water. Instead, wash it round your mouth and spit it out. If you swallow you get more thirsty.'

'I know,' Brian replied.

'Also, it is best not to urinate. Save this as much as you can.'

'There is no need to worry,' Brian answered. 'We have enough water.'

'You cannot tell when you will have enough until you return home and see how much is left. That is how much enough you have.' A faraway look entered Nchembe's eyes. 'It was important in the forest ...'

He fell silent, realizing what he had said, and Brian, looking sideways at him, saw Nchembe gazing at the ground before him, at the blotch on the soil where he had spat.

'What was it like in the jungle?'

Nchembe made no reply for a moment then answered, 'Not good.'

'Tell me about it,' Brian prompted.

He was suddenly curious, now Nchembe had mentioned it, to know what it had been like to be a terrorist. He would not have dared broach the subject had not the African done so, albeit so tentatively, in a moment when his guard had dropped.

'Why should you want to know?'

Nchembe was immediately suspicious and Brian could see he was upset. He had to defuse the situation quickly.

'I want to know,' he said truthfully, 'because you are my friend and I want to know things about you so I can share more with you. Your time with the Mau Mau will not have been good – even you admit that to fight that way for your freedom is wrong. If you talk of it, perhaps it will not be so bad ...'

'It is true you have this reason?' Nchembe asked. 'You have not been ordered by the inspector to ask me this?'

'No, Matthew. I am not a member of the police or the prisons department.'

Again, Nchembe was silent.

'You do not have to tell me. I am not a spy for them,' Brian assured him.

'I will tell you a little. But later.' Nchembe pointed to a shady patch under a big bush. 'First, we have the lion to hunt.'

Brian was ashamed and, with sheepish laughter, admitted allowing his attention to wander and miss the spoor: not twenty feet from them were the all-too-evident signs of a lion having spent a good part of the early hours lying on that very spot. The grass blades were bent and crushed, with no sign of there having been dew on them. Small branches had been snapped off and, on a group of three thorns the size of small nails but as sharp as needles, there hung a tuft of mane. From the shade, across a sandy patch of soil, led a set of fine male pugmarks.

The water bottle closed and back in Nchembe's possession, they set off side by side, following the tracks. Brian, despite Broomhall's warning, loaded the rifle and put a bullet in the breach, the bolt home and the safety catch on.

The lion travelled for half a mile in a southerly direction until it came to a *donga* in which pools of water had formed. There it had lain on its belly and lapped at the water, stood up, faced about, walked forward, turned, walked back to the water's edge and again gone down to drink. Its night-time thirst quenched, it set off in a westerly direction, walking steadily. Once, it disturbed a herd of waterbuck which crashed off through the undergrowth, but it made no attempt to follow them: its pugs, at their even, steady pace, cut right through the area of scrabbling and sharply dug hoof marks.

Near to a large *donga*, still flowing with a shallow stream in the middle, the lion joined its pride. Nchembe had suggested at first that the animal they were following was a solitary male, a juvenile: he was clearly not an old lion for his pads were not badly scored or cracked. However, the pride he joined – with a bit of scuffling – was quite large and he was possibly a junior male in its hierarchy. Brian and Nchembe fanned out along the stream and traced the pugmarks of eleven females, four cubs, of which one was not over six months old, and two other males, one a huge lion.

Now they knew they were after a pride, not an individual, new precautions had to be observed.

'They are not yet close,' Nchembe commented, studying the pugmarks where one of the cubs had entered the water, drunk standing up, then returned to the bank. Its pugmarks were mainly dry but with a hint of dampness at the very centre of the pads.

'One hour,' Brian suggested.

'Maybe longer,' Nchembe answered, judging the temperature of the sun by turning his face to the sky and closing his eyes.

'We can stop here and rest,' Brian decided.

The sun was by now well up and the lions would themselves be searching for shade in which to lie up for the heat of the midday. They would not go on the move until late afternoon and then they might hunt. It would be best to let them settle and then stalk the pride, picking out a target at comparative leisure. Furthermore, with Nchembe accompanying him – and Brian feeling somehow responsible for the African – it would be best to let the lions settle. He would not mind being alone in an area of roaming lions, but he did not want the added responsibility of Nchembe's safety.

They sat under an acacia tree and Brian, taking the satchel from Nchembe, unbuckled it and removed the food, breaking the bread and cheese in two with his hands and offering half to Nchembe who accepted it and began to eat.

'The bread we eat in Wamumu is very ... harsh.'

'How do you mean? You mean it is coarse?'

'Yes. There is grit in the flour. This bread is good. Do you buy it in Nairobi?'

'Oudu made it,' Brian said, adding as explanation, 'our houseboy.'

No sooner had Brian spoken than he regretted it. To mention his servants was to establish another barrier in what he thought was still a frail relationship. Why, he thought suddenly, did Europeans call their servants *boys*?

'Is he Kikuyu?'

'No, he is a Luo.'

'It was dangerous in the war to employ a Kikuyu servant,' Nchembe mused. 'They were often asked by our agents to poison their *bwanas*, put glass in their food, or rat powder. Not many did this ...'

'You were going to tell me about your life as a Mau Mau ...' he thought to say "terrorist" but changed his mind, '... soldier.'

'What do you want to know? I will tell you some things if you want to know them,' Nchembe offered.

'I don't know,' Brian answered. It dawned on him that he had little real knowledge of the terrorists. 'Tell me what you like ... I know nothing of Mau Mau except what the newspapers say.'

'Soon you will know everything,' Nchembe replied, 'for there is a report being written about Mau Mau. The man who is writing it visited me and asked a lot of questions. His name is Corfield. Do you know him?'

Brian rapidly reviewed a mental list of his parents' friends. 'No.'

'I think he is a lawyer. Lawyers are powerful ...'

Despite their presence, a waterbuck appeared on the far bank of the stream and nervously dipped its head to the water. It drank quickly then bounded back into the bush.

'When you join the Mau Mau,' Nchembe began, 'you take an oath. An oath giver – an *mzee* who knows magic – conducts this and you go through the ceremony with those others who are joining. It is a business of strong magic. Some people were made to join and some joined because they wanted to. I was one of these.'

'What happened?'

'This affair is at a special place,' Nchembe said. 'First, a goat is killed and the new members eat its meat. Then the

137

meat and blood of the goat are put on your ...' he lowered his hand to his groin and cupped his genitals, his fingers pressing through the cloth of his shorts, '... and then you insert yourself into the meat and you move as you would in a woman. When this is done, you eat again of the meat.

'When this is over, you eat of more meat that is from a man. He might be an enemy of the tribe, or a man killed because he would not join. Then you drink his blood which is warm from him – just a little sip, to touch the lips – then you line up and each of you jumps over his body seven times and on the last time you say "Mau Mau is as ants to the enemy: we can kill at any time." After this, you drink *pombe* and go to sleep or go back to your village.'

He looked up and over the stream, avoiding Brian's eyes.

Brian said nothing. The rites were bestial – articles in the *East African Standard* had stated so often enough – and beyond the bounds of the printed word, but he had not realized quite how primitive they were.

'The oath is very powerful,' Nchembe added. 'Telling this to you would have had me killed by magic.'

'Do you believe so?'

'Yes. I was only fifteen when I took the oath. And, at first, when I was put in prison, I would not talk and the police stuck wires to me connected to big batteries. Even fixed to the light in the cell. When I still would not talk of these things, the police brought in another *mzee* who removed the power of the oath. So now it is safe; I have told others and no harm has come to me.'

From the satchel, Brian removed two of the passion-fruit, slicing the tops off with his sheath knife. He handed one to Nchembe and began to suck the sweet, pip-filled pulp out of his own. Nchembe merely held his and continued to speak.

'In the jungle, we ate wild fruit and the animals we caught or the food we obtained from villages,' he went on. 'Even the villages which were protected by the army and the police ... We could get in to them and the people brought us food, leaving it in hiding places in the *shambas*. Those villages were bad places. They were like Wamumu. They were like prison camps with long hours of curfew. Sometimes twenty hours a day. Maybe more. And there was starvation in them. People had no clothes ...'

As he spoke, he absent-mindedly twisted the fruit between his fingers.

'I had a colobus monkey coat. It is still safe in the jungle. I hid it where no one can find it. One day I shall return for it. When the war is finished. This will be soon now. Dedan Kimathi will soon be caught. And they will hang him. Then Jomo Kenyatta will be released and will be our leader and we shall have our land.'

'Will it really be so simple?' Brian queried.

'I think so. *Uhuru*. It will come.'

'"*Uhuru*"?' Brian repeated. 'What is that?'

'It is freedom. We will be one nation. Not like today, with the tribes apart so. It is the British idea – to divide the people and rule them. Even the Kikuyu people are made into two – the Mau Mau and those who want liberty and those who are foolish and want to go along with the British idea. It makes Kikuyu fight Kikuyu. This is a civil war. It exploits the ignorance of our people. It is a wise and clever way to govern. It worked well in India ...'

Brian was amazed at Nchembe's grasp of facts, of his astute knowledge of politics and political tactics. He had not considered the problems so clearly himself.

'The trial of Jomo Kenyatta was unfair. It was arranged. And after he was put in prison, bad men took charge of Mau Mau. Remember, in 1952, Jomo Kenyatta cursed Mau Mau. He knew it was not the way to go. But Mau Mau was good for the British. It showed the world how bad are the Kikuyu. They even fight themselves ... Think of the murder at Lari in 1953 ...'

As he spoke, Nchembe did not look at Brian but at the far bank of the stream, as if across it, with the waterbuck, lay a promised land towards which he was striving. But, on mentioning the infamous Lari massacre, he turned to stare earnestly into Brian's eyes.

'This I have told to no one,' he said. 'I was there. At Lari. Ninety-four Kikuyu were killed. Chief Luka was burned to death. *Toto*s were crucified, alive.'

Brian caught his breath. Here he was, in the middle of nowhere, a loaded Rigby by his side with one slug up the spout, sitting breaking bread with one of the perpetrators of perhaps the worst of all Mau Mau atrocities. Yet, at the same time, mingled with his apprehension, he felt a compassion for Nchembe which was touched with both fear and sympathy.

'It was bad. It was then I saw this was not the way.'

He paused, lowered his eyes, then looked again into Brian's face.

'One girl *toto*,' he said, his voice quieter, 'was held against a post and her hands pulled back behind. One of the men then nailed her hands to the wood. She was screaming and another pushed grass and earth into her mouth to make her stop. Then they cut her open with *panga*s. Just a little, so the insides only just began to come out...'

From his eyes tears welled, and he rubbed at his cheek with the stump of his arm.

'She was a Kikuyu *toto*. I was one with a knife ... I killed a *toto* of my own people. Not an enemy or a British soldier or a Kikuyu traitor. A *toto*. I was fifteen then. Almost a *toto* ...'

He choked and sobbed. Brian felt tears brimming his own eyes.

They neither of them spoke. There was nothing to say and, for a quarter of an hour, Nchembe sat leaning forward, motionless, his hand still holding the passion-fruit. At last, as if wakening from a dream, he sat up and, squeezing the fruit, poured the seeds and juicy orange pulp into his throat.

'It has been many months since I ate this fruit. How is it called in English?'

'Passion-fruit.'

Nchembe laughed wryly.

'It is a good name for what we have been speaking of.'

'I will tell no one what you have told me,' Brian said as Nchembe tossed the empty shell of the fruit into the stream where it tumbled slowly over in the lazy current.

'I know this. You are my friend ...'

Their meal completed, they set off once more after the pride of lions.

Crossing the *donga*, the lions had headed into thick bush.

To follow them through such cover, in which they might be lying up, was suicidal. Brian and Nchembe skirted the area and arrived, on the far side, at the edge of a grassy plain dotted with acacias. Two miles away, in the haze of early afternoon, a line of trees indicated another, possibly water-filled, *donga* which would be a likely place for a pride to lie up. They would be close to water, be afforded the shade of the trees and probably be near a drinking pool to which game would be attracted.

Nchembe agreed the pride could well be in the vicinity of the distant trees but pointed out there was little cover between the two of them and the wooded banks.

'It will be hard to get close,' he said, eyeing the Rigby, 'and your gun has range but no telescope. If the air is hot and dancing, it will be hard to kill.'

The only alternative was to approach the trees by keeping to the cover on the edge of the plain. It would mean fast walking for at least twenty minutes.

They started off and soon came upon a heavily trampled game path at least six feet wide. Many creatures had used it and left their signatures in the dust – warthog and bush pig, antelope, zebra, Thompson's gazelle, buffalo, giraffe, water-buck and bushbuck, dik-dik and, for a short distance, an old leopard lame in one hind foot which he dragged slightly, unable to lift it clear of the ground with each step.

Bending over, Nchembe spoke very softly even though their voices could not carry far in the hot air.

'The *chui* has broken his leg. A long time ago...'

The leopard's tracks went off into the cover and they proceeded towards the trees.

Coming round a vast baobab, in which was perching a large bird of prey – Brian was unable to identify it for the glare from the sky – they discovered an even wider game path, marked with the round, serving dish-sized footprints of elephants. Their own route joined this natural highway which was thick with dust and heading towards their goal, the line of trees.

'If we walk on the side of this we can get close. The *simba* will not smell us,' Brian half whispered.

Nchembe nodded his approval of the plan. A hot breeze

was blowing along the game path, whipping up tiny spirals of dust. They could do with some camouflage for their scent.

Brian kept to the left-hand side and Nchembe the right. It was better for them to be apart for, now they were drawing closer to their quarry, both could watch out ahead for signs of the pride.

The game path, having been well trodden, consisted mostly of loose dust and dried dung. Each step Nchembe took caused a small plume of dust to drift away from his bare feet, blowing in front and to the side of him, warning Brian the wind was not entirely in their favour. He regretted not having gone straight across the grass-covered plain.

There were only four hundred yards to go and Brian's nerves were taught. He walked in a semi-crouch, his head below the level of the grass. He cast a quick glance at Nchembe. Across the game track he too was walking with his head up but his back bent.

Carefully, Brian opened the bolt to check the Rigby was loaded. In the breech was a bright bar of brass and the circular base of the cartridge. He eased the bolt shut before the extractor could flick the ammunition free. A bead of perspiration fell onto the gun metal and remained there, its meniscus tucked in where it came in contact with the smearing of gun oil.

Out of the corner of his eye, Brian saw Nchembe jump, his back straightening and his stump of arm waving frantically in the air. He screamed, an unearthly and high-pitched sound which echoed even in the hot air. From ahead came a roar and a thrashing of undergrowth as the resting lions, grazing gazelle and a small herd of zebra stampeded through the grass, the antelope leaping high in the air.

Again, Nchembe screamed.

'What is it?' Brian shouted, covering the ground to his friend in three strides.

It was only when he reached the African's side that he saw.

Nchembe, keen to keep his eyes on the trees, had not seen a puff adder lying half submerged in the dust, the chevrons on its back dulled by a coating of dust and, Brian noted, not so obvious in any case as the snake was a female.

142

'Oh, God!' Brian swore.

Nchembe staggered. The bush jacket had slipped from his shoulder and he had shed the satchel and water bottle which were lying on the game path.

'*Nyoka!*' he said in a wailing voice. '*Nyoka! Nyoka!*'

From somewhere in the recesses of Brian's memory, he heard someone tell him Africans could die of the thought of a snake bite, not necessarily the venom.

The snake was not moving. Brian put the muzzle of the Rigby just above the shield-like top of its skull and pulled the trigger. Nothing happened. He released the safety catch and pulled again. The snake's head disappeared into a stain of blood and tissue. The ground smoked around where its head had been. He dropped the rifle into the dust, reaching for his sheath knife.

'Sit down! Quickly!'

Nchembe fell to his knees. His hand tried to reach his ankle but could not. His black face was ashen and his eyes rolled with fear.

'Keep still!'

Nchembe thrashed his foot about as if the snake was somehow locked on to it and he had to dislodge it. He moaned loudly.

'Keep still, for Christ's sake!'

Nchembe ignored him so Brian spun him round and sat on the African's thighs. He stuck his knife in the ground and began to tug his belt out of the loops on the waist of his shorts.

'Which leg?' he bellowed. 'Which leg?'

The knife scabbard fell to the ground as the belt cleared it.

'... *Kushoto*,' Nchembe mumbled through his groaning.

Brian passed his belt around Nchembe's left leg and tightened it through the buckle, wrapping it round and tucking the loose end in. Where the metal buckle pressed into Nchembe's flesh, grey flakes of skin began to fall away.

Grabbing Nchembe's foot, Brian twisted it to one side and upward. Just above the Achilles tendon, on the back of the ankle, Brian saw two puncture marks, one above the other. The snake had turned its head to bite. In the lower puncture was one of the puff adder's fangs, broken off as Nchembe had jumped.

Pulling the fang out as if it were a splinter, Brian prised his knife out of the ground and, with a deft movement, made an incision from one fang-mark to the other. As the blade opened the skin, Nchembe hit Brian in the small of his back with the stump of his left arm.

'Shut up and keep still!'

He bent over and squeezed the incision until it ran with blood. Then, leaning forward, Brian sucked as hard as he could at the wound, spitting the blood, venom and dust out, praying he had no cavities in his teeth. As he sucked, he promised God he would clean his teeth regularly after this. Daily. Twice daily. After every meal. After every bar of chocolate.

For five minutes, he sucked and breathed deeply, gradually loosening the belt. Finally, hoping he had removed most of the venom, Brian got up and, picking up the water bottle from where it had fallen from Nchembe's shoulder, rinsed his mouth thoroughly and gargled. This done, he drank a draught and handed the bottle to Nchembe.

The African was still sitting in the dust, leaning back on his right arm. The belt was loose around his thigh. It was as if he were frozen with fear.

'Get up now,' Brian ordered. 'It's nothing to worry about. The poison is mostly out.'

'*Mimi ... Kufa ...*' Nchembe chanted softly, his eyes still rolling.

'Rubbish!' Brian shouted at him. 'You will not die. Get up!'

He helped Nchembe to his feet, replaced his belt and put the sheath knife back in its scabbard. From the top pocket of his bush jacket, Brian removed three long sticking plasters – his emergency supply – and, wiping Nchembe's slashed heel with his handkerchief, pulled the wound together with the adhesive strips.

'Can you walk?'

Nchembe looked at him as if he was a stranger.

'*Ndio, bwana,*' he said.

Before they set off, Brian emptied what remained of the food from the satchel and dropped the dead snake into it. Then he hoisted the satchel and water bottle over his shoulder, picked up the Rigby and they started back to the Land Rover.

For a while, Brian held Nchembe's right arm as they walked as quickly as the African could manage. He was unsteady for the first mile but, after that, he was able to walk on his own.

Neither of them spoke until Nchembe was in the passenger seat of the Land Rover. By now, it was four in the afternoon and the sun was beginning to go down.

As Brian put his hand on the steering wheel, Nchembe took a firm hold on his arm.

'Why?' he asked.

'Why what?' Brian replied.

Nchembe, letting go of him, made no answer.

Brian started the engine.

'You have saved me from the snake. You put your mouth to my foot and took the poison into your own body. My feet are not clean ...'

'I did what had to be done. If you act quickly, you can save someone from snakebite. Even from the puff adder.'

'But I am a Mau Mau ...'

'You *were* a terrorist,' Brian corrected him. 'Now you are Matthew Nchembe and I ...'

There was nothing to be said. Nchembe placed his hand over Brian's, tightening his grip so harshly Brian's fingers hurt, crushed on the black steering wheel.

'*Asante*,' Nchembe said, simply.

'There is no need to thank me,' Brian replied. 'We are friends.'

8

The headmaster sat upon the stage. Behind him ranged the staff and before him, seated on the floor, were the first-year boys now at the end of their 'new bug' year. Next term, they would be second formers, initiates, old hands with the knowledge and power to make miserable the lives of the new intake. To either side of the hall, the sun shone brightly upon the quad and the main school entrance. Under its small, angled roof, looking more like the top of a wishing well, the school bell hung in shade, the polished brass glinting with reflected light from the windows of a parked car.

Behind the junior boys were ranked the remainder of the school, the seniors seated on metal-framed chairs. The piano played tinnily the opening bars of Hymn 523 and the school, at the chaplain's signal, broke raggedly into the song:

> *Lord, dismiss us with thy blessing;*
> *Thanks for mercies past receive;*
> *Pardon all their faults confessing;*
> *Time that's lost may all retrieve ...*

Brian did not join in. There was a lump in his throat for, although there was much he did not like – had not liked – about The Duke of York School, it had been his home for the better part of each year for seven years and he knew he would never see it again as it was that sunlit morning.

This was the last day he would wear the maroon blazer and grey slacks, the silver and maroon tie. Already, up the hill by Lugard, the Land Rover was parked, loaded with all his belongings packed into cardboard boxes – his books, games kit, spare uniform, Combined Cadet Force webbing belt which he had succeeded in thieving after the final inspection the Thursday before: he wanted it for a souvenir, nothing

146

more. It was a reminder of his school-days with their almost military discipline.

He wondered, as the first verse of the hymn faded and the pianist thumped out the intermediate bars, if Stadden would confess his faults and be other than a racist and a bully, or if Chopping would ever retrieve the sleep he had lost worrying about Micks.

The boys around him began to sing again, lustily shouting out the final verse, in deep-throated counterpoint to the unbroken shrill of the juniors' voices.

Let thy Father-hand be shielding
All who here shall meet no more:
May their seed-time past be yielding
Year by year a richer store:
Those returning ... Those returning
Make more faithful than before.

The gusto with which the schoolboys attacked the last verse was filled not so much with religious feeling as with the desperation of getting the whole proceeding of Final Assembly over with so they might get back to their packing, their parents' cars, the buses which would take them to Nairobi railway station or Embakasi airport.

In his heart, Brian could not wish any father-hand to shield some of those with whom he had spent his seven years, especially the Afrikaners: Stadden, Pederson, the Krugers; in the final analysis, he wished them ill.

When the final chord had died, the boys expectantly silent, the headmaster – 'Pansy' James, whom Brian both admired for his teaching and despised for his ignorance of the boys' common lives in his school – bade his pupils an earnest farewell, reminding them, as he did at the close of every term, that the holidays were a time of relaxation but not stagnation. The first day of the next term, the new school year, was the eighth of September. By then, Brian thought, the Duke O., as they called it, would be but a memory and he would be – he prayed – on his way to the spires of Oxford.

As he walked by the school bell for the last time, Brian squinted through the glare. How many times, he considered, had he rung that bell as a part of his prefect's duties, pulling the whitened rope to one side, all the while staring at the deep-cut engraving – "HMS Duke of York" – and thinking of the calls of the drowning sailors it had absorbed into its metal; the bell had been lifted from the wreck of the famous battleship. Every strike, signifying the end of a teaching period, had released some of those screams of despair just as they released pupils from the agonies of their lessons.

'Well, Brian? The end of chapter one and the start of two ...'

He turned to find his housemaster, Mr Hesketh, catching up with him.

'Yes, sir.'

'A sad day when one leaves a school. But for you there are greater challenges ahead. I wish you the very best of luck,' he offered his hand, which Brian accepted gladly, 'and would like to thank you for the support you've given me in the house. You have been a first-rate prefect, a stabilizing influence on your peers and those junior to you. You've been a credit to the school.'

'Thank you, sir.'

'The school won't stay like this for long, you know. In the next year or two,' he waved his hand over the expanse of grass lawn between the drive and the gymnasium, 'we'll have a chapel built here. But after that ... Independence is sure to come in the next ten years. Or less. Then it'll all change.'

There was a sadness in the teacher's voice which did nothing to settle Brian's own mounting inner nostalgia. The beatings and sessions of Pres' PT, the tackyings and canings he had received or meted out faded into a dim blur of unpleasantness. In its place, he recalled more human or wonderful memories: the first time he had watched the shy forest deer, the Suni Pygmy Antelope, feeding in a clearing beyond the area known as 'The Happy Hunting Ground'; his first *Charaxes* butterfly, caught with the aid of a bowl of bait, beer and sugar-water boiled gently over the prefects' hotplate when they were at a house meeting; the lions he had seen briefly on the hockey pitches; the pennies he had had flattened by town-bound freight trains.

148

There were two routes he could take to Lugard. One was to follow the main school drive down the hill, past the sanatorium and the headmaster's house, over the *donga* and up the hill by the railway bridge. The other was known as the 'Burma Road', a path which snaked through bushes between the school rifle range and the staff houses on the lower slopes of the Speke–Lugard hill.

For old times' sake, for the final time, he walked along Brooklands to the steps down to the swimming pool, squash and tennis courts. Junior boys from Kirk were larking about outside their boarding house as he descended the steps. The swimming pool had been drained for painting, the diving board removed and the fountain silent and dry. At the bottom of the steps, he turned right, past the corner of the armoury and the parade ground, and went over the roadway, down beside the range. As a first year, he had rummaged in the butts for dented, misshapen scraps of lead and copper, and he had been tackied for it.

The path was dusty and he kept an eye open for any puff adders which might be lurking there. He did not want to suffer Matthew Nchembe's fate.

He had, he considered as he walked, slipping into a reverie as he often did when strolling along ways he knew by heart, done the right thing with Nchembe. God only knew what he had risked contracting from the African's foot, for Nchembe had been walking all day through elephant droppings, over a multitude of germs and filth. Where there were animal droppings there was always tetanus. His mother had insisted on him having a booster injection as soon as he arrived home from Wamumu. Broomhall had been both shocked and surprised when he heard the story and Nchembe had immediately been given a shot of anti-venom. Then he had praised Brian for his quick thinking, his bravery and his efficient application of bushcraft survival tricks.

Brian had remained the night at Wamumu. Nchembe ran a high fever in the evening and was almost delirious, but Broomhall assured Brian this was shock and fear rather than any haemotoxin left in the African's body. By morning, he was weak but well on the way to recovery. Very briefly, Brian had visited Nchembe in his hut.

'I am well,' the African had said with a certain edge of amazement to his words. 'This is due to your braveness. I know this. My life is due to you.'

'Bravery, Matthew,' Brian had said, quietly. 'You must get it right for your book.'

Nchembe had smiled.

Brian's arm brushed a bush but the rustle it made was far greater than a mere touching of the outer twigs. Suddenly, Stadden was standing on the path before him, one of the Krugers by his side.

'How's your kaffir comrade?' enquired Kruger, a sneer on his lips. 'Been to see him in jug again?'

Stadden made no comment and Brian realised by his silence that he was bent on revenge. The animal that makes a noise, stamps its feet, paws the ground or starts a charge is usually bluffing. Kruger was bluffing. He was not going to initiate any action. But Stadden was motionless. Even his face muscles were still, set in a leer.

Brian made no reply and stopped walking.

'How long since you kissed your kaffir's feet?' Kruger mocked.

At that remark, Brian half-smiled: if they only knew the truth of it, he thought.

'Or his arse,' Kruger continued.

Stadden brought his right hand round from behind his back. He was holding a long-bladed razor.

Brian still did not speak.

'Thought you'd got away with it?' Stadden murmured, barely audibly. 'Thought you would leave without seeing me?' His voice rose just enough for Brian to hear him clearly. 'Sneaking down the Burma Road to avoid me? Afraid to keep to the drive? That was your mistake, you *pongo* bastard. Down here there's no one to help you or come running ...'

'Still need your army?' Brian observed quietly, nodding slightly in Kruger's direction. 'Still unable to do your own fighting?'

'Pik's here to see fair play,' Stadden retorted sarcastically.

'Got a razor for me too have you, Kruger?' Brian asked.

Stadden lunged at Brian, but he was ready. He had expected a quick strike when it came. He jumped backwards by one step. Stadden straightened and advanced one step. Brian knew from his face that his temper was controlling him, not his reason. He was white on his cheekbones and prominent forehead and his jaws quivered and moved from side to side with anger.

'You know how kaffirs scar their faces?' Stadden asked. 'They think it makes them beautiful. Those lines that decorate them. Well, seeing you love kaffirs, we thought you should look like one. For you, it'll be bright pink lines on your lilywhite skin ...'

He lunged again, but Brian was again ready. Stadden, expecting him to move back once more reached too far forwards and Brian hit his forearm with all the strength he could muster. Stadden grunted, recoiled, but did not lose his grip on the razor.

'Not good enough!'

Kruger stepped forward now with a short, thick stick in his hand. He swung it at Brian, who ducked. As he did so, Stadden came again, the razor slicing down towards Brian's scalp. He twisted his head and the razor cut through the shoulder-padding of his blazer but not as far as the lining.

With a deft thrust of his arm, Brian reached out and grabbed Stadden's genitals. He closed his fingers as hard as he could through the tight material of Stadden's trousers and squeezed with all his might. Stadden dropped the razor and squeaked. His hands flew to Brian's, his bitten fingernails clawing at Brian's wrist but unable to get a purchase. He was breathless from the shock and started to stagger away, but as he moved, so the pain intensified. Brian stood up, but still held on. Stadden's hands were loose now, trying to press into his belly above his penis, seeking to alleviate the scorching agony. He squeaked again.

Suddenly, Brian let go. Stadden doubled over and Brian brought his knee smartly upwards. It connected with Stadden's bulging forehead: the shock of the impact jarred his leg.

Kruger, who had kept aside not knowing what to do, again swung the stick at Brian, cursing him in Afrikaans mingled with English.

'You fucking kaffir-lover! You fucking nigger-screwer ...'

Brian's fist hit the side of Kruger's temple. The Afrikaner lost his balance and let go of the stick. Brian caught it in mid-air and rammed it end-on into Kruger's ribs.

'One day,' Brian prophesied hopefully, throwing the stick away, spinning like a propeller through the air towards the *donga*, 'a black's going to see to you. I only wish I could be there to watch it. Time you yarpy sons-of-bitches got what was due to you.'

He turned to Stadden who was lying on his side, both hands to his crutch still and his ugly, protruding forehead gushing blood from a cut over one eye. 'As for you, Stadden, your balls are barely big enough to grab. You're not worth shit.'

With that, Brian stepped around them, went over the *donga* and up the slope towards Speke and Lugard, the stuffing from his shoulder-pad working free and tickling his neck.

As he drove under the railway bridge, Brian cast a quick look at the driving mirror. The school badge and motto over the bridge were back-to-front and, with enjoyable irony, Brian spoke out loud, translating the Latin in reverse.

'The best but nothing,' he mocked.

The school drive ran parallel to the forest for half a mile then came to a T-junction with the Ngong Road. Brian slowed. It was an historic road. Not a mile to the right, Lord Errol had been murdered for the love of Lady Delamere – or so they said – and Mrs Mordant's hedonistic world started to crumble; not much farther on lived Armand and Michaella Denis, the naturalists whom Brian admired for their wildlife and safari films; and near there Baroness Karen Blixen-Finecke, who loved Africans, and wrote some famous books, had had her house. Brian wondered, as he spun the steering-wheel of the Land Rover to the left, if Karen, the name of a village of well-to-do houses in the forest, had been named after the Baroness, who had tried to grow coffee there in the shadow of the Ngong Hills.

The road to Nairobi crossed the edge of a flat plain. On the right, behind trees, was Nairobi Racecourse; to the left was an expanse of grass and some bushes. Half-way to the city boundary, on the side of the plain, was a shallow depression which, in the rains, filled with water. Driving past it, Brian recalled how, in the green-brown water there, during his second year at the school, he had seen a dead man lying against the bank, his head and arms under the surface. Police askaris were standing about on the verge and his father had said, briefly, 'One terrorist less. Poor benighted sod!'

At the crossroads at Dagoretti corner, over the railway line and past the showground where the Royal Show was staged annually, Brian crossed into Burnbrae Road, down the steep side of the valley, over the bridge under which trickled a tiny, weed- and rush-choked stream grandly entitled the Kirichwa Kubwa River, up the other side and across another junction into St Austin's Road. From there it was not a mile home.

'Really! You are clumsy, Brian!' his mother chided him. 'Look at your blazer. Some end-of-term japery, no doubt.'

He did not admit to the cause of the tear but said, 'It doesn't matter. Throw it away. I don't need it any more.'

'I'd like to keep it,' she responded. 'A memento of when you were young ... Oh, Brian!' she added wistfully. 'You've become a man so very quickly. I can remember ...'

She hugged her son and he realized then, perhaps for the first time, he was taller than his mother.

As he entered his bedroom, carrying a cardboard box full of books, Brian discovered the houseboy crouching over an open leather suitcase, carefully folding shirts.

'What are you doing, Oudu?' he said, taken aback.

'Surprise!' exclaimed his mother from the doorway. 'We're going on holiday. Tomorrow. Your father's got some local leave due and we've been saving it. We're going to your favourite place – a sort-of goodbye present before you leave for Oxford.'

'If I leave ...'

Brian was immediately filled with dread. The examination

papers would, at that very moment, be in the hands of the markers and adjudicators back in England.

'You'll do well. We're certain.' She turned to the houseboy. 'Everything okay, Oudu?'

'*N'dio, mem'sahib*. All ready.'

He tucked in the sleeves of a shirt which had slipped out and closed the suitcase.

'Well, you'd better be off or you'll miss your ticket. *Bwana kido* —' She stopped herself. 'I mustn't call you that now, must I? You're not the small master any more.' She gathered herself as if about to make an important pronouncement. 'Oudu, *Bwana* Brian will take you into town.'

'So we're going to …' Brian began.

'Yes,' his mother interrupted. 'We're going to Malindi.'

The plan was the same every year. The evening before the Titchners set off, Oudu said goodbye to his wife and *toto*s who lived in the servants' quarters behind the garage, and was taken into Nairobi where he caught the overnight train to Mombasa. Once there, he would catch a bus which wound northwards along the coast road to Malindi. He would arrive at the beach house in mid-afternoon and his employers would turn up towards dusk, all being well.

It was not a good time to drive to the coast. So soon after the rains, the bottom of the many drifts – long, steep-sided valleys which the Nairobi–Mombasa road crossed at right angles – would still be muddy and it might require both skill and luck to get through them; any bridge would still be doubtful as the bridges would not necessarily have been restored in the few weeks since the last of the heavy rains fell. To make the journey in the open Land Rover was out of the question, although the vehicle had four-wheel drive. The only alternative to the train was a saloon car.

The next morning, before light, Brian and his parents left the house in their black Humber Snipe. It was a heavy car but fast and Mr Titchner hoped it would be powerful enough to negotiate the drifts between Mtito Andei and Voi. In the boot, in addition to their suitcases, were two broad spades and some lengths of sacking, thirty yards of stout tow-rope and a full tool kit. Hanging from the front of the bonnet was a canvas water bag while, in the rear of the car, beside Mrs Titchner, were several rows of beer and water bottles; on the seat was a hamper of food.

They drove through Nairobi, the headlights picking out two hyenas tipping over a dustbin in Valley Road, near the Greek Orthodox Church. By All Saints' Cathedral, a jackal ran across the road in front of the car. At the roundabout by the D C's Office, they turned right down the broad Princess Elizabeth Way and, as they passed the Nairobi Game Park, dawn broke.

For the first twenty miles or so, the road was blessed with tarmacadam but, not far short of Stony Athi – named after the river there but a more appropriate description of the road surface – the tarmac ended.

As the Humber approached the end of the smooth road, Brian's father remarked glumly, 'Two hundred miles to the next bit. Now for dust, dents and din.'

With a thump that rang the bottles together, the car dropped from the metalled surface onto the murram. Instantly, the tyres kicked up a plume of dust which billowed behind and the suspension bounded and thudded. Stones cascaded against the floor and inside the mudguards. The corrugations in the road surface set up a rhythmic dunning sound that killed all opportunity for conversation.

The back windows were kept shut but the front were opened and a cool breeze whistled in. Brian balanced his arm on the sill and looked ahead down the road. The sky was grey but the forecast was for a sweltering day.

By nine o'clock, they had gone through Sultan Hamud, ninety miles from Nairobi. The landscape changed from savannah to scrub and the few animals Brian had seen in the grassland would now be invisible. On the road, from time to time, he saw piles of dung made by crossing elephants. Occasionally, antelope would appear far ahead but were long gone by the time the Humber drew level with them and roared by.

At half past ten, they reached Makindu and, twenty minutes later, Kibwezi where a village surrounded the road on either side. Mr Titchner slowed for, in settlements, children or chickens were likely to run out, not to mention dogs, cats, goats or adult Africans, wobbling on heavy black Raleigh bicycles.

A few *duka*s lined the verge, well back from the main carriageway. In the shade of the overhanging roofs, Africans were sitting about. Outside a workshop, two Africans and an Indian in a turban were animatedly discussing an up-turned cycle from which the front wheel had been removed.

'Twenty-seven miles,' shouted Mr Titchner over the temporarily reduced noise.

Brian nodded and looked over his shoulder at his mother. She was asleep, her head deep in a pillow wedged between the back of the seat and the door.

As they travelled further south from Kibwei, the scrub became more dense and Brian kept a look-out for rhinos: it was ideal rhino territory. His interest was not merely in the sighting of one: it was also to warn his father. Rhinos, on occasion, attacked cars or ran in front of them. To collide with one was as bad as hitting a train or a lorry. No one survived a high-speed collision with a rhino.

Watching for the risk brought to Brian's mind the photo on the desk in the guard's office at Wamumu and he wondered what Matthew Nchembe might be doing at that moment or if he had yet been released.

Whenever a vehicle advanced towards them, both Brian and his father could see it coming from several miles away. It signalled its approach with a distant cloud of reddish dust. As the vehicle drew near, sometimes flashing its lights, and both drivers returned to their correct side of the road – for one drove on the smoother side, not necessarily the left – both Brian and Mr Titchner wound their windows up. Then the Humber was enveloped in dust. They opened them again half a mile later. Despite this precaution, by the time they arrived in Mtito Andei, they were caked with a fine dusting of soil which had penetrated their ears and nostrils.

Mtito Andei, approximately half-way between Nairobi and Mombasa, consisted of a railway station, three petrol pumps, a restaurant and little else.

156

Mr Titchner slewed the Humber off the road and halted by the middle pump. An African dressed only in navy-blue shorts appeared.

'*Tafadhali jaza tanki,*' Mr Titchner ordered, opening the door, stepping out and stretching his arms and back. '*Angalia mafuta na maji.*'

Brian left the car and opened the bonnet for the African.

'Coffee?' Mrs Titchner asked in a drowsy voice.

'You're back with the living then, Dotty?' her husband said.

'Just about.' She peered out of the window. The sunlight was hazy but brilliant, nevertheless. 'We at Mtito Andei already?'

'Yup!'

'*Mafua na maji muri,*' said the African, closing the bonnet. '*Unaweza kusafisha kioo cha gari.*'

The African went for a *dhebi* of water, a cloth and an oblong of plywood upon which was stencilled "oke Bon". He began to rinse and rub the dead insects off the windscreen. A number had dried hard and he had to scrub them off with his improvised scraper.

The car attended to, they drove to the restaurant. There was no one seated at the tables but two Europeans, both in khaki bush clothes, were sitting at the bar, glasses of lager before them.

'What's the road like towards Mombasa?' Brian's father asked them.

'Not too bad, as a matter of fact,' one of them replied in a rounded English accent. 'One drift about five miles this side of the Tsavo river's a bit tricky, but – what do you have?'

'Humber.'

'Should be okay. I'd keep to the right if I were you, where someone's chucked in a load of branches. Another one near Ndi's a bit dicey but again, it's drying out. The rest are passable. Anything north of here?'

'The road's fine.'

'Jolly dee!' exclaimed the man and he returned to his beer, saying to his companion, 'Tea in the Norfolk?'

Refreshed with sweet black coffee and toast, the Titchners

set off once more. Brian now took over the driving, keeping the Humber off the worst of the corrugations and maintaining at least fifty miles an hour for as long as he could. The philosophy was either to go at two miles an hour and gently coast over every corrugation but getting nowhere, or fifty miles an hour and hit only every eighth rut.

By one o'clock they had crossed the Tsavo National Park, passed the Taita Hills and driven through Voi. Only a small herd of elephant had caused them to stop and then for not more than a quarter of an hour. At Mackinnon Road, for some unexplained reason, there was a strip of about five miles of tarmac but it soon ended and, at three in the afternoon, they arrived at Mariakani where the road divided; straight ahead was Mombasa, to the right was Kinango and, ultimately, Tanganyika. To the left was a lesser road to Gotani. It was the latter they took.

The air was hotter and much more humid now they were nearer to the coast: in Nairobi, six thousand feet above sea level, the atmosphere was seldom sticky or damp. The red murram earth had given way to a grey soil and the roads, although dusty, were less rutted. The landscape was more luxuriant, with well irrigated *shamba*s of cotton and maize lining the road, interspersed with fields of sisal and vegetables.

After thirty miles, the road met the coast highway running north from Mombasa, though 'highway' was hardly a befitting noun for a single-lane dirt road running on white compacted coral which produced a dazzling albescent, rather than a cloying red, dust. Increased by the proximity of the dense coastal jungle, which grew right up to the side of the road, the heat became oppressive and was only relieved when Brian halted at the Kilifi ferry.

'Forty more miles to a dip in the ocean,' Mr Titchner commented as they stood leaning on the car while the chain ferry made its laborious way across the creek.

Not a marvel of modern engineering, the ferry was a large, raft-like structure floating on a bed of oil drums lashed together with metal hawsers. Through a runnel on the deck ran a cable which spanned the creek, a distance of some three hundred yards. An antiquated marine diesel motor propelled the ferry at a very slow speed and, when this broke down, it was moved by muscle power, a line of Africans hauling on ropes.

The shores of the creek were hidden in green jungle, creepers hanging to the water and the trees leaning over.

Tropical birds with brilliant colouring darted through the shade or winged across the water. Brian's father, waiting for the ferry to cross, indulged himself in fifteen minutes' bird-spotting.

North from Kilifi, the road continued through lush forest, the sides banked up with coral dust, deceptively dangerous: if one pressed one's foot gently against the bank, it sank in as if into snow but, if a vehicle skidded and hit the dust bank, it compacted instantly like concrete and the passengers risked an overturning.

Brian drove past the turn-off to Gedi – which he longed to visit as soon as he could – and, soon afterwards, he was heading along the side road to Silver Sands, north of Casuarina Point.

The house was just as they had left it six months before. A simple building, it consisted of a huge sitting-cum-dining room, three bedrooms and a bathroom. A deep-set verandah faced the beach, which was barely twenty yards off, and the sea which, at high tide, was forty-five yards away. There were no gardens or fences, just a wide tree beneath which Brian halted the Humber and beeped the horn. The sound fell flat in the jungle, here less luxuriant than on the road but still dense. Oudu came out from the small hut behind the tree. He had already settled in, his belongings stored in his room, and had purchased salad vegetables, washed them in dilute potassium permanganate solution and put them out in bowls on the table on the verandah.

As soon as Brian had eaten, he left his parents and, dressed only in his swimming trunks and a vest, with a pair of tackies on his feet, he walked to the sea. The shoes were essential for the white sand was unbearably hot late in the afternoon and, once in the water, he did not want to stand barefoot upon a spiny sea urchin. The tide was still just on the ebb, as he could tell from the muted sound of the breakers on the reef a quarter of a mile offshore.

He sat on the edge of a coral pool about ten yards square and five feet deep with a sandy floor. Without lowering his legs into the pellucid water, he waited for the occupants to re-appear. The first to show themselves were small fish with neon-blue stripes on their sides. They were followed by two angel fish and a crab, its shell encrusted with minute barnacles. On the coral and rock, the cowries unsheathed their mantles.

This was the peace he wished the whole world could own and, as he sat there, thoughts of Stadden and Kruger, the Duke of York School and the examinations, of Dedan Kimathi and the Mau Mau drifted into insignificance. Even Matthew Nchembe moved to a distant corner of his mind. This was Malindi, which the Arabs had called the 'Slave Shores' and the Chinese the 'Heavenly Coast', a thousand years before the British knew it existed. To Brian, this was paradise.

A change of tone on the reef, an increase in the volume of sound made by the breakers, told him the tide had turned and it was time to return to the house.

For a week, Brian snorkelled in the tide pools. He borrowed an aqualung from the Cecils, who lived further along the beach and collected tropical reef fish which they kept, in temporary captivity, in a vast tank in their house – a tank so big it filled one wall of the living room, interrupted only by a portrait of their dog who, at the given command, would leap into a nearby chair and pose as it had for the artist.

With the diving gear, Brian was able to explore the deeper pools, discover the beautiful but lethally poisonous lion fish, hiding eels, octopi and the multitude of fish living in or on the coral, their colours so gaudy yet so subtle, so utterly indescribable. The coral itself was magnificent, shaded with pinks and reds, greens and yellows, some of it spindly and fragile, some fern-like and some shaped like unskulled brains. The sea-shells were numerous: he was fortunate to find two leopard cowries as well as a large number of cream, orange and green money cowries, a small conch and half a dozen

160

clams; the biggest, which took him thirty minutes to prise off the rock, was a foot across. In one pool, not fifty feet square, he found a four-foot-long hammerhead shark, trapped by the receding tide. He swam in the water with it, grabbing hold of its smooth fin and its rough T-shaped head, the eyes on each end. It was not dangerous to play with such a small shark. His only real fear, other than the lion fish, was of meeting a sea snake for the venom of which, like the fish, there was no known antidote.

On the morning of his last day, Brian drove the Humber to the ruins of Gedi, ten miles away. Not long rediscovered, they were only partially cleared of the forest which had overrun them after the city was abandoned by the Arabs in the early sixteenth century. Many of the buildings were unexcavated.

Under the shade of the jungle trees, Brian followed the paths which wove between ruined mosques, a palace, houses and pillared tombs. In the market place, he paused and watched the butterflies dance and dodge in the sunlight. One, an iridescent green and black, landed on his shirt front.

Once, as a child, he had been chased by a green mamba in this market place, now occupied only by snakes and the ghosts of slave traders long dead. And perhaps the genie who lived in a *fingo* pot, recently discovered in the palace.

Other memories of his holidays in Malindi came to him – his little, bright yellow Jetex speedboat which had raced along the biggest tidal pool he could get to, forced forwards by its solid fuel pellet lit by a fuse set off with his father's cigarette: when it reached the sand bar at the head of the pool, it skated right over it, across the next miniature lagoon, over a second bar and then sank, a hundred yards away. He remembered a wooden motorboat he had owned, which had also sunk, and the first shark he had landed from the reef. And the smell of Nivea cream. His mother always insisted he rub his nose and cheekbones with it to keep his skin from peeling. Even now, seated on his own in the ruins, he could distinguish the scent of that morning's application lingering through the smells of the tropical flowers and damp wood.

'Had a good week?' his father asked him that evening as he

swung to and fro in the hammock suspended from the twin palms by the verandah.

'Yes, Dad. I have. Thank you very much. Indeed. Both of you.'

'It's been good to see you unwind, Brian,' said his mother. 'It's been a tense time.'

'Not as bad as I thought, somehow. The exams weren't as ghastly as I expected.'

'That's a good sign.' His father reached over to the table for the jug. 'Another tot?'

'Please.'

It was Brian's favourite Malindi drink – fresh coconut milk, fresh lime juice and, now that he was old enough, Bacardi. The ice rattled on the lip of the jug.

'Will you be sorry to leave Kenya?' his mother asked.

'Yes, I will.'

'Understandable, Dotty. Been the lad's home for a long while.'

'What'll you miss most, do you think?'

'Masses of things. Thousands. The animals, Malindi, having servants, hunting ... Both of you.' He smiled and his mother's eyes moistened. 'But I'll be back for the holidays. Sometimes ... I hope!'

'Not so,' his father replied.

Brian was surprised. Though it had never been discussed, mentally he had been counting on his father flying him out for at least the long vacation each year.

'Let me explain,' Mr Titchner went on, recognising the worried look in his son's eyes. 'It's not that we don't want you. It's just that we won't be here. Kenya's had it for the likes of us. We've been good for it, I think. But our days are numbered here. A few more years – five or six, perhaps – and Kenya'll have its independence. In a new, black Africa there won't be any room for us whites.'

Brian opened his mouth to speak, but his father raised a hand.

'Let me finish. When the day comes, there'll be a mass exodus of Brits – all heading back to the UK. Some'll be dodging what they fear will be a blood-bath, some'll be surrendering to their fate. Many won't have jobs and they'll have a hard time adjusting. And there won't necessarily be the jobs for them, either. Not much use for an irrigation expert in Esher or a coffee planter in Caithness. So ...'

He gazed out at the sea. The evening sun was low beyond the peninsular upon which Vasco da Gama had landed centuries before, starting off the white exploration of eastern Africa.

'So we're going back to the U K now. Before the rush starts. I've been offered a job as a consultant to Crown Agents in London. Government job – pin-stripe suit, rolled brolly over me arm and a bowler hat on me bonce. But it'll be safe. It's very highly paid and we'll be set up for the future.'

He made light of it, but Brian was aware the prospect of working in a London office did not excite his father any more than it would him.

'We'll have a bit of cash, because I'm getting a nice little handshake from here. We've bought a cottage in Surrey and I can commute. If that's awful, we've also purchased a mews flat in London ... Though that's really an investment.'

'For you,' his mother said.

Brian could say nothing. His emotions were mixed, for now he realized this evening would be the last time he ever saw Malindi. At least like it was now.

'I think you're wrong,' Brian ventured, after a pause.

'How do you work that one out, son?'

'When Kenya does get freedom, they'll still need Europeans to run the businesses, to help establish the new government. To attract foreign investment. They won't just throw us out.'

'They may well need us, Brian, but they won't want us. Old Jomo won't take kindly to keeping on the race which threw him in clink. Tom Mboya and that lot ... The Kenya African Union and so on. They will require us to stay but they'll make it damn hard. The farms'll be nationalised – given to the Africans – the industrial base, such as it is, likewise. When Kenya's her own mistress, we shall be at the end of the queue for everything.'

'No. They'll accept us. They know they can't run things without us.'

Mr Titchner poured himself more of the coconut and rum punch.

'Don't misunderstand me, Brian,' his father answered shrewdly, appreciating the source of his son's argument. 'I don't mean this unkindly. But just because your chum in Wamumu might have said whites'll be welcome after independence doesn't mean they will be. He's not a politician. He's an idealist. A smart one, perhaps. But not a realist.'

'He did say that,' Brian admitted. 'He said when they get *uhuru* – that's what they call freedom – the whites will be welcome to stay.'

'That's as may be, Brian,' said his mother. 'And it may be his opinion. But it'll not be the common thought. Even for liberals – moderates like us, for example, who have the African interest in mind – it'll be hard. You see, the African's not going to think of us who try and do a bit of good in the system. They'll only remember the Afrikaners ...'

'And the gung-ho settlers,' his father butted in. 'They won't remember those of us who stood up for them, or gave as well as took. They'll remember the whites who rioted outside Government House and gave Baring a hard time after the murder of the Ruck family. They stubbed cigarettes on the arms and faces of the askaris – the same askaris as are now fighting the Mau Mau. The Sultan of Zanzibar was staying there at the time – remember that, Dotty? – and appeared at a window. One white in the crowd bawled out, "Look! The bloody niggers are in the place already!" That attitude won't die, and neither will the African view of it. And we'll all be lumped into the same mould, fair or not.'

'Well,' said Brian, 'at least I'll have you in England with me.'

'And you'd better invite me to a guest night at your college at least once a term, my boy. Or else!'

'If I get in,' Brian answered.

'You'll do all right. Don't you worry about that.'

Later, by moonlight, Brian walked along the beach. At the approach of his steps, the transluscent white ghost crabs raced for their burrows in the sand, reappearing after he had passed. The phosphorescence on the breaking waves glinted at him just as the fireflies did in the littoral brush beyond the high-tide line of washed-up coconuts, palm leaves and dried seaweed. He was sad and the night breezes in the palms seemed to sigh with compassion. Returning to the house, he saw, far down the beach, a leopard running ahead of him. When he reached the spot where it had been, he stood and studied the pugmarks in the soft, still-warm sand.

One day, he vowed to the leopard, he would come back.

9

The day the examination results arrived, Brian opened the air-mail envelope with trepidation. His hands shook and his face drained of blood. His grades were typed upon a folded sheet of crisp foolscap, the examination board letterhead at the top and the stereotyped signature of the chief examiner printed at the bottom.

He had spent the morning in the forest at Langata, releasing Diana, the chameleon, and her two surviving offspring back into the wild. With his inevitable departure for Britain drawing closer – for if his results were poor he would still be sent back to the United Kingdom to enter what his father quaintly termed 'a commercial career' – he felt it important he let go the animals he kept as pets. To release them in the grounds of the house would have been to condemn them to a quick death at the hands of the servants as soon as he was gone: that had been the fate of a harmless tree snake he had once owned for a while. Although the arrival of the results was imminent, he tried to press them to the back of his mind and his morning in the forest, setting the reptiles free, had helped him forget them.

For fully a minute, Brian stared at the sheet, his fingers smoothing out the folds, his elbows resting on the edge of the lunch table, his cup of coffee getting cold.

'What does it say?' his mother asked, her voice strained with tension.

Speechless, Brian handed her the paper. She took it and turned it round to read.

'Oh, Brian!' she exclaimed, handing it back to him. 'That's wonderful. I'm so glad for you.'

His father pulled the sheet from his wife's fingers and quickly scanned it.

'And proud of you, Brian. Nothing between you and Oxford now. You've exceeded the grades required. I'll put through a call this afternoon and give them the results. Just to be sure they've got them . . .'

'You could have phoned me,' Brian muttered.

'Wouldn't have been the same. The letter came in the office box number and I wanted you to open it – hence my unusual return home at luncheon on a Wednesday. Now,' he picked up his briefcase from beside his chair, 'I must get back. Celebration tonight, eh?'

Brian nodded.

'Yes,' he said, 'I'd like that.'

'Dotty,' his father continued, 'ring round! The Holborns, the Mordants . . . All the usual gang . . . I'll order some champers from Aladdin Lalji.'

'And we'll need more brandy,' his wife said. 'And cashew nuts, peanuts, maraschino cherries – red and green. And some pickled gherkins. Oh! And sodas – we're nearly out of sodas. And cheese crackers —'

'Write it all down,' Mr Titchner interjected with exasperation.

As soon as his father had departed, Brian backed the Land Rover on to the drive from where it was usually parked beside the banana trees, next to the washing lines. He told his mother he was going out: she did not ask him where he was off to, assuming he was doing the rounds of his friends, comparing results, sharing similar joys or commiserating with those less successful.

He reached the outskirts of Thika within an hour and, by a quarter to three, he was approaching the junction with the road going down the hill towards Wamumu.

Half-way from the main road to the camp, there were signs of a new village being erected. A thorn *boma* with a wicket gate had been constructed and a shallow pit in the ground showed where the earth had been extracted to make the three round mud huts half completed beside the *boma*. One had no door and the other two only skeletal roof beams. In a stack was piled the thatching straw, a bicycle leaning against it. Beyond the *boma* and across the other side of the road, cleared scrub and a patch of burned grass showed where the early preparations for a *shamba* had got under way.

As Brian drove by, the garden to Inspector Broomhall's bungalow was being tidied by two *bibi*s, their bodies bent double as they picked at weeds in the flowerbeds before the verandah and crushed clods of earth into powder, the dust drifting at their feet. In the shade of the verandah sat a European woman, a wide-brimmed hat hiding her face. She was reading a book. Brian waved but she appeared not to see him.

As he reached the entrance to the camp, a platoon of askaris marched across the parade space and lined up at the main entrance where a lorry was parked, its back in the prison compound but its cab outside. All the askaris were carrying their Lee Enfield .303 rifles at the slope. As they reached the lorry, the N C O in charge barked an order in Swahili and his men halted, shifting their rifles to be held at the waist.

The Land Rover parked in the shade of the office, Brian knocked on the closed door.

'*Ingia*! Come!' called a voice.

Brian turned the handle and entered to find a European officer seated at the desk, the telephone receiver in his hand.

'Yes,' he said to his caller, looking up at Brian as he did so, recognising a fellow white and beckoning him to be seated, 'I'll see to that. I've a three-tonner here. One's due from Embu in about an hour ... No. K A R truck. Our driver ... I see. That's fine. Cheerio!' He hung up and continued, 'And what can I do for you, young man?'

'Can you tell me where Inspector Broomhall is, sir?'

'Down at Taveta, I'd say. He's in charge of the police station on the border.'

'When did he move?'

'Just gone. Two days ago. Lock, stock and truncheon. The C O down there had a nasty contretemps with a hippo in the Ruvu. Didn't you know?'

'No, I didn't,' Brian replied and realised his next question would most likely fall on deaf ears.

The askari sergeant entered the office, saw Brian and smartly saluted him.

'*Jambo, bwana*!' he greeted Brian. '*Habari*?'

'*Mzuri sana*,' Brian answered, raising his hand in acknowledgement of the salute.

'You two know one another?'

'Yes, sir. I often shoot in this area.'

'Good sport about? I'm not averse to a bit myself when the rota allows.'

'I shot my first leopard here,' Brian announced.

'Fine! Fine! Now – forgive me, but I'm terribly tied up in things. Is there anything I can do for you?'

'I wonder,' Brian asked tentatively, 'if you might give me permission to go into the detention centre? Inspector Broomhall allowed me ... You may ask his wife for confirmation, sir. She's up at the bungalow.'

''Fraid not! That's my wife ... We've got the quarter now. As for going into the camp – 'fraid not again. Things in a bit of turmoil.' He shuffled the papers on his desk as if to prove the point. 'But tell me, why should you want to go in?'

Brian sensed that to give the real reason for his request would be to arouse suspicion and, possibly, get Broomhall into trouble. He had no idea as to whether or not his previous visits were allowed under the rules.

'I want to pay a prisoner some money I owe him. My leopard was skinned by a detainee and I promised, with Inspector Broomhall's permission, to come back.'

'What's the boy's name?' the new inspector asked.

'Nchembe. Matthew Nchembe.'

'Hold on a tick ...'

Once again, the police officer shuffled through his papers, turning lists over and sliding his index finger down them. He closed one folder and opened another, licking his thumb and flicking the flimsy pages over.

'Trouble is,' he said, 'the *karani* had filed some under first name, some under second. And half the spellings're up the shoot. Ah! Here we are! Nchembe, M. That yours?'

He pulled the papers loose, the clip catching on the next sheet down and tearing the corner off. He held it up for Brian's inspection. On the top of the page was a printed box containing smudged thumb print a beside a fading photo of Matthew Nchembe.

'Yes, sir.'

'Well, he's not here. Discharged.' He looked at the date stamped in the bottom of the sheet in red. 'Just over a fortnight ago.'

'May I see the form, sir?' he asked.

He thought of his own recently-received paper and how he had wanted to share the information with Nchembe. He wanted to tell him he had done well enough to go to the British university and that, one day, he might return, for he had set his mind on a course of study which could be of use to Africa.

'Not supposed to really, but – why not?'

Brian quickly read down the column of typing. It gave no information he did not already know. At the bottom was Nchembe's signature in an almost childish hand.

'Does he have a forwarding address?'

The inspector laughed loudly.

'This is a detention centre, not the New Stanley Hotel! They don't leave addresses for their mail to be sent on to!'

'Have you no idea?'

'I'd forget it, if I were you,' the inspector advised. 'I'm sure he has. I'll bet he'll not miss your few shillings in his joy at being back in the *bundu*.'

'It's not just that . . .' Brian began, but paused and said, 'Do you have ID cards on file? They must have an address on them.'

'Maybe. But we don't keep those records here. And they as like as not give incorrect information. And it's not so good at the best of times that you could send them a postal order. They don't have box numbers in the bush.'

'No, of course,' Brian said. 'I'm sorry to have bothered you. Thank you, sir.'

'Not at all. Sorry you've had to come all the way out here. From Nairobi?'

'Yes, sir.'

'Well, have a good drive back.'

Brian left the inspector in conversation with the askari sergeant and stepped outside. Lying stretched in the sun, just as it had on his first visit to Wamumu, was the dun-coloured pi-dog.

The lorry was starting up, blowing grey clouds of exhaust smoke into the camp. Brian could see the vehicle was crowded with what were now ex-detainees. He started the Land Rover, determined to drive up the road ahead of the truck; he would otherwise be in its dusty wake.

'Hold on a moment!' the inspector called, walking quickly towards the Land Rover, the sergeant marching behind carrying a cardboard box tied with cord. 'You Mr Titchner?'

'Yes.'

'Fancy that! Your prisoner has left this box with your name on it. The sergeant here drew it to my attention. Broomhall was to have got it to you.'

The sergeant put the box on the seat next to Brian. As he let go of it, the cord fell off.

'Sorry about that. We had to check it.' He tied a knot in the cord. 'Can't chance it, even if they are supposedly rehabilitated. If you ask me, there's no such thing.'

'Thank you,' Brian repeated, putting the Land Rover in to gear.

'That's all right. No bother at all.' The officer looked at the box. 'God knows what you'll do with that.'

At the junction with the main road, Brian went left towards Fort Hall, Thika and Nairobi. The lorry followed him but, at Sagana, it veered off to the right on the road to Nyeri.

Pulling up at the side of the road, Brian let the Land Rover idle while he opened the box. The inspector's knot was loose and easily undone.

Opening the cardboard flaps, Brian found a piece of brown paper. On it was written in pencil, in the same childish hand as the signature on the discharge sheet:

This is for my friend, Brian Titchner. In memory of our friendliness. Maybe we shall meet again in a Free Africa. Your friend Matthew Nchembe.

Under the note was a package wrapped in newspaper.

Lifting the package out, Brian placed it on top of the box and tore it open. Inside was another note. It read:

This has come from the forest for you.

From the newspaper fell a jacket of supple, correctly-cured, black and white colobus monkey pelts.

Oxford, England: 1966

10

The room was in darkness except for a single candle burning
with a flickering flame on the table at the far end. It was a
thick candle such as one might find on an altar and the flame
gave the top inch or so of the wax a pallid glow as if it were
made of flesh which had never been in sunlight. Beneath it,
opened out and off-white like water-ruined vellum, was a
leather-bound volume of some antiquity. At the opposite end
of the room, over the door, glimmered two sticks of Indian
jasmine incense. The scent permeated the darkness.

'Are we gathered?' asked a voice, disembodied by the
darkness.

'We are,' came the answer from the door.

'Then it is time to bar the gate.'

The latch on the door clicked shut; the candle was
extinguished by an unseen hand. The lingering smell of the
candle wick mingled with the perfume of jasmine. From the
darkness came a new voice speaking in strong, clear words.

'May the spirits of the elements approach – and such a
tempest of fire and thunder, hail, rain and wind pour down
upon the city, that all may go to wreck in a moment.'

'May it be wrecked that it might be raised anew and with
fresh fortitude,' replied several voices in response.

'I now call upon Rhydisel, The Devil of Oxford, to cease
his thrusting of the mutilated dead down the well in front of
the Anatomy School of old ...' these words were met with
suppressed laughter in the darkness '... and request those
Learned Imps present, past and lively be up-standing to raise
a glass to Satire and Edmund Spenser.'

There was a shuffling in the darkness and the sound of
chairs shifting across a carpet.

'The Learned Imps,' toasted the chorus.

A match struck in the blackness and the candle was re-lit.
The crystal glasses scintillated in its light.

175

'Now, let there be light upon the city so we might wreck and build.'

'Wreck and build!' echoed the others.

The lights were switched on: not bright, they were wall-bracket lamps in dark green shades, each bearing a low wattage bulb.

The five men present, their glasses raised, drank the toast, each draining his fluted glass.

'Roll call, gentlemen. Rhydisel asks for you to announce yourselves. Mr Charles Runciman B Sc., Learned Imp; Mr David Schofield B Sc., Learned Imp; Mr Michael Thomas Barnstow M A, B Sc., Learned Imp Extraordinary; Mr Jeffrey Crane BSc., Imp in Orders; Mr Brian Titchner B Sc., at present Learned Imp and Confessor to Rhydisel. Apologies for absence from Messrs Stephen Collard, Patrick Delahaye, Auberon Havelock and Philip Boston – all plead detention by the will of their gods.'

'All present,' the men chorused.

'Then we may commence to set the world to right, topsy-turvy the ills and see the light.'

The diners were dressed in a kind of uniform. All wore dark, pin-striped trousers over black shoes, with white socks which showed as they sat in unison, tugging their chairs back under themselves. Their jackets were white as were their shirts but they wore black bow ties. The only colour about their dress was in their waistcoats which were gaudy in the extreme. The man who had switched on the lights, David Schofield, wore a silk waistcoat of blue and yellow paisley patterns on a red ground. The man seated next to him wore a waistcoat of brocade, a gold dragon curling across his chest over a jet-black ground. The American facing him – who insisted on calling his waistcoat a vest – sported one made of cream raw silk with embroidered scarlet lilies. Another wore a bottle-green waistcoat of velvet. The fifth man, at the head of the table and master of ceremonies for the evening, had the least colourful but the most unusual waistcoat of them all. His was made of black and white fur, long and quite obviously well groomed for it hung in combed strands over his cummerbund.

'Our menu this evening,' he pronounced, lifting a white card from the silver stand before him and showing it to the others. It was bordered with a black line like a Victorian mourning card. On the top was printed a black-and-white check-dressed harlequin figure with the devil's head.

'Aigo Boulido; Les Palourdes, Sauce Mornay,' he read from the menu, 'Foie de Veau Farci – Fenouil de Florence; Cervelle d'Agneau, Sauce aux Câpres; Glaces Canadiennes; Les Croissants Anglais.'

'Thank you, Rhydisel,' said the man in the brocade waistcoat. 'For my part, the wines are as you chose from our host's list. The champagne tonight is Mumm's Cordon Rouge.'

'That sounds pretty damn fair!' exclaimed the American in the raw silk vest. 'Is it always this good?'

'Indeed it is,' answered the man sitting opposite him with a cultured, almost affected accent. He paused then added, with a slight stutter, 'In fact, it is often even b-better depending on the season and the availa-ability of the s-seafood. The t-trouble with Oxford is that it's such a long w-way from the s-sea.'

'Long way!' retorted the American. 'Hell! You should come from Omaha.'

The door opened and two waitresses entered. As if in keeping with the diners, they wore black dresses and stockings, white aprons and white caps. Behind them came the wine waiter.

The first course, by tradition and the rule of the club, was taken in silence. Bread rolls with the soup were broken, not cut and no butter was served. Conversation only commenced with the baked clams. Again, there was a rule to observe. As long as there was food on the table, the talk was restricted to everyday matters and, through the second course and the first entrée, it revolved around the chances for Oxford in the Boat Race, due to be run in three weeks, the vagaries of dons – particularly one in Brasenose College who had heavily criticised the latest chapter of one of the diners' thesis – and Christopher Hassall's biography of Rupert Brooke.

'Rupert B-Brooke is famous,' declared the man with the

stutter, 'for having written the w-worst p-poem in the English Language.'

'Is that so, Charles?'

'It most certainly is!'

'And can you recite it for us?' asked the chairman in the hairy waistcoat.

'Of course he can!' Michael Barnstow retorted. 'Charles can recite anything. He's a fund of p-poetry, aren't you, Charles?'

'There's no need to mock the afflicted,' Charles Runciman responded without the slightest stammer and began to recite.

All in the town were still asleep,
When the sun came up with a shout and a leap.
In the lonely streets unseen by man,
A little dog danced. And the day began.

All his life he'd been good, as far as he could,
And the poor little beast had done all that he should.
But this morning he swore, by Odin and Thor
And the Canine Valhalla – he'd stand it no more!
So his prayer he got granted – to do just what he wanted,
Prevented by none, for the space of one day.
'Jam incipiebo, sedere facebo,'
In dog-Latin he quoth, 'Euge! sophos! hurray!'

'That really is utter bosh,' complained the man in the paisley-patterned waistcoat. 'Utterly mawkish senti-mentality.'

'You've heard n-nothing yet. Listen to the last verse,' replied the reciter and continued,

When the blood-red sun had gone burning down,
And the lights were lit in the little town,
Outside, in the gloom of the twilight grey,
The little dog died when he'd had his day.

'I will place a wager ...' began the man in the bottle-green velvet waistcoat.

'Look out! Mike's going to place a bet!' exclaimed the master of ceremonies.

'His t-trouble,' commented Charles Runciman, his stutter returning, 'is that he comes from All Souls'. They've b-been b-betting there since time immemorial. He's b-been reading Oman's b-book, *I'll* b-bet.'

'So what's your bet, Mike?'

'I bet I know of a worse poem in the English Language. Worse than that drivel of Brooke's – who was ever a man of dubious talent.'

'We can't accept a wager depending for its proof upon the taste of the punter,' declared the master-of-ceremonies. 'There can be no truth in artistic judgement.'

'Pretty far-fetched bit of logic, that,' the punter complained, 'but I'll accept it. Yet I know the very poem.'

'What is it?' Charles Runciman demanded to know.

'Keats's "Lines on the Mermaid Tavern" which, I'll allow, I might not be qualified to comment upon, being a man of science and truth,' he glanced at the master of ceremonies, 'but which was given to me by a schoolmaster who formerly had to put up with me as being so. I recall its lines which go:

> Souls of Poets dead and gone,
> What Elysium have ye known,
> Happy field or mossy cavern,
> Choicer than the Mermaid Tavern?

'That is bad,' agreed the American, shaking his head. 'I'm glad to say we have nothing as base in American literature. Save perhaps some of Edna St Vincent Millay's poems.'

'There are more bad poets than there are good ones,' stated the man in the brocade waistcoat. 'Just as there is more imperfection in the world than perfection. Or beauty.'

'Which brings us to coffee,' said the master-of-ceremonies and he gave the signal to the waitress who was standing bemused beside the serving table.

When the coffee was poured, the percolator replaced upon its electric ring and the decanter of Taylor's port on its journey around the table, the waitress left, quietly closing the door. The men removed their black bow ties and jackets, unbuttoned their waistcoats and settled themselves more comfortably into their seats.

'Our discussion topic this evening,' the master of ceremonies stated, 'is as follows: Is it our duty to continue colonial patronage of former colonies after they have received independence and, if so, in what form should this patronage be given? Quite a broad-ranging basis for discussion. And, I think,' he consulted a folded, white oblong of card which he removed from a pocket in his hairy waistcoat, 'it is your turn this month, Jeff, to start the ball rolling.'

The American, Jeff Crane, put down his coffee cup and, reaching over backwards, lifted the percolator off the serving table. He took his coffee black and sweet.

'Some irony you got there. The Old Colonial talking of a subject close to his great-great-gran'daddy's heart.' He replaced the percolator which immediately began to bubble. 'What one has to consider here, firstly, is the reason for the desire of independence. Why do nations, who seem to have had it good under foreign rule, want to chuck it out? The U S of A is a good example, in some respects. We didn't do too badly out of colonial rule, as I see it. We paid taxes to London, sure. But we got in exchange military defence against the French in the north and south; we got funding from London; we drew upon the old country – the occupying power, so to speak – for our blood, our injection of people: our population. We were, for a long while, English overseas. The reason we finally fought against England was because we, as settlers, took all the risks but the centre of power – fiscal, legal, governmental – was in London. We wanted some degree of self-determination. We fought the Injuns, opened the forests, felled the trees and trapped the rivers, grew the tobacco, the cotton, the sugar ... But the main profits went east to Britain.'

'One of the differences – and it's unfair to use America as a b-basis for argument' – Charles Runciman pointed out, 'is that those who fought the B-British were, by and large, British. It wasn't a war of independence. That's what we c-call it in the U K. The Americans call it the Revolutionary War – the War of the Revolution. You can see the p-plaques on veterans' tombs in any New England graveyard. They

180

weren't running a freedom fight; they were operating a revolution, an overthrow of the p-powers-that-be. It's interesting to remember that the American Indians didn't fight for independence ...'

'The hell they didn't!' Jeff Crane said, forgetful of the rules of the Rhydisel Club. Being an Imp in Orders, which was to say a new member and learner, he was unused to the laws which governed meetings. 'They fought to stay free ...'

David Schofield reached for the port; the neck of the bottle chimed on the side of his glass.

'Fulmination and vituperation are forbidden in discussion once coffee is served, Jeff,' he remonstrated politely.

'With the newer colonies, things are very different,' Michael Barnstow said. 'In these countries, the indigenous populations are made up of a majority of local natives, so to speak, not expatriates who have settled there for one reason or another. This makes an important difference, for these are the largely exploited nations, those who have had colonial domination placed upon them, rather than – as it were – exporting it with themselves to a new land. It is this type of situation to which we must address our attention at this meeting.'

All agreed and the discussion changed course towards assessing the need for these countries to continue receiving aid after independence.

'The decision boils down to whether the developed world – that is, the former rulers – give hard cash aid, either in money or trade credits or easy tariff controls, or aid in kind by way of expertise, technological advancement and infrastructure upon which development can take place. Or the whole shebang!'

'I reckon cash alone,' Jeff Crane said, 'makes for trouble. You can see what happens to the hard currency handed out by the US in order to combat Communism. It goes into the Swiss bank accounts of the new rulers, the élite of whichever country. There's an old Peace Corps saying, 'One month's aid equals six Mercedes Benz' – with armour-plated chassis, bullet-proof windows and a bar in the back for the booze.'

'Is that always the case?' Charles Runciman began, intent on attacking the comment, but Jeff Crane cut in.

'Not always. Take Vietnam. There the cash – and God knows how many millions of bucks are pouring into Saigon from D C – goes into buying more guns, more ammo, more missiles – as well as Buicks, Cadillacs, Lincoln Continentals.'

'But hard currency can do good,' Michael Barnstow rejoined. 'And if you give aid, you are invariably giving yourself aid, too. Thereby, the country receiving the aid actually does the donor good – we give Nigeria a railway, for example, but in doing so we give employment to thousands of our peopled at Swindon, or Crewe, or wherever they make rolling stock and engines. Yet that's really – isn't it? – surely just another example of colonial exploitation, but at a distance.'

'Possibly, but it does give them a railway,' David Schofield pointed out. 'The Chinese are doing this now in Kenya. Roads, bridges, improved communications, irrigation … If that's not the same …'

'C'mon,' said Jeff Crane, 'of course it's the same. You think we white guys are the only ones with colonial aspirations? Look, you take a country of uneducated people with a tiny minority – ruling class – of smart-assed bastards. Those at the top don't give a damn for the masses. They don't care who foots the bill so long as they have the power and the luxury. What you have to fight in many of these places is a medieval concept of rule, not the beneficial rule of your Harold Wilsons here and your Socialists. You don't get Socialism in other countries – no National Health system, no national education system, no power-to-the-people. That's whitey talk, as they say in the South.'

'The best thing to give is aid,' David Schofield announced after a moment's pause, 'even if we do benefit from it ourselves. It might improve our industrial base to build cars for Africa or tractors for South America or even just ploughshares for India. But, beyond that, we can be sure aid reaches the people. We can't assure money does. I mean, a tractor has to go to a farm …'

'And what,' Jeff Crane interrupted, 'if, on the way, some

son-of-a-bitch gets hold of it and sells it to the farmer instead of just passing it on as a gift from the Yanks or whoever? What then?'

'So the greedy and corrupt make a buck.' Michael Barnstow spoke with a hint of resignation. 'That's hard to avoid. But at least the end product is a pricey tractor digging up the pampas, not a B M W or a Jaguar driving the streets of the capital city.'

'Tell you something else.'

Jeff Crane was calming down after his outburst, reminded by another severe look from David Schofield of the rules of the club.

'What's that?'

'Well, Michael,' the American continued, addressing the last speaker, 'my cousin's been serving in 'Nam. Got out of the last big battle of Hué in a chopper gunship – and they're a form of aid, not cash – and wrote me the month before last. A long letter. Getting it off his chest. That's one dirty war out there – dope a-plenty, V D rate as high as the insanity one. Anyway, the Peace Corps or somesuch some time back thought the Viets looked hungry and malnourished. They flew in hundreds of tons of dry milk powder. Must have been a glut in the U S of A or something. Anyway, it was all shipped over and distributed to the starving locals. But now – well, not many drank it, let's put it that way. Some sold it back to the U S troops, the rest used it as a form of underground currency and it passed from hand to hand in lieu of money. Some of it was used to cut the dope, too. Result? Nobody puts on any weight. And were they hungry in the first place? Probably not, except in the refugee camps. Vietnamese, my cousin says, are skinny little beggars all the time. Even the whores, and they're loaded.'

The coffee percolator was emptied into the cups and the port circulated once more. In the centre of the table stood a pineapple on a bed of grapes. Charles Runciman reached forward, lifted the crown of hard, saw-edged leaves and extracted the first slice, cutting it on his side plate with a fruit knife and fork.

Brian, who had been silent through most of the discussion so far, agreed with part of it and disagreed with other aspects.

'I believe just doling out money is wrong,' he began. 'It's like paying for a whore, to keep Jeff's allusion going. That has happened in Kenya, I hear. A good deal of the money that's gone in has subsidized the politicians and been channelled into private funds. And aid isn't necessarily good, I think, unless it goes hand-in-hand with technical expertise. So much of what we do is short-term. It's no use whatsoever to give a country an electrical system, from a hydro-electric dam through to a light bulb in a mud hut unless you provide the technical back-up – the education. Look at India. They're just twenty years into independence. When I was in Uttar Pradesh, the power supply was always failing, the telephone system was near collapse and you couldn't effectively place a call outside the immediate exchange area ... If you give a nation electricity, you've got to show them how to keep the river running to drive the turbines ...'

'And the wife in the mud hut how to change a fuse,' Michael Barnstow suggested.

'And m-make a f-fuse when the supplies in the shops f-fail,' Charles Runciman added.

'The British Empire failed as a colonial institution in one major respect,' David Schofield said. 'We gave those countries we ruled a great deal – law and order, roads and communications, better farming methods, industry, social conscience, financial institutions, education, improved medical health. But what we didn't teach them was how to run their own countries. We taught them how to run them for us, not for themselves. Now we spend our aid – money or not – trying to bolster the collapse which is inevitable, in my opinion. Just look at India for that ... Brian and I were out there eight years ago with the university hockey team. Remember?'

'Indeed, I do,' Brian answered. 'Very well ...'

'A shambles, that country. Nehru's done his best. Gandhi's dream's more or less come true, bar the partition of Pakistan – another instance of listening to the politicians, not to the people – for which may Mountbatten be cursed. But the roads are in terrible disrepair, the railways have no schedule except on paper, the power and communications systems are at breaking point, as Brian's said, and – worst of all – the Indians have accepted and developed to the *n*th degree the curse of all British administrations: bureaucracy. Buying a train ticket takes three forms, two ticket inspectors and a flash of your passport. Not to mention your wallet, if you get my drift. The universal *buckshee*. Getting into the country with a hockey team – complete with sticks – took almost a major diplomatic exchange.

'I think we gave freedom too liberally, with too little forethought. We didn't ready the natives for it. We just handed it over. Look at Brian's beloved Kenya! The Colonial Office spent less than five years "Africanising" black governments. Five years! They thought to educate people in running their own lands, at twentieth century standards, in less than the time it takes a medic to get his bachelor's. In my book, that was criminal, as bad as slavery ...'

The others nodded general agreement and then, as if to prove not only the Third World was a place of ineptitude and technological poverty, the bulb in the wall bracket over the serving table popped loudly and failed.

'M-made in Japan,' quipped Charles Runciman and they all laughed except for Jeff Crane.

'You mark my words,' the American said, not as lightheartedly as the occasion might have demanded. 'Listen to the Yankee Prophet. Twenty years from now, we'll be worried about the goddam Japs and their transistorised world. We've only seen the start. Wait until their goddam car industry ...' David Schofield raised his hand. 'I know already! No fulmination and vituperation. Still think this is one helluva funny club where you can't cuss mildly in favour of your argument.'

'Tradition,' Charles Runciman reminded him. 'We live on tradition, it is the backbone of truth and Oxford. And Oxford is the ultimate truth.'

In the distance they could hear the little mechanical figures on the clock in Carfax striking the hour.

'Saved by the bell,' muttered Michael Barnstow, 'from Charles's diatribe on truth, trust and St Trinian's.'

'Enough!' Brian interjected and banged his dessert spoon like a gavel on the much-battered first edition copy of Henry Johnson's *Rhydisel* where it lay open by his now-empty glasses.

The others fell silent.

'It is my onerous and solemn duty to call Rhydisel home, to withdraw him from out of our presence and to hold him dear until the time arises for him to wing abroad once more. Unbar the door.' David Schofield turned the handle and pulled the door ajar. 'Return, Devil of Oxford, to await the call, once more, at time pre-determined by calendar and clock, of your Learned Imps.'

He raised the book in front of his face and slammed it shut. A fine eddy of dust drifted over the dirty plates, empty bottles and the half-eaten pineapple.

Later, as he and David Schofield walked down Cornmarket, Brian said suddenly, 'I wonder if it will ever improve?'

'What?'

'The lot of the poorer countries.'

'I expect so. It'll take time ...'

'And money, and investment, and support or aid. We really should be doing something. Now.'

'There's Oxfam,' David Schofield said, 'other charities.'

'They don't want charity. They want help.'

'We'll be giving it to them. I was approached by those Brazilians last week – the firm I told you about, met them when they were head-hunting last term. But I think I'm going to go for the fertilizer people. Either I C I or Fisons. Haven't decided which to run with. Not yet. I like I C I but my research hasn't impressed them all that much and Fisons like my work on the natural deterioration of phosphate salts.'

They crossed the street by Frewin Court, the alley which led down to the Oxford Union. The pubs were clearing. The Carfax clock had struck eleven and it was a Saturday.

'Fancy a night-cap?'

'Don't think so. Besides,' Brian added, 'we're not members.'

'I am.'

'You are?' Brian exploded with laughter. 'Joined the Union? You ought to be ashamed! Apart from the debates, it's for young old fogeys and would-be politicians ... You're not going to turn into a political animal, are you?'

'I wonder – sometimes – if I might not do more for the world by turning to politics rather than organic phosphates.'

'I'd like to talk over your phosphate research some time – if you'll let me. The manner in which it's retained in the soil or drains off with leaching interests me. My current reading is ...'

Brian's words were drowned by the squeal of a bus's brakes as it pulled in to a stop.

'Okay. Might as well talk before I head off canvassing for support with a rosette on my lapel...'

'Hold on. Keep a true course,' Brian advised. 'It's a passing whim. A puff of wind from the darkness of the storm.'

'Maybe it's Rhydisel.'

They shouted with laughter and their hilarity drew the attention of a crowd of undergraduates making their way up Market Street towards Exeter College. They shouted back and pointed at them, waved and disappeared into the ill-lit street.

Parting by the Martyrs' Memorial, Brian said, 'See you in a fortnight? I think we all agreed last time to have an intermediate meeting before the end of term beano.'

'I'm rowing. The "X" Team, rather than the "A". I'm just filling in a seat. Ballast really. See you before that, though. Lucy's party next week. I'll have the bends by then.'

'I had forgotten her do! Good! See you then. Don't overwork. Or row.'

David Schofield walked off up the tree-lined side of St Giles and Brian went down Beaumont Street, turned right at the traffic lights by Worcester College and, within fifteen minutes, was unlocking the door of his digs in Jericho.

Beyond the desk, through the window and across a small,

neatly-tended suburban garden stood a row of trees, the buds still hard and the branches skeletal against the grey water of the Oxford Canal and, beyond that, the River Isis. The fields were just as grey in the light drizzle which was falling, obscuring distant Cumnor Hill. As Brian looked out of the window, scratching some order into his hair, his dressing-gown hanging loose from his shoulders, a train pulled out of Oxford Station and started to rattle along the line heading north to Stratford-upon-Avon.

He had stayed up late for the three nights since the meeting of the Rhydisel Club, reading a number of texts in depth, learning from them and lifting information which he incorporated into his thesis. The daylight hours he spent in the laboratory on South Parks Road, analysing samples drawn from the ground by an auger and packed into cardboard sample tubes.

Across the desk, a huge mahogany leather-topped piece of furniture with heavy drawers and claw feet, was strewn the debris of his work – sheafs of file paper scribbled over with notes, open and shut textbooks, a pile of photographs of cross-sections of trenches dug into a variety of soils, several of the cardboard cylinders and test tubes. Some grit from one of the samples had spilled onto the leather and he scooped it up with a sheet of blank paper, dropping it into the remains of a cup of chocolate. A milk bottle stood on the edge of the desk, beneath the reading lamp which was still switched on.

Moving the milk into the centre of the desk and switching off the light, he sat down, leaning over his evening's work. His Parker fountain pen had been left open, the nib dried solid. He shook it to get the ink running again and began to scan his night's work carefully. He was now revising the final draft of the thesis upon which his doctorate would depend.

The erosion of soil is generally initiated by mankind and his farming practices. Mostly, it begins with the destruction of natural vegetation by domestic grazing, timber-felling or bush burning. Once the natural cover – with its roots – is removed, erosion can set in. The vegetation not only holds the soil together with its roots, but also protects it from direct rain and wind influence. Erosion, similarly, affects fertility ...

He looked up, gazing out of the window. He thought of the dusty red earth of Kenya, of the murram roads with their tiny rough pebbles of silica catching the sun as if the surface were scattered with chips of glass.

At the back of the room, the toaster clicked and a square of warmed bread ejected upwards. He pushed it back in and depressed the switch, checking as he did so that the electricity meter was not about to run out. It was not, but to be on the safe side he inserted two more shilling coins to keep it going. When the toast was brown, he removed it, buttered it and smeared it with Cooper's Oxford marmalade.

Seated again at the desk, Brian balanced the toast on the rim of the work surface and flicked through a file of loose sheets. He read through his mention of laterites, of how the soil type was rich in iron and aluminium, how bauxite was a laterite, how sometimes, because of upward motion of water through such soils, chemicals were brought into the A-horizon, the topmost layer of the ground where the best deposits of saltpetre could be found.

Saltpetre! – he was day-dreaming once again – was that how Matthew Nchembe had managed to get a store of the chemical with which to cure the leopard skin? He looked through the door into his bedroom. There, hanging on the wall, was the very same leopard.

He returned to his thesis and read on.

Gully erosion, on the other hand, is more localised than sheet erosion and is caused by water cutting grooves into the earth, especially in semi-arid regions. In eastern Africa, the gully – known in Swahili as a *donga* ...

Beside the notes, pinned to the page with a brass-coated paperclip giving the illusion of gold, was a black and white photograph of a deep *donga* near Stony Athi. The acacias standing on the bank attested to its depth of over thirty feet.

He thought of the shifting cultivation and over-grazing, Masai *ngombe*s browsing the bushes, the goats eating everything, no *boma*s or permanent settlements: nomadic wandering ruining the earth. And he thought of the Kikuyus – sworn enemies of the Masai – increasing in numbers, needing more land, more food, more cultivation, more denuding of the bush, more grazing, more erosion, more damage, less fertility, less food. It was the eternal cycle of destruction.

He picked up the whole pile of papers and turned them over. On the top was the title page of his thesis – it was neatly printed in Letraset: *Eternal Cycles: Erosion and Destruction of Soil in East African Rural Environments.*

There came a gentle knock on the door, the sort of knocking made by one student aware that another might be engrossed in his work and not want any interruption.

'Hold on a minute!' he called and wrapped his dressing-gown around himself, tightening the cord about his waist. 'Come in.'

He never locked his door for the other lodger could be trusted and no one left the front door open which closed on an old-fashioned automatic spring-loaded hinge. The house, divided into three flats, was occupied by students with the exception of the ground floor in which lived the widowed Mrs Rattle, the owner of the house and once the wife of a college porter who had been astute enough, during the war, to use a small legacy to buy a house near the centre of the town. It not only provided him and his wife with a place to retire to but also a continuous source of income which, if not handsome, was at least adequate. Houses for rent had been at a premium in Oxford for seven hundred years – since the university was founded.

The door opened slowly and a head peeped round the side of the panelling.

'Are you verging on the decent?'

'Verging. How did you get in?'

'Your Canadian archaeologist chum let me in. He was going out with a small sarcophagus under his arm.'

'He's studying mummified animals,' Brian said. 'It's falcons this month. Cats last month. Next month it'll be ibises. Come on in. There's a howling gale out there.'

The door opened fully and Lucy Haycraft entered. She shut it behind her, the draught hissing as the door met the frame, and perched on the horsehair sofa strewn with cushions, many of them covered in printed batik.

'You look frozen,' Brian said. 'And wet.' He glanced out of the window where the drizzle had developed into a thin cold rain.

She unknotted the scarf under her chin and, pulling it aside, shook it. A fine mist of dampness flicked off it and on to the cushions. Dark spots appeared on the batik. She rolled the scarf into a ball and played out her shoulder-length blonde hair. Unlike many nineteen-year-olds, she did not use lacquer but left her hair to swing naturally. Her complexion was smooth but dampened by the rain, her long neck hidden in the wide collar of an angora pullover.

Brian sat at his desk as she shrugged off her overcoat. Beneath it, she wore jeans – as she usually did – with a broad leather belt like a man's, the buckle an oblong of polished brass with a picture of the Wells Fargo stagecoach in relief on the metal. Her only jewellery was a pair of pearl stud earrings and a gold Longines wrist-watch on a black leather strap.

'Brian!' she criticised him teasingly. 'You haven't even lit the fire. How long have you been up? Or have you run out of shillings? Were you working late?'

'No, the meter's okay. I've been up about twenty minutes; and yes, I was working late.'

'You should have a word with the mummy-man down-stairs,' she said mysteriously.

'What about?'

'Gas meters.'

'What about them?'

'He's invented a gadget – with an engineering post-grad – which slows the meter down though you still get the normal flow through. I don't know how it works but he told me about it at a party. It's a sort of magnet, I think. You put it on the window where the little dials go round – stick it on with Sellotape. And then you plug it into a wall socket. He says it saves him pounds a week.'

Brian took her overcoat and hung it from a hook on the back of the door. As he lit the gas, the elements quickly glowed red-hot, one of them spitting tiny sparks into the air.

' You've not used that very much lately.'

'How do you know?'

'The dust's burning on it. I can smell it. And see it.'

'I prefer not to work when it's hot,' he explained. 'I like to be cold. I suppose it comes with living so much of my life in the tropics.'

'I suppose so,' she replied, adding, 'Have you made any coffee yet?'

He shook his head and she jumped up, the horsehair sofa creaking.

'In that case, I'll make some while you get dressed. Or would you rather I got undressed?'

Brian laughed.

'Well, which is it to be?' she answered, pouting.

'I'll get dressed,' he decided.

'And shaved. Your face hasn't seen a blade in days. Then I'll let you kiss me.'

He ran his hand over his stubble. Where he had cut his finger on a sheet of foolscap, opening a new packet, the bristles stuck into the wound and made him wince.

While he shaved, the electric Ronson snagging on his stubble, she talked to him through the bedroom door as she made them a pot of coffee on the Baby Belling cooker which was inside a cupboard at the rear of the living room.

'How's your thesis coming along?'

'All right, I suppose. I've a good bit on erosion in the White Highlands and am into the section on erosion where savannah has been destroyed.'

'Will you be done on time?'

'I've set myself a deadline,' he said over the buzzing of the razor. 'Prof. Talbot wants the first half by the end of the second week in June – for the long vac I'd guess. The typist says she can do it in a fortnight, with two carbons.'

'That'll be expensive ...'

Brian knew it would not be cheap, but a professional could do it so much more quickly than himself. And he did not lack the money. Since the death of his parents the year before, in a light aircraft crash in Sussex, he was well-off. His inheritance made him wealthy, in fact. He had sold his parents' house and the Chelsea mews flat, traded his father's share portfolio and re-invested the money in bonds. He had kept his father's car – the MG B-GT he had promised himself and Dotty as a retirement present – but little else. Their furniture was in store against the day when Brian set up a home of his own.

Lucy Haycraft pushed open the bedroom door with her elbow and entered carrying two steaming mugs on a tin tray printed with an Aubrey Beardsley figure in trailing folds of material. Sitting herself cross-legged on the bed, she balanced her mug on her knee and put Brian's on the bedside table. That he was dressed only in his socks and brief black underpants did not perturb her in the least.

'Your bed's a mess,' she commented, picking up the tangled sheets and letting them drop. 'And it smells of you.'

'Hardly surprising,' he answered, pulling the razor out of the two-pin plug he had inserted into the light socket and replacing the bulb. 'I sleep in it.'

'It looks as if you fought in it last night.' She gave him a leery look. 'You didn't have a woman in here last night, did you? Not that Melissa from L M H?'

'No, I did not,' he remonstrated with her. 'And there's nothing between Melissa Mee and me. Or I. As the case may be. Should be.'

'You sound flustered, Brian. I didn't know twenty-eight-year-old doctoral sloggers got so easily ruffled. Guilty conscience...'

'Rubbish!'

He pulled on a pair of tight, fading jeans and a striped blue shirt over which he tugged a heavy polo-neck sweater. His feet thrust into a pair of Hush Puppies, he sat next to her on the bed and winced as his lips met the piping hot coffee.

'If you want to know ...'

'I do,' she said, her voice no longer teasing or vexed, but serious and, he realised, possibly loving.

He was never totally sure of her emotions. At times he believed her to be in love with him yet, at others, he felt jaded – it was as if their relationship was shallow, being only a temporary or passing affection. There were moments when he felt very insecure.

'I had a restless night because I was dreaming.'

'Let me guess. India this time?'

He shook his head.

'Kenya?'

'Yes,' he admitted. 'The nearer I get to completing the thesis, the more I remember it. I suppose it comes from looking over all the photos again, thinking of it in such detail, writing of places which are mere dots on the map but which I know so well – the petrol pumps in Mtito Andei, the escarpment above Lake Magadi ...'

'It can't help to have that leopard hanging over you all the time.'

'No,' he agreed, 'I suppose not ...'

'Why don't we go for a walk?' she suggested suddenly. 'You need to get away from your thesis and I'm bogged down in Milton. And I've no tutorial today because my tutor's got 'flu' Half Wadham has it, I'm told.'

As she stood up, taking his half-drunk coffee from his hand, she bent forward and kissed him very lightly.

'You taste of toast,' she remarked and he smiled.

He opened his wardrobe. It was a huge, Edwardian cupboard with carved panels on the front which reminded him of the façade of provincial English cinema architecture. On the inside of the door was mounted a three-quarter length mirror, the silvering turning black in the right-hand top corner as if some fungus, deadly to glass, was eating into it.

Next to his college blazer hung his rack of waistcoats. The topmost one was that made of colobus monkey skins.

'You are longing to go back, aren't you?' she asked as they reached the end of the avenue of trees leading from Christ Church to the river, turning left to walk along the bank path.

'Yes,' he said pensively. 'I suppose I am. I've not been back to Kenya since I left to come up to Oxford. That's almost ten years ago. I've had a few jaunts abroad playing hockey, and a trip to India for the Overseas Aid people, but never to Africa.'

Across the river, on the south bank where there were some

194

cricket fields, a rowing coach appeared on a bicycle, one hand holding a megaphone, the other the handlebars. He pedalled furiously down from Folly Bridge to halt opposite them. He had difficulty slowing and stopping single-handed. He wrenched himself round in the saddle and pressed the megaphone to his mouth.

'Come along! Come along!' he yelled up-river. 'Number three. For God's sake! Keep the stroke going ... Cox! Think, man, think!'

Three swans sailed by on the river, a flock of ducks in mid-stream taking to the wing as the college boat bore down on them.

They walked on in silence, satisfied with each other's company and, as they reached the Botanical Gardens, the drizzle lifted and a weak, late winter's sun shone wanly through the trees.

'Once, a long time ago, when I was in my late teens, I had a man warn me about his wife ...' Brian said suddenly.

'Go on!' Lucy exclaimed. 'You and another man's wife! And you in your late teens, too!'

'Not quite.' He gave her a mock-indulgent smile in response to her tease. 'He was an inspector of police. Or in the prison service. I don't think I ever knew which ... His wife had a dream. She dreamt of an Africa unmolested by mankind. In which she could photograph wild animals until her camera grew too hot to hold. She tried to talk me into it ... I suppose, in a manner of speaking, she did. She was envangelizing – her husband said so. I guess I must have taken in a bit of her creed.'

'You want Africa to be covered in wild animals?'

'Perhaps ... No! I want ...' They stepped between cars parked in Rose Lane and, as they came to the High, two pigeons erupted from beneath a car and flapped towards the grounds of Merton College. 'I want a balance of mankind and nature: a harmony in which both can exist side by side, benefiting each other, making the most of what the environment has to offer. You know, Lucy, there are fewer more beautiful sights than a pair of cheetah hunting. Or a leopard.'

'Is that why you shot one?' she chided.

'No. I shot one to prove myself to myself. And that's done and I think now it was wrong. My father always painted birds. Never shot them ...'

'I'd like another coffee, Brian,' Lucy demanded.

She kissed his cheek, let go of his hand and started to walk faster up the pavement, past the Examination Schools building, grimacing up at the buff stonework as she did so.

11

'What is it, Dash?' Brian asked, picking up the strand of light blue, tube-like beads, allowing it to hang between his hands. 'Is it a necklace?'

'You take care of that,' Dashiell Nye exclaimed quickly, his mid-West Canadian accent turning on the words and rounding them off. 'It's fragile.'

'It weighs nothing.'

Brian moved his fingers and the beads slid against each other, a fine powder dropping from them on to the table.

'It is a necklace,' Dash confirmed, 'but don't move it too much. This talc-like substance might be the material the beads're made of.'

'That was going to be my next question. What is the substance? The shades of blue are quite beautiful – I don't think I've ever seen anything quite like it. This bead,' he wiggled his thumb against one at least an inch long, 'is almost colourless with only a hint of faint blue while this one,' he moved his little finger, 'is deep royal blue, almost cerulean. And they've a shine to them, some of them, where there's no patina. Yet there's no pattern to them ...'

'Faience,' Dash said. 'A kind of porcelain. Glazed earthenware. What's its age?'

'Knowing you, Egyptian.'

'Right on! Now – how did I get it?'

'Borrowed it from the Pitt-Rivers?'

Dashiell Nye, whom all his acquaintances nicknamed Dash not only because it was an abbreviation but because he was a fast mover – on his bicycle around Oxford, on his Harley-Davidson around England and, in the vac, around Europe, with the girls – was working on an archaeological thesis so vague and yet so seemingly complex Brian had never come fully to grips with what it was really about. Working with mummified animals seemed an intrinsic part of it; beyond

197

that, his studies appeared to be a maze of academic arabesques and esoteric conundrums ideally suited to a brilliant, unquestionable thesis and a top-rate doctorate at the end of it.

'Nope! Try again.'

'Nicked it from the Pitt-Rivers?'

'C'mon! Be serious.'

'Found it on a wizen falcon or cat or monkey. Or ibis. Anything like that.'

'Getting warmer, pal. Try again.'

'It was an offering to the hippopotamus-faced goddess of revenge and childbirth: Tauret the Terrible. Anyone who touches it gets cursed by the Oath of Osiris. Your fingers drop off and your ears grow big as cabbages ...'

'And your lips thick as Mick Jagger's. Are you taking the piss, good buddy?'

Brian laughed, admitted he was and added, 'But you've got to admit you ask for it. All this proddle about mummified birds and so on.'

'Well, this one's completely different. I'll tell you...'

Very carefully, he lifted the necklace from Brian's hands and laid it on a sheet of velvet spread on his work table. With his forefinger, he prodded it cautiously into a circle about twelve inches in diameter.

'Last vac.' he began, 'I went out to Egypt on a dig with some buddies I met on the Smithsonian expedition last year. Stayed near Akhmim, fifteen Ks away or so. Near the Nile bank. Shortly before I got there, the last party – we were working on two week shifts and I really only wanted to brush up a bit on my technique ready for the summer and my son-of-a-bitch thesis –' he thumped his hand despairingly down upon a fat spring-loaded binder almost breaking at the spine with the strain of containing so many pages '– had uncovered a burial chamber and part of a temple complex. Nothing grand, you understand. The burial chamber had been grave-robbed within thirty years of the interment – probably thirty days, knowing how it could be! – but the temple left as it was. There was beneath it a catacomb system, again not very big but absolutely loaded with mummified fauna.'

'You must have jumped at that one.'

'Sure did! Gave me the first opportunity I've had of picking the buggers up out of the sand with my own bare hands. Technique practice was shot! I spent the first four days down the caves rummaging about, sticking labels on them and cataloguing all I could. They were stacked six feet high and three or four cases deep against a wall about twenty yards long. Many weren't in wooden cases of course but tubes of wood or cylinders of clay. Some just stuck there in their windings.

'When I'd listed the first layer and that sexy little Spaniard I told you about from Salamanca had drawn the area and photographed it, I started removing the goodies. Up in the military tents the Egyptians had provided, I set about undoing some of the mummies. Couple of monkeys were the first ones. Then there were ten or so ibises from the river swamps. And four small crocs. Nothing new, nothing to write home about or shove in the son-of-a-bitch thesis. But then I came upon a larger-than-average cylinder.'

He paused for effect bending over from his chair and turning the gas up in the fire. The white, honeycomb elements cracked and clicked as they expanded and reddened. The gas hissed loudly.

'This one contained a baboon. Well mummified, in fairly good condition. Hair still pliable, skin and tissue rigid but not as desiccated as you usually find them. Viscera removed. Unguents still a little sticky, if anything – like paint almost dry. Ever so slightly tacky. Now, Brian, I've found baboons before ...'

He became serious. The usual joking attitude Dash Nye applied to everything in life was dropped for the temporary intrusion of scholarship. Like many of Brian's friends – and like Brian himself – he was deeply fascinated by his work which he seemed to dismiss as a light distraction from his general enjoyment of a good life but which was, in truth, central to his every day. Even when he was high on pot in one of his many girlfriends' houses off the Cowley Road, his dreams and thoughts revolved around sacrificed, mummified creatures.

'So what was new about this one?'

'That was,' Dash replied, looking at the necklace and prodding it again with his finger. 'The baboon was wearing it round its neck. I've never seen that before. It's a bit of human jewellery, no doubt about it. I've seen them on mummified people often – and bronze rings and bangles and all sorts. But never on an animal. What it means I don't know.'

There was a knock on the door and he shrugged as he stood up.

'But what it does mean is that it provides a big imponderable that fucks up my son-of-a-bitch thesis good and proper!'

He opened the door. Standing on the landing, clasping a parcel to her bosom, was Mrs Rattle. She was breathing heavily, her arms underneath the package with her fingers holding it in to herself, only half her face appearing over the top of it.

'Good morning, sir,' she greeted Dash. Seeing Brian seated by the gas fire she added, 'Sirs. Postman's been and left this blessed parcel for you, Mr Nye.'

'You shouldn't have brought it up the stairs, Mrs Rattle,' Dash chided, reaching for it. 'I can come down.'

'It's heavy,' she warned, releasing her grip on the edges. 'But, well, I had some letters to bring up for Mr Titchner, so I thought to make the trip. Books, is it?'

Dash lifted the parcel from her hands and weighed it thoughtfully. The stamps were Spanish and covered in smeared black postmarks.

'No. Things for my work,' he confided, furrowing his brow and narrowing his eyes. 'Dead bodies sent from the tombs of Ancient Egypt. We're starting a coven up here, Mrs Rattle. Nightly witch-cult dancing in the nude, spinning spells around the pentacle to bring a blight upon those creatures of the underworld we find to be our enemies.'

She wheezed a hoarse laugh and said, 'You are a wicked man, Mr Nye. I don't know what Mr Rattle would say to you. Naked dancing in the rooms ...' She winked obviously at Brian. 'And who are these enemies of yours, then?'

'Not you, Mrs Rattle!' Dash lowered the parcel to the unmade bed where it pressed a deep dent in the rumpled sheets and blankets. 'Greater enemies even than yourself to the poor clerkes of Oxenford. No!' He waved his finger magisterially in the air and pointed to the ceiling. 'I speak of – dare I utter the word in the presence of such innocent ears as your own, Mrs Rattle? – I speak of ... postgraduate supervisors!'

'You should show respect for them that's cleverer than you,' she answered, yet she knew he was teasing.

Brian accepted his mail from her, opening it when she had gone and while Dash was cutting open his parcel with a Stanley knife: there was a letter from his bank informing him of interest earned in the last quarter on his deposit accounts, and a bill from Blackwell's Bookshop demanding at least a partial settlement of money outstanding on his account.

'It's from that bird in Salamanca,' Dash exclaimed. 'I knew she'd come through!'

'I heard she had,' Brian remarked, folding his letters into his pocket.

'Hell! Did she! Fantastic in the sack! Even wanted to do it down the goddam catacomb. Not my scene! But you know the saying: lie with 'em and they'll lie for you.'

Inside the heavy brown paper wrapping was a cardboard box within a wooden crate such as one saw full of oranges or cucumbers in a greengrocer's. Layers of newspaper lined and protected one box from the other. Copious strips of brown adhesive tape held everything together.

'How's she lied for you?'

'Getting this lot through. Here.'

He handed Brian the parcel wrapping. On the customs label the contents were stated to be clothing and personal effects.

'So? You left her your laundry.'

There was a ripping sound as Dash tore off the last strip of tape and lifted open the flaps. Inside, nestled in layers of crumpled paper and cotton waste, and surrounded by rolls of corrugated card, were six clay cylinders.

'Baboon and friends!' Dash announced with glee. 'More for the collection. Now I don't need to pinch bits from the Pitt-Rivers as you so ungentlemanly suggested, O Brian of Little Faith and Soil Erosion.'

'Those are mummies from your dig?'

'Sure are! Straight out of the ground, brought safely through the Mediterranean by fair Spanish hands on fair Spanish hands' father's oil tanker, across the burning plains of central Spain and the cool airs of the upper atmosphere, courtesy of British European Airways to the city of spires.'

'What do you mean, the collection?' Brian asked.

'You have your core samples and test-tubes of dirt. I have my deceased menagerie of wonders … *Voilà!* And I'm not French Canadian, either!'

With a flourish, he raised the blankets drooped over the side of his bed. Beneath, next to his suitcase, were stacked over a dozen clay cylinders.

'My own catacombs!' he announced proudly.

Brian was speechless for a moment, unable to collect his thoughts. It was preposterous and hilarious. Every night, Dash slept over his mummies, made love to his girlfriends over his mummies.

'What animals have you there?' he asked at last.

Dash, grinning with the pleasure of his surprise, said, 'Including today's batch: a baboon, four cats, two crocodiles, three ibises, three falcons, two other unidentifiable birds both a bit far gone – cheapo embalming by a poor worshipper, no doubt – a puppy, a monkey and a baby.'

'A baby what?'

'A baby baby. Human. What else? Want to see him?'

'Yes,' Brian said cautiously, wondering if Dash was playing a joke on him yet, at the same time, overwhelmingly curious.

From the back of the space under the bed, Dash produced a wooden mummy box half again the size of a violin case. It was tied round with sisal string. Tugging at the knot, Dash removed the string and lifted the lid, giving it to Brian. It smelt of dust and dryness but there lingered on it a taint of something not unlike cinnamon.

In the case lay a form wrapped no longer in linen strips but in a clear polythene bag. Around the dark body were little white cotton bags of silica gel such as one found in the packaging of Japanese electrical goods. As if it were his own child, Dash lifted the corpse carefully, almost lovingly, from the case, and laid it across his knees. In the bottom of the mummy case, in more polythene bags, were the shroud cloths.

He opened the bag on his lap and removed the child. It was not so much a baby as an infant of perhaps two or three years of age. Its skin, much darker than it would have been in life, was the colour of strong, black tea. Upon its head were fine strands of black hair and its feet, though discoloured and shrunken under a taut skin such as covered the remainder of the body, looked as if they had been recently alive. The creases under the toes were plainly visible and even the lines on the heel.

'Do you know how he died?'

'Not really. I've done an autopsy on him with my supervisor – last year – but we couldn't be sure. The internal organs – most of them – have been removed as was customary. But we reckon he drowned in the Nile. There was silt in the body cavity that could have come from the lungs and in no way corresponded to the site of the burial. We do know he ate some grapes for his last meal – found some pips in a section of bowel. Here,' he held the child out, 'you take him.'

Brian held out his arms as if he was accepting a living child. Looking at its dark form drawing nearer to him he thought how much it resembled a black *toto*.

Lucy reached over the side of the bed, her hand circling in the air until her fingers touched her glass. Raising it from the floor, she gazed into it and awkwardly tipped the last vestiges of the malt whisky onto her lips. There was just sufficient to wet them.

'So Dash really does have a mausoleum under his bed. Kathy told me as much but I didn't believe her. She found it once, rummaging about for her shoe.'

She rolled on to her back, the sheet clinging to her skin.

'What so surprised me was it was so light,' Brian said. 'It was quite shocking, like holding a silhouette.'

'That's very poetic.'

'Stuff poetry!' Brian exclaimed. 'It was horrifying. He laid it in my arms and my hand automatically went under its spine to support it. As if it were alive. And my whole hand went inside it.'

She poured more whisky into her glass and struggled up against the pillow, her blond hair ruffled against the cotton, a strand of it sticking to her cheek.

'Do you want a scotch? Or would you rather have a joint?'

'A scotch,' he replied absent-mindedly, continuing, 'It was grotesque. I felt as if I was being sacreligious. Profane, somehow. After I got up to my room, I scrubbed my hands. It wasn't as if they were dirty but impure. And I had a weird dream that night.'

'Tell me about the dream,' she said. 'Dreams are your psyche manifesting itself in reality.'

'Psyche or not, it was real enough. Real people, real places, real events . . .'

He swung his legs over the side of the bed and crossed the room to the mantelpiece where he had left his tumbler before they made love. The late afternoon spring sunlight was washing through the window and on to the wall above the bed, illuminating a large painting she had completed as a part of her 'A' Level Art practical. It was an oil of two beech trees between which rose a tall pillar on an outcrop of grassy hillside.

'I do adore a man's bum,' she declared and, as he turned to face her, added, 'amongst other things.'

'You are a naughty little girl,' he answered and, squatting on the bed beside her, kissed her lightly.

She let the sheet drop to her waist and his hand ran down her side and pushed between her skin and the pillow, arching into the small of her back.

'What don't you like about me?' she asked.

'I don't like that bloody awful painting,' he replied, casting his eyes up at it. 'Other than that, not a thing.'

'I only keep it because it covers the dust square where the last one hung. It's an example of my lost psyche. I was in a phallic phase when I painted it. Still a virginal schoolgirl . . .'

'Have you ever left it?'

'No,' she admitted, 'not really. Now tell me about your dream.'

'I was back in Kenya – pronounced *Keen*-ya then – and out hunting with a boy I knew in those days. His name was Chopping: I've not thought of him for years but ...'

'But he's still in your mind. Go on.'

'We were in a clearing in the bush and we shot a baboon – Dash has got a few in his collection – and it jumped about like a dying man in the movies. Gunfighter hits baddie. John Wayne triumphs again! Staggering to and fro, clutching at the wound, barking and screeching like they do. Chopping shouted, "Got him! Got him!" and I looked at him: he was blowing the smoke out of his revolver like cowboys do. His rifle had turned into a revolver, you see. We walked closer to the baboon and, as we got nearer, I saw it had the face of a boy I went to school with. A nasty bit of work, he was. An Afrikaner called Stadden. Yet it wasn't quite his face.'

'What do you mean?' Lucy questioned, genuinely interested. She had been reading Graves's *The White Goddess* and Frazer's *The Golden Bough*; now dreams fascinated her to such an extent she maintained her own dream diary in which she recorded those she and her friends experienced.

'He was nicknamed *Mbuzi-kuu* – Swahili for a big goat – because his forehead was prominent like a goat's. And this dying baboon, thrashing about on the ground, had his features yet it also had its own dog-like snout and baring teeth. We shot it again. At least, Chopping did. This time it yelled an African word. It shouted "*Uhuru!*"'

'That means freedom, liberty.'

Brian nodded. His hand shook as he poured out a measure of whisky into his glass.

'When it was dead, I picked the baboon up. They can be heavy – weigh up to fifty pounds, sometimes more if it's a big male – this was a male. And, as I lifted it, it turned into a human African baby, its chest shot through. I turned round and found I was not in the clearing any more. I was in a village and all around me were dead Africans – all women and *totos*, no men.'

'What's a *toto*?'

'A child ...'

The sun reflected off the painting and shone on his face but Brian did not flinch at it.

'Watching me were African men. They didn't do anything to me. They watched me in silence. And the dead *toto* weighed nothing and I looked from them to it and it was Dash's damn mummy and my hand had fallen into its hole. Then I dropped it and ran away through the clearing – and my hands were covered in blood. Over my shoulder, I could hear that Afrikaner lout shouting at me.'

'What was he shouting?'

Brian did not speak. Lucy put her hand on his arm and shook it softly.

'What was he shouting, Brian? It might be important.'

'It was, in a way,' he said after a long pause. 'He was shouting "Kaffir-lover!" over and over again.'

After a few minutes of silence, Lucy kicked the sheet off herself and stood up, stretching as widely as she could, her arms and legs spread. Then she bent over in front of Brian and touched her toes three times.

'Let's get dressed,' she suggested. 'I want to go out for what's left of the sunshine.'

As they strolled along the bank of the Cherwell, towards the pond at the northern end of the University Parks, Brian broke a ten-minute silence by asking, 'Was it good for you this afternoon?'

'Yes,' she replied in a distant manner. 'It was okay.'

'Aren't I good enough for you? I sometimes feel – not exactly inadequate but something of a minor disappointment to you. I'm not as experienced, perhaps ...'

'Don't talk about it,' she interrupted him. 'You were fine, honestly. And yes, I've had better lovers but ... Oh, what the hell! Just don't worry about it so.'

They sauntered slowly down the avenue of trees parallel with the backs of the houses in Norham Gardens. The trees had broken their buds, the boughs ghosted in soft, bright greens and browns. Birds sang in the branches and across the newly-mown cricket field waddled a parade of ducks heading for the river, the sun striking the azure feathers of the drakes.

Brian loved Lucy. He had had little time for women in his undergraduate years, concentrating instead on his degree course, his membership of a university photographic club and having only casual affairs which came to nothing. If they seemed as if they might develop further, he had terminated them. When he went down and entered employment, he was too busy, too bound up in his work to be bothered with girlfriends. Some of the laboratory assistants and clerks from the administrative office had sought him out, tried to date him, and he had gone with them for short periods but again regarded none of them as serious. When his parents died, the will to find someone to love died, too. It was only when he met Lucy that he found a spark of feeling unlike any he had known previously.

She had taken to him, too. He had travelled with her to meet her parents, with whom he got along well. They had liked the serious soil-man from Oxford, the wealthy young man who, despite the climate of the Swinging Sixties, did not squander his inheritance.

Her father was a well-known artist: his portraits of industrialists, millionaires, rock stars and even nobility were famous. Her mother, one of his former models, was a striking woman, tall and very slender with sharp but not cruel features: Lucy's father often referred to her as his living Modigliani, his own thin, Parisian waif. Their relationship was stormy as the result of artistic temperament rather than adultery or drink, the more prevalent of artists' vices. This caused Lucy to be quick-witted, alive with the electricity of amorous confrontation.

With such a tempestuous but secure background, Lucy believed herself immune from romantic harm, protected against the ill winds of life by the good fortune of her beauty, her father's fame and her own playful femininity. She was adept at the art of being a woman, toyed with all men, teased a few, yet promised her allegiance to none. The new liberty, as one of her feminist movement friends termed it, was an aspect of modernity which she was only too ready to exploit. Permissiveness was a ball and chain, her friend's motto went, but, for Lucy, the permissiveness of society was her liberty.

Brian was the nearest she had allowed a man into her life, the only one over whom she felt slightly guilty when in bed with another. She did not keep herself exclusively for him but she settled her conscience by sleeping with him far more than any other. He was not the most expert of the lovers she had experienced but he was, with the exception of the son of one of her father's subjects of commission, the wealthiest; and he was, certainly, one of the kindest and the most considerate. He did not lavish gifts on her and when he did they were small, almost trite presents – a new book of verse by one of the up-and-coming new poets, a bottle of champagne and a box of her favourite brandy-snap biscuits filled with cream, a cheap Mexican silver bracelet from the little jeweller's shop in St Michael's Street, a cheap art nouveau ornament or a bunch of flowers for her flat, the top floor of a terraced house in the maze of streets between Iffley Road and Cowley Road, a few hundred yards over Magdalen Bridge.

Only the champagne and brandy-snaps, she thought as they passed through the iron railing gate onto South Parks Road, had an ulterior motive. Champagne as well as pot, she considered, made her randy.

'You are coming to the party, aren't you?' she asked as they stepped through a throng of cyclists outside Rhodes House. A demonstration against the Vietnam War was to occur that evening and knots of students were beginning to collect – or, as Brian's undergraduate moral tutor had put it, to coagulate – at street corners, outside the coffee houses, wine bars and the pubs which were just opening for business.

'Of course. Do you want a hand setting it up? I'm not planning to do anything tomorrow afternoon except to check over a report on some samples I had sent for analysis. A friend in Imperial College, London ...'

She wasn't listening. He could tell by the way she was looking down the road rather than tilting her head towards him. His work bored her. It was not artistic, it had no heart and no passion – it was as dry as the desert, the African dirt of which it consisted. That it meant something to him, that through it he could follow his own passion for Africa, was not of concern to her. Her emotional rewards had to be more immediate than a long-term dream of turning Central Africa into the food bowl of the world.

'No. Thanks, though. Janet's going to help and I've a little caterer man from near the football ground doing the food and delivering it. I can't be bothered. All paper plates and cups.'

Janet, Brian thought: poor, dowdy, lack-lustre Janet.

Niece to a senior Liberal Member of Parliament, Janet McFarlane was one of Lucy's fellow students at St Hilda's. She was a plain girl who wore her hair in bunches as if she was ten rather than twenty, a girl who disapproved of all Lucy admired or sought – beauty, sex, fun, even a tan. She seldom shaved her legs and was famous for informing any would-be beau at the start of their date that she was agoraphobic and had to travel by taxi if a private car was not available. These traits ensured she had no steady boyfriends and little enjoyment. For her, a party was an opportunity to work hard at something other than her studies, and to succeed in them she had to struggle whereas, for Lucy, the course work demanded for her degree came easily and afforded her ample opportunity for hedonistic pastimes. Someone like Janet, who bathed in the reflected glory of Lucy, was an added asset for she could be put upon in a way most acquaintances could not. She would be the one to do most of the preparations for the night of partying.

A young man on a bicycle, at the periphery of the noisy crowd, balancing his machine against the kerb with one foot, parped his cycle horn at her and waved.

'Hi, Luce!' he called.

She returned his wave but paid him no further attention. Brian noticed the young man's slightly crestfallen look and wondered who he was.

'You won't forget to bring a bottle, will you? I've ordered fifteen large tins of beer for those who row and kick inflated bladders about fields, but the rest would like wine. But that's so expensive. Even the plonk.'

'No, I won't forget.'

They parted on the corner by the New Bodleian Library building. Lucy kissed him fleetingly on his cheek and whispered into his ear. 'See you tomorrow at the party, then.

It'll go on all night, I'm sure. And you will stay, won't you? And you will bring bubbly, just for us?'

He nodded.

'And you were good this afternoon. Honestly. I loved feeling you slip right up and into me.'

She winked raunchily at him and squeezed his arm painfully.

She didn't mean it: not the first sentence, anyway. He knew as much as he stood at the road junction watching her walking quickly down Holywell Street, past the music shop and around the gradual curve in the road behind New College.

Brian set off in the direction of Jericho. He felt disconsolate and low, unsatisfied not just with how he had spent his day but with his life. He knew he was trapped by his love for Lucy, the artist's daughter and girl-about-Oxford, yet he could do nothing to reach out and snap open the lock. Dash had given him a warning not long after he began his affair with her.

'Heed the advice of an old hand!' Dash had said. 'I know girls like that,' he pronounced it *goils* as if he were a New York mobster discussing his moll, 'from way-way back. Dey ain't no good, man!'

Brian had laughed at his wagging finger and inept impersonation of James Cagney.

'Seriously,' Dash had gone on, 'you want to watch that one. "Hearthbreak Hotel" on legs. That's what she is. An Oxford bicycle.'

'A bicycle?' Brian had responded.

'*Bicyclus oxoniensis*. Moves like greased shit through the town, and everybody rides it.'

Brian had taken umbrage.

'That's a bit bloody unfair,' he had complained. 'You hardly know her.'

'Reputation! Reputation rides ahead of the wind of scandal. Don't get grit in your eye, pal, when it starts to blow. Just before the storm hits, take cover!'

'Reputation is usually slander under the protection of implied truth.'

'As you will, but don't say you weren't given due notice. I'd not like to see you hurt. Just use her. That's what she likes. I'd do so myself, given half a chance. But she's not into my type. Not enough ...' He fell silent for a moment then added, 'Told her you love her?'

'I don't see what business it is of yours!'

'It's not,' Dash had answered, 'but have you?'

'Yes, as a matter of fact. And I do.'

'And she returned the compliment?' Dash had questioned, his voice not so much curious as concerned.

'Yes!' Brian had retorted with fierce indignation.

As he walked past the gates of Trinity College, glancing in at the smooth lawns and neatly-tended flower beds, he tried to remember when she had last said she loved him. If, indeed, she ever had. He regretted having told the lie to Dash. At least, he thought, commiserating with himself, she was constant in her inconstancy.

By the Martyrs' Memorial, standing in the road and blocking the traffic, was a crowd of several hundred students. The evening sunlight, casting a warm glow on their colourful college scarves and the stone walls of Balliol College, picked out their shadows. A cordon of police were advancing from outside the Randolph Hotel. Further up Beaumont Street were five mounted policemen, their horses stamping and restlessly tossing their heads. As he skirted the demonstration, noticing not all the scarves were those of Oxford colleges – at least three London University red, white and blue scarves shone in the sunlight – and walked past the entrance to the Ashmolean Museum, one of the horses bucked and kicked the kerbstones, sparks flying from its hooves.

Wars, Brian considered as the chanting of the demonstrators faded in the distance, eroded the spirit as rain wore away at the earth.

The party was theoretically by invitation only but, as was always the case, the news spread until the original thirty savants had grown to a hundred guests and the size of the party was restricted only by the confines of the venue and the provision of drink or dope.

211

Lucy's party began officially at eight, but no one arrived for at least half an hour. This did not concern her – as it did Janet who needlessly fretted that no one would actually turn up – for she knew the ways of party-goers: leave home at seven-thirty, drive to a pub, have a few drinks to get into the mood, drive to an off-licence and buy a bottle or two, drive to pick up those who had begged a lift, arrive at the party an hour later. From then on the evening, indeed the whole night, would be spent circulating from one party to the next. After several hours of dancing, eating, smoking and drinking at one host's expense – of electricity as much as food, 'grass' and alcohol – the first-comers would disappear, to be replaced by the second wave of arrivals, most of them already well into revelry. The ebb and flow of guests was not obvious. It was just that, over the space of an hour, the keen and sober observer would notice those who had begun the party were now absent.

The departures and arrivals were announced not by a knock on the door or even a tread on the stairs – no one would hear either over the blast of music – but by a flavour in the air of the room. Perhaps the stink of beer might change to one of wine or whisky, the smoke be less dominated by tobacco and more by marijuana, the experienced able to tell by one whiff whether the source of the drug was Turkish, Indian or Moroccan. The scent of perfume, after-shave or eau de cologne might change and the taste in music alter although, as the night wore on, it invariably turned from loud rock and roll to less loud and more evocative rock and roll. The volume of the music would be reduced, too. No one wanted to disturb those living nearby, for irate neighbours inevitably called the police, the police would soon smell the 'grass' drifting in the air, and everyone would be busted. The Magistrates' Court on Monday would then be crammed with students facing a fine, the castigation of their parents and the possibility of rustication from the university. No one was prepared to risk that fate merely for the satisfaction of a desire to numb their eardrums after eleven o'clock. Besides, there were other things to do in the late or early hours.

Brian arrived a little after time, a package under his arm.

The house was vibrant with music. Brian could hear the party from the end of the street, and the throbbing of the music and the sound of voices straining against it grew as he drew nearer to the building. The front door was open, a dim orange light casting an oblong across a tiny front garden entirely filled with a holly bush, a hydrangea and Dash's Harley-Davidson upon which was perched a girl in tight blue jeans and a T-shirt across which was printed *US Kill Babies In 'Nam* in the colours of the Stars and Stripes.

The occupants of the downstairs flat, two Chinese-Malay engineering students on Commonwealth bursaries, on being told what a party involved, had surrendered to circumstances and joined in. For them it was Hobson's Choice and, for the price of six additional party cans of Watney's bitter, they had invited some of their own guests. A group of bemused and reserved Oriental students, eating Ritz biscuits from a bowl, had gathered at the foot of the staircase as if afraid to enter the mêlée above: the music was upstairs, the food and drink downstairs. Such a gathering was not what they were used to in Singapore.

Under the stairs was a cupboard in which the occupants of both floors stored a communal Hoover and in which were housed the electricity meters. Brian opened the door, depositing his package carefully behind two empty suitcases to which were pasted Qantas labels.

As he climbed the stairs, there was a lull in the music. Conversation quickly rose to fill the void only to be drowned out, as Brian reached the landing, by the opening bars of the Rolling Stones' "Satisfaction", the bass guitar so loud the floorboards by the door vibrated.

Against the bannister rail leaned Dash and his current girlfriend. She was hugging herself close into him, his fingers playing up and down her spine as if on the fretboard of Keith Richards' guitar. His hand missed two chords to acknowledge Brian's arrival.

'Where's Lucy?' Brian enquired. The hand missed another two chords to jerk its thumb in the direction of the music.

Forcing his way between two couples swaying against each other in the doorway, he reached the sofa. All the furniture in

213

the room had been shoved against the walls, the Indian carpets rolled up and the floorboards showing bare in the centre where the varnish had not been applied. The lights were out except for a dim bulb in a reading lamp draped with a red cloth. The sofa, the two armchairs and the space between them were wedged with bodies, an androgynous mass in the semi-darkness. Another mass was gyrating and pulsing to the music.

A hand forced a way between his arm and ribs, then ran smoothly round to his stomach, stroking the flesh through his shirt. Lips pressed into his neck from behind.

'You're late,' a voice said, close to his ear.

'I'm sorry. I was working and the time just slipped away. I didn't notice until the daylight faded and then I had to wait for Dash to get out of the bath. He'd used all the hot water and the immersion had run out of shillings and ...'

'Excuses, excuses!' Lucy teased. 'Now you're here, dance with me.'

It wasn't a request but a command and he obeyed it.

Two hours later, as they stood in the tiny kitchen, hemmed in by people and empty, half-empty and still unbroached tins of bitter, bottles of wine and cider, and half-eaten food, Lucy asked him where the champagne was.

'Hidden,' he said, enigmatically.

'Where? Don't you think we could open it now?' She looked at her watch. 'It's after eleven.'

'Okay,' he agreed.

The stairs were crowded with people sitting on the steps talking, drinking and smoking. The light on the upstairs landing had been switched off and Brian found it hard to see where he was putting his feet.

Only once did he stand on someone's hand, the owner exclaiming in the half-darkness, 'Look where yer puttin' yer fuckin' feet, will yer! I'm no' a fuckin' car-pit!'

'Sorry,' Brian apologized automatically.

He found the champagne undiscovered, removing both bottles from their wrapping. The man who wasn't a carpet had watched his movements carefully. Any experienced

214

party-goer knew to be on the look-out for clandestine fumblings in cupboards. Such movements could mean either a private store of booze or a stash, both of which were fair game.

'You've got two!' Lucy said with delight as he returned to the kitchen.

In the room with the gramophone – he could not bring himself to think of it as the living or sitting room any longer, for the noise precluded ordinary life and those not dancing were not sitting but sprawling over the sofa, the chairs, the cushions and the floor – the record playing was The Who's "My Generation", the dancers and sprawlers all singing with the chorus.

> Why don't you all f-f-fade away.
> Don't try d-d-dig what we all s-s-say.
> I'm not trying to cause a big s-s-sensation.
> Talking about my g-g-generation.

Some, like miscreant schoolboys corrupting the words of Christmas carols in school chapels, shouted over Roger Daltrey's line, altering it to, 'Why don't you all just f-f-fuck off.'

Taking one of the bottles of champagne, Lucy thrust it under the kitchen dresser with her foot.

'That'll be safe there,' she decided. 'We'll have it later. Open your one now, then.'

As he poured the champagne into two paper cups, the bottle warm from the heat in the cupboard, Lucy gave the kitchen door a push and it swung shut, marginally reducing the sound of the music.

'Isn't Janet handy?' she said, emptying the cup at once and holding it out for Brian to refill.

'Why do you say that?'

'Well, she's so good with the music.'

'You mean she's working the record player?'

'Best place for her!' Lucy replied unkindly. 'That way she's in the swing of things but doesn't have to worry about males. She's not the sexiest ...'

215

There were times when Brian despised Lucy. She used those around her, took advantage of their innocence, their weaknesses and their generosity. Dash, he supposed, was right to some extent. He knew he was used by her and wondered if she ever spoke to her friends about him in such terms.

'He's not the sexiest of my lovers,' he heard her say in his imagination, 'but he's not bad. He's ... well ... He's well-hung, if you get my drift.' He could hear, too, the giggles of her less-worldly female audiences.

As midnight approached Janet, at Lucy's suggestion, turned the volume down much lower and started to play quieter songs. This brought about the gradual departure of the noisier guests, the men with no partners and those couples in search of a more swinging end to their evening.

Lucy drank half the bottle of champagne and plied Janet with all Brian had not poured for himself. By half-past midnight, Janet was no longer in control of the music and those who wanted it simply put on whatever LP came to hand. Several times, Lucy placed the Walker Brothers' recent number-one hit on the turntable and stood next to Brian, in the centre of the other dancers. No one took any steps. There was insufficient space. They merely stood on their allotted part of the floor and moved against each other.

'You're staying the night, aren't you?' she asked him, her head on his shoulder and her hands around his hips, resting on his buttocks.

'If you want me to. Or you can come back to my place ...'

She made no reply, half-twisting him on the spot.

'Janet's finally got herself a man,' Lucy observed as they turned.

In the haze of red from the subdued lamp, Brian noted it was not so much a case of Janet having got herself a man but rather the other way around. She was seated on someone's lap: Brian could see the man beneath her had his hand under her skirt. As he watched, the hand moved downwards and he caught sight of a lace frill. Janet was wriggling but whether with enjoyment or in protest he could not judge. As Lucy turned him again, Brian noticed the hand, now disappearing

216

up Janet's skirt again, belonged to the man upon whose fingers he had trodden on the stairs.

'Do you know him?' Brian asked Lucy.

'Who?'

'Janet's groper.'

'I don't really. I think he works in the car factory at Cowley. Makes M Gs or something. Maybe he'll take her for a ride ... I do like this song.' She began to sing the refrain quietly in his ear. 'The sun ain't gonna shine anymore ... The moon ain't gonna rise in the sky ...'

As the music faded, Lucy said, 'Scott Walker really is quite dishy.'

'Who?' Brian asked.

'Scott Walker.'

'Is that his name?'

'Whose?'

'Janet's groper.'

'No!' she retorted, adding a little sarcastically, 'You really are a bit square, Brian. He's one of the singers on that track. My father's been asked to paint his portrait. Perhaps I'll get to meet him at a sitting.'

No one put another record on the turntable. Janet was too preoccupied and everyone else uninterested or similarly engaged. The dancers either sat on the floor or remained vertical, hugging each other as if the music continued.

'Bedroom,' Lucy muttered. 'Via the kitchen.'

With the second bottle of champagne, she led Brian to the bedroom door. It was dark inside but, as the door swung shut behind them, he could hear people rustling. The room smelled of sweat.

'Over here,' she whispered.

Brian stepped gingerly through the darkness, his feet catching on coats fallen or pushed off the bed. Someone, near the bed, grunted once. Another sighed. After a moment his hand came into contact with Lucy's, more by chance than design. She guided him around the bed and towards the wardrobe, knocking the drawn curtain as she brushed by it. A moment of bleak street lamplight illuminated the room and, by it, Brian caught sight of two semi-clothed forms making love on the bed. The bright light caught the arch of the girl's legs.

Beneath the window lay a haphazard pile of coats, pillows and several cushions. They were warm. Lucy drew him down to them and he knelt on the floor. She relinquished his hand and he listened to her moving awkwardly. Then her hand found his again and she pulled him on top of herself, pressing his fingers on to her belly. She had pulled her dress up to her waist and had removed her panties: she was bare beneath him.

'Don't wait,' she whispered, almost inaudibly. 'I don't want you to wait. Just do it now.'

When Brian awoke, his back ached. So did his head. His mouth tasted as if he had been eating one of his soil samples. His shirt was rucked around his chest, his tie was gone and he was naked from the waist down but covered by an overcoat. His watch had worked its way around his wrist so that the face was on the inside of his arm. He peered blearily at it. It was precisely nine o'clock.

Lucy was not by his side but she must have only just left him, for the huge cushion and the gaberdine raincoat next to him were still warm; on the latter was a light stain, testament to their love-making.

He leaned on his elbow and rubbed his face. His stubble rasped.

There was the delicate smell of hashish in the room.

The bedroom door opened and a girl whom Brian had never seen before came in. She was wearing nothing but a man's shirt and, from where he was lying, he could see the bushy hair below her smooth tummy. In each hand, she was holding a mug of coffee.

'Wakey! Wakey!' she said cheerily. 'Sunday's come and the bells are ringing. It's a sunny spring day and all's well.' She sniffed the air. 'Whose got some left?'

'I have,' said a muffled voice from the bed.

'Can I have a puff?'

'Of course. Certainly you may.'

The girl stepped over the debris of clothing, bedding and

218

cushions on the floor and bent over to give Brian one of the mugs.

'Hi, you must be Brian. I'm Angela.'

'Good morning, Angela,' Brian replied.

'Lucy's making breakfast in the kitchen,' she announced. 'Fried eggs, bacon and tomatoes. Your trousers are over the back of the chair.'

He lay back, the coffee balanced on his chest and his head reeling. He closed his eyes.

From the tangle of sheets and blankets on the bed rose a black arm in the hand of which was a joint. The girl sat on the edge of the bed and, exchanging the roll-up for the second mug of coffee, sucked at it greedily, inhaling hard.

'This is Brian Titchner,' she said, after her first long pull at the joint. 'Lucy's boyfriend.'

The man in the bed sat up and peered over the girl's thigh. Brian opened his eyes to stare straight into the face of Matthew Nchembe.

12

As Brian drove his father's green M G along Woodstock Road, he studied Matthew Nchembe from the corner of his eye.

His hair was longer than it had been in the detention centre at Wamumu, the tight, wiry curls combed from a parting on one side. His skin looked a darker black, his eyes brighter: when he grazed his wrist against the top of the car door, lowering himself into the bucket seat, Brian noticed his skin did not flake or stripe grey as it had.

He was no longer dressed in the ragged vests and shorts of his days of captivity. His stump arm he kept hidden by a chocolate brown blazer with plain brass buttons, the sleeve tucked into the pocket. He wore a pair of well-tailored Daks, the creases sharp, a white open-necked shirt with the collar folded neatly over the jacket; his shoes were not cut from old car tyres but were of high-quality leather which had been well polished. Around his right wrist was a Rado watch on a stainless steel strap. Next to it was a black bracelet of woven elephant hair.

Less obviously, Brian sensed, Nchembe was self-assured. He was certain of himself, moved with decision and was utterly at ease.

At Wolvercote, Brian turned the car off the main road and through some suburban streets and lanes, halting in the car park of the Trout Inn. It was a favourite weekend haunt of those – both town and gown – at Oxford who did not while away their Sunday mornings reading the newspapers, gardening, studying, singing in college choirs, attending services or punting on the Cherwell.

As he pulled up beside a brand new Jaguar V8 sports car and switched off the engine, Brian remembered how he had last halted a vehicle with Nchembe in it, the African terrified that he might die.

They had not spoken as they drove out of the town, but now Brian broke their silence.

'I did go back', he said. 'To Wamumu.'

'I know that. I was told.'

'You weren't there. They had let you go and had no record of your whereabouts.'

'I know that too. None of us gave our destinations.' He looked at the pub with its tubs of flowers, the dying daffodils moving to and fro in the breeze. 'Some did,' he corrected himself, 'but they were foolish. I did not want to be traced. It was not that I was going back into the forest – no one was left by then except some intransigent maniacs ...'

'How did you know I returned to the detention centre?'

'Someone in the camp told me. One of the men I shared my hut with ...'

He opened the car door, leaning across himself with his right hand. Then he swung his legs out and, gripping the top of the windscreen, hoisted himself up, his stump of left arm pressing through the blazer sleeve on to the back of the passenger seat.

'You got over the *nyoka* okay,' Brian observed.

He had not used a Swahili word for so long: uttering one again, in the presence of Nchembe, he realized how many years had passed them both by since the day of the snake bite.

'I was ill for several days. An old man – the camp *mzee* – gave me some medicine but, in retrospect, I doubt it did any good. It was you who had done that, Brian.'

Nchembe walked around an Austin A40 so that the car separated him from Brian.

'I wonder ...' he said.

'Wonder what?' Brian asked.

'If that is the first time I have ever addressed you by your name. I would say in the camp I always called you *Bwana*.'

Brian laughed. 'You called me both Brian and *Bwana*. I remember that clearly.' As Nchembe regained his side, Brian struggled to recall smaller details of their meetings in Wamumu. 'And don't you do otherwise.' He laughed again, adding, 'Call me Brian – as opposed to the other!'

'I shall, friend,' the African responded.

221

Nchembe sat on a bench by the river bank. In front of the pub, water splashed over the weir, several swans and a multitude of ducks riding the rough waves below the terrace, begging for crusts from lunchtime sandwiches or the shaken crumbs from packets of potato crisps. Brian went in to the crowded bar, reappearing after ten minutes with a tray upon which were two rounds of beef sandwiches and two pints of bitter.

'I hope you like this.' Brian slid the tray on to a table in front of the bench, thrusting aside half a dozen empty glasses. 'It's English beer. A bit of an acquired taste.'

Nchembe turned back from the river. His loose sleeve had come out of the blazer pocket and he deftly thrust it back in without twisting it.

'Do you know,' he said, 'I have a scar on my ankle? Whenever I have tended my feet, or put on my shoes or socks, I have seen it and been reminded of you. And your bravery. Do you realize, if you had had a bad tooth or a sore gum, the poison from the puff adder might have entered into your bloodstream and killed you?'

On the instant, that fateful afternoon flooded back into Brian's mind. He could see the wide, dusty game path, the round footprints of elephants overscored with the small, pointed hoof-marks of antelope. He could smell the dry bush, the lantana, the earth itself where the wind was spiralling it into dust devils. He could hear the distant grunt of a lion and then Nchembe's scream of horror and terror.

'It was a risk. Not that I gave it a thought at the time – mind you, I did afterwards. At the time, I acted by instinct.'

'My instinct,' Nchembe admitted, 'was to die that day. It is the way with Africans who know no better. For the African, all snakes are poisonous.'

Brian raised his glass of bitter.

'Now, try a different kind of poison. And have a sandwich.'

Nchembe lifted his own glass of bitter and drank deeply from it. Brian had held his glass in one hand and a sandwich in the other, but realising Nchembe could not do likewise, he lowered his glass and made a mental note not to be so tactless again.

222

'Like it?' Brian enquired, noticing his companion had drunk a quarter of the beer.

'Of course. But this is not the first time I've drunk bitter. I've become quite accustomed to it. And beef sammies with Colman's mustard are not a new experience either.' He picked one up and ate half of it before continuing. 'I'm not recently arrived in England, you know.'

'How stupid of me! I assumed you were new somehow. How long have you been here? In fact, tell me the whole story of life after Wamumu.'

'All of it?' Nchembe asked.

'All!' Brian nodded. 'It's two hours to closing time.'

'There is not much to tell. When I was released I went back to my mother's *shamba* at Rumuruti. She was not there. I was told she had moved to Mweiga where she was working as a servant of an Afrikaner farmer. I went there but she had been dismissed – I do not know why as no one would tell me, but I suspect because the farmer discovered I was a detainee – so I went back to Rumuruti. I was then told she was in Nakuru. In Nakuru I was told she had been killed in a road accident.'

'I am sorry.' Brian was aware how shallow his sympathy must seem.

'It does not matter. Anyway, I then went to Nairobi and – well, I joined the KAU, the Kenya African Union. You know of it?'

'Yes. One of the main political parties fighting for *uhuru*.'

Nchembe helped himself to another of the sandwiches. The beef was rare and smoky flavoured, the mustard harsh.

'I worked as a clerk for a government office,' he went on, 'then for the post office and then for the railway. Then for the Union. They gave me more education as well as work and, just before *uhuru*, I was sent to university.'

'In Kenya?'

'No. I was sent to university in Leningrad. For three years. When I left there, I was awarded a degree in law. So now I am a lawyer.'

A young girl with hair to her waist, dressed in a mini-skirt and T-shirt, came out of the bar and started to collect the empty glasses from the table.

223

'Excuse me, miss,' Nchembe addressed her. 'Could we have two more pints of ... What was it, Brian?'

'Worthington,' he answered.

'Worthington,' Nchembe ordered.

The girl smiled acceptance of the order and added, 'Do you want any more sandwiches?'

'Can you do two ploughman's?' Nchembe enquired.

She said she could.

'Then two, please, without pickled onions. That okay for you, Brian?'

'Fine. Thanks.' He reached for his wallet.

'No, no!' Nchembe exclaimed. 'My shout...'

When the girl had gone, taking the clutter of empty glasses with her, Brian said admiringly, 'You've certainly learnt some English ways since you've been here. Not to mention the idiom! How long's that been?'

'Just since last September. This time ...' Brian was about to ask how often Nchembe had travelled to Britain, but the African continued, 'I'm at Magdalen, doing post-graduate work – international law. I'm here on a Commonwealth scholarship. There's a quota system, I believe, and I'm part of the Kenyan allowance.'

The girl returned with another tray carrying two pints of bitter and two plates of cheese, tomatoes, cress, large hunks of bread, a pot of butter and a bowl of pickle. Nchembe handed her a five-pound note.

'I'm really very fortunate,' he said, 'as I receive a generous grant for my studies and I saved money when I was working.'

'It could not have been easy. Clerks don't get paid kings' ransoms in Nairobi.'

'Indeed, they do not. But I was able to keep most of my money because I lived in Bahati. It was not good, to be truthful. In fact, Wamumu was more comfortable. I shared a room in one house with four other men. It was a ghetto, really. The P W D housing the British had put up was of poor quality and very over-crowded. After that, so as to save more, I built myself a shack on the outskirts of Nairobi, beyond Bahati, between the railway line to Thika and Eastleigh Aerodrome. The Nairobi River runs through there. It smelled badly even in the cold weather. But I saved much and,' he grinned broadly, 'in Russia there is not much to spend your money on.'

'You were lucky you did not have your money stolen in Bahati,' Brian commented. The place was a semi-slum of African buildings, a no-go area for the police and the army unless in strength. The police station on Ngiya Road was one of the best protected in the capital.

'I had my money invested. Not in a bank,' Nchembe added enigmatically. 'And, because I was from the forests, even though I was not with Dedan Kimathi or General China, people respected me. Perhaps because of this, too.' He wiggled his left shoulder.

The clientele of the Trout Inn was thinning. It was nearing one o'clock and those who were to return to their families or their colleges for lunch were departing in cars, on motorbikes or bicycles. Within fifteen minutes, more than half of the customers had left.

'Brian, may I ask you to break the bread for me?' Nchembe requested. 'It is the drawback of ploughman's lunches for the likes of me.'

As Brian picked up one of the knives from the tray, Nchembe said, 'Don't bother with the knife. The crust is always hard and knives in restaurants are always blunt. Use your hands and just pull it into four pieces. After all, we are friends.'

They ate and drank in silence for some minutes. When he had consumed his bread and cheese, without butter but with a liberal smearing of pickle, Nchembe swept all the crumbs onto the paper napkin in his lap and shook them into the river. The flapping of the napkin at first alarmed the ducks but their fear evaporated as soon as the morsels hit the surface.

'Now tell me of yourself, Brian,' Nchembe demanded, turning back to the table, draining the rest of his beer and starting on a third pint which the girl had delivered while they were eating. 'Do you go back to Kenya now the people have their own land?'

'No. I've not been back since I left school.'

'You should. Things are not so bad. Many of the

Europeans were afraid that Kenya would be like the Belgian Congo, with many whites murdered, their homes and businesses plundered or nationalized. But this was never the case. Our leader, Jomo Kenyatta, would not allow it.

'There was talk, I know, of Africans having all the Europeans' possessions after *uhuru*. Some evil men started to spread rumours that this farm would be up for grabs, or that farm, that Africans would own the Europeans' cars, homes, wives even. But it was all nonsense. No one with any intelligence regarded the rumours and they were quickly put down.'

'I've nothing to go back for,' Brian explained. 'My parents are now dead...'

Nchembe did not offer his condolences as Brian had done earlier. Instead, he smiled broadly and said, 'That is good. Now we are even more equal. Both of us are orphans and we have no ties. We are the free agents who can work for the world. What have you been doing in England, Brian?'

'I came to Oxford after leaving The Duke of York School...'

'Now it is Lenana School,' Nchembe interrupted.

'And studied agricultural sciences – agronomy, agricultural economy, a bit of bio-chemistry, that sort of thing. I got a First, much to my amazement, and went to work for a company making fertilizers and farm chemicals. After a while, I left them and went abroad – to India. Then back here. Not very exciting.'

'What are you doing now? Does it interest you? Is it important? Will it be of use to the world?' Nchembe quizzed him.

'I'm studying edaphology.'

'What in God's name is that?'

'The study of soil, basically.'

'And what are you studying it for?'

'Because it interests me.'

Nchembe was quiet for a moment, then said, 'Do you never think of East Africa, Brian?'

'Yes,' he replied. 'I think of it. And, from time to time, I

226

have remembered you and wondered what became of you. Now – since this morning's massive surprise – I know.'

'I mean, do you never think of East Africa, the land? Not your life there?'

'Again, yes. My thesis relates to East Africa amongst other places. It's about soil erosion and destruction in the tropics.'

'What kind of destruction?'

'All kinds: over-grazing by goats, centralization of water supplies and therefore population concentrations, problems of nomadic communities, deforestation, leaching of soils, desertification. Every aspect of soil degradation.'

Nchembe banged the stump of his arm down on the table, the loose sleeve flapping below the amputation. The glasses rattled and some sparrows, foraging beneath the table, took to the wing, chirruping with annoyance.

'What you write could be of great importance to Kenya,' he exclaimed in an excited voice.

'If anyone reads it,' Brian replied ironically. 'It's a thesis, not a book commissioned by a publisher.'

'What you write will reach the eyes of authority,' Nchembe declared. 'I shall ensure it. Then you must return to Kenya and implement your ideas.'

'I couldn't —' Brian began but Nchembe cut him short.

'Of course you could! There is a place in Kenya for the European. We have not nationalized your farms or businesses,' he winked, his cheek creasing, 'nor your wives and bicycles. We welcome you staying on, sharing in the prosperity of the country. Making it grow, alongside the Africans. We are a team of people working together to bring about political and social harmony and well-being. You would be welcome ...'

'It's not that,' Brian interjected.

'Then what?'

'I don't know. I've no firm plans yet. Some ideas, but ... First things first: I want to write the thesis and get my D.Sc. Then, maybe, I could continue to research here. Or at another university. Get a fellowship at my college – St Peter's. They would view my application kindly, I'm sure.'

'Lock yourself away!' Nchembe exploded, his stump arm

banging once more on the table. 'What good can that do? What use is research if it is never applied?'

'It will be applied ...'

'By whom? A company taking advantage of your learning to make money out of the Third World – if the governments can afford it.'

'That's unfair!' Brian responded, anger rising in him at Nchembe's implied criticism. 'Nothing can advance without research and to suggest it will subsequently be used merely to line pockets is unjust. Someone – something – must finance any research and a modicum of profit must be made to cover the initial outlay. But after that ...' He searched for an example. 'Take penicillin. That's sold to Third World countries at a very low price. Smallpox vaccine, prophylactics for malaria, fertilizers – they are often given away in foreign aid. The companies manufacturing it might be making a profit from it, but from the donor, not the Third World countries.'

Nchembe drank from his glass of beer. Before he replied, he wiped the froth from his lips.

'You cannot believe that, Brian. Think! If Britain, for example, gives a thousand pounds to Kenya in aid, and the aid takes the form of – for the sake of argument – smallpox vaccine, and the pharmaceutical company charges a full profit-margin price to Britain, the result is that although Kenya might get all the vaccine it needs, the value in real terms is reduced. If the vaccine was sold at *cost* price, there would be a balance left over which could go into education, or other medicines, or other aid.'

The customers having mostly drifted away from the pub, there was less food being thrown to the ducks. In order to make up for the deficiency, five ducks and a drake had flown off the river and onto the pub terrace where they were scavenging under the tables and benches, eating crumbs and spilt crisps, competing with the sparrows for every morsel.

'Companies steal from the mouths of the poor,' Nchembe said. 'Just as that pretty barmaid's broom will soon sweep up the crumbs from the tables so the ducks cannot get them. Apart from what it can grow for itself, make for itself, Africa is like those ducks – it survives only on what the rich countries in the industrialized world give it – but the aid is not surplus like those crumbs, it is simply a means of increasing profit. Or dumping sub-standard goods ... It is colonialism at second hand.'

'It sounds to me as if you are displaying your Russian education,' Brian answered, noticing as he did so a small enamelled badge shaped like a flag pinned on Nchembe's lapel. It was so tiny the colours merged into each other. 'And that badge,' he pointed to it, 'looks like a Communist Party badge. Are you a member?'

'No. That is ... a club badge.'

'What club?'

'Just one for students. Like the Christian Union or CND or Oxfam. The usual sort of thing one gets tied up with as a fresher,' he explained convincingly. 'It is nothing. But, tell me, as we speak of parties and politics – are you a Tory, Brian?'

He laughed dismissively and said, 'Not a chance!'

'Then you are a socialist?'

'I vote Labour,' Brian informed Nchembe. 'That is the way to look after the masses but within a capitalist society. There is nothing wrong with making profits so long as the benefits are shared, if not equally, then at least fairly. The strong must look after the weak. Isn't that often the way in much of nature? In the higher animals?'

'Yes,' Nchembe agreed. 'The baboons look after their young, elephants will stay with a dying member of their clan; but the human is a selfish animal.'

As Nchembe had foreseen, the barmaid came out on to the terrace with a tray, a dustpan and brush. The tray was laden with empty glasses; then she proceeded to sweep the tables clean, but she did not cast the crumbs on to the ground. Instead, she collected them in her dustpan and emptied them onto the tray where they fell into the dregs of drink in the glasses.

'Sometimes, even the waste is not given away,' Nchembe observed.

'I am sure,' Brian said, returning to the earlier theme of

their conversation, 'my work will be applied. In the long run. My thesis will form part of the corpus of learning about soils, about understanding the management of the earth.'

'You were disparaging just now,' Nchembe retorted. 'You said, "If anyone reads it." Make up your mind, Brian. Either your work will be utilized or it will be ignored – and something which might save Africa will exist but be hidden in the libraries of Oxford. Then, a thousand years from now, when Africa is a desert or covered in concrete, some scholarly man, digging into the musty, leather-bound volumes of the Duke Humphrey's Library, will discover your work and be able to say, "If only someone had read this ..."'

Brian drank the remaining beer in his glass: as he did so, he could hear the landlord calling for last orders.

'A quick one?' Brian offered, hoping to draw the conversation away from the direction it had taken. He had been looking forward to talking about their Kenyan days, not being drawn into a political argument.

'Yes, I'll get them,' Nchembe said, standing. 'Will you have the same again?'

As he walked into the pub, Brian wondered how Nchembe would manage to bring two glasses of beer out with only one hand. He thought of going to help him but decided against it. He was peeved at Nchembe's insistence he get out of Oxford and do something. As if he was not doing anything now. He was. His thesis was paving the way for more research – by himself or others – which would, in the long term, form a body of knowledge to be used and not necessarily merely to make profits for multi-national corporations. What his studies were unfolding was a pattern of soil destruction and, although in his heart he wondered if his thesis would ever be regarded by other than fellow workers in the same discipline, he believed he was doing good.

The barmaid held the pub door open for Nchembe who returned to the table carrying two glass tankards of beer, both the handles grasped in his one hand. As he placed them on the table, Brian could see how taut the sinews were between his fingers and recalled, as they relaxed, how the same fingers had flexed around the razor which skinned his leopard.

'I am sorry,' Nchembe apologized. 'I did not want to bring our discussion to such serious matters.'

'It doesn't matter,' Brian said, inwardly relaxing. 'I understand.'

'I hope so,' Nchembe answered. 'But also I hope you will reconsider. Africa needs experts. Like you and me. I am needed to bring law and justice to injustice. You are needed because you can save the land. We all must earn our right to live and I hope to do this when I am qualified further. And you?'

'I hope to, also.'

'Let's drink to that.' Nchembe raised his tankard, spilling a little of the beer. 'To us, who must create stability and wealth and earn our share of it.'

'To us,' Brian echoed.

Neither of them spoke for a few moments, then Nchembe asked, 'Do you still have the leopard's tooth?'

Brian ran a finger around inside his collar and pulled on his gold chain. The tooth, set in a mounting of rose gold, had stopped on the clasp and he had to work it round from the side of his neck. He lifted it out, over the top of the shirt. Nchembe grinned with pleasure.

'And yours?'

Nchembe opened the space between the buttons on his shirt: between his thumb and index finger, hanging from a silver chain against the black skin of his chest, was another canine tooth.

'Through all of the years, I have kept this, to remind me of the man who saved my life.'

'And the scar.'

'Yes! And the scar.'

He brushed some crumbs from their sandwiches on to the ground. A sparrow flew deftly under the table, picked up the largest and sped off with it to the branches of a willow overhanging the river.

'What are your studies involving, Matthew?' Brian asked. As he did so, he realized it was the first time he had used Nchembe's given name. Or, he thought, taken name.

'They are complicated,' he said, as if not wishing to go into

231

them. 'I am studying – I suppose it is best summed up as legal equality.'

'What does it cover? It seems pretty vague.'

'Well, the theories of equality. As they are viewed by the law. I believe the only way for Africa to be free is for every man to have the right to vote – that equality of opportunity be legally constituted.'

'You don't believe all men are equal, do you?' Brian replied, a hint of disbelief in his voice. No one, he believed, could be so naive.

'No. Of course not. Some are not as clever, some are too devious, or too lazy, or too ignorant, or too bigoted, or not as well endowed,' he lifted his stump, the sleeve hanging over the blunt end, 'as others. But they must all have the opportunity to achieve their potential. This is the only way they can gain their dignity, the only means by which they can justify themselves. This is the only way for them to understand justice, to have a chance at it, to know they live in a system which allows them to do their best. That is the only way to combat violence ...'

'Are you still against violence?' Brian asked.

'Of course! But not merely the use of the gun and the *panga*, but also the violence against the soul. The corruption and crushing of hope is greater than the destruction of the flesh. That is why I am a lawyer. I want to stop this kind of violence. I have already renounced the tenets of the bullet.' He laughed. 'I sound like a biblical prophet. Like one of the fathers in the mission school ...'

His voice faded and Brian could see he was remembering his schooldays, before he took the oath and thrust his penis into dead flesh and drank the blood of a murdered man.

'Maybe you are,' Brian remarked, 'but of the bible of peace rather than the holy one.'

'Maybe ...'

A cloud moved across the sun and the breeze blowing from the river was immediately chilly. A papier-mâché beer-mat lifted from the terrace wall and sailed into the river, floating upside down. Several ducks – they had returned to the river after the sweeping up of the crumbs – swam rapidly across to it and one pecked at it tentatively, flicking it over. The badge of the brewery glimmered through the water as it sank.

'The children of the present are the masters of the future,' Nchembe said suddenly.

'How do you mean?'

'Those who are young now are later to be the leaders, the decision-makers, the men of power. Once we were young, when we met. Then we had dreams. Ideals.'

Brian nodded. The sun came out from behind the cloud and warmed them. It was as if talking about the days in Kenya heated the very air.

'What were your ideals when we first met?' Nchembe asked.

'To give freedom to the Africans.'

'How did you feel in Wamumu? When you entered the camp?'

'Apprehensive. Afraid, I suppose ...'

Nchembe interrupted. 'I mean, how did your conscience feel?'

'Oppressed, sorry, in a way ... It's hard to put into words.'

'When I first entered Wamumu I was in handcuffs,' Nchembe reminisced. 'I was in a van with five others and two guards. They were English soldiers, not askaris. There were no windows through which to see where we were going and I was afraid. Much had been done to me since I was captured – my life had been saved, but my arm cut off. I had been beaten and abused, insulted and violated. For many hours I was given no food and questioned endlessly about things I knew nothing of.

'Once in the camp, my fellow detainees – those who had been genuine Mau Mau: many were not really terrorists but just petty criminals or unfortunates who had been rounded up through their own stupidity or because to live in the camp was better than to live on the *shamba*s – they welcomed me. They knew I was a real Mau Mau, had fired a gun. I told no one of ...'

He paused and lowered his voice just as if he was still in the camp, still wary someone might overhear him and act on the information. Along the terrace sat two couples in their late

233

twenties – as he and Brian were – but they were listening intently to one of the two men telling what was, judging from the laughter greeting the punchline, a risqué joke.

'... Lari. Only you know that!'

'I have told no one,' Brian assured him.

'I knew you would not.' He went on, 'I was seen as a sort of hero but my fellow ex-Mau Mau became a little cool towards me when I started to explain my ideas. Yet they were afraid of me because I was a real fighter, from the forest. They respected me but were scared.

'But I am digressing from my point and that is not the way for an international lawyer! How did you feel towards the Africans in Wamumu?'

'I felt sorry for them. I wanted to help them in some way. It was like – it was like going into a hospital and seeing sick people and wishing you had it in your power to cure them.'

'Exactly!' Nchembe exploded. 'You wanted to help. Do you not want to help them now? What has happened to change your mind? To alter your opinions?'

'Nothing ...' Brian started to say.

'Nothing! That is it! Nothing! Nothing at all! And that is why you must return to Africa – to Kenya, which you know – and share your knowledge to free the people. Much as you would have liked to free the detainees – and you took me out for one day, which I shall never forget – so now you can free the people. From the ruination of their land through ignorance, from starvation, from poverty. Believe me, in twenty years, Africa will be starving. What you see now in small areas will be widespread.'

Nchembe held his hand out over the table.

'Take my hand,' he said.

Brian went to shake it but Nchembe grasped it at an angle, clasping his fingers tightly. It was the grip of two men about to arm-wrestle. Yet the African did not push to one side or the other but raised their hands between their faces. Automatically, Brian's fingers also clenched.

'You see! Brothers!' Matthew declared. 'Under the skin, all flesh is red.' He released Brian's hand. 'Think about what I am saying. Think of coming back to Africa.'

'I'll think about it,' Brian promised, smiling.

Yet Nchembe was not smiling in return. His face was set and earnest.

'Parson's Pleasure is downstream.'

As Brian spoke, a slight breeze came off the right bank gently to buffet their punt.

'You'd make an excellent guide to Oxford,' remarked Angela without turning her head. 'If they fail your thesis you could start a tour company and be rich.'

'There's little chance of that.' Lucy opened her eyes and squinted against the sun. 'Theses are seldom failed. Never, even. It's not like finals ...'

'When I was a second-year,' Brian confided, 'I actually worked as a tour guide one long vac. It was awful. I did not only Oxford but Stratford as well. And Blenheim. The tips were all right, but the tourists ...' He looked up to the sky in mock exasperation. 'The Germans were the worst. And the Americans wanted to keep stopping to photograph every-thing. It threw the coach timetable to blazes.'

The summer sun was hot and both girls had unbuttoned their blouses to the waist, though keeping the two halves across their bodies. They both wore jeans, were barefoot; Angela balanced on her head a boater with a college ribbon glued around the crown. Nchembe was dressed in grey flannels with a light blue shirt, Brian in faded, flared jeans and a T-shirt upon which Lucy had printed the design of the underside of a mushroom in red and blue. It was a trendy design – magic mushrooms and L S D were in.

'That T-shirt looks good on you.'

She complimented herself as much as she did Brian. A number of her friends, including Angela, had asked for a copy or a similar garment in different colours. Fluorescent inks were available in a few of the London art shops or more locally – if one knew whom to approach – from certain undergraduate members of the chemistry faculty.

'I like it.'

In either direction along the river Cherwell, there were other punts, most of them separated by twenty or thirty yards of water. Almost all were heading upstream at a leisurely rate. Between them wove ducks. Every so often, the surface of the river was disturbed by a rising fish, the circle of ripples expanding from the broken water, competing with the low wakes of the punts to be the first to rock the lily pads and marginal plants. In against the reedy banks scurried moorhens; water voles streaked along their muddy tracks; frogs plopped into the water at the approach of a bird or human voices.

No one spoke loudly. It was not the way of the river in Oxford. This was no watercourse for sport, jollity, holiday revelry. It was a peaceful channel of muted discussion and friendly, nonsensical talk. This was the quiet river, away from the scullers and eights, the river of lovers and friends, amicability and relaxation.

Brian's bare feet shifted on the flat stern deck of the punt. He swung the long pole behind the square stern and ran it upwards through his hands, water pouring off it and down his arms to the elbows where it dripped off to splash at his ankles. He dropped the pole into the water and thrust down, letting it slide through his hands as the punt moved forwards.

Nchembe half twisted his head to look up at Brian. He and Angela were facing forwards with their backs to him: it was Lucy, alone in the bow seat, who was looking at him in silhouette against the sky.

'What about Parson's Pleasure, Brian?'

'It's a beach or bank on the river. I've not been that way since I was a fresher. In the old days, before God and the Church had invented bathrooms, the dons used to go there to wash, swim, relax ... Or so rumour has it. I don't think they do it now. The idea was that they could bathe naked there. It's given rise to a lot of apocryphal stories ...'

'Tell us one!' Angela demanded. 'If you tell a good one you'll get a good tip at the end of the tour. Better than you got from all those tourists.'

Brian ducked a bough of willow. They were approaching a

right-hand bend in the river and the trees were growing nearer together in the strait leading up to the corner.

'Well ...' he began. 'If you're all sitting comfortably, I'll commence. Parson's Pleasure's one of the stretches of river where women are not allowed to pass. If you have a member of the fair sex in your punt, you are obliged to drop her off at a certain point – I seem to recall there used to be a jetty-like structure there, all rotting and swaying. Anyway, you drop the ladies off and carry on past the bathing spot. The girls walk round a wood and rejoin you downstream where there was another jetty affair.'

He knelt on the punt deck as a particularly low branch loomed closer, the leaves brushing his face, a fine hail of twigs falling on his back.

'One day, a punt-load of undergraduates, either out of devilment or ignorance, did not allow their ladies to disembark but poled on by the spot where a large number of dons were marking essays, starkers. Imagine the scene!'

He was about to embroider the narrative when another punt drew level with his own. It was occupied by five youths who were travelling as fast as they could. The punter at the back was working his pole with a clumsy haste and the wake they made rocked Brian's craft gently in towards the willows.

'Cheers, mate!' one of the occupants shouted sarcastically. 'Make way for the motorway punt.'

'Get on with the story, my man!' Angela insisted. 'No gripping yarn, no grateful gratuity.'

'Imagine the scene,' Brian repeated. 'Piles of essays, opened textbooks white to the sun, bottles of claret wedged into the grass tussocks, goblets of wine balanced on tomes ...

'Ghastly white bodies without academic gowns spread-eagled on the sward,' Lucy interrupted.

'That sort of thing. Anyway, one of the dons – it was one of those glorious thirties summers when the sun never set – who will remain nameless as he's still about the city of spires – in spirit if not in body – was a noted homosexual. And thereby hangs the crux – the crutch – of my tale. All the dons see the girls. Pandemonium! Grabbing of copies of *The Times*, *Manchester Guardian*, *News of the World*, essays, chapters of thesis and dissertation. Papers – some brilliant academic treatises, I'm told,' Brian was warming to the telling, 'were thrust over the genitalia of the aristocracy of international academia. Pressed against the finest classical groin in Oxford was an interpretation of the Odes of Horace, possibly a paper on the Pubic – sorry! Punic – Wars; over the privates of the professor of Politics, Philosophy and Economics went a fundamental – perhaps one might say seminal – assessment of the causes of the Great War. But not our noted queer gentleman don! He grabs a copy of a fellow Fellow's newspaper and thrusts it down over his head. Asked later about this display of eccentricity and sheer exhibitionism he explains that it was the most sensible action for him to take as his face was the only part of his anatomy by which ladies might know him.'

Angela's single hoot of laughter echoed briefly from the right bank where there were no willows leaning over the river. It briefly broke the peacefulness of the river, alarming a moorhen which thrashed through the reeds. Lucy laughed lightly, less brashly, and Ncheme chuckled in a deep-throated manner.

'You have earned your tip, Brian,' Angela decided. 'Punt on, good charioteer!'

As the punt turned the bend in the river, the breeze caught it again and Brian had to work the pole hard to keep the vessel on course.

Not only had he to propel it against the wind, maintaining the forward momentum, but he also had to steer by hanging the pole to one side or the other of the stern, at various angles to the hull of the punt. The pole, over twelve feet long and six inches in circumference, and soaking wet, was so heavy the effort took away his speech.

'At least the breeze's warm,' Lucy called to him and he bobbed his head in agreement.

She would have preferred Brian to be sitting next to her in the prow of the punt. Then she could rest her head against him, slip lower in the seat, lie her hand on his thigh and squeeze his skin gently through the denim of his jeans. Her other hand she would trail in the water, flicking it at his face

239

when his eyes were shut. Small fish – if the punt slowed – would rise to nibble her fingertips, and ducks would paddle in to see if she held bread to the surface. That, she considered, was the traditional way in which to take to the river.

But Nchembe could not punt one-handed and Dash had opted out of joining them, deciding instead to meet them at their destination, reaching it on his motorbike with his latest girlfriend balancing on the pillion, her arms clinging around his waist and her fingers tucked in behind the wide, brass buckle of his belt. A Harley-Davidson, he declared insistently whenever an afternoon's punting was proposed, was the way a real man travelled with broads.

A left-hand bend soon followed the right-hand one but, once through this meandering chicane of slow currents and past a swan's nest tucked safely onto a bed of reeds, the Cherwell straightened again, running parallel to a track across the fields, one of the many country walks around Oxford, the footpath from Marston to Sunnymead.

'What time is it?' Brian enquired.

Nchembe wriggled his wrist out of his shirt sleeve. His watch caught on the inside of his cuff. Angela worked it free for him.

'Twelve-fifteen.'

'Great!' he exclaimed. 'Perfect timing. Another ten minutes…'

Ahead of them appeared a knot of punts. There was distant shouting and calling, the occasional laugh and the dull clunking noise of punt hull against hull.

'Traffic jam?' Nchembe guessed.

'Parking space,' Brian replied. 'That's the Vicky Arms!' He held the punt pole vertically to act as a brake, moving it from side to side to keep the craft in the centre of the river and on a straight course. 'Time to get dressed, ladies!'

The Victoria Arms, a public house set in fields half-way between Marston and Summertown but on the Marston bank, was a favourite destination for punters. It was ideally situated and student rumour had it that the building had been so sited in the days of the rising popularity of punting – at the height of Queen Victoria's reign – to be at just the right spot for refreshment. Before this, the punters would not be thirsty; beyond, they would be too tired to continue and would turn around to drift down the way they had come, riding with the current. Even being upstream of the town was wise – those with a few drinks in them would have the gentle current to carry them home.

The jam of punts began to sort itself out as Brian drew his slowly nearer. The chaos had been caused by the five speedsters who, not knowing the etiquette of the river, had first of all barged into the queue of those waiting to run against the shore, and then attempted to dock their craft bow-on to the bank. It was the custom to leave a punt lying alongside, held in place by the pole thrust into the mud amidships. Subsequent arrivals would moor alongside the other punts until three or four lay abreast. At the Vicky Arms, there was some competition for bank space as the pub had only some eighty feet of suitable shoreline. If one had to pull in short, a jump was required to make it safely to the meadow.

Much jostling and reprimanding forced the five youths to comply with the unwritten laws of punting and, by the time Brian nudged his punt against two others, the arguments were over and most of the protagonists had walked up the sloping field to the pub.

'Here we are,' Brian told Nchembe. 'Your first trip to this one. I had to take you somewhere for the first time.'

Brian pulled on his socks and shoes and they gingerly stepped over the other two punts and strolled to the pub. On the terrace above them, the tables were crowded and on the grass of the meadow there sat or lay groups of drinkers.

'My round,' Angela stated. 'My tip for Brian.'

'Let's have champagne,' Lucy suggested. 'And I bet they've got ...' she looked among the drinkers at the tables until her guess was confirmed, '... yes, they have! Strawbs! You two find a bit of smooth field with no thistles and we'll get the drinks.'

'Okay,' Brian acquiesced. 'Female liberation suits me fine. Come on, Matthew, we'll stake out our pitch on the field. The Vicky gets busy as hell on a day like this.'

To prove his point, six more punts arrived virtually

simultaneously and jockeyed for position. There was insufficient space for the last two which were obliged to moor by the rough bank. One of the passengers, a fat undergraduate carrying a thick book under his arm, misjudged his leap to the shore and fell into the muddy bed of reeds. His book flew ahead of him on to the meadow.

'Are you all right?' shouted one of his companions.

'Fine!' he bellowed. 'I'm just fine.' There was a sucking sound from the mud as he moved his feet. 'But is Polybius?'

His companion found the book and brushed it cursorily with his handkerchief.

'Bit of cowshit. Nothing that won't come off.'

This information was met with a groan of despair from the fat man and much laughter from his friends as they dragged him clear of the ooze.

'What are strawbs?' Nchembe asked as they found a satisfactory spot on which to sit, half-way to the river and near the hedge of hawthorn and hazel which ran from the pub to the riverbank.

'Strawberries. They're strawberries. You must know strawberries.'

Nchembe nodded.

'We grew them in our school *shamba*. A long, long time ago. The priests liked them with sugar.'

'And cream. You'll see.'

They sat in silence for a few minutes. Somewhere overhead, a lark was singing and Nchembe gazed upward, trying to see it.

'Blithe spirit,' Brian, Nchembe remarked. 'I'm not much of a one for poetry, but thinking of strawberries made me remember Father ... He used to read us English poetry. And Irish. Keats, Shelley, Byron, Yeats ... How utterly futile it was, I used to think. Teaching European poetry to African boys in the bush. For most of them, it was a waste of time. They should have been digging the *shamba* or learning to count. But for me, I see now, it meant something. Although I only understood it when I came here. Take that lark ...'

It had ceased its song. He scanned the sky until it began

again, somewhere over the tallest of the stands of hazel in the hedge.

'There it is!' Nchembe pointed to the bird. 'By the dent in the cloud hanging directly over the highest tree.' He started to recite the poem.

Hail to thee, blithe spirit!
Bird thou never wert,
That from heaven, or near it,
Pourest thy full heart
In profuse strains of unpremeditated art.

'I can't see it,' Brian said, but Nchembe ignored him.

'Shelley wrote it,' he said. 'Shelley was a socialist. His wife was a socialist, too. One of the first of the major free-thinkers ...' The lark stopped singing again and Nchembe lowered his face. 'The lark is like freedom. It is forever present, unseen but alive and beautiful. I like poems of freedom ...'

Brian made no comment. It seemed inappropriate to disturb his friend's thoughts.

'Hello, you two. Hi, Matt! How's it going?'

They turned to discover Dashiell standing behind them, a tray in his hands and a girl on his arm. She wore a black mini-skirt well above her knees and a cotton blouse with lace trim at her throat. Her black hair was trimmed to a pageboy cut and her eyes were lined with deep mauve.

'This is Debbie,' he introduced her. 'She works in the damn great fancy drugstore in Cornmarket.'

'Boots?' Brian queried.

'Yeah! That's the one. Say hi to Brian and Matthew.'

'Hi!' she whispered shyly. 'Nice to meet you. Can't shake hands, I'm afraid. Got them a bit full.'

She held an ice-bucket with two champagne bottles protruding from the top.

'Hello,' Nchembe said, rising to his feet, his loose left sleeve catching her attention. 'Shall I take that from you?'

His fingers gripped the side of the silver-plated bucket and lowered it to the ground.

243

'Girls're on their way. Waiting in line for the straw-berries.' Dash broke the word in two. 'I've got the rest.'

He shuffled Debbie's hand off his arm and bent over, handing the tray to Brian. On it stood six fluted glasses, two plates of lightly-buttered brown bread, the butter melting in the sunlight, a wadge of paper napkins and two one-pint beer tankards filled with crushed ice and prawns.

'Nothing like peeling prawns, downing champers and stuffing in the straw-berries afterwards.' He turned to Debbie. 'You like that?'

'I don't know, really,' she said. 'Never had prawns before.'

'Now's the time, then.' He surveyed the grass where Brian was sitting. 'Nip up to the bike, baby. It's next to the VW bug. Remember? Get the rug. It's in the pannier. Left one ...'

Obediently, she went off up the field towards the car park.

'Where did you meet her?' Brian asked.

'At a party someplace. Then I saw her in Boots.'

'Doesn't have a lot to say for herself,' Brian observed.

'You don't want them to talk, do you? Hell, but she's a hell of a goer, Brian. I tell ya ...'

'How old is she?' Brian asked.

'Sixteen.'

'She says ...'

Dash grinned.

'Sure she is! Or she's been reading for a doctorate in the Kamasutra ...'

Debbie returned with a tartan rug just as Angela and Lucy appeared across the field carrying six punnets of strawberries, a saucer of sugar and a small plastic pot of double cream.

They all sat around the edge of the rug, drank the champagne and peeled the prawns, eating them either by themselves or rolled into the bread and butter. As soon as they began on the prawns, Brian felt a twinge of embarrassment and sympathy run up his back; it was the sort of feeling he had when he saw a cripple in the street or a mentally handicapped child in a shop, holding on to its mother's hand in blind, primitive trust. Nchembe could not peel the prawns. Yet, no

244

sooner had they begun than Angela understood his problem and peeled a dozen for him before starting on her own.

The field was getting crowded. More punts had arrived, more vehicles had driven down the dusty lane from Marston. The terrace was packed with people. Conversation, laughter and the sounds of eating and drinking drifted over the meadow.

The champagne finished, Brian walked up to the bar to order another two bottles. He had to wait a quarter of an hour to get served. On his way back down the field, making his way through the crowds sitting or lying on the grass, he came upon the five youths who had raced by their punt to the Vicky Arms. They were sitting, not far from Dash, Nchembe and the girls, surrounded by empty beer mugs. As he passed them, one of them spoke.

'Three nice bits of fluff, them.'

He wondered if this had been said for his benefit: if it had not, the next sentence certainly was.

'That brown-haired bint's wasted on a coon.'

Brian ignored them. They were, he thought, the worse for wear from the bitter. Their come-uppance would come when they had to punt back down the river; punting when half-cut, as every undergraduate discovered sooner or later, was no easy task. He hoped they might sink the punt and lose the ten-pound deposit all hirers had to pay the owner.

As he pushed the champagne into the bucket, a loud voice said, 'Did yer watch "Till Death Do Us Part" the uvver night?'

'No,' came a drunken chorus.

'Ole Alf Garnett's got the right idea. He's talking to that long-haired son-in-law of 'is. On the telly. Says, "Proper blackies are th' ones born in th' jungles. Th' na'ives. Don't tell me they're educated. 'alf of 'em are still eatin' each uvver."'

'I think Enoch's is the bes' idea,' another voice blurted out. 'Send 'em all back to the jungles. Kick 'em out. We don't want a load of jungle bunnies over 'ere.'

A third voice said, 'Best thing the Yanks ever did. All them white blokes beating the shit out of niggers in Mississippi. Civil rights! Monkeys ain't got no rights.'

'Bastards!' Brian swore under his breath. He spoke through gritted teeth. 'Little bastards!'

'Leave it, man!' Dash pressed his hand on Brian's arm.

'It doesn't matter, Brian.' Nchembe held out his empty glass and looked pointedly at the ice bucket. 'If you were black like me, you'd learn to ignore it. They are ignorant.'

Lucy smiled at Brian and said, 'Don't bother with them. There's a whole field of hundreds of people and only five pricks. Open the champagne.'

Brian undid the wire and pressed the cork up with his thumb. It exploded free of the bottle, sailed into the air and was deftly caught by one of the fat student's friends.

'You're out,' he announced. 'Caught and bowled.'

Brian waved and called back, 'For a duck. Your innings.'

Joking with the students made him less antagonistic, less angry, but his rage was soon rekindled by a new comment from the youths.

'Ever heard of the one-armed bandit?'

Nchembe laughed quietly and so did the others except for Brian and Debbie. From the long-lost past, he could hear the same phrase being spoken by.... He sought to recall the inspector's name then got it – Broomhall – yet without such rancour and cruelty.

'I don't think that's nice,' Debbie declared. It was the first time she had spoken without being drawn. 'You shouldn't mock those less fortunate than yourself. I feel really ashamed ...'

Nchembe laughed again.

'There's no need. I am quite inured to such taunts and, for once, they don't know how near the truth they are.'

'Do you think he pays out?' mused one of the louts.

'What's "inured" mean?' Debbie asked Lucy, a puzzled look in her eyes.

'Used to it, accustomed to it.'

'Well, I don't think it's fair,' she said indignantly.

Getting to her feet, Debbie walked deliberately over to the youths. They fell silent, had not expected one of the girls to approach them. She stood over them, her arms akimbo and her lacquered hair unmoving in the summer breeze.

246

'Why don't you wankers shut your gobs!' she exploded. 'It's as obvious as the bollocks on a bulldog that you're all pissed. Which must be why you,' she pointed to the largest of the youths, 'are such a fucking great piss-artist!'

With that, she turned on her heel and marched back to the others.

Her sharp tongue and home truths had stung the youths. The injury to their pride was compounded by loud guffaws of laughter and a smattering of applause from a large number of the surrounding people.

Having lost so much face the youths left and headed for the punts.

'Wouldn't wan' yer sister to marry one, would yer?' observed the one who had been most put down by Debbie, passing close to her. She stuck her tongue out in response.

As they reached the water's edge, one of them yelled back, 'D'yer like 'is big black cock up yer, darling?'

They stumbled into their punt and cast off from the bank, having difficulty in turning the long craft around. It swayed to and fro but, to the disappointment of many of the onlookers, none of them fell over the side.

'I still don't think it's something to laugh at,' Debbie said as the youths set off down-river.

Now she had spoken she was no longer afraid, no longer shy in the company of people who were – as she believed – so much cleverer than she was.

'It was the irony of what they were saying,' Nchembe explained.

'What do you mean?' She was puzzled again.

'Have you ever heard of Mau Mau, Debbie?' Nchembe asked.

'No, not really.'

'The Mau Mau,' Brian interrupted, 'were a band of terrorists who fought against the British in Kenya about ten years ago and caused the British government to give Kenya its freedom. It's just that – well, Matthew here was one of those terrorists. So to say he was a one-armed bandit is rather funny.'

Debbie giggled, then her face became serious.

'Is that how you …' She was embarrassed to mention it. '… how you lost your arm? Was it shot off?'

'In a way,' Nchembe confirmed with a grin. 'I shot it off with my own gun.'

The look of incredulity upon her face made the African laugh all the more and he leaned over, resting on his right arm, and kissed Debbie's cheek.

'Now you can say you've been kissed by a terrorist.'

She blushed and they all laughed at and with her. Angela, taking Nchembe's hand in her own, tightened her fingers on his.

From the direction of the Vicky Arms came the sound of a bell. Some of the scattered groups of people began to stand.

'Time to go. All good things come to an end,' Brian said. 'Matthew and I'll get the punt out and you lot can do the rest.'

'Trust you to get the easier job!' Lucy chastised him but he reminded her then who was going to have to propel the punt back down the river.

Dash and Debbie left the car park in a roar of dust and ethylene vapour and, when Lucy and Angela had returned the tray, ice-bucket, empty bottles and crockery to the terrace, they walked to the river bank and settled themselves in the punt.

'I hope your day's not been ruined by those pigs,' Angela said to Nchembe. 'We all wanted it to be a new experience for you.'

'No. I'm not at all bothered,' Nchembe replied. 'Wherever you go there are racists. Even in Russia, where they are supposed to be more … I just accept it.'

'You're not knocking the good old U S S R, are you?' Brian spoke from the rear of the punt. 'The K G B'll be after you.'

'Not all systems are perfect, Brian,' Nchembe said philosophically. 'It's wisest to take the best out of them all and build it into your own.'

The current in the centre of the river was sluggish. Brian allowed the punt to drift, steering it with the pole. He did not have to provide any motive power until they reached the first bend.

Where the willow trees hung over the bank between the

two corners, he let the punt slide under them, halting it by the bank and tying the front ring to a projecting root by the short rope provided. He pushed the pole along the inside of the punt and slid down to sit next to Lucy, putting his arm around her. She rested her head on his shoulder.

'You need a shave.'

He made no reply.

'You also have a quick temper.'

'When it's aroused,' he concurred.

For an hour, they lay in the shade of the willows, watching the punts pass by, dozing, gazing up at the sun through the foliage and listening to the birds in the branches. Once, a water vole passed within two feet of the side of the punt. Keeping motionless, they watched it pause, preen its whiskers, then disappear behind the roots of the trees. Ducks occasionally inspected them but nothing else disturbed the quietude.

'We'd better be getting back,' Brian observed at length. 'I don't want to forfeit the deposit.'

He poled the punt out from under the willows, turned it downstream and set off at a good speed. It was easier now for the breeze, strengthening as the afternoon wore on, was behind him.

As they rounded a bend, a punt slid out of the reeds ahead of them. In it were the five youths.

'Trouble,' said Brian, quietly.

Nchembe and Angela, who were sitting in the bow seat facing backwards, looked over their shoulders.

'The paddle,' Brian said.

Nchembe's hand fastened on the four-foot-long paddle provided for each punt in case the punter accidentally dropped his pole.

The youths were not as vociferous as they had formerly been: an hour of waiting had silenced them, somewhat sobered them, sharpened their anger and hardened their resolve for revenge.

'Gonna teach you a fucking lesson, student,' one of them called as Brian braked the punt with the pole, dragging it on the bottom of the river.

'Where's the little tart with the big mouth?' enquired another.

With the aid of their paddle, the youths started to move their punt towards Brian's. He raised the pole from the water. It was too heavy and cumbersome to use as a weapon and the youths knew it.

'Thinks he's gonna pole us!' The ringleader snorted derisively. 'Not a monkey's chance! Hey, lads! Monkey's chance! Get it?'

Yet none of them laughed and Brian realised then that they were serious. He slid the pole for safekeeping along the gunwale and, as he did so, saw one of the duckboards was loose.

The punts met bow-on then began to slip alongside each other with a grinding of wood. Nchembe got to his haunches and, as one of the youths grasped the side of the punt, he smashed the blade of the paddle, side on, into his face. Brian leapt forwards, grabbed the length of boarding and swung it at the youth who was standing up, ready to cross from one punt to the other. The board missed him, but in avoiding it, the youth lost his balance, waved his arms about in a comical show of attempting to regain his equilibrium and fell forwards. The punts were drifting apart and he hit his shoulder and neck on the stern deck of Brian's punt and tumbled into the Cherwell.

Only one of the other three louts attempted anything. He hit at Nchembe with his own paddle, but Nchembe dodged it, dropped his paddle, reached over the increasing width of water between the punts, dragged the youth by his hair and then struck him on the back of his neck with his stump of arm. The youth howled. Nchembe let him go. He too fell into the water.

'Want to make anything more of it?' Brian shouted.

The two surviving youths made no response.

The stern of Brian's punt rocked. The lout he had missed was trying to climb in. Brian, standing now, got hold of the punt pole, withdrew it from under the seats and, using it like a lance, ran it at the youth. It struck him in the chest and he let go of the punt, slipping back into the water.

The fight had taken less than ninety seconds and Angela and Lucy had kept out of the way. Now, as the punts drifted apart, Lucy reached for the louts' punt pole which was projecting out of the rear of their craft. She grasped it firmly and tugged hard. It came free and she quickly ran it through her hands. The youths, dumbstruck by her action, made no move.

She stood up, the pole over her head.

'Give us that back,' one of the youths demanded weakly.

'Certainly,' she replied exultantly and hurled it downwards like a spear at the inside of the punt. There was a splintering of timber.

'Shit!' yelled one of the youths. 'You've holed it!'

'Goodbye deposit,' Lucy teased.

Brian gave his punt a long push down the river.

'Where did you learn to throw like that?' he asked, astounded at Lucy's success and strength. 'I've never found those biceps.'

'At school,' she replied. 'I held the javelin record for three years. And you don't need strength so much as balance.' She sat down at his feet, perching herself not in the seat but on the edge of the boards of the stern deck. 'More like poise, I'd say.'

Nchembe fell back in his seat, grinning broadly.

'Now my day is most definitely not ruined. Indeed, as the saying goes, it is made,' he declared with a noted degree of satisfied pleasure in his voice.

14

As the evening approached, the woods along the lane from the cottage gradually became steeped in the scent of late honeysuckle. In the shadows of the trees, a sudden warm breeze rustled the undergrowth, disturbing bees hovering over the campion in the verges and the last of the blackberry blossom. Already, under the shade of the thorned leaves, hard green fruits were swelling and the first one or two, where the branches had been brushed aside by a passing car or torn at by an inquisitive cow as it meandered towards the milking shed in West Milton, were beginning to blush from exposure to the sun.

Over the lane swung bats, their zigzag, crazy flight easily seen against the sky yet invisible against the trees. Over Swyre Hill, the sun had set, the sky a wash of delicate pinks and blues.

As they walked, they did not speak. Matthew Nchembe tickled at grass-heads with a stick he had picked up in the ash and beech copse they had passed near Loscombe. His attention was taken by the birdsong drifting over the fields, hidden in the coverts and woodland.

Brian was lost in his thoughts, glad to have moved into the cottage at last. For the first time ever, it seemed, he had a home, a place where he could sink roots and feel secure. Although he had lived for so many years in Kenya, and Africa was still deeply engraved on his mind and ran in his blood, he had never seen that country or continent as his home. Whatever he did had set him apart, reminded him he was a foreigner, an impermanent resident at best. The colour of his skin, the manner in which he spoke Swahili, the fact that every third year his parents and he had taken 'home leave' reinforced in him the feeling that Britain was his real place, his natural home on the planet.

Now, with the purchase of the cottage, he had a base to

which he could always return, which was not his grandparents' house, his uncle's flat, a rented apartment or suburban semi-detached on the outskirts of London. This property was his own, the deeds in his name, his name for the cottage on the gate, burned by a poker into an elm board left over from the repairing of the upstairs floor.

He had bought the cottage when it was nearly derelict. The previous owner had been Mr Hastings, a widower in his eighties, a fiercely independent old man who refused help from village neighbours. He did not collect his old age pension from the Post Office. He turned away the Meals-on-Wheels service with a curt – and some said somewhat crude – retort to the volunteer who drove the Morris van with its containers of stew and rhubarb-and-custard, and he grew as much of his own food as he could in the small, sloping garden behind the cottage. What he had as surplus he sold from a tray mounted on the rear of his decrepit bicycle, cycling over the rolling Dorset hills to Maiden Newton where he illegally set up his pitch outside the railway station. The policeman deliberately ignored him and he did a fair if seasonal trade. When the winter came and he was short of supplies, the postmaster gave him credit, subtracting what was due from the pension the old man refused, placing the balance in a Post Office savings account in the old man's name. It was, like his customer's vegetable selling, against the law but it was deemed best by the vicar, the social worker from Dorchester and those in the village who loved or hated but respected the old man.

When he died, he surprised all the villagers by leaving a will. There was not much in it. He left everything to another octogenarian in Askerswell, a widow whom he had known from childhood. Within three months, she too was dead and her sixty-year-old son, a garage proprietor in Wareham, sold off the old man's house. He had no use for a tumbledown cottage in which the previous occupant had existed in only two of the rooms. The man might have had a different view had he known the old man was his father.

Out of respect for the previous owner, Brian had named his

cottage Hastings House. It was a grand name for a tiny building.

As soon as he had signed the deeds and paid over the four hundred and twenty pounds purchase price, he commissioned a local builder to strip, renovate, repair and extend the cottage. The outside lavatory remained as a feature of the garden, but a new one was added at the end, above the extension to the scullery. The kitchen was enlarged, the original sixteenth-century fireplace restored with its seating round the hearth. An Aga stove was installed, the roof re-tiled, the stonework re-pointed, the plumbing re-piped and the wiring re-laid, the garden dug and terraced with stone walls. Over two months, the house was transformed. By the summer, Brian had what he wanted, although he did not move in until the end of the academic year. Now, like all the other students, he had a home to go to in the vacations. Nchembe, much to his delight, was his first weekend guest.

'What is that bird?' the African asked, breaking into Brian's thoughts.

'Which bird? I wasn't listening.'

They stood still for a minute. A blackbird shrilled through the hedgerow, dipping low over the road.

'Not that one. Wait a moment.'

From far over the fields where there had once been a castle floated a fluid tremble of birdsong.

'A nightingale,' Brian said. 'You usually hear them at night but they sing all the time. You can hear it now because many of the other birds are falling silent as darkness comes.'

To prove him wrong, a cock pheasant chirped loudly back along the way they had come, where the lane crossed the single track railway line.

'It is very beautiful music,' Nchembe said quietly. 'It reminds me of my home. I wonder if they have such birds in Kenya ...'

They walked on, again not speaking. It was enough for both of them to be together. Since they had met at Lucy's party, they had seen a good deal of each other, both in the company of the girls and about Oxford. They had met attending debates, had bumped into each other in the

Bodleian Library, had had lunch together and had gone to parties together. They had not, after their first river outing, gone punting again.

'You know, Brian,' Nchembe commented as they started to climb the hill towards the cottage, 'we have become very staunch friends.'

'Yes, we have.'

'Do you not think this is strange?'

'No, not at all,' Brian replied, puzzled. 'Why on earth should I?'

'We did not truly know one another before. In Kenya.'

'Didn't we?'

'I do not think so.'

'I always saw you as a friend ...' Brian began.

'But?' Nchembe answered, sensing something unspoken in Brian's words.

'Can I be frank, Matthew?'

'Of course. Friends cannot exist without being frank with each other.'

'Well ... Don't take this personally, will you?'

Nchembe shook his head and added, 'I do not take things personally. It is a good defence.'

He smiled and Brian had second thoughts about speaking. Nchembe sensed this, too.

'Don't worry,' he assured Brian. 'Just say it. Words are but words. They are not actions.'

'When we were in Kenya, I thought of you as my friend. My Mau Mau friend. My own terrorist. It was so unusual for someone like me to have an African friend – not to mention one from the forest. In a way, I regarded you as something very important. I didn't know why. I don't think I do now! But I saw you as special, a special friend. I thought we had a special relationship.'

They stepped onto the verge as a car approached them up the hill, one of its headlights broken. The gearbox ground and yammered against the steep gradient. Once it had passed and they were walking again, leaning forwards against the slope of the hill, Brian continued.

'When you skinned the leopard, I felt a friendship growing

255

in me. I don't know why. I know I should have hated you as you were a Mau Mau, but it didn't enter into it somehow. I was – like Victorian priests were with prostitutes – curious to understand terrorists and know them, see what they were like. I was curious about you. One knew of Micks – I mean, Mau Mau: that was the slang for them – but one never saw any. Except maybe the photos of Dedan Kimathi in the *East African Standard*. But he didn't count, somehow. There was so much propaganda blown up about him.'

They reached the cottage, Brian inserting his key into the polished brass lock on the kitchen door.

'So you were curious,' Nchembe mused. 'And how do you think I felt?'

'I can't imagine!'

'Like you in a way. Curious. You were our enemy. Or so it was supposed to be. But I never fired my gun at a European. Not until I was captured. Until you came into the camp at Wamumu, I had never really been near an ordinary white person.'

'Not one?'

'No. Except the interrogators and the fathers who were my teachers in Rumuruti.' He chuckled. 'And they were not exactly ordinary.'

'Is that why you agreed to skin the leopard?'

'Ndegwa thought I was crazy. Do you remember him?'

Brian turned on the electric kettle by the Aga stove, removing two mugs from hooks screwed into a beam running along the wall.

'I remember him. He fixed the *gari* with you ...'

'He hated you. You were the young oppressor, though he would not have been able to put it in so many words. You were simply an object of hatred for him. But to me you were a fascination. I wanted to see what you were like.'

'And I you,' Brian admitted.

The sky was bristling with early stars in the half-light as they went into the garden, side by side on one of the terrace walls. In the rockery behind, which Brian had laid the week before, newly planted alpines nestled among pieces of granite, sandstone and blue lias. On the terrace wall, Brian and Nchembe rested an oak biscuit barrel with a silver-plated lid which had once belonged to Brian's grandmother. A silver-plated shield on the side embossed with her initials. He removed the lid and put it on the stone wall, the metal ringing.

'They're digestives,' he indicated the barrel, 'chocolate on one side.'

'Like our hands,' Nchembe observed with a grin, helping himself to a biscuit. 'Tan on one side, black on the other.' He bit into it, crumbs scattering on his trousers. 'What are our plans for this evening?'

'Same as yesterday and the day before? Pub after a spot of food. Or ... I've an idea. There are badgers down in the valley.' Brian pointed with his coffee mug to the ash and elm copse surrounded by a dense hedge of hazel. 'We could try and see them. Fancy that? They'll be coming out soon. Their den's in the middle of the trees but there's a path through.'

'Do you remember honey badgers?' Nchembe asked.

'The ratel. *Mellivora capensis.* Been around since the Pleistocene. Burrows under the ground and smells like hell. I once watched one following a honey-guide bird showing it where there was a wild beehive. And a boy at school had one as a pet, but it could turn nasty very easily and, in the end, he let it go in the Kikuyu reserve. They are vicious little brutes ...'

'I had a friend in the forest,' Nchembe said by way of contrast, 'who had a coat made out of their skins. He smelt of the animal. We called him *Nyerege*. And he was vicious also ...'

An owl called briefly from the badgers' copse, its hoot cut short as if it was, in mid-call, alerted by a vole in a bank or a fledgeling floundering on the dead leaves of the wood, cast out of the nest and doomed. Brian, remembering honey badgers, found his mind returning to the night of the lion under the fly-sheet. Then there had been an owl in the acacia. Suddenly, he could hear it again and the Dorset twilight – for just an instant – took on the mystery of an African moonlit night.

'Kenya is a very beautiful country,' he remarked distantly.

'I sometimes dream of it, of the wild animals and brown grasslands.'

'Do you remember,' Nchembe gazed in the direction of Swyre Hill, the last of the sunlight reflecting off-white where the land touched the sky, 'how clouds looked before the rains? I have never forgotten that ...'

'You could see the rain coming, sometimes a day ahead. Even more,' Brian replied. 'Then, as the weather front drew nearer, the air cooled and a wind would start in the bushes or the tall grass. The trees would shiver. And in the sky there would be a huge bank of dark cloud ten thousand feet high, with a grey haze beneath it. And it would roll forwards like ...' he searched for a metaphor '... like dough being unfolded. It would stretch from horizon to horizon, like smoke, not rising but billowing horizontally.'

'And the birds would fall quiet and stop flying,' Nchembe continued. 'The snakes would come out of their holes in the ground or the low-lying places – or so the *mzee* would say – for they did not want to drown. And the butterflies would hide under the leaves. And the zebra would stamp their feet and all of the animals would wait. Then – do you remember? – the first drops ...'

Along the road across the valley drove a small car, its headlights picking out the hedgerows. As they watched, the bomb-shape of the owl dipped low through the beams and disappeared against the dark shadow of the hills. Brian let the sound of the car die before replying.

'Always huge. So huge! Where they hit the dust of the drive or the road, they cratered a hole two inches across, as if a stone rather than a liquid had landed there. And the blob of water would remain for a moment before being blotted up by the murram.'

'Then the downpour.'

'Yes, then the skies opened. Sometimes there would be lightning dancing in the encroaching billows, and muted thunder ...'

'In Africa,' Nchembe said, authoritatively, 'the thunder is not as it is in Britain. There it is *Ngai* himself calling to the land to be ready, and his voice is not terrible.'

'The rumble is lost in the vastness of the sky ...'

'Whereas here, thunder is dominating and threatening. Not kind. No wonder the Viking peoples who invaded your land called the thunder Thor, the god of war. For us, he is not so ...'

'It rained for days.' Brian emptied the dregs of his coffee into the alpines behind him. 'The black cotton soil so good for roses and strawberries – according to my mother who jealously nurtured our Nairobi garden – turned into a glutinous morass bogging down the cars and even the wheelbarrow. The red murram ran with water and the roads turned into rinks of mud ... The culverts overflowed. And then came the frogs.'

'*Chura*!' Nchembe exclaimed.

'And toads. Where they came from, God only knows! You seldom found them in the garden during the rest of the year. You never saw them in the waterholes in the Kikuyu reserve or, come to that, in the deep ditches down the sides of our garden. Yet as soon as the rains came and the lawn flooded there appeared hundreds of them. Hopping in the grass, diving into the ditch, swimming and bloating and snapping at flies and mosquitoes. And copulating. Every puddle was soon decorated by strands or globs of spawn. And the racket they made!'

Nchembe laughed and said, '*Chura* songs. All animals sing when they make love.'

'There was one species in particular,' Brian went on, 'which I could never identify – as soon as you tried to get near them, they stopped, like cicadas do – which made a sound like someone dropping a glass marble into a tin bucket. And there was another which sounded like a very loud cricket. And another like a child popping its finger in its mouth. They were endless. All night long.'

Brian rose to his feet, rubbing his behind with his hand.

'That stone's hard,' he observed.

'After the rain, though. What about then?' Nchembe got up and shook his legs. The stone had numbed him also.

'Then the bush turns green. And the *dongas* run with red earth.'

'Like blood.'

'Yes,' Brian agreed, 'like blood, the life of the land washing away.'

Nchembe laughed.

'Even in the long vac you can't escape from your thesis.'

'It's upstairs in my study, waiting for you to go.' He walked across the narrow lawn towards the kitchen door which was split like a stable entrance. 'Now for a drink – or the badgers first?'

'A drink,' Nchembe decided. 'Let the badgers alone in their world and we shall stay in ours.'

Under the bank, where the river turned in a lazy curve beneath a strand of willow, the water ran slower. The surface was broken by the trailing wands of the willow boughs reflected on it, the water being deepest there, and black. On the short bank opposite the willow was a reedbed and, projecting into it, a rickety wooden platform of split and rotting planks balancing upon posts rammed into the mud. In the reeds was the remains of a swan's nest, the edges smattered with guano, the centre decorated with flecks of bedraggled feather down.

Standing cautiously upon the platform, Brian was casting a Blue Dun upstream of the deep water, allowing the fly to drift on the current, working it out from the trailing willow branches as it neared them, avoiding snagging the bank.

For several days prior to Matthew Nchembe's arrival, he had noticed a trout rising beneath the trees. Some of the time it was coming up for flies lifting from the water, at others it was after small grubs falling from the branches overhead. Occasionally it ventured into the centre of the current or over towards the platform, seeking larvae coming downstream or out from the reedbed.

The afternoon had been still and hot but, as the sun began to lower, a small breeze had started to blow along the valley from the direction of Cerne Abbas. With the ripples on the water, the trout had begun to feed again.

At first, Brian had tried to tempt the fish with an Orange Governor, hoping the colour might attract it. It had ignored

260

the lure. Next, because there was a swarm of gnats hovering under the willows, he had cast with a Black Gnat and then a Black Butcher; again, he had no luck although the trout twice approached the latter but refused to bite. He also tried a Green Caterpillar and a Rusty Spinner. Eventually, noticing a small insect with whitish wings appearing in the reedbed, he knotted the Blue Dun to the leader and cast out. The fish instantly came at it, but swerved aside at the last moment.

As he fished, cast the line, played it, drew it in and re-cast, Brian thought of little. Fly fishing was for him a relaxation. He was not a serious fisherman, one for whom the art of the cast and the hunt was more important than the end result. For him, it was an opportunity to allow his mind to wander or go blank, a chance to watch the fish and riverine animal and bird-life. With good fortune too, it would culminate in trout and almonds with new potatoes back at the cottage.

When his thoughts did form, they centred upon his delight with his way of life, his pleasure at having acquired the cottage, the impending completion of his thesis. He fought against thinking over his academic work. Every so often, his mind turned to Nchembe who was fishing with a coarse rod three hundred yards upstream where the river was wide and sluggish.

He pitied his friend for not being able to fly fish – it was definitely a two-handed sport. Instead, for him, there was just the throwing out of a line with a hook baited with a maggot, the bale arm on the reel locked. He had nothing to do then but watch the float.

They had laughed as Brian had tackled up Nchembe's rod for him. The float was made of a porcupine quill with a painted fluorescent red tip and a tiny rubber band to hold the line in close above the lower ring, glued to the thicker end of the quill.

'If I had known of this,' Nchembe had joked, 'I would have spent my last months in the bush collecting spines from the ground. They are everywhere – cast off by their owners. You only need to look around a porcupine burrow ... I could have become a millionaire in fishing floats. I wonder,' he had then considered, 'why the Africans have never used a quill as a float. I've never seen them so used.'

Being with Nchembe resurrected memories Brian had long since forgotten. Everything Nchembe did or said he related back to Africa, to Kenya, to his childhood or his time in the Aberdare forests. Brian did not find this irksome – he enjoyed having his own nostalgia invoked – yet he often wondered if this perpetual series of comparisons was made with an ulterior motive.

Several times, as they sat drinking in the village pub, where Nchembe was accepted by the locals with much the same curiosity as might be afforded to a Martian – the only comment they heard clearly was from a local farmer called Dickson who stated to his exiguous wife and all who would listen, 'They bloomin' niggers! Oi'd not trust a one of they. And that one's bein' educated at some 'oity-toity uneevercity. Drive they out if Oi 'ad my way,' – or sitting in the cottage with a brandy, the hi-fi playing quietly in the corner, Nchembe had broached the subject of Brian returning to Kenya after his doctorate was granted, using his knowledge for the betterment of the African farming system, or the preservation of soil quality, or the teaching of agricultural methods and husbandry. So much expertise was so badly needed in East Africa, he repeatedly said. It did not exist among the locally-trained government officials, was non-existent in the bush where farming was subsistence agriculture at best. The country – no, he had insisted, the whole sub-Saharan continent – desperately needed vets, farm technicians, agronomists, experts in forestry and irrigation, water conservationists, game conservationists. It needed innovative thinkers, scientists with a vision of Africa having the rich future which was assuredly possible.

To all of this, Brian paid more than lip service. He was gradually coming round to agreeing with Nchembe.

He had planned for himself more of an academic career in Oxford than a practical one in the field. He was working in an expanding discipline. His learning and expertise would be increasingly in demand in the future. Starvation was already rife in Biafra and in India: someone was going to have to grow more food. And yet, as soon as he accepted this, he realized – or believed he realized – the problem had to be tackled at source. Firstly, before the food-growers could materialize, they would have to be educated, and that was where he saw his future.

The more Nchembe talked, however, the more Brian began to waver in his ideas. Perhaps, he was beginning to accept, it would be better for him to go back to Africa, to work in the field and gain practical experience. With this, he could then return and teach. In the meantime, he would have done some concrete good. And, he reasoned, he might learn a lot more back in the bush that was relevant and as yet undiscovered or unconsidered.

The Blue Dun had reached the end of the willows. Brian started to pull the line in, coiling it automatically on the unstable pier at his feet. Most of the line in, he recast upstream. The trout had continued to rise, on several occasions within a few feet of the fly, but after its initial engagement with the hook, had ignored it. Brian decided, if it made no pass at the fly in the next three casts, he would change the lure back to the Black Gnat. He was certain the fish was going for gnats now.

As he coaxed the Blue Dun past the willow, the trout took it. The rod tip bent and quivered. Brian struck, firmly but not harshly. The line went slack but he was not fooled and kept the tip high. Then it tautened as the trout raced for the bank. Brian let it have some line then curved the rod to the left, forcing the fish to turn. If it gained the haven of the bank, the line would soon be snagged in roots or weed.

The trout, annoyed at having been turned, swam upstream. Brian had to work his hand quickly to keep the line from slackening again. Then, once more, he turned the fish. For the first time, it broke the surface with a dull splash.

Until now, Brian had thought he was dealing with a fish of two pounds at the most. But, as it fell back below the surface, he realised it was much larger.

For ten minutes, he played the fish, steering it clear of the reedbed downstream and the roots of the willows, keeping it in the centre current, trying to exhaust it. Twice he thought he had succeeded but, each time, it veered away at the last moment, its spotted flank showing clearly in the water.

Finally, the fish succumbed and with only a few thrashings of fear or anger was safely in the landing net. Brian carried it to the bank, his feet slipping on the crumbling planking, where he killed it with his lead-cored priest. It required several severe blows to the head: the average trout took only one.

Holding the fish by a gaff through its gills, he reckoned it weighed just over four pounds. It would be more than sufficient for both of them.

His fishing tackle broken down, Brian walked upstream to where Nchembe had caught two perch which he had succeeded in dropping into his keep-net.

'That's a hell of a fish!' he congratulated Brian. 'I trust you don't want me to skin it? The penultimate time you went hunting and involved me, I wound up preparing the trophy. And the last time ...'

He shuddered.

'Only the adder's poisonous in Britain – and it's not a puff adder. The bite rarely kills. As for preparing the trophy, I'll oblige you.'

As they walked back to where the MG was parked Nchembe observed, in the distance, the chalk figure of the Cerne Abbas giant on the hillside.

'What is that? I saw it when we arrived.'

'It's a giant. The ancient Britons made it about two thousand years ago.'

'He seems particularly well – how shall I put it? – engenitalled.'

'He was a god, or so some say. Others believe it's a caricature of the Roman emperor. Whichever, they used to say if young wives went up to the giant by the full moon and sat on the end of his penis they would conceive.'

'What!' Nchembe roared with laughter. 'And I thought it was we Africans who were superstitious, and are supposed to be randy. And well endowed in the groin. You whites seem to be doing okay after all.'

264

They ate the trout, fried by Brian in almonds with a touch of garlic, served with new potatoes sprinkled with fresh mint from the garden. It was accompanied by a bottle of good Muscadet purchased from a reputable wine merchant in Oxford – "purveyor of wines and spirits to His Majesty King George IV" was printed below the royal insignia on their invoices. Then they both settled before the hot stove and leaned back in their chairs. Between them stood the scrubbed deal table littered with empty plates and dishes.

'It was very good,' Nchembe complimented his host. 'I have not eaten fish that way before. Nor, I think, have I had trout. It is a dry meat, but with the potatoes and butter … And the burnt nuts.'

'Roast, not burnt,' Brian replied, feigning a sense of hurt.

'A question, Brian,' Nchembe said after a few moments of silence.

'Fire away.'

'Forgive me, but in my room upstairs there is a trunk. I opened it to see if I could put my clothes in it. It has many wooden boxes in it …'

'It was my parents',' Brian explained. 'We used to call it the treasure chest. In it are our family – well, heirlooms, I suppose. There is some of my mother's jewellery there: she always wanted to give it to my wife. Some of my father's things are in there, too. A few paintings and drawings. Nothing of great value. The boxes contain slides.'

'Slides?' Nchembe was puzzled. 'Microscope slides?'

'No, transparencies. Pictures. For a projector. There're some movies there, too.'

'Movies?' Nchembe was puzzled. 'What movies?'

'Our holidays, birthdays, similar events. My father had an eight millimetre cine-camera. A Bell and Howell, I think it was. I've still got it somewhere. It was silent, of course.'

Nchembe pushed his plate aside and put his half-empty wine glass in its place.

'How did you ever see these movies? In the cinema?'

'No, of course not. My father wasn't the Governor of Kenya!' He smiled briefly. 'We had a projector to show them on. And a screen. I think the projector's with the camera. In the attic. I've put a lot of junk up there, out of the way. Stuff I haven't got around to bunging out.'

He picked up the Muscadet bottle and tipped it over his glass. There was no wine remaining in it.

'I've an idea,' Brian announced suddenly, dropping the bottle in the pedal bin by the sink. 'Why don't we get out another bottle? You'll be off in the morning and I'll not want it. I must get on with my thesis after this happy interlude of hedonism.'

Agreeing, Nchembe cleared the table of dirty crockery, rinsing the glasses in preparation for the new bottle. Brian left the room to collect the wine from the cupboard under the stairs. He was gone for five minutes before Nchembe went after him. The cupboard door was ajar and the bare, low-wattage bulb was burning in the recess beneath the stairs, but Brian was nowhere to be seen. Nchembe was about to call out to him when he heard a sound from the top of the stairs. It was a soft thud, as if a body had been dropped onto the landing carpet.

'Brian?' he called out tentatively, but received no reply.

By the bottom of the stairs was a rack for umbrellas and walking sticks. Instinctively, Nchembe grabbed the heaviest looking stick and jerked it from the stand. The handle was loose and lifted: he discovered he was holding a sword-stick. Carefully, and as silently as he could, he withdrew the blade and, grasping it firmly, carefully mounted the stairway.

The vision of the ignorant farmer and a repetition of his words came to him. It would not be impossible for the man to have entered the cottage: as it was built into the valley-side, the second storey could be entered from the garden over a small, wrought-iron bridge which led into the study.

Another sound issued from above where the lights were not switched on. The vestiges of late twilight gave the landing a dimness more foreboding than complete darkness might have been. The second noise was of something heavy being dragged.

As Nchembe reached the head of the stairs, a faint glow gradually illuminated the landing. It seemed to come from

266

above, as if reflected from one of the bedrooms onto the ceiling. He raised the sword in readiness.

In the centre of the landing was a Windsor chair. It was usually to be seen against the wall by the bathroom door.

'Brian?' he called again.

There was a muffled, gagged response. It appeared to emanate from the bathroom.

Nchembe burst the door open. The light was on, but there was no one in the room. On the rim of the bath were footprints, clear on the white enamel.

'Brian!' Nchembe shouted. 'You okay?'

'A black Porthos!' exclaimed a disembodied voice. 'I thought all three musketeers were froggies. Have at thee, sir!'

Nchembe looked up. Through a square hole in the ceiling he could see Brian's face peering down at him, a background of tiles and felting behind his head.

'Going to do for burglars with a sword? Better use a *panga* ...'

As soon as he spoke, he regretted it. Most of the victims of the Lari massacre had been *panga*-ed.

'I was worried for you. You were gone a long time and I heard noises. And the man in the inn ... In some places, to be the friend of an African is not good for a white.'

'This isn't Pretoria or Durban,' Brian said defensively. 'Some of them might not like inter-racial friendships in this village but they'd not bring out the sjamboks. You've heard the cliché, "An Englishman's home is his castle"?'

'Then where are your ramparts?' Nchembe answered. 'And what are you doing?'

'As I was getting the wine, I thought I'd take a leak. Up here, looking at the trap-door, I had an idea. Here,' he pushed the corner of a cardboard carton over the rim of the opening, 'Can you help me down with this?'

Nchembe propped the sword against the cistern, stood astride the bath, as Brian had done, and clasped the box between his hand and the side of his head. It was heavier than he had anticipated. He balanced himself by pressing the stub of his left arm against the towel rail.

Brian swung down from the trap-door and, standing tiptoe

on the lavatory, replaced the door, pushing the brass bolt home with a click.

'What is this?'

'You'll see, Matthew. A surprise.'

The wine poured into the rinsed glasses, Brian removed the spice rack and a knot of corn dollies hanging on the wall beside the stove. He opened the cardboard box and lifted from it an Eumig eight millimetre film projector.

'Movies!' he declared. 'I thought we'd look at a few reels of my parents' home cinés. Show you how the colonials lived ...'

Nchembe shifted in his seat, re-arranging beneath his spine the cushion which had slipped to one side.

'Excellent! I should like to see them very much. You as a boy. And Kenya ...'

It took Brian some time to thread the film into the projector. The instruction book was missing and it was largely guesswork. The guidelines marked on the machine itself had worn off with over-use. At last, the film was in safely with the sprocket holes fitted over the teeth of the wheels and the loop loose, to prevent the film tightening – that much he remembered from an evening of broken films and blue language from his father. He switched off the light and snapped the switch. The motor clattered, the reels turned and the bulb came on, casting a hazy-edged square of light onto the whitewashed wall. After a few seconds of squiggled lines and bright orange ghosting to the side of the square, a coloured picture of a house appeared. Brian focused the image.

'This was my home. Outside Nairobi,' he explained.

Across the wall strolled the houseboy, his white *kanzu* flapping against his shins, his bare toes showing through with each forward step.

'Our servant, Oudu. In the garden.'

'A Luo,' Nchembe announced authoritatively. 'And he has a military moustache!' He laughed quietly.

'He was in the army before he came to us.'

The camera panned to one side, following Oudu. Sitting at a round table under the shade of several banana trees was a group of four Europeans. They waved silently at the camera.

'Who are these people?'

'The lady in the pink dress is my mother. The other woman is Gia Holborn, a lawyer's wife. And the man's her husband ...'

'And that is you!'

'Yes,' Brian admitted, embarrassed.

'How old are you here?'

'About twelve.'

'Where is your father?'

Oudu placed a tray of drinks on the table and grinned sheepishly at the cameraman. Brian's mother spoke to Oudu. She touched his arm. He grinned more broadly, faced the camera and bowed. Then he, too, waved. The camera jerked slightly.

'My father's taking the pictures. It was all in good sport.'

Brian was worried the film showed Oudu performing for the camera like a pet animal.

'Yes,' Nchembe said. 'I can see that.'

He was silent for a few moments. The Europeans drank their drinks. Across the lawn behind them, slightly out of focus, passed the shadow of a cloud.

'Did you like your servant?'

'Yes. I did. We all did.'

'How many years was he with you?'

'Twelve, I think.'

'What happened to your servant before him?'

'He didn't come back from his annual holiday.'

'What tribe was he?'

'Kikuyu.'

'Perhaps he ran away to the forests, to be with his brothers.'

'Perhaps.'

The wall whitened. There were more scrawls of lines.

'My father never edited his films. He just spliced them together, year by year. The reel cans have the date and the year scratched on them.'

Next, a black American saloon drove across the kitchen wall. It had bulging headlights and white-wall tyres. It halted by a bougainvillaea bush, dark against the backdrop of purple blossoms. From the car issued a woman.

'That's old Mrs Mordant! She was one of the old set. An old Kenya hand. A real harridan!'

No sooner was she out of the car than the scene changed completely. In glass-clear water swam a hippopotamus, obviously filmed from an overhanging tree. A leafy twig came into shot and was brushed aside by the movement of the lens.

'A clever juxtaposition?' Nchembe suggested. 'Your father was a witty man.'

'Yes. He was fun.'

The reel ran out and Brian rewound it and loaded another.

For the next hour, a cavalcade of fleeting moments of Brian's life jittered or flickered or washed across the wall: swimming at Malindi, climbing the walls of the ruins of Gedi, marching with the CCF at the Duke of York School, sitting reading with a chameleon clinging to the book. Views looking out over the Rift Valley, panoramas of Mount Kenya and Mount Kilimanjaro, African villages of round, thatched huts built against the green forests or the red earth, street scenes in Nairobi and Mombasa, the Norfolk Hotel in the capital, the Nyali Beach Hotel north of Mombasa and the Outspan Hotel at Nyeri – they all danced upon the white wall. His mother, his father, their friends came and went mutely to the clicking of the projector which made less of a racket once it had run a few reels. Few of Brian's own friends appeared. Interspersed between family scenes came elephants and rhinos crossing the Nairobi-Mombasa road at Tsavo, their footprints smoothing out the washboarding of the surface, lions mating on an ant-hill, two cheetah sitting in long grass, a crocodile with a bloated antelope carcass, flamingoes standing in their own reflections on Lake Nakuru, zebra and wildebeest, impala and kudu, Thompson's gazelle and gerenuk, giraffe and hartebeest, geckoes, warthogs, snakes, butterflies, baboons, turtles in the Tana river and a tortoise. The final sequence of the last reel showed Brian standing proudly beside the skin of his leopard.

'That's the lot,' he announced, the film spinning round in the spool, the leader flapping against the projector casing.

Nchembe reached up and switched on the lamp hanging over the table. He picked up the wine bottle. It was empty.

'Get another, Matthew.'

While Brian rewound the last film and put the projector aside to cool down, Nchembe brought through a bottle of Niersteiner.

'No Muscadet left?'

'None.'

'Never mind.'

The bottle uncorked, they sat facing each other in silence. Nchembe broke into Brian's thoughts.

'Those are historical films.' He looked at the reel tins piled against the cardboard box. 'I very much doubt if many people have such a collection. You should not keep them in the roof of this cottage. They may get damp. Already a few seem to be losing their colour.'

'No. They are nothing. Just memories, really.'

'But, Brian,' Nchembe was insistent, 'they show a world which no longer exists.'

'Colonials don't exist, that's true!'

'Neither do other things. The animals are fewer, Nairobi has many new buildings. In the bush, lots of people are roofing their homes with corrugated tin, not grass. The film of the Rift Valley – it is not like that now. You show it as just bush – dots of trees and scrub. Now, it is being made into *shamba*s. It is all changing. The real revolution is now. Mau Mau only started it, the politicians only gave it impetus. It is the people who are doing this now. And not always for the good.'

'The films may be of interest,' Brian conceded, 'but they could never be made into anything worth showing. In the cinema. On TV.'

'No, maybe so. But they are cameos of a life and a land now gone or going quickly.'

They fell silent again. Brian opened a window. The heat of the projector as well as the stove had made the kitchen stuffy. Through the open window drifted a hawkmoth to hover by a pot of flowers growing on the sill. From down in the valley came the single curt bark of a fox.

'Africa is being raped,' Nchembe said, his voice slightly louder from concern and the third bottle of wine.

271

'How?'

'By change. Everything is altering too fast. No one is thinking of the future. Now we are free of domination, we are going too quickly. Trying too hard. We are losing our heritage. Our land. Our animals. We are greedy for change. And a land with no past has no future.'

'But it is the Africans who are doing the taking now,' Brian said. He slurred together 'the' and 'Africans' for the wine was affecting him, also.

'Yes,' Nchembe allowed. 'We have learned from the whites. The land is for taking, not giving. We must give something back. Exchange what we take for something good.'

'Maybe I should give the flicks back?'

Nchembe grunted his incomprehension.

'Flicks. Movies. The cinés. Give back the pictures. Make the tin roofs into thatch. Un-tarmac the roads and make them bumpy once more.'

'That's not possible,' Nchembe said disdainfully. 'How can pictures become life over again? That is a foolish thing to say.'

His hand knocked against the stem of the wine glass. The moth circled the light and settled upon the copper shade, its wings fanning so rapidly they were only a blur.

'But,' Nchembe mused, 'it would be good if we could make the leopard alive again.'

'How?' Brian repeated.

'In fire, the soul can arise ...'

'I do not understand ...'

'In the flames, the spirit can be re-born. The spirit lives in the smoke. As the smoke rises perhaps a new leopard will be born.'

'In Dorset?' Brian asked incredulously.

'In Africa. Back in Africa ...'

They drank the remainder of the bottle without speaking. When it was finished, Brian dropped the two bottles into the pedal bin. They hit the first empty and all three broke.

'Le's do it.'

'Do what?'

'Le's give my le'par' back to Africa.'

272

Brian walked unevenly out of the kitchen and up the stairs. He returned, stumbling down the steps, carrying the leopard skin draped over his shoulder like an exotic scarf.

'Outside,' he ordered Nchembe and bent over to rummage in the cupboard beneath the sink.

Together they went on to the flagstones before the house, overlooking the valley.

'This is for the dead animals,' he muttered, pushing the leopard skin into a heap against the stone garden wall.

From his pocket, he pulled a tin of cigarette lighter fuel, sprinkled it over the leopard and dropped a match on it. The fuel flared and the two men staggered backwards. As the flames died, Brian squirted more liquid onto the pelt, re-igniting it. The flames sought to travel up the stream of fluid but could not reach the can. There was a pungent stink of singeing hair and skin.

'When I was a boy. In Nairobi. I use' to kill *siafu* with Ronson lighter flui'. Spray it on the trail. Whoomph!' His hands mimicked an explosion. 'All the an's running here and there. Soldier an's trying to sting things ...'

The flames of the burning leopard reflected on Nchembe's face. His eyes were wide, the whites prominent. Where his tight curled hair met his forehead glistened beads of sweat.

'Are you sure you've got to go?' Brian asked as the train pulled in to Maiden Newton station. 'You're more than welcome to stay. Gives me an excuse not to get on with the thesis.'

'No. I must go. Business.'

'Angela business?'

Nchembe smiled.

'No. African business.' He looked at the station clock. 'I've only three hours to catch my plane.'

'Secret African business?'

'In a manner of speaking. The fight goes on, Brian, even if the war is over. You will know of it one day.'

'Moscow?'

Again, Nchembe smiled.

'Not Moscow. But Europe. Western Europe. I'll be back by the start of term. Have a good summer, Brian.'

They shook hands. Brian noticed how both of them still had soil under their fingernails from burying the remains of the leopard skin in the garden.

'You, too.'

'And get the thesis done, Brian. Remember it's for a cause, not just a scarlet academic gown.'

'Yes, Matthew. I'll not forget.'

As the train left the station, gathering speed northwards, Brian felt a pang of sorrow at his friend's departure. Yet, mingled with it, was a sense of foreboding he could not quite justify.

15

'One of the great advantages of a British Museum reader's ticket,' Brian's undergraduate tutor had told him as he signed the referee section of the application, 'is it gives one access to the only clean gent's convenience in London – apart from the ones in the Dorchester and Claridges, which don't count. Of course,' he continued thoughtfully, 'one doesn't have free bottles of cologne, a barber on hand and Imperial Leather soap, but one does have fresh towels in one of those new-fangled roller-box affairs and there isn't, as one tends to find so prevalent these days, a two-and-sixpenny condom dispenser. Anyone would think the masculine nation is bent on nothing in life but fornication. Still,' he handed the form back to Brian, 'looking around the university, that might just be possible. The waiving of rules in some colleges is scandalous. We'll all be *co-ed* – a simply ghastly Americanism – in twenty years at this rate. Disgraceful! Over my corpse be it! Quite takes away the traditional skills of drain-pipe scaling and wall traversing.' He gazed almost wistfully at the application as Brian folded it into his pocket. 'Enjoy your B M days, dear boy. Enjoy them ...'

Whenever Brian entered the Museum, between the huge iron gates, through the colonnaded main entrance and the heavy brass doors, he thought of Dr Proctor and his scatological conversations. Whatever the topic, he could skilfully turn it to lavatories or copulation and, ultimately, the demise of the male preserve. The world may rot, nuclear war break out, pestilence rule the land and the Church be overrun by infidels but he cared not, so long as Oxford colleges continued to exclude 'the female gender', as he put it.

The main entrance lobby to the Museum was crowded with tourists. Some gazed about themselves in awe, others consulted the information board, the layout map of the building or one of the uniformed guards. A dense throng

275

packed the Museum Shop on the left, purchasing postcards and replicas of gold Viking brooches in brass or the red wax Great Seals of the Kings of England re-cast in red resin.

Brian made his way through the crowd, skirting a party of Belgian schoolchildren and diminutive Japanese business-men – there was not a woman in their number; Brian noted with wry humour that this would have pleased the recently-deceased Doctor-proctor, as he had been known.

Entering the narrow corridor leading to the Reading Room, Brian always felt self-important. The notice bearing the card "Readers Only" separated him from the rabble of holiday-makers and culture-curious. Out there was the planet of common ignorance while ahead of him through one set of doors, past just one guard, lay the universe of knowledge.

The guard, an elderly man with a thin string of medal ribbons on his jacket, glanced at Brian's reader's ticket and nodded approval.

Beyond the door was the round Reading Room under a vast dome inset with windows grimed by the city air. Sixty feet high or more around the walls were bookcases reached by narrow catwalks.

Brian searched for a seat, found one, noted the number and placed his briefcase upon it to denote ownership. It was not yet ten o'clock but most of the seats had already been filled. If he had arrived at nine, when the gates opened, he would have had to queue with the most eager of the day's scholars.

In the centre of the Reading Room, several hundred feet in diameter, was the circular librarians' desk and it was to this that Brian made his way, over the dark blue carpet and past the ranks of red-spined catalogues standing on shelves under blue, leather-topped reading surfaces. The sun, misted by the dirt on the windows, cast weak beams onto the brass lamp fittings and the grille at the collection point.

No one spoke except in very subdued tones and then only to a librarian. Any noise created in the Reading Room echoed, amplified by the books and the dome. A dropped volume, a cough, the click of a briefcase catch were reproduced perfectly but came from the void above rather than any one identifiable spot in the room.

'Titchner,' Brian said quietly to the library porter, a spotty-faced youth wearing a khaki coat ingrained with dust lines.

He left the stool upon which he perched and surveyed a line of shelves, eventually removing half a dozen books from it. Brian had ordered them the afternoon before, knowing it would take some hours for them to arrive from the stacks. Some of the volumes would have come not from the museum premises, the long corridors of shelves and cases in the basement and betweeen the Reading Room and the North Library, but from depositories half-way across London.

'Seat number?'

'Gill.'

The youth handed over the books. From between the pages of each flapped the carbon copy of the order slip.

Returning to his seat, Brian put on the reading light, pulled out of the wooden panelling before him the blue leather-padded book rest, shoved the blotter pad to one side and opened his briefcase, careful not to let the catch snap. Any echo, if he caused it, always made him self-conscious. With his sharpened pencils lined up like weapons and the pad of foolscap spread, he lifted the covers of the first book, found the page he needed by consulting the index and began to read.

Time slipped by. The beams of sun travelled the walls and catalogue shelves. The foolscap gathered scribbled notes and diagrams, lines of communication joining one idea to another like tracks upon which trains of thought might steam. When Brian first felt a pang of hunger and thirst, it was a quarter past five in the afternoon. He closed the books but left them at his seat. The Reading Room would not shut until nine that evening and he planned to return.

The air was muggy when he stepped outside. At some time during the afternoon there had been a shower of rain and although the road and pavement had dried, there were puddles in the gutter. He walked over the pedestrian crossing between the museum gates and the YWCA building, went by the magic trick and joke shop, the window crammed with Dracula teeth sets, itching powder, collapsible wands, tumblers of unspillable liquids and Oriental Magic Wallets, and entered the Museum Tavern.

Although the pub had only just opened, it was already crowded. The barmen were hard at work serving home-going businessmen, labourers from a nearby building site and other students whose biological clocks, like Brian's own, had informed them that evening licensing hours had arrived. All the clientele, except for three secretaries, were male.

Brian balanced his briefcase on one corner of the secretaries' table, went to the bar and ordered a pint of bitter, a scotch egg and two rounds of beef sandwiches. When he returned to his case, he found it had been lowered to the floor, the spot taken by two office boys intent on trying to pick up the secretaries. One sat on a stool and the other lounged against the frosted glass panel of the Victorian window. The girls were obviously keen to be rid of their attentions and Brian's arrival, laden with plate and glass mug, gave them the opportunity.

''ere! You moved 'is case,' one of them accused the office boys. 'That was 'is place.'

'Right!' The office boy saw his chance. 'Shift up then, an' we'll all get a seat.'

'Can't!' the girl stubbornly refused. 'B'linda's got 'er bag 'ere. Can't put it on the floor. It's got china in it. Init, B'linda?'

'Yeah! It 'as,' confirmed the girl in the middle of the bench seat on behalf of her friend who was hugging a bag to her side.

Brian remained standing by the corner of the table.

'Sorry 'bout this, mate,' said the taller of the office boys. His hand started to push the glasses aside on the table to make room for Brian's plate and beer. The boy's hand was smudged with mauve indelible ink.

'Cheers!' Brian replied and lowered his plate and glass, checking as he did so that his briefcase was safely under the table. The seated office boy showed no intention of relinquishing his stool.

''ere, B'linda,' said the secretary at the end of the bench. 'Move up. Put that bag o' files on yer lap.'

'Thought they was china ornaments,' challenged the standing office boy.

'They ain't. They're china files.'

Brian squeezed in next to the girls; the office boys chest chagrined glances at him.

'Think we get the message,' one of them declared.

'At last,' Belinda commented sarcastically, speaking for the first time.

'Yeah!' said the one in the middle. 'Why don't yer piss orf?'

The girls smiled at Brian as he ate but made no attempt to talk to him. For that he was grateful. He was anxious not to lose his concentration on his work.

As he got up to leave, thanking the girls for the seat, he saw a face peer quickly around the street door then disappear. The action was not unusual. People did this all the time, looking in to see if their drinking cronies had arrived, if there was room at the bar, if there were single girls present – or single young men – if food was being served yet. What caught Brian's attention was the fact that the face was black and looked like Matthew Nchembe's.

If the bar had not been so crowded, he would have called out. Instead he picked up his briefcase and forced his way across the room. As he reached the door and stumbled into Museum Street, colliding with a porter from the vegetable market in Covent Garden, he saw the African climbing into a taxi half-way down the street towards the occult bookshop, its sign swinging gently in the breeze caused by the passing cars.

'Matthew!' he called out, but the man did not hear. 'Matthew!'

The African turned in the doorway of the shining black taxi and pulled the door shut with his right hand. His left would have been easier. Through the rear window of the taxi, Brian saw the man sit back next to another figure with shoulder-length hair. The driver pulled the taxi into a gap in the traffic and the vehicle disappeared down the street, turning left at the junction with Bloomsbury Way.

Walking back into the British Museum, Brian wondered if it really had been Nchembe. He had had so brief a glimpse of him. And yet Nchembe was out of the country, had been for a week, somewhere in Europe, he had said. But, somehow, Brian was certain it had been Matthew he had just seen getting into the cab.

Once seated at G11 again, he dismissed the brief encounter. There was nothing he could do about it. He did not know Nchembe's London address – if he had one – and could only contact him through his college in Oxford. In the meantime, he had work to do. This was, he told himself, for a cause, not merely a fancy gown.

When the library closed, Brian walked out with the remaining readers. Many had already gone home. He did not bother to have the books held over for the next day: one day's concerted effort had been sufficient. He had, in his foolscap pad, all the references and notes he required.

By the museum gate, he halted to fasten one of the clasps on his briefcase which had brushed against his thigh and opened accidentally. Setting off once more without looking up, he stepped in the way of a fellow reader.

'I'm sorry,' he apologised automatically.

The reader was an African woman in her late twenties, dressed in the toga-like traditional costume of Nigeria. She was slender with almost oriental cheekbones, her skin less black than Nchembe's or that of most East Africans. She, too, was carrying a briefcase with a lady's umbrella tucked under her arm.

'That's quite all right,' she answered with no trace of an accent. 'I saw your case was undone as we came down the museum steps, but didn't like to tell you.'

Then a passer-by jogged her arm and she dropped her umbrella. Brian bent to pick it up.

'Here you are.'

He handed her the umbrella and, as he did so, his attention was attracted by an enamel badge she had pinned to the colourful material wound around her shoulders.

It was very similar to the badge Nchembe sometimes wore in his lapel: a flag consisting of three horizontal bars. The topmost was black, the middle green and the bottom gold. This badge differed from Nchembe's, however, in that in the middle of the flag it had a clenched brown fist and beneath it the inscription "ANC 912–621".

The woman was turning away, putting up her umbrella. It was beginning to drizzle.

'Excuse me,' Brian said.

She turned.

'Yes?'

'That badge you're wearing. I couldn't help noticing it. What is it?'

'It's a few years old now,' she replied. 'It's for the fiftieth anniversary.'

'Of what?' he asked.

'The A N C.' She could see this meant nothing to him. 'The A N C,' she repeated. 'The African National Congress.'

16

The trees along the bank and towpath of the canal had lost most of their leaves by the second week in October when Brian returned to Oxford. What the autumnal weather could not achieve a severe storm did. Not only the trees suffered, for the street near the church of St Barnabas, just round the corner from Brian's digs, was littered with tiles and slates from the houses and the church tower.

In his digs, which Brian had kept on during the summer although he had not used them, a window frame had leaked and badly stained the wallpaper and carpet.

'Such a nasty mess, Mr Brian,' Mrs Rattle had said as she let him in to his room. 'If my hubby was still here he'd have seen it all cleaned up. But you can't get people in these days. Not like it was. I had this lad come in and do as much as he could but he was an idle little blighter.' She tugged on the sash window and raised it an inch. 'Room needs airing a bit.'

'I'll get it painted, Mrs Rattle,' Brian offered. 'The whole wall. The whole room if you like. It'll not bother me. I shan't be up for long this term —'

'Your thesis nearly done then, is it?' she interrupted.

'Yes. Nearly done.'

'You will,' she said shrewdly, 'remember you have to give me a month's notice, won't you?'

'Of course I will.' He lowered his suitcase to the floor and laid his briefcase and portable Olympia on the table. 'And I've not forgotten the rule about typing late at night.'

'Your house nice, is it? Just as well you took most of your precious things with you. The floor was awash, it was. And the walls went mouldy. Would have been the ruination of your lovely lion skin.'

'Leopard. It was a leopard.'

'Yes, that's right,' she said absent-mindedly. 'Now, I'll light the fire and get a bit of warmth in.'

She slammed the window down, a flake of paint dropping from under the sill and drifting to the bare floorboards where the carpet had been rolled back. She knelt down, her apron catching under her knees and struck a match to the gas fire. The white, cracked elements soon began to glow as the gas hissed through the jets.

'Is Dash up yet?'

She rose from in front of the fire, put the box of matches on the narrow mantelshelf and smoothed her apron over her dress. Brian noticed how the sleeves of her pullover had worn through.

'Dash? Oh, you mean Mr Dashiell. Oh, no. Terrible! Hasn't nobody told you?'

'Told me? No, what ...'

'He went out to some Arab place. You know how he was always digging up relics and such. Well, he went there and was digging in the desert and the sand fell in on him. Buried him alive. His native porters or whatever dug like navvies to get him out but it was no use. It was all in the *Oxford Mail*. Headlines, it was.' Her eyes were misty. 'I was so sorry. Mr Dashiell was a real Oxford gentleman even if he was an American.'

'Canadian, Mrs Rattle. He was a Canadian,' Brian corrected her automatically, too shocked to respond appropriately to the news.

She wiped her eyes with the hem of her apron and brushed away a fleck of dust adhering to her cheek.

'I wrote to his family and I had a lovely letter from his mother. Then his father came over from there and paid me rent through to now. And he took all his things away but he left me his motor-bike. And what was I to do with that? It's still in the garridge Mr Rattle used to rent in Juxon Street.'

'You could sell it.'

'Oh, that'd look fine! Who'd think it was any good, an old Oxford dame like me flogging a huge machine like that? Besides, I'd have to deal with them rocker types with leather tassles hanging from their arms. I'd be scared ...'

'Leave it to me, Mrs Rattle. I'll advertise it and get it off your hands.'

She thanked him and went down the stairs to brew him a cup of tea.

As he removed his clothes from the suitcase, hanging his jackets in the wardrobe and placing his shirts in the chest of drawers, Brian felt the emptiness of loss. He had known Dash for two years. They were good friends, had shared many hours together, dated undergraduates together, got drunk and smoked dope together. Now, as suddenly as if his death had only just occurred, Dash was gone, never to come back up at the start of a new term. It was not the common university parting: at the end of a course, students left vowing to keep in touch though seldom doing so. Yet they would often meet again, years later, at a guest night, a reunion or in a corporation boardroom. With Dash, this could never be and the realization pained and saddened Brian immeasurably.

By the time he had unpacked his suitcase, Mrs Rattle was back with the tea on a tray. Beside the pot was a plate of hot scones.

'You shouldn't have gone to so much bother!' he chided her, at the same time grateful. It had been a long drive from Dorset and her kindness helped force the sadness from his thoughts.

'It's no bother, Mr Brian. I've only the one gentleman to look after at present.'

'Have you another lodger lined up?'

'Well, I had a lot of enquiries,' she admitted, 'and – yes, I've got another lodger. Did you see the notice on the bathroom door?'

'No, I didn't.'

'It's a pretty little notice. One side says ENGAGED and the other VACANT. It's to stop any embarrassment. The lock's never been very good and I didn't want that idle little blighter trying to fix it.'

'Do we need it?' Brian asked.

'We do now. The new lodger's a lady.'

'What would Mr Rattle think!' Brian mocked.

'Must move with the times, Mr Brian. And she's a very nice girl, so!'

As Brian went to leave in the early evening, Mrs Rattle stopped him by her door.

'Do you have a moment, Mr Brian?'

'For you, Mrs Rattle, always. What can I do for you?'

'Come in a tick.'

She opened the door and he entered her cluttered sitting room, not as big as his own room upstairs. Every level surface was littered with knick-knacks, souvenirs sent from abroad by the generations of students she and her husband had cosseted, criticised, looked after, given alibis to (for both the police and the university bulldogs) and generally guided through their university years.

'I need your advice,' she said, closing the door.

From under her upright chair before her small television set she produced a biscuit tin. It was decorated with roses and a pair of Persian kittens.

'What do you think this is?'

She handed him the tin. It was heavy and he noticed two holes drilled in the side.

'Take off the lid.'

He did so. Inside was a jumble of wires, electrical bits and a dry cell battery. He could understand none of it but he guessed what it was: a meter-slowing device.

'Where did you find this, Mrs Rattle?'

'In Mr Dashiell's room. It's not a bomb, is it?'

'No,' Brian assured her.

'What is it then? Is it something ancient? It doesn't look old ...'

'I think it's a radio,' Brian lied. He was loathe to destroy the old woman's memory of his friend, the "real Oxford gentleman" she had harboured as she had so very many others. 'Dash wanted to make a radio to go on his motor-bike.'

'I don't think it'll work, will it?' she questioned him.

'No, I don't think so. I'd throw it in the dustbin if I were you.'

'I believe I'll keep it,' she said, taking the box from his hands. 'The bits might come in useful if my radio or the blessed telly go on the blink.'

Over her shoulder, Brian saw the vertical hold on the television set had slipped and the picture was flickering.

After a sandwich and a pint in the Lamb and Flag on St Giles, Brian walked in a cold wind down Broad Street and Holywell Street, along Long Wall Street and on to Magdalen College. In the porters' lodge, he asked for Matthew Nchembe.

'I'm sorry, sir,' the porter informed him politely. 'Mr Nchembe has not yet come up. We expect him to return early next week. And he will not be taking rooms in college. We understand he has rented accommodation – if you will excuse me, sir?' The porter leaned over, took a key from a hook and handed it to an undergraduate standing behind Brian. He then lifted a black, hardcover notebook from under his desk, opened it and ran his finger down the columns of copper-plate writing. 'Mr Nchembe has rooms in Gordon Street, sir.'

Brian moved the book around so he could read the address for himself.

'Where is Gordon Street?'

'Down the Abingdon Road, sir. Between Vicarage Road and Lake Street. On the right just before you reach U C sports fields, sir.'

'May I leave a message?'

The porter handed Brian a pad and he wrote upon it, *"Welcome back from Darkest Europe. How about dinner? My shout. Or a drink? I'm at the same address. Brian."* He folded the note, unfolded it again, and added, "PS. Dash died on an arch. trip to Mid. East."

From Magdalen, he walked over the river and down Cowley Road in the direction of Lucy's flat.

He had received several postcards from her during the summer. Her father had taken a house in the mountains of Italy and she had spent her summer there. Some of the postcards bore Italian stamps, others Swiss or French. A few had been mailed in Britain although they were photographs of Rome or Florence.

He turned into St Mary's Road just as the street lights came on. From the house next to Lucy's blared Georgie Fame's "Get Away".

'Lucy's not in,' the girl who opened the door informed him. Brian had never seen her before.

'Are you in her college? Can you give her an urgent message?'

'I'm at the Poly,' the girl replied, 'but I'll give her a note.'

'Just say Brian's back.'

'Okay. Brian who?'

'She'll know.'

The girl closed the door. Making his way down the street, Brian looked over his shoulder and saw the curtains pulled across the front-room window of Lucy's flat.

Mrs Rattle's new lodger was what Dash would have called a nubile broad, usually shortened in his terminology to a *nube*.

She was a postgraduate Mathematics student at Lady Margaret Hall and came from Bedfordshire. Her father was a farmer and she had attended Bedford High School for Girls. She had a sister who was a fresher at Girton College, Cambridge – reading Archaeology and Anthropology – and an older brother who also farmed.

This much Brian was told by Mrs Rattle before he had either set eyes on or even heard the girl moving about in her room.

'Ever such a nice young lady,' Mrs Rattle proclaimed. 'A real little poppet.'

It was a pity, Brian thought, that Dash was no longer with them – if he had failed with the mathematician, he could have worked on an introduction to the younger sister. He would have shown her his mummifiedl baboons and baby and taken it from there. He claimed once the baby was a great turn-on for girls whom he managed to get as far as his room: it aroused their mothering instincts, or so he said.

'When is she moving in?' Brian enquired.

'Two days ago, Mr Brian. She already lives here. I'm surprised you two haven't bumped into each other.'

On his return from looking for Nchembe and Lucy, Brian had met a girl descending the stairs. She was short and not quite podgy, with her hair tied in a plait, and round, steel-framed spectacles of the sort John Lennon had taken to wearing. He had bade her good evening but she had hurried by him, mumbling an incomprehensible reply.

'I think we may have, Mrs Rattle. She wears glasses.'

'Only for reading, she told me. It must be all those numbers and signs and things. The papers she leaves lying about in her room look for all the world like those Middle Ages geoman-thingamejigs's ways of turning stone into silver.'

'Lead into gold,' Brian corrected her. 'Alchemists sought to turn lead into gold.'

'Whatever,' Mrs Rattle replied. 'That's what her sums look like. And she has ever such a lot of books.' She gave Brian a pointed look of mock disdain. 'Many more than you and Mr Dashiell, God bless him, ever had.'

As Brian went up to his room, he heard for the first time a movement in the girl's room. There was a shuffling sound followed by a very low playing of Wagner. He knocked on the door.

'Half a mo',' came a muffled voice.

As he waited, the record player was turned down even lower so it became almost inaudible. The shuffling recommenced and he regretted his interruption. Perhaps she had her boyfriend with her.

The door opened.

'Hello,' she said. 'I'm Judy Lockyer and you must be Mrs Rattle's earthman from upstairs.'

Brian was more than taken aback and his surprise must have shown on his face.

'I am sorry.' She misinterpreted his silence. 'You must be looking for the Canadian archaeology post-grad. I'm afraid ...' she paused, choosing her words '... he doesn't stay here now. If you have a word with Mrs Rattle downstairs ...'

The girl was not the bespectacled, pig-tailed one he had met. She was about Brian's height, had straight, dark brown hair cut in a Mary Quant pageboy style, and wore a heavy, loose Arran sweater over tight black jeans. Despite the draught which swept under all the doors in Mrs Rattle's house until one invented a stocking-dog or nailed on a felt strip to exclude it, she was barefoot. Her eyes were shadowed in light blue and her long eyelashes touched with mascara. As she held out her hand to shake his own, Brian noticed she wore a heavy gold-link bracelet.

'No. I wasn't looking for Dash,' he assured her as he took her hand. 'I was – I thought I'd welcome you. I am the earthman from upstairs – as opposed to Mrs Rattle's Venusian.'

'You certainly don't look like the Mekon,' she replied. 'Would you like a cup of earthwoman's coffee? The kettle's just boiled.'

The room contained none of the furniture Dash had used. The bed was a brass-framed Victorian double with brass lamps mounted on the head. It was the only old piece of furniture. The armchairs were modern with bright cushions strewn on them, there were Indian rugs on the floor, several contemporary watercolours hanging from the picture rail and the curtains were decorated with tiny flowers. The three-tier bookcase – one of Mrs Rattle's fitments, screwed into the wall – was packed with books, and beside the gasfire more shelves had been constructed from planks lying between blocks of plain building bricks. Where there weren't books there were small modern art sculptures and figurines.

'Do sit down. Isn't that bed hideous!' she exclaimed. 'I know it looks awfully out of place but I do like it. It was my grandmother's and I do like sleeping in a double bed. One can stretch out all the way.'

Brian thought of Dash at that moment, wondered if his ghost was somewhere in the room, cursing its ill luck.

'How did you get it up the stairs?'

'It comes to bits. It has its own spanner, and you can reconstruct it. But even then the bits are heavy.'

They drank coffee and talked in the exploratory way single people of the opposite sex do when meeting for the first time. He found out about her family and farm, her school and her holidays in Crete; she found out about his background in Kenya, the death of his parents and the purchase of his cottage.

'I should very much like to see your cottage one day,' she said as he left her room. 'It sounds idyllic.'

He returned to his own room, undressed and prepared to go down for a bath. Mrs Rattle seldom came upstairs after nine in the evening. Then he dressed again: it was no longer a male house. By the time he reached the bathroom, the mathematician had been in there and the room smelt of perfumed talc. There was an outline on the linoleum where her feet had stood as she had powdered herself. There was just sufficient hot water left for him to have a skimpy, five-inch-deep bath.

For three days, Brian received no word from Lucy. He assumed she was busy arranging her timetable, planning her term, deciding which lectures to attend, sorting out matters with her tutors. On the fourth day, as he was leaving the Radcliffe Camera, trying to decide whether or not to visit her, he saw her standing alone at the end of Brasenose Lane. She was looking in the direction of Turl Street and did not see him as he approached.

'Lucy?' he said tentatively.

She spun round. He saw her cheeks whiten then blush.

'Brian! How long have you been up? I had no idea you'd returned to Oxford.'

'I left a message at your flat. Couple of days ago. I gave it to the girl who's at the Poly.'

She had turned away from him anxiously glancing down the lane. A number of cyclists were steering into it, dismounting from their machines, leaning them against the wall as near as they could to the street light and locking the wheels to the frames or to iron hoops set in the stonework. It was getting dark early and the light was on.

'I don't know a Polly.' She spoke absent-mindedly.

'That's not her name,' Brian said with exasperation. 'I don't know what her name is. She's at the Polytechnic.'

'That's Jo-Anne. She's forgetful. She'd forget how to boil a kettle if it wasn't for the three-pin plug.'

The conversation was not going the way Brian wanted. He was not interested in the amnesiac Jo-Anne and her inability to carry out simple tasks.

'You've not been in touch.'

'No, Brian, I'm sorry. Things're piling up. You know how it is in your third year. The pressure's on.' She cast a quick look down Brasenose Lane again. 'And time seems so short. The third year's only from October to May. Six months. I feel as if I've done nothing for yonks.'

'Are you doing anything this evening?'

'I've got to meet someone.'

'Who?'

He could hardly not ask. His curiosity and annoyance were as great as his increasing feeling of desolation.

'Olivia Kelvin-Kelly. Do you know her? She's reading Geography at L M H. Though we all say she's reading Divinity. Always says "Divine, darling!" when you ask her something. You must know her or have heard of her. Her father's big in building skyscrapers.'

She waved briefly down the lane.

'Never heard of her.' Brian's annoyance was growing. 'Can't you put her off?'

'No. We're planning a party. You'll come, won't you?'

'If I'm not busy ...' he replied peevishly.

'Good! Now – I just saw her go past. Must rush or she'll miss me. I said I'd meet her at the other end.'

She ran off down the lane, her unbuttoned coat flapping behind her.

Brian was in two minds whether or not to follow her, to meet the divine Olivia, but he resisted the temptation. He knew he was being stood up – but, there again, the start of the third year was indeed a time of concern, fear and anxiety. Lucy need not necessarily have been giving him the brush-off.

As he started to walk through the Schools Quadrangle towards the Sheldonian, a voice called his name. It was Charles Runciman, Learned Imp of the Rhydisel Club.

'B-brian! How are you? How w-was your vac.?' He clapped his hand on Brian's shoulder. 'And how's the house? And the p-parturient thesis?'

'Fine but miffed; fine but brief; fine; fine but not yet fruiting. In that order. And you?'

'The d-d-dreaded *vacance en famille*! Or whatever the

French is for a b-bloody time with relations. My parents, getting on in years and tired of – and I qu-quote verbatim – "that awful little Wilson man in the g-g-gaberdine mackintosh", have decided to up roots and transplant their English oak in s-sunny Portugal's v-vineyards. They – and my uncle and his b-blousy and b-boring wife – 've bought a pompous-looking villa on a hillside near Caminha, on the Mino estuary. It's rather like the k-kind of house c-criminals on the run buy as a hedge against inflation and extradition. As c-close to Spain as they can get without actually b-being in it. My mother's turned Roman C-candle in her dotage and that's as near as they can get to Santiago de C-compostela without coming under Franco's tax laws. They've even got a B-BVM in the dining room. Sits on the dresser like a g-garden gnome.'

'BVM?' Brian asked.

'B-blessed Virgin Mary. Has a candle before it. It's m-most m-macabre. Like a film set for one of those Hitchcock films. Enter B-bette D-davis in b-black, with fangs. I couldn't wait to get away. But one must pay homage to the Old Folk.'

They stepped side by side through the gate by the Clarendon Building, between the car exhaust- and time-consumed stone busts balanced atop stone columns.

'You know,' Charles commented, looking up, 'I love my p-parents dearly. They've had a b-bugger of a life. But I do find them not a little trying. In fact,' he pointed at the unrecognizable visage on the nearest pillar, 'old Whatever-the-hell-his-name-is up there b-bears a striking resemblance to my f-father. As a younger man, you understand.'

Brian laughed. Charles had, with his light conversation, driven away the irksome thoughts aroused by Lucy's snub.

'When do we next meet? The Imps?'

They crossed Broad Street and Charles stopped outside Blackwell's bookshop, using the light from the window to consult his diary. As he thumbed through the pages, Brian surveyed the display of books – the central volume was Graham Greene's first novel in five years – entitled *The Comedians*, it had a dull, almost military green cover with what appeared to be the painting of a hybrid cactus-cum-artichoke on it.

'Super book!' Charles declared, his diary open in his hand. 'I read it last night. In one sitting. Rare for me, that! I'm not usually into modern novels. But G-Greene! He's different. It's set in Haiti with the T-tonton Macoute secret police. Say no more! Thursday week. Fancy a p-pint?'

Brian gladly accepted the invitation.

'Have I mentioned Matthew Nchembe to you?' Brian said as he sipped the froth off his pint of bitter.

Charles Runciman shook his head and Brian related the tale of Wamumu and the leopard, with a précis of Nchembe's life including his law degree from Leningrad, how he lost his arm and how he was now up at Oxford, furthering his law studies. While he spoke, Charles drank his beer and listened. By the time Brian was finished with his story, Charles had emptied his glass whereas Brian had barely touched his own.

'Another one?' Brian offered. 'You bought the first round.'

'In a minute.' He placed his hand over his glass. 'I never realised you'd had such an exciting life, B-brian. Leopards and g-guerrillas as pals. You must find Oxford a bit stultifying. And so must he. All us insular, j-jingoistic p-provincial-ites . . .'

'Nothing like it! And you've been to Portugal for the summer and I've been to deepest Dorset.' Charles grimaced, feigning displeasure. 'Besides, Rhydisel would never let it happen. Now – same again?'

By the time Brian returned from the bar with two more pints, and as he started to down his first in order to keep up with his companion – the cardinal rule for any aficionado of eating and drinking societies like the Rhydisel Club was that members never lagged behind – Charles had had an idea.

'I say, B-brian. Do you think your chum'd like to address the Imps? Or even b-become one? I don't think there's ever been a c-coloured Imp. What do you think?'

'I can suggest it to him.'

They left the pub at nine, their two pints of bitter having expanded into four pints and a scotch. Charles Runciman walked most of the way back to Brian's rooms in Jericho. He had taken digs on Leckford Road, not far way.

No sooner had Brian closed the door of his room than there came a gentle knock upon it. He opened it to find Judy Lockyer on the landing.

'I'm sorry to bother you ...,' she began but Brian interrupted.

'That's all right. What can I do for you?'

'Nothing really ... But if you're not working, would you like a coffee? I heard you come in and guess you've been in the library all day.'

'Actually, I've just had a few pints with a friend. But I'd like a coffee – and it's my turn. Come along in.'

'Your room's very spartan,' she observed as she sat on one of Mrs Rattle's chairs.

'Most of my stuff's at the cottage.'

'Where is it?'

'In Dorset.'

'Yes. You told me. I remember now.' She reached over to the table and scanned a page of his notes. 'What are you working on?'

'Soil erosion and leaching.'

Brian lit the gas fire, drew the curtains, switched on his reading lamp and extinguished the bulb hanging from the centre of the ceiling. The electric kettle boiled and he made two cups of coffee, taking from his cupboard a bottle of college port and two glasses.

'Cheers!' he said, filling the glasses and raising his. 'Welcome to Mrs Rattle's home for waifs and strays.'

She smiled and lifted her glass to chink against his own. They talked of his research until after ten-thirty when she rose to leave.

'Tell me,' Brian asked as she put her hand on the door knob, 'do you know a woman at L M H called Olivia Kelvin-Kelly? Apparently, they all call her Divine.'

She paused thoughtfully for a moment and then said, 'Never heard of her.'

'I was saddened by your note. Dashiell was a good compan-

294

ion. There was much of life in him.' Nchembe stirred sugar into his cup and prodded the fresh cream eclair with his cake fork. 'It must have been a terrible death. But very quick. And it is good to die for what one believes in, or doing what one wants. There is nothing worse than dying pointlessly.'

'I sent a letter to his parents.' Brian toyed with his Danish pastry. 'It seemed the right thing to do. I signed it for both of us. I didn't think you'd mind.'

'No. I do not mind.'

Nchembe forced the bladed prong of his fork into the eclair. Cream oozed out of the rounded opposite end and squirted onto the rim of his plate.

'And now! How was your trip to Europe? I missed you when I came up.'

'It was good. I met some friends and we made plans. African friends, that is. There are some very good clubs in Paris where black people can go. As it was for artists in the twenties and thirties so it is now for what governments are calling ethnic minorities.'

'Where else did you go? I was hoping you'd send me corny cards of the Eiffel Tower or that gauche pissing child in Belgium.'

'Oh, I was all over. I went through Belgium on my way to Amsterdam. And I was in Munich and Vienna, Geneva, Zurich, Berne, Warsaw, Bucharest, Berlin, Milan, Rome ... I was everywhere! And nowhere. But I sent no letters to anyone. There was not time and – it was not convenient.'

Brian let the matter drop and ate his pastry, the sugary coating sticking to his lips.

'And you? How was it for you after I left?' Nchembe enquired.

'I've done a huge amount to my thesis. Typed up whole chapters, sorted out the rest of it as well as the cottage. Redecorated the bathroom, which needed it. Planted some trees – a weeping silver birch and two six-foot ash trees. I even built a garage at the top of the garden.'

'Built a whole building? So quickly!'

'A bit of a cheat,' Brian admitted. 'It's a wooden one and came in prefabricated units. I just had to put them up, screw them together, and paint the whole edifice with creosote. I smelt of it for days. But it works. The M G goes in with plenty of room to spare. The worst part was hanging the doors. I had to dig away the earth outside so they could open.'

'You did this on your own?'

'Not quite. I got a teenage lad from the village to lend a hand. It took us from eight in the morning to ten that night.' He rubbed his fingers on the paper serviette and tipped the sugar dispenser over his cup. It delivered one measure of crystals. 'It sounds awfully domestic. Hardly the life of a jet-setter.'

Nchembe pushed the remainder of his eclair around his plate.

'I'm sorry ...' He paused but did not look Brian full in the face. It was unusual, for generally when he spoke to anyone he watched their eyes, judging their reactions.

'What are you apologising about?'

'Sorry I didn't call on you directly I returned to Oxford. Or England. I still had some business to see to.'

'When did you return? I ask because I thought one evening I saw you in London.'

'Did you?'

Nchembe was immediately alert.

'How do I know? I was working in the B M and popped out about six-ish for a pint and sandwich in the Museum Tavern. It's right outside the main entrance. It was crowded as hell but, as I was leaving, I could have sworn you looked in, saw it was packed and decided against it. I pushed my way out and saw you getting into a taxi. It had obviously been waiting. But it mightn't've been you.'

'When was this?'

Brian thought, rummaged in his briefcase and took from one of the document flaps a much crumpled book-ordering slip from the library. He showed it to Nchembe.

'That was the day. Date's there on the top.'

Nchembe studied it, replying, 'No. It could not have been me. I was in Rome then.'

As they settled their bill in the coffee house, Brian asked

Nchembe if they might have dinner together one evening. He could bring Lucy and Nchembe Angela.

'It would be good,' Nchembe answered. 'But not with the girls. Angela and I aren't seeing each other. It was a bit of a short affair. And my going away ...'

'Well, just us two then? I'd like to talk over a bit of my thesis. And my thoughts ...'

'Yes!' Nchembe eagerly interrupted. 'That would be fine. I should like it. And to discuss your thoughts. I'll drop you a note or call round at your digs. Next week?'

'That's okay. As regards dinner – I might have a rather unusual invitation for you instead of a tête-à-tête in an ordinary eating house. I'll drop it in at your place.'

'No, don't bother.' Nchembe spoke, Brian thought, a little too quickly. 'My digs are way out of town. Drop it at Magdalen. I have to come in to the centre every day. Do you receive mail at your college?'

'Of course. I often dine in hall. It saves cooking on Mrs Rattle's Baby Belling.'

'Next week then. Or watch for a note from me.'

Brian sensed, as they parted, something amiss. It was as if Nchembe was being guarded about something. Brian began to ponder, as he made his way towards the Bodleian Library, just what Nchembe's summer wanderings across Europe might have involved. After all, he had been through the Iron Curtain even though Brian was sure he had originally said he would not be leaving the West.

Nchembe wore a dark blue suit over a blue shirt and a black tie out of deference to the rules of Rhydisel. The other men wore the customary uniform of pin-stripe trousers, white jackets, and black bow ties. Each, as he sat, unbuttoned his jacket to display his waistcoat. As Brian opened his own, Nchembe happened to glance at him; then the African laughed loudly.

The master of the evening, Charles Runciman, tapped the table with his soup spoon.

'M-might I inquire after the cause of jollity?'

Nchembe placed his hand on Brian's shoulder.

'This waistcoat,' he said, everyone's attention upon him, 'was my last gift to Brian in Africa. The skin is colobus monkey. I wore this in the forest when I was a freedom fighter against the British. I caught and killed the monkeys with my own hands, except – take your coat off, Brian!'

Brian stood and removed his jacket.

'Turn around!'

Brian faced the side table upon which were arrayed the evening's bottles of wine, open and breathing or leaning in ice buckets.

'Except this one. You see this mark?' Nchembe spread the fur with his fingers. Beneath the hairs was a deep scar in the pelt. 'This is a burn. The monkey was electrocuted on power lines running beside the Naro Moro to Nanyuki road.'

Brian replaced his jacket and sat down.

'You don't mind, Matthew?' he asked.

'Mind what?'

'My having had it made into a waistcoat ...'

'Of course not. For you it is a special waistcoat. And for me, also. I have nothing left from my days in the forest.'

During the meal, conversation concerned the war in Vietnam, the increasing size of jet airliners, "The Tibetan Book of The Dead" and the predilection of the Roman Catholic Church, in ancient times, for assassinating any pope who displeased the cardinals who had voted him into office. Poetry was also discussed.

'Last term,' Charles Runciman announced, 'when our impish b-brethren P-patrick and Auberon were *in absentia*, I b-brought up the matter of the worst poem in the English Language. I'd now like to introduce you to what I c-consider to be one of the very b-best.'

From his pocket, Charles produced a paperback book.

'This is the p-poetry of the future,' he announced. 'It is by an Ulsterman. This is his first volume.'

An Oxford Corporation bus ticket marked a page and Charles carefully withdrew it, spreading the book on the table as he did so, pinning it open with his side plate.

'This is the start of the title poem.' He smoothed the pages under the plate. The book had been so well read they did not

298

spring up. He concentrated on the lines, temporarily suffocating his stutter. 'It goes like this:

> All year the flax-dam festered in the heart
> Of the townland; green and heavy headed
> Flax had rotted there, weighted down by huge sods.
> Daily it sweltered in the punishing sun.
> Bubbles gargled delicately, bluebottles
> Wove a strong gauze of sound around the smell.
> There were dragon-flies, spotted butterflies,
> But best of all was the warm thick slobber
> Of frogspawn that grew like clotted water
> In the shade of the banks ...

That, to me, has the v-vitality lacking in so much m-modern literature. The writing is evocative, capturing experience rather than merely d-documenting it.'

'Who is it by?' Patrick Delahaye, a junior fellow in English was fascinated. 'You're right it has verve.'

'Seamus Heaney,' Charles informed him, 'one of the most important p-poets of the next q-quarter of a century. I'd b-bet on it.'

'And you not an All Souls' man!' Jeff Crane commented, not willing to miss the opportunity of getting at the evening's Confessor.

'Listen to the ending,' Charles advised. 'To g-get the best you can't have me reading it. You have to d-do it for yourself. But the last lines are quite st-stunning:

> The slap and plop were obscene threats. Some sat
> Poised like mud grenades, their blunt heads farting.
> I sickened, turned, and ran. The great slime kings
> Were gathered there for vengeance and I knew
> That if I dipped my hand the spawn would clutch it.

He sees the frogs as seeking revenge for his b-boyish stealing of their eggs to hatch in j-jam-jars. It's entitled "Death of a Naturalist" ...'

'Quite makes you think of the caviare we've just consumed ...' Auberon Havelock said thoughtfully.

'And that's just it! The p-poetry is alive. It d-deals with events and occurrences to which we can relate. It is universal.'

The table was then cleared by the waitresses and coffee served, with a tray of white and pink cubes of Turkish Delight rolled in sugar dust, and a bowl of fruit. Those who did not take brandy received glasses of mauve Parfit d'Amour.

'It now b-befalls me,' Charles declared, his eyes glinting in the candlelight, 'formally to introduce our guest. He is, as you all know, Matthew Nchembe, who rises from the dark continent, the world of camelopards and those beasts with teeth upon their noses and others such as only Rhydisel has seen, a friend of many years of our b-brother B-brian. They met initially when Brian was a youth in Kenya. He was then a redoubtable white hunter and Matthew was undergoing at Her Majesty's p-pleasure a course of rehabilitation from his ways as a M-mau Mau fighter. These two met when Matthew skinned Brian's leopard and I d-defy anyone here to come up with a more outrageous event over which a friendship might be forged ... Matthew Nchembe.'

Nchembe rose to his feet, pushing back his chair with his right hand. His left sleeve, tucked into his jacket pocket, was working loose.

Brian cast his mind back over the years, wondering at the course their lives had taken and the manner in which fate had brought them together again in such an unlikely venue, at such a time in their lives: it was, he considered, almost as if some force had planned it, was even now seeking to establish a future for them both.

'Gentlemen,' Nchembe began, 'I am honoured to be invited to your gathering. As an outsider, I am conscious of the courtesy being extended and thank you.'

He looked about at the up-turned faces, white in the candlelight.

'Let me tell you of my first meeting with Brian. It was a meeting that must have been cast by the stars. I was indeed what was known as a Mau Mau detainee, held in a camp of tin huts and barbed-wire, called Wamumu, about seventy miles east-north-east of Nairobi.

'My days as what you would have termed a terrorist, and

300

what we consider to be a revolutionary liberty fighter, were not long and were brought to an end not by the security forces but by my own ignorant ill-luck. My home-made rifle exploded in my hand, hence ...' he raised his left stump in the air; the sleeve came completely out of his pocket to flap obscenely in the air '... my blunted arm.'

He picked up his coffee cup and sipped from it.

'By the time I met Brian,' Nchembe glanced at his friend, 'I had renounced violence as a means of obtaining *uhuru* – freedom – for my country. It was not a matter of rehabilitation but a realization of how things really were. Violence begets violence. There had to be a way of compromise and reason. This was the eventual course taken and, as a result, there was no blood-bath, no killing of whites or Asians, no driving out of the colonials. There was simply a transition of power. Today, all races live harmoniously in Kenya and together they are making the country strong. But only as strong as they can. There is much lacking. Communications, irrigation, improved mining, agriculture, medicine and technology, natural husbandry and conservation ...

'Yet, how do we get these?' Nchembe continued. 'Our gross national product in Kenya is low. We export coffee, tea, cotton, tobacco. We earn from tourism but this is insufficient.'

Around the table, in the candlelight, the men were intently watching him. Even as they drank their coffee, sipped their cognac or liqueur, their eyes remained on him.

'We have three choices. One is to accept charity and therefore be vulnerable to exploitation – which is to say, colonialism in one form or another. Are we not seeing this in Kenya now with the presence of the Chinese? The second alternative is to develop our own agricultural and natural resources technology, but for this we require an educated élite who can assess the problems of our rapidly-swelling society. Our third alternative is to do without and slide into poverty, starvation and degradation.'

Jeff Crane shifted in his seat. At salient points in Nchembe's speech, he had nodded agreement which Brian had noted with pleasure; his friend was impressing the members.

'I ask you,' Nchembe went on, his voice becoming impassioned, 'to consider this: Africa needs you – your expertise, encouragement, humanity. I suggest ... come to Africa, bring your knowledge, skills and ideas. Do not bring these as conquerors or rulers – as colonials – but as men willing to share. Come and be Africans. Your colour is immaterial. After all, under the skin, all our bloods are red.'

Nchembe sat down to a stunned silence. His brow was beaded with sweat, his hand shook as he lifted a glass of mauve liqueur to his mouth. A little spilled onto his fingers.

As he and Brian walked through the streets, the sky clear and the air frosty, Nchembe said, 'I hope you are considering what I said this evening, Brian?'

'I've been thinking since you left the cottage.'

'Africa is changing fast and urgently requires guidance. I was thinking of this when Charles read the Irishman's poem. The title is apt for Africa – "Death of a Naturalist": an innocent youth who knows no better until his conscience revolts at the sight of the frogs coming, as he thinks, to seek retaliation. Africa will do this to the people who, with their naivety and guileless ignorance, know no better and will not learn otherwise unless they are taught. Africa needs you, Brian.'

They parted at Carfax as the figures on the clock chimed midnight. Brian watched his friend set off along St Aldate's. Even as far down as the entrance to Christ Church he could hear the toecaps of Nchembe's polished shoes striking off the pavement.

Lucy was quarter of an hour late. When she did finally arrive, it was by taxi and not on the white bicycle she usually used to get about Oxford. She stepped from the cab, paid the driver and slammed the door.

Brian had been sheltering from the rain under the canopy of the entrance to the Oxford Playhouse. She had asked him to meet her there for she was, she said in a hurried call from a telephone call-box, the pips demanding more money and

302

cutting short her last sentence, due in the theatre at seven-
fifteen for a full rehearsal.

'Can we have dinner together afterwards?' he had
requested, but the line went dead before she could hear him.

The taxi made a U-turn, splashing water over two
pedestrians from an oily puddle at the corner of St John
Street. One of them shook his fist at the driver who, seeing
this, beeped his horn and jumped the traffic lights by the
Martyrs' Memorial.

'I'm sorry I'm late.'

'That's all right,' Brian forgave her, but she felt the need to
excuse herself further.

'The taxi was held up by a road flooding. It's a beastly
night. I'd rather be tucked up in front of the fire with a book.
Still – the show must go on. Can't resist the roar of the
greasepaint and the smell of the audience!' She threw back
her head and laughed once at the posters beside the theatre
entrance doors: her name was prominent on the cast list. 'And
I've only got a few minutes.'

'Dinner after?' Brian offered again.

'I can't. The run-through'll go on until well after ten.
Eleven even.'

'I'll come back with the M G,' Brian offered. 'I can easily
book a table at ...

'No. Honestly, I can't. Cordelia needs so much.'

Brian looked at the poster. The Oxford University Dra-
matic Society were putting on Shakespeare's *King Lear*;
according to the poster, Robert Boscowan was '*the mad king,
driven to death by ill-luck and his two minxish daughters*' with
Alan Stantington as the Fool and Lucy Haycraft as Cordelia.
From the advance write-up the play had received in *Isis*, the
university magazine, it was going to be a major production,
the first 'for some time' – the critic had been at pains to point
out – 'which treats the Bard's script not as a tragedy but as a
black comedy'. It was also to be performed in modern dress
on a stage without props or a backdrop.

Lucy tugged on the handle of the main theatre entrance
door. It was locked.

'Damn!' she exclaimed. 'I'll need to go round the back.'

'I've an umbrella.' Brian unfurled the black material. 'I'll take you to the stage door.'

'That's awfully kind of you but – well, could I borrow it? This rain's forecast all night.'

'Then let me bring the MG round? I'll park it ...'

'No ... Well, you see – I'm not actually going home tonight,' she admitted.

'I see.'

Brian felt the chill shiver of rejection pass through him. He had known it was coming, had sensed it since she had met him in the lane by the library, but it was nevertheless a shock.

'I'm sorry, Brian. I was going to tell you. It's not easy because we've had such a good time, but ... You know how it is.'

'Frankly, I don't.'

'Don't make it more awkward than it is.' She spoke almost sharply. 'It's not easy for me.'

'It's no barrel of laughs from my side, either,' he replied ruefully. 'I just wish you'd told me when we met. Or at least sent me a note.' He grasped at a last straw. 'Perhaps a farewell dinner after the rehearsal?'

'Don't be silly, Brian. That really wouldn't be on.' Now she was being curt. 'Just understand ...'

Someone knocked on the inside of the theatre door and pointed eagerly to the rear, mouthing at them through the glass. She gave them a thumbs-up.

'I'm sorry, Brian,' she said again. 'I must go. Really. Maybe I'll see you around? It's ...'

He opened the umbrella and handed it to her.

'Keep it,' he said.

She accepted it, smiled wanly at him and walked out of the protection of the theatre canopy, the rain and water flowing from the roof sounding a sudden tattoo on the stretched segments of the umbrella. She walked briskly round the corner into Gloucester Street.

Brian followed after her at a slower pace. By the time he reached the corner she was nowhere in sight. He traced her steps, still visible on the wet pavement. As he reached the alleyway at the rear of the theatre, he saw her go in through the stage door, the light cast from within briefly illuminating the pelting rain.

'Oh, sod it!' he muttered bleakly.

Before he regained Beaumont Street, his hair was plastered to his head and his feet were wet. Rain was leaking through the lace-holes in his shoes and ekeing into his socks. By the time he arrived back at his digs, he was soaked through to the skin.

He was miserable, his feelings hurt and his ego bruised. She had, he said to himself as he retraced his steps, the rain seeping down his collar, abused him cruelly. He had given her so much, had grown used to her ways, her foibles and tastes, her body even. Now he had been spurned almost callously, briefly, with no explanation or apology. His disconsolation compounded by the pelting rain, he grew to hate her, to search for flaws in her and yet, no sooner did he find a fault in her, than he forgave or justified it and this increased his aching sense of loss.

17

Brian's note was terse and he walked across Oxford in bright, late autumn sunlight to deliver it.

As he made his way down St Aldate's and Abingdon Road, over the Thames, past the cricket fields and the football ground, municipal workmen were clearing the rubbish left by the previous evening's mid-week match crowd. He felt inwardly calm, terribly pleased with himself.

For the first time since his parents had died he felt he had a direction to his life, an aim more than merely the goal of academic achievement or recognition amongst peers. He was, he considered, doing something positive. Not only would he soon complete his thesis and be awarded a doctorate but he was also to return to Africa and do something definite with his now considerable body of knowledge.

So caught up was he in his thoughts that he went a hundred yards past the turning to Nchembe's digs before he realised he had gone too far.

At the door to the African's lodgings, he rang the bell. It sounded janglingly from inside but nobody came to answer it.

He removed the note once more from its envelope. It was more than a brief letter to him. It was an affirmation for the future, an idealistic contract he was making with himself, with Nchembe, with a whole continent.

Unfolding the note, he read it again:

Dear Matthew, I've given your speech at the club and your words before and since much thought. In the end, I have come to agree with you. As soon as I have my doctorate, I shall seek work in East Africa – preferably Kenya, which I know so well – and see if I can't be of some use to the common good there.
Brian

Folding and re-inserting the note in its envelope, he licked the flap, sealed it with the ball of his thumb against the door and thrust it through the letterbox. Through the frosted glass he could make out its hazy outline lying on the hessian mat inside.

The evening traffic was heavy. The end of the Michaelmas term was close with the round of parties and dances, many of them spiced with the anticipation of Christmas. The pubs were hung with decorations and, in the cold evenings, served pokered cider and hot buttered rum. The shops stayed open later to accommodate Christmas shoppers. It was the season of going out, of entertaining and entertainment. Carol singers loitered outside churches or gave concerts in college quads, candles in lanterns hanging from their hands. Students from the polytechnic dressed as Santa Clauses or reindeers or – if they were attractive girls with long legs – Santa's helpers from his grotto near the North Pole, and paraded the streets collecting money for charities or advertising various shops and stores.

At Carfax, Brian parped the horn of the MG at two cavaliers, an archbishop and a pirate on their way to a fancy-dress party. One of the cavaliers jabbed two fingers in the air at the car in a markedly un-royal gesture of defiance.

There was no place to leave the car near the dance. Early-comers had taken any available kerb spaces and a policeman was patrolling the sections of the street where parking was prohibited. Brian halted by him to ask if he might suggest an alternative street.

'They'll all be chock-a-block tonight, sir,' the constable replied, bending down. His civility was due to his noticing Brian was not only smartly dressed in evening wear but was obviously older than the average student. 'I could suggest Longwall Street, but it'll still leave you a long walk back.' He looked up and down the street. 'Tell you what sir, slip in here behind the Hillman and I'll move the notice down a bit. No harm so long as your vehicle's still under the light. What we don't want are cars left in darkened side streets.'

Brian expressed his gratitude and reversed the MG against the kerb.

'No bother at all, sir. And might I warn you, sir, of the

dangers of drinking and driving? Hate to ruin your Christ-mas, sir.'

'Thank you, officer. I'll be careful – though I've only to go to Jericho to get home.'

'Still in control of a motor vehicle, sir. Good evening to you.'

The constable walked off down the street, his gloved hands behind his back, his breath misting in the night air.

The dance had already begun as Brian and Judy entered, she resting her hand on his arm. At the door, they surren-dered their guest ticket and were met by Charles Runciman.

'B-brian! How good to see you – b-both of you! You look q-quite debonair and gallant, my dear chap. And Judy,' he made a slight, formal bow, 'you will be the b-belle of the b-ball.'

He took her hand and kissed it.

'You'll melt hearts tonight, Charles,' she teased him. 'To have one's hand kissed is …'

'I d-doubt I shall be in the p-position to need to th-thaw one,' he replied, adding, 'Hearts aren't exactly my cup of tea. I'm more a man of l-letters rather than le-lechery. However, we shall see …'

'You're already sozzled, Charles,' Brian remonstrated with him. 'Been at the green chartreuse all afternoon, have you? Like those decadent Victorian poets you like.'

'N-nothing so sordid. Merely g-gin and tonics starting with my supervisor before a t-tolerable imitation of Christ-mas fare in hall. Then the rounds of p-pals in the f-faculty. And so on … I did have tea – and c-crumpets, would you believe? – with the dean of degrees at five o'clock. So it's not been one B-bacchanalian orgy after another.' He looked through the crowds of people leaving the dance floor: the music had stopped as Brian and Judy had arrived. 'Now! You are on my table and I've s-some people for you to meet whom you don't know …'

They followed him through the throng to a table on the edge of the dance floor but as far from the band, a quintet, as was possible. Charles Runciman approved of the waltzes and the foxtrots, but not of what he knew would follow later in the evening when the rock group arrived.

'Stuart Holland, M-mandy Hauser, may I introduce B-brian Titchner and Judy Lockyer. Stuart is a Harvard man and is really "Junior" because he's an American and he spells his name as the k-kingly dynasty did. You Americans will do anything to g-get a b-bit of aristocracy.'

The man rose from the table.

'Charlie still thinks we're a colony and ought to be taxed. Or whipped for the war of the revolution,' Holland announced in a cultured Boston accent.

They shook hands, the girl at the table smiling her welcome, tossing her long fair hair and moving her chair so Judy could squeeze between the tables.

'I hear from Charlie you're a soil expert,' the American remarked as Brian sat and Charles poured out glasses of champagne.

'In a manner of speaking.'

'D-don't be so modest, Brian.' Charles wrapped the champagne in a napkin and stood it in the centre of the table beside the candle burning incongruously in an empty bottle of the same vintage and from the same chateau. 'B-brian's one of the top bods on soil erosion in Africa. He's so much in the know that m-most of the continent is b-begging for him to go back and save it from disaster.'

'Charles is a little too gracious in his compliments,' Brian was quick to assert. 'I'm working on a doctoral thesis but it's not submitted yet.'

'My d-dear Brian, the submission – in your instance – is certain to be a mere f-formality.'

'Begging you to go back?' Holland's companion queried. Her accent was also American but not Bostonian. Brian wondered where she came from.

For twenty minutes, they talked of Africa and Brian's childhood there. Holland, before entering Harvard, had been to Rhodesia on a lion hunt and they spoke of this before conversation turned to hunting moose in Canada and grizzly bears in the Rockies.

The quintet was taking a break and speech was possible

despite the hubbub of the five hundred members of the college and their guests. However, when the musicians returned to their dais and commenced to play again, conversation became awkward. Holland asked Judy to dance and Brian escorted Mandy Hauser on to the dance floor.

As they spun in the midst of fellow dancers, Mandy questioned Brian about Charles Runciman.

'Is he queer?' she asked.

'You've not met him before?'

'Never. He knows Stuart through their bridge circle. They often partner each other. And they belong to the same gentleman's club in London.'

'If by queer you mean is he a poof, then the answer's no,' Brian told her. 'Not really. He's not interested in women, but then he's not particularly bothered with men either – he's not a homosexual.' He turned her to avoid another couple. 'At least, not in the active sense of the word. He's,' he found the right description, 'that unique product of this place, an Oxford eccentric.'

'I've seen a few since we got here,' she admitted.

'How long have you been in Oxford?'

'Just this term. Stuart's here for a year on an exchange fellowship – he's a professor at Columbia U – and I've come with him. It gives me a chance to study up my field ...'

'Which is?'

'Archaeology. Specifically the Middle East at the time of the Romans.'

The music stopped. They let go of each other and applauded. Making their way back to their table, Brian thought of how Dash would have given much to show yet another blonde his finds; then he remembered how he had had the same thought on first meeting Judy.

While they were on the dance floor, Charles had produced another bottle of champagne and a tray of assorted canapés. Once his guests were settled, he requested the next dance of Judy and the two of them stepped on to the floor.

'Charlie's very quaint,' Mandy remarked, 'and one hell of a dancer.'

On the floor, Charles and Judy were spiritedly dancing a tango.

'He is rather gay,' Brian agreed.

'But you said he wasn't! I mean, is he or isn't he?'

'Which?' Brian was confused. 'No. He's not a homosexual. Yes, he's very gay. Can't you be one without the other?'

Holland interrupted, 'You two are talking right away at cross purposes. In San Francisco jargon, Brian, gay means a queen, a queer. Over here, honey,' he told Mandy, 'gay still just means happy as hell.'

The leader of the quintet switched on a microphone placed on the dais during the tango. He was a man in his forties wearing a dinner jacket and black bow tie. He might have been an older member of the college were it not for the violin and bow in his right hand. Behind him, on the oak panelling of the hall, hung oil portraits of past masters of the college.

'Thank you, ladies and gentlemen.' His words were responded to by enthusiastic applause. 'The next number will be our last until the early hours. Would you all care to take your partners for a dance I'm sure will liven up your joints and prepare you for the group following after the break – ladies and gentlemen, the Gay Gordons.'

At this announcement the Americans exchanged quizzical glances and Brian bit the inside of his mouth to prevent his laughter.

The tables emptied as everyone took to the floor, Holland and his companion joining them. Judy remained with Charles, mingling with the mass which was gradually evolving into a circle round the hall. Brian, remaining seated, lost sight of them.

As the music began, Brian leaned forward to refill his glass and banged his shoe against something beneath the table. He raised the white linen cloth to discover a large picnic freezer box on the floor, a gentle frost of carbon dioxide seeping from the lid and catching the half-light under the table. He lifted the lid. Inside were four more bottles of champagne.

This ball, Brian thought, was like all those his father had attended, and his grandfather before him, part of a tradition, as much of a tradition as academic gowns, Oxford bicycles and elderly dons. The ghosts in the college that night, he thought, would be suffering from severe déjà vu. Yet, if Nchembe was proven right and the world went on, it would soon all be different, irrevocably altered and probably, Brian reasoned, for the worse.

A ring of dancers brushed past him and, suddenly, in the mass of evening dresses, dinner jackets, bow ties and white fronts, bare arms and almost bare breasts, he caught sight of Angela. She had her arm in that of a tall undergraduate with shoulder-length hair brushing the sleek collar of his jacket. Just as Brian saw her, she noticed him and he waved. Her hand waved from beneath her partner's arm but the smile on her face froze for an instant. She might have seen a ghost.

The Gay Gordons came to its climax. The applause was deafening and the dancers halted, or fell about, or whistled, or cat-called, or hooted.

Through the jostle of people returning to their tables, Brian saw Angela coming towards him, briskly side-stepping couples in her way.

'Hello, Angela ...' he began.

'What on earth are you doing here? I didn't know ...'

'Whose the flower-power?' he asked, ignoring her question.

'Nigel – but who do you know here?'

'We've come as Charles Runciman's guests. He's a post-grad here and ...'

'You're n-not chasing other women now are you, B-brian?' Charles interrupted good-naturedly. 'I've b-brought back your own.'

Brian took Judy's hand and, one by one, introduced those at his table to Angela. She smiled and shook hands, her demeanour suddenly changing. Her boyfriend then arrived at the table to guide her away. As she went with him, she looked anxiously over her shoulder for a moment, and stared meaningfully at Brian.

Charles produced yet another bottle of champagne and, leaving the table, returned a few minutes later with a second tray of canapés. They were all of one sort. Holland picked one up and ate it.

'I'm very sorry,' Charles apologized, 'but it's Iranian S-sevruga, not Russian B-beluga. So you can b-both eat it without any p-pangs of conscience whatsoever.'

'Chilled as well,' Holland complimented him. 'If this was what the cold war was all about, let's have more of it. Where on earth are you getting all this from, Charlie?'

'My s-secret.'

'Go on, let us in on it,' Mandy demanded.

'It's q-quite simple. I've employed a c-caterer to do for us this evening. He's ensconced in my r-rooms with a c-crateful of goodies.'

'I do wish you had a partner tonight,' Judy said.

'My p-partner will arrive later,' he announced confidently and with an air of mystery. 'They were unable to g-get here because the t-trains were running slow. Or something.'

'I thought you weren't going to thaw any hearts.' Judy took the spirit of Charles's secrecy and kept her voice low. 'You've not got yourself an assignation tonight after all, have you?'

'Sort of. And I rather hope it's already th-thawed itself out on B-british Railways.'

Upon the dais was a commotion of activity. The rock band had arrived and were setting up their equipment, positioning loudspeakers and trailing wires. The work was done by three roadies, men in jeans and printed T-shirts with shoulder-length hair and tattooed forearms. Within fifteen minutes, the group was ready and started playing. Their first number was Martha and the Vandellas' "Dancing in the Street".

For half an hour they played non-stop – Beatles and Stones, the Animals and the Who, Otis Redding and the Kinks – before taking a short break.

No sooner had the music ceased than Charles left the dance to return a few minutes later with his partner. Brian and Judy exchanged cautious glances; Stuart Holland and his American girlfriend looked at each other with bemused amazement.

'M-may I introduce you all to B-bridgette?' Charles said.

The girl by his side was hardly unknown and heads from a number of the surrounding tables turned to look at her. She had appeared, over the past few months, on the front covers of all the best glossy magazines. For *Harpers & Queen* she had modelled scanty swimwear, for *Vogue* evening gowns, and she had appeared on the cover of *Time* in a feature on the Swinging Sixties. Her auburn hair was curled inwards in a cut shaped by the best salon in London. Her gown was tight-fitting and elegant. Her make-up was flawless and her skin softly tanned. She was Brian's height and, as he took her hand in his, she did not avert her eyes but looked into his, own.

'Welcome to Oxford.' Brian was at a loss as to what else to say.

'Thank you,' she said, her voice light. She cast a quick glance around her and those at other tables who had not been able to tear their eyes off her now did so. 'I believe you also go to lectures?'

'Only on the odd occasion,' Charles assured her. 'We usually just j-jive about and m-make merry hell.'

'Your train was held up?' Holland asked, nearly speechless with awe in her presence.

'My train?'

'My little j-joke. B-bridgette actually d-drove down, didn't you, my dear? She has one of those very large sports cars which g-glares at one from the front. It's made in B-birmingham from which it takes its name.'

'Now Chas is teasing you again.' She held his hand and gently tugged on his arm. 'It's made in Newport Pagnell and I bet he knows it.'

Brian thought for a moment: Newport Pagnell was the town in Buckinghamshire where Aston Martin-Lagonda had their factory.

'Now that is one in the eye for the sceptics,' Judy remarked as the others danced to the first number of the band's next set, leaning into Brian's ear to be heard over the music.

'She's certainly one up to Charles.'

'Oh, no!' she retorted, 'you get at least ten points for an international model.'

With the arrival of the rock band, most of the lights in the college hall had been extinguished. Each table was lit by its own candle, but the dance floor was in semi-darkness except for flashes of light from equipment linked to the amplifiers. It was not until the next long break for the band that some of the lights were switched back on.

Brian left his seat to find the gentlemen's lavatory and, as he did so, across the tables, he saw Matthew Nchembe standing by the bar. He was talking to another African student and a Sikh in a dinner jacket and a saffron-yellow turban. Standing at Nchembe's side, with her arm through his, was Lucy, dressed in a long white ball-gown. Around her neck was draped an azure feather boa: even at that distance, Brian noticed her eye-shadow matched the dyed feathers.

At first, he made no move and Judy, finding him not walking away, followed Brian's stare. She tried then to grasp his sleeve but he stepped out of her reach, striding across the dance floor.

By the tables on the opposite side of the dance floor, Angela accosted him.

'Forget it, Brian,' she urged him, touching his arm, but he ignored her.

Nchembe only saw him when he was within ten feet.

'Hello, Brian. I didn't know ...'

'Evidently.' Brian cut him short. 'I want words with you. Outside.'

'We don't want any trouble.' The Indian was on the defensive, obviously used to having to fend off an attack he saw building up.

'You keep out of this, *chut*,' Brian hissed, the insult rising from the dim recesses of his childhood memory.

'How dare you speak to me in this manner?' the Sikh complained.

'Then keep your nose out of matters that don't concern you.'

'You're drunk, Brian,' Lucy said. 'Why don't you go away and leave us alone.' She looked up at Nchembe. 'Let's go. I've had enough dancing for one evening in any case.'

'I'll see you tomorrow, Brian,' Nchembe offered. 'Why don't you come round to my place at about ten?'

'Now. I want to talk to you now. And as for you ...' Brian glared at Lucy but made no comment, then made his way to the exit. Nchembe walked between the tables, following him. Behind him were Lucy and the Indian.

'J-Just let it go, my d-dear fellow,' Charles advised at the door, trying to head Brian off. 'These things happen all the time. *C-c'est la vie, c'est la guerre* is, I think, the p-popular aphorism for such a state of affairs.'

Yet Brian made no reply. He merely walked past his friend, white with anger.

The procession went across the quad and through a low stone passageway to a door. Brian, knowing the college, was aware it led into the fellows' garden. In the summer, it was a haven for the college teaching staff, a leafy escape from the pressures of students and their demands. The flowerbeds would be ablaze with bedding plants, the bushes alive with bees. Now, in the winter, the trees were naked and the beds bare earth with twigged bushes rising against the stone wall every ten feet or so.

Ignoring the notice forbidding students and guests from entry, Brian pushed the door open and went through. When it closed behind him, he turned to see Nchembe, the Indian and Lucy standing on the path.

'How long's this been going on?'

'That's none of your business,' Lucy said caustically.

'I suppose you were seeing her before she and I broke up.' He addressed Nchembe but received no answer. He turned to her. 'I suppose ...'

'Suppose all you will, Brian. You were getting very boring with your bloody thesis and I – I can do as I like. If I was seeing Matthew it was nothing to do with you.'

'Please, let us leave this disagreeableness and return to the dance,' the Sikh suggested. 'None of you can achieve anything by this.'

'Shut up!' Brian muttered.

A light came on in a room at the end of the fellows' garden.

'If you must know, I was seeing Matthew last term. And in the long vac. – we met in Italy and he stayed with me and my father at our house in Fivizzano. And we went ...' She was warming to her speech, revelling in her vindictiveness.

'Enough!' Nchembe raised his hand and she fell silent.

Nobody spoke for a moment. Brian was vaguely aware of the door to the garden opening. He stepped closer to Nchembe.

'So this is how you show friendship,' he said sarcastically. 'You stay in my home, spin some bullshit tale about having to go abroad on business and then you spend the rest of the summer making it with her.'

Someone drew heavy curtains over the distant window and the light was extinguished.

He glowered at Lucy, beside himself with rage. 'I suppose you liked a foreign fuck, did you?' He jabbed a finger in Nchembe's direction but did not take his eyes from her face. 'Is it true they have big cocks?'

She said nothing and he returned his attention to Nchembe, searching through the irrationality of his anger for the most maleficent words he could find.

'It was good, was it? Fulfilled the promise that after *uhuru* you'd get a white woman? Did you get the bicycle on offer as well?'

'Why don't you piss off, Brian?' Lucy was ready to drive home all the viperous spite she could muster. 'You never were any good between the sheets.'

'You'd know.' He spat the words out at her. 'You've had enough experience to judge. But as for you ...' He looked at Nchembe. 'You two-faced bastard – double standards just aren't in it, are they?'

Nchembe made no attempt to defend himself.

'What price your friendship then?' Brian stormed at him. 'It's worth just what you can get out of it. A woman and the ability to say you've white men as acquaintances. All that talk about doing Africa good – doing you good, you mean!'

He paused to allow Nchembe to refute these slurs. The African still did nothing, said nothing.

'No answer! Someone cut your tongue out like they did to the *toto*s and screaming women at Lari? Like you did at Lari. You screwed your own people then – those who supported you in the forest, your own tribe, your friends – just as you're doing now. I wonder what your friends in the Aberdare Forest were really like. Like you? Dependable? Trustworthy?

317

Loyal? Some band of freedom-fighting brothers they must have been! No wonder Mau Mau fell flat on its face ...'

'It was not like that.' Nchembe spoke softly, his emotion totally under control. 'We were brothers. Like you and I ...'

'Your tribe ...' Brian paused to catch his breath, losing the thread of the insult he was planning next. Casting a sideways glance at Lucy, he saw she was crying. His voice lowered. 'You didn't even have the guts to tell me yourself.'

With a swift thrust of his hand, Brian reached forward, grabbed Nchembe's evening shirt and tore at it. The pleated front ripped, the studs breaking free of the cloth. Against the African's chest hung the chain bearing the leopard's tooth.

'And I'll have that back.'

Brian closed his fingers on the canine, his own nails like claws scoring the African's smooth chest. The chain snapped as he pulled hard at it.

Nchembe, startled by Brian's action, was slow to try to prevent it.

'Here's what I think of you and your fucking friendship!'

The chain flashed as Brian threw it on the grass and ground it in with his heel.

Removing the tooth was an act of catharsis but it was not enough revenge. His temper finally snapping, Brian swung his fist hard at Nchembe's face. The African raised his stub of arm, the sleeve of his jacket hanging grotesquely from it, but the remaining bone was too short to divert the blow. Brian's fist hit the African on his cheekbone and the corner of his eye. Then, with one movement, Nchembe brought his only arm round, the hand not clenched but cupped. He caught Brian on the ear and sent him sprawling onto the ground, into a pile of dead leaves sodden by the recent days of rain. The air trapped in the cupped hand had formed a pressure in his ear which partially deafened him.

Brian got up, aided by Stuart Holland who had come through the garden door, closing it behind him. The American brushed the dead leaves off Brian's jacket and when Brian looked up, the others had gone, the door swinging open on its hinges.

His pyjamas lay in a heap on the bedside carpet and he put them on, struggling with the tangled knot in the waist cord. Over these he put first his thick winter dressing-gown then an overcoat lying across the back of the rocking-chair by the window. Before pushing his feet into his shoes, he pulled over them a pair of thick socks from a drawer in the dressing table. The wood squeaked as he opened it.

From the top shelf of the wardrobe, he lifted a package wrapped in brown paper and tied securely with twine.

He avoided the weak creaking step on the stairs, passing through to the kitchen, unbolting and unlatching the door. The freezing night air took his breath away as he went outside and up the garden towards the garage, his breath making clouds before his face as he fumbled with the side door. Within, he rested the parcel upon the long bonnet of the M G and removed a bottle from a shelf.

At the end of the garden, he dropped the parcel on to the heap of compost he had piled there, uncorked the bottle, sniffed at the neck and sprinkled the contents over the paper. He went back to the kitchen to return a few moments later.

'I hope you were wrong, you black son-of-a-bitch!'

He spoke aloud and a rodent in the hedge scuttered across frozen leaves at the sound of his voice. He stopped what he was doing and peered into the network of twigs and twilight. He had noticed a rat-run weaving through the hedge towards the inn. He knew the publican kept chickens: just as in any part of Africa, where there were hens there were rats. The difference was, he thought, in Africa there would be snakes to prey upon them.

He struck a match, tossing it on to the package. It flared dully in one spot then the flames spread along the paper, jumping from splash to splash of the liquid. The black fumes of burning paraffin rose into the clear air, cooled quickly and hung over the hedge, obliterating the stars. Soon there came to him the stench of singeing hair.

'I hope fire is the end of everything.'

The twine burned through, the contents of the parcel unwinding to fall across the compost heap. It might have been alive, the way it seemed to spreadeagle, arching back, the long white and black hairs stark in the starlight and flickering yellow flames.

He stood by, shivering, prodding the flames with a stick, holding the burning mass up so the fire might get under it, not going in to the house until he was certain all the waistcoat had been completely burned.

Zambia: 1987

18

The house on the outskirts of Lusaka was set back a quarter of a mile from the metalled Leopards Hill Road, surrounded by eucalyptus, frangipani and citrus trees, bougainvillaea bushes and an assortment of low shrubs. To one side of the rear of the house was the swimming pool, a little up the gentle hill upon which the whole estate was situated. The grounds, totalling about five hectares, were contained by a metal link fence eight feet high which, wherever they could, ground creepers had colonized, giving the bare chain mesh a faint resemblance to a recently-trimmed hedge. Two kilometres away, across the shallow African valley, a range of low, wooded hills lined the horizon.

He eased the new Mercedes Benz from the tarmac strip of the road to the murram track, the suspension rocking the car and the rear wheels pluming up dust, spattering gravel into the scrub. Keeping to the smoother side of the corrugated track, the saloon travelled at about fifty kph, dodging the deeper ruts and potholes, until it arrived at the gates set in the link fence. A gardener, at the approach of the car, had opened the gates and now stood to one side to allow the vehicle to enter, the driver steering to avoid the central concrete plinth raised several centimetres proud of the surface of the track. As soon as the Mercedes was through into the compound, the gardener swung the gates shut, bolting them to the plinth.

The car halted under the cover of trees by the side of the house, the accompanying dust-cloud drifting into the branches and settling on the Peugeot 405, the white Jaguar XK120, two Toyota safari vehicles and a beige and brown Range Rover: the last three, in the way of Africa, had front-mounted power winches. As soon as the smooth engine died, there appeared from around the house a servant dressed in a white shirt, his khaki trousers visible only when his white apron flapped aside. He was barefoot. Upon his head he wore a small, white, pork-pie hat.

'Good morning, boss.' He surveyed the Mercedes. 'This new car is very good.' He stroked the chrome metal of the door mirror.

'Morning, Tom. Two boxes in the boot. Can you have them brought in?'

On the verandah, ensconced in one of the comfortable wicker chairs arranged around low tables, sat a European in his late twenties. Before him was a silver tea pot and milk jug, a half-empty cup and a plate bearing the remains of two croissants. He was dressed in a pair of khaki shorts and a short-sleeved bush shirt from the buttoned-down pocket of which projected the top of a gold Parker roller-ball, the stylized arrow of the clip outlined against the drab colour of the material. His legs were covered by long khaki socks and, on his wrist, as obvious against his tanned skin as the pen clip, was a gold Seiko watch.

'Morning, Mr Titchner.' He rose from the chair to greet the arrival. 'How was the airport?'

'Hello, Peter.' Brian climbed the steps. 'As ever. The Q Z flight was over an hour late – apparently there's an immigration officers' go-slow in London. And they were a long time getting the D C 10 unloaded. You know what the cargo boys are like.'

He poured himself a coffee from a percolator standing on the bar to one side of the verandah. 'When did you get in from Harare?'

'About an hour ago.'

'Good flight?'

'Not too bad. There's an alert on or something, so I had to divert and fly in the long way, but I'd been given warning by air traffic control in Harare. Came across the border east of Kachalola, changed course to Old Mkushi, down to Chongwe and in from there. Left the Cessna at the flying club and came straight here in the second Toyota. One of the boys met me. I radioed in just after you'd left for the airport.'

The gardener who had closed the gate shambled around the corner of the house with a teenager; they were carrying a wooden box between them. It was not large but it was heavy and they staggered to the steps of the verandah.

'Thank you, Thadeus. Where's the other one?'

The gardener, an old man with a partially-withered right leg, pointed towards the parked vehicles.

'Bring it here, too.'

'They've come then?' Peter Peal asked.

'Indeed they have. And not before time. It took two cartons – cartons, mind you, not packets – of Peter Stuyvesant to get the consignment dealt with promptly. Not to mention a bottle of aspirin for the handler's cold. But it'll be worth it. The delays are a pain...'

He cut the binding round the box with a serrated knife from the bar. The packing of polystyrene shells clung to his bare arms by static and he shook them free.

'Here's one of them.'

From a wrapping of plastic bubble foilpaper bound with strong rubber bands, Brian removed a steel box set with several gauges and knobs.

'Is that it?'

'That's it.'

'Hardly looks anything. And it's so small.'

'The probe,' Brian ran his finger over the rod taped to the side of the box, 'is super-sensitive. For our purposes it's more than adequate. I've bought six of them.'

'Six!'

'For use in the research stations as well as in the field. They'll last a year or two, with luck. Unless they get pinched first – so keep your eyes on them. They weren't cheap.'

'How much?'

'A hell of a lot. Let's put it this way, Peter – if I was short of the ready, I'd have to make a serious choice between these and the new Merc.'

Peter Peal sucked his breath, hissed, and changed the subject.

'What new Merc? You've not bought another car ...'

'You'll see. Now I'm going to have a shower, a bit of a swim and breakfast.' He called through the open window to the lounge. 'Tom! Breakfast in thirty minutes, please.'

'Yes, boss,' came the muted reply from the kitchen.

'I'll leave for Harare this afternoon,' Peter informed his employer. 'I've got to pick up a few things in town. Can I use one of the Toyotas?'

'Check it's tanked up. One of them came back nigh on empty. If I don't see you before you go, have a safe flight. Take two of the analysis kits and good luck with the sampling. See you next Saturday ...'

Brian waved his hand as he entered the house.

While he was taking his morning swim, lazily propelling himself through the water after the obligatory five lengths which he had set as his daily target for the month, Brian heard the Toyota start, die and start again. He made a mental note to get it serviced.

Towelling himself dry, he sat at the edge of the pool. The sun was higher now and had warmed the wall around the pool patio. Over a dozen lizards were basking on the stones.

He patted his belly. The weight he had put on in Washington the month before – due to too much good food and a shopping spree at the Sutton Place gourmet store – was almost gone now, the muscles toned up again. His skin shone, he thought, more healthily at the age of forty-nine than it had at twenty-nine.

When he had eaten breakfast, sitting on the verandah with the shadow of the house shortening visibly before him, he went into the office which led off the verandah, taking with him a tumbler of fresh orange juice.

During the night, the telex had printed out a number of messages from his offices in Washington and London. He raised the dust-cover from the machine, quickly scanned them, wrote his replies on the blank areas at the bottom of each print-out and slid them into the correspondence tray. Rebecca, his secretary, would deal with them when she arrived. He switched on the ansaphone and leaned back in the chair behind his wide desk, sipping the juice. The messages were mostly social – invitations to drinks, to dinner, to go for a fishing weekend in the lower Zambesi. One was more important than the rest. It came from State House and requested a report from him on the maize project. He shuffled through the previous day's typing, found the required report, pinned a compliment slip to it and put it in an envelope. On the outside he wrote, neatly, 'By hand. His Excellency the President.' He propped it on Rebecca's typewriter. She would see it was delivered to the president's private secretary before lunchtime.

The leaning sign at the gate was made of enamel, the lettering and company logo blue on white. Where the sun was striking the notice, an olive-green and gold-striped skink was clinging. As Brian halted the Mercedes by the gate, and beeped the horn twice, the lizard zigzagged from one word to another like the dot following the words on English Language television lessons.

'Afriground (Zambia) Ltd, a branch of Titchner Agrisoils, Inc. Lusaka Research facility. No Admitt —' Brian read to himself, the final word half-covered as the reptile came to a stop.

A bulb flashed on behind a shattered green glass plate, hooded like a traffic light. Brian was annoyed the glass had been broken again only a few days after being replaced: he knew the reason – the traffic lights in Lusaka suffered a similar fate – for the local Africans were smashing them, breaking the glass into small fragments and trying to pass them off to tourists as raw emeralds.

He drove the Mercedes through the gates which closed electronically behind him. Security was important not only to halt the pilfering of fruit and vegetables by local people but also to prevent the stealing of technology, plans and ideas by those in competition.

In stark contrast to the surrounding countryside, which was composed mostly of scrub bush and sunburnt grass with the occasional African smallholding haphazardly dotted about in it, the research station was an oasis of plenty. Under squat glasshouses, the panes of which darkened or lightened automatically according to the intensity of the sunlight, shifting their colour much as liquid crystal displays might, grew rack upon rack of grasses, wheat fronds and maize plants, none more than twenty centimetres high. Over the surrounding grounds were laid tunnels of polythene, the plants within them greenly hazed under a fine spray of water.

Rather than take the road up to the research buildings on the crown of the hill, Brian went slowly down a track between two areas of plastic tunnels. Reaching a junction of tunnels, he turned left, the suspension on the expensive car gliding over a cast aluminium ramp beneath which ran the water-piping ducts. Ahead of him was parked a mud-spattered Nissan four-wheel-drive pick-up, the rear offside suspension low. He pressed the switch on the Mercedes door; the window lowering, hot, dry air surged in to combat the air-conditioned coolness of the saloon.

'How's it going, Gary?'

From a trench at the end of a row of tunnels appeared a head of tousled blond hair. A hand rose, ruffled the hair and a shower of dirt fell from it.

'Bloody! There're big rocks in this one. Taking an awful time to shift them. And the shaft on the cement mixer's bent.'

An African head rose next to the European one. The tight black curls of hair were tinged the colour of weak coffee from the soil.

'How did it happen, Simon?'

The African shook his head and shrugged.

'Cement mixer buggered!' he announced laconically.

Brian left the Mercedes and climbed down the ladder into the eight-foot-deep trench at the bottom of which two Africans were attempting to prise loose from the sub-soil a boulder the size of a car wheel. They had already buckled a crowbar. A third man was standing by watching dis-passionately.

'How much farther to go?'

'Six metres – just over. Down to the marker.' Gary de Witt mopped his forehead with a dusty handkerchief. Sweat had made channels in the dust adhering to his back.

'End of the week?' Brian enquired.

'No sweat!' Gary's accent was, like his laugh, short and curt. 'I'll re-phrase that! Pints of sweat but we'll make it, easy.'

'Any other problems?'

'Only the damn Nissan. Another leaf's gone in the spring. I tell you, Mr Titchner, the only Jap wheels that are any good are the Toyotas. They take stick. But those Nissans are crap.'

Promising to arrange for two new leaves to be fitted to the pick-up, Brian climbed out of the trench, slapped the seat of his trousers clear of dust and returned to the Mercedes.

In the laboratory, he delivered two of the analysers to one the technicians and seated himself at a desk in a side office upon which was arranged an I B M terminal. Punching in the codes, he obtained a screen menu and called up the latest figures for maize. The next month's report would be up-to-date, so far as it went – it would do for the government servants and the president in any case; they would want it for their own report to whatever source was funding the agricultural budget. There were, Brian thought as he scrolled through the screen read-out, so many devious paths for foreign aid to travel before it reached him.

The figures looked good. He pressed the printer command and watched as the Epson tractor fed itself with paper and the bar graphs and pie charts appeared on the sheet. They would have had to be positive regardless of the actual results, for a negative or lack-lustre result would have put the financing in jeopardy. Yet Brian knew, as do all shrewd politicians and those who live in the same tight universe of truths and half-truths, that there can be a world of possibility between the actuality and the statistics.

The print-out torn from the machine and placed in a card folder tucked under his arm, Brian left the office and made his way to the control room from where the water and chemical flows were controlled by computer. A young white American, the daughter of a diplomat, working for the company during her holiday out from university in Colorado, was watching over the screens, the oscilloscopes and the flow gauges.

'How's it going, Peta?'

He startled her and she turned quickly in her her chair, her eyes scared until she saw who was speaking. She had been in Zambia only a few weeks, was still afraid of Africa with the fear imbued in all diplomats who are employed by the super-powers and ever-conscious of terrorists and coups d'état.

'Mr Titchner!' Her face relaxed. 'Everything's fine. And there's little to do. It's all done by them,' she pointed at the computers, silent save for the occasional momentary hum of a disk drive, 'the number crunchers. I feel almost redundant – and guilty. I'm hardly earning my keep.'

'Sorry,' he apologised, 'I didn't mean to make you jump. But you don't need to be so edgy. This isn't Nigeria – or New York! And the facility here's safe as houses. So long as you don't break down in the dodgier parts of town on a Friday night, you're okay. And that goes for most places these days.'

'It takes a bit of getting used to,' she admitted.'I've not been out of the US or Europe before. Except for the Caribbean which is the US really, isn't it? Father,' she gave the single word a degree of formality, 'has never had a real Third World posting before, nothing on which we could go along.'

'You enjoy Africa,' Brian advised her, marvelling at her assurance that the whole Caribbean was as good as an unchartered state of her native country. 'It's a very wonderful continent. As for earning your keep – you're just what we need at the moment, to fill in. Iris will be back from the UK in a fortnight – her mother died, you know – and then you'll have a bit of cash to see the place. As for it being an easy job – well, it may be, but it's vital. If something goes wrong, the number crunchers, as you call them, can't scream for help. You yell out if something goes on the blink. Gary'll be up like a flash.'

'Does this liquid actually provide all the plants need? I find it hard to believe you're growing crops without soil.'

'Hydroponics,' Brian explained. 'Everything grows in a liquid medium. It's common in Europe and the US where they grow salad vegetables and the like – in Saudi they grow salad greens in the desert for the meals service on airlines operating out of Riyadh and Bahrain. But here it's a new venture, especially growing mealies. Maize, that is. It's a bit of an exploration.'

'I think it's miraculous. Quite wonderful, Mr Titchner. You're doing so much for the Africans. They need our help, our technology.'

'Yes,' Brian replied noncommittally. 'They seem to.'

He left the laboratory, stopping to check the supply of liquid fertilizers stocked in drums in a warehouse shaded by eucalyptus trees. Several drums had – as Gary had put it – 'walked of their own volition and done a bunk in the direction of the bush', the theft making a mockery of the computer stock-taking process which was now unreliable and would remain so until Rebecca could get a few hours off to set matters to rights; and that would not be possible until Gary, who would have to advise her, had finished the trench and installed the pipeline.

The radio in the Mercedes was one of the best available. It not only received local stations but also short-wave broadcasts and, as he drove the car along the dirt road from the research farm, the power steering removing all the effort of avoiding the worst ruts and potholes, he pressed the control knob.

'This is the BBC World Service,' he heard. 'The time is one p.m. Greenwich Mean Time. Here is the world news read by ...'

A mamba sped across the road, the fluidity of its black body looking like a wave form on one of the oscilloscopes. He neither braked nor swerved to avoid the snake, yet neither did he accelerate to see if his wheel could hit it before it reached the dust-blown grass on the verge. He simply ignored it.

'In Washington, the Irangate hearings continue with testimony being given by Colonel ...'

Brian ignored the news item. Whatever alleged fixing of the figures, doctoring of the books, skullduggery and subterfuge had been going on in high places, it did not bother him. So long as his company was not involved in the imbroglio he was not concerned with the outcome. It was but another instance of aid funding going astray, of a power-broker's meddling. Arms to the Contras and hostages had no bearing upon agricultural loans and grants to Africa. He was glad he had no dealing with armaments, although he was certain some of the chemicals Afriground (Zambia) Ltd held in supply could be used to fashion crude explosives.

He pulled the Mercedes onto the forecourt parking lot of

the Kabulonga supermarket and slid it into a clear space near the entrance. Before he had turned the ignition off, a pair of small boys dressed in tattered shorts were standing by the door, offering to look after the vehicle while he was in the store.

'All right. You look after the car,' he agreed. 'One kwacha each.'

They grinned their response at his generosity – tips for such a service were usually counted in ngwee – and waved away several other would-be guards, who, undeterred, were then insulted with a rapid string of invective.

In the shop, Brian purchased a case of tonic and three cases of beer. He also took from a rack by the check-out a plastic bag of biltong. It was labelled 'K3.60. Game'.

'You sure this biltong is game?'

'Yes, sir,' the man at the till assured him.

'You sure it's not beef from Kafue?'

'Antelope from Serenje.'

Brian doubted it; no one would risk transporting game meat so far. He bought it all the same.

A youth carried the beer out to the car for him. He unlocked the boot and swung the lid up.

'Very good car,' the store porter complimented him, the suspension dipping marginally under the weight of the crates.

From his wallet, Brian peeled out an olive-green two-kwacha note and two black one-kwacha notes. With the former he paid off the porter and with the latter the two guards who were stood behind the car and beckoned him out of the parking space. He ignored them. As like as not, they would from ignorance rather than malice guide him into another vehicle.

Rebecca was sitting at the telex when he arrived back at the house in Leopards Hill Road. He handed the keys of the Mercedes to Tom, asking him to unload the cases, and went into the office.

'Anything important?'

'Nothing really,' Rebecca replied. She was what would have been termed a 'Cape coloured' were she still living in her native South Africa, her accent a mixture of the African and

332

the Afrikaans. 'London has shipped the nitrates. They should get here some time in early September. In addition, there's a message from Pacific Metals Trading in Yokohama confirming the piping was shipped on the tenth as requested. It's a Taiwanese ship ...' she consulted the sheaf of telexes '... the *Okinawa Virgin* via Manila, due in Mombasa next Thursday.'

'We need that piping yesterday,' Brian thought aloud. 'Gary de Witt is damn near at the end of his trench. I want it all laid before we get rain and the sides of the ditch cave in or it just dries and silts up.'

He opened the packet of biltong and offered her a piece. She took one and put it on a Barclays Bank D C O coaster by the side of the I B M keyboard.

'I know. I've arranged for onward shipping to Dar then rail to Lusaka. Assuming all goes well it'll be here a fortnight on Thursday.'

'A big if!' He put a slice of the biltong in his mouth, pushing it into his cheek with his tongue. 'You know, I think Afriground would go to ground if it wasn't for you.'

'Flattery will get you everything,' Rebecca answered; the telex began to chatter again under its perspex dust-cover.

By good fortune, Brian was able to park the Mercedes immediately outside the town office in Chachacha Road. From the window, through the vertically-hung slat blinds, he could keep an eye on the car. It was not that anyone would steal the entire vehicle, just the accessories, the windscreen wipers or the wheelcovers. The latter would make excellent decorations for one of the long-haul lorries that raced or snailed along the busy highways to Lilongwe, Dar es Salaam, Harare or Lubumbashi. There was no vandalism in Zambia as there was in Britain. No one damaged property needlessly, for the sheer destructive fun of it. In poor countries, whatever is worth the taking is worth the having. Vandalism, Brian thought as he watched a young African lad through the blinds, casing the car but not touching it, was a luxury only the rich could afford. He tapped on the window and the would-be door-mirror owner looked at him sheepishly and walked briskly away.

'So where is the hitch?' he asked, returning to the conversation.

'In Bonn.' Jim Hannington thumbed through the papers in his briefcase which he was balancing on his knees. His eyes were red with having spent the past fourteen hours either in a 747 or waiting for one. 'It seems the finances are clear and a full allocation has been made for the scheme exactly as planned and projected and within the guidelines. The trouble is they're only prepared to release the capital in the stages outlined in their proposal. This means ...'

'I know what it means.' Brian was irritated. He did not suffer fools gladly and bureaucrats less, be they white, black, brown or yellow. 'It means, in short, we get the funding in dribs and drabs, having to wait months for the paperwork to release the next chunk while investment in stock is lost. When will these bloody bankers become *au fait* with the problems we face? This isn't the Rhineland or some dairy-rich valley in Switzerland. You can't count on things here. Besides ...'

Another lad was studying the car. Again, Brian knocked on the window but this time with no effect. Either the lad was unaware of his tapping or assumed it was nothing to do with him. He knelt down quickly and jammed his fingers in the veined sides of the wheel covers, giving the metal a firm wrench. Brian picked up the telephone receiver and banged it hard on the glass. The lad looked about, unable to assess the direction of the noise but now aware of its meaning, and ran off.

'Besides,' Jim took up where Brian had left off, 'if we don't get a sizeable proportion of the money in at the start then potential financial investment will be lost. And that bungs up ...'

'Precisely. The drain-pipe.'

A third party at the meeting between Brian and Jim Hannington, his international trouble-shooter who saw to the European end of Afriground, would not have understood the allusion to a drain. Yet they might have guessed, from the manner in which Brian lowered his voice at the metaphor and from the look of resignation in his eyes, that it was something 'not quite kosher' as Senator Rosenblaum had put it when discussing the matter of currency dealing with Brian in Washington. The problem existed in Zambia, for some white businessmen with international connections, of how to export earnings. Currency regulations were draconian. A departing passenger at Lusaka airport was as likely to have his wallet searched for kwacha as to have his briefcase emptied in search of emeralds or his suitcase for plastic explosives. Any loopholes which could be exploited were exploited. Any roundabout ways in which money could travel, being laundered in the process, were closely and jealously guarded by those who had discovered them. For Brian, the balancing of foreign aid capital against earnings within Zambia was, for all its convolutions and arabesques, his favoured method of making sure his income was high and mobile.

'So we present a case again?'

'It looks that way, Brian.' Hannington opened a pack of cigarettes, tearing along the ribbon in the cellophane wrapper. 'I think it'll wash. And I'll stress the urgency.'

'Relate it to the growing season.'

Hannington nodded sagely. He knew all the arguments, all the persuasions, all the facts and statistics and reasons – both real and imaginary – to convince the funding organizations that they should be parting with their money in large and comparatively prompt lump sums.

'Do you want any of it transferred here as cash?'

'Better bring in a reasonable percentage. I'll leave it up to you. By the way, I've had a tip a few people would like a Singer sewing machine. There's a new digital one out or somesuch. You can programme the stitches with a knob. Something like that. Half a dozen of those would not go amiss.'

'I'll buy them through Twiga Dealing in Nairobi. I'm flying up in the morning on Air Zimbabwe. Going off to Harare in a couple of hours.'

He prepared to leave the office, closing his briefcase and pulling his tropical-weight jacket over his short-sleeve shirt.

'Have a good trip, Jim. When are you back?'

'Last week of the month, with luck. I've got to look at our

cane project in Costa Rica. Apparently they're having labour problems. Lot of absenteeism.'

'I heard of it in D C,' Brian remarked. 'What's the market like?'

'If we fire them, there's plenty more to be hired.'

'Good. But try and avoid it if you can. I don't like to be seen hiring and firing locally-recruited staff of any position. It upsets the overall profile of the firm. Mind you,' he had cause to tap on the window a third time, 'we might have to shed a few staff here. But I'll look into that.'

'How long are you stopping here?' Hannington asked.

'Until mid-September. See the dry season through. I need to keep an eye on things – see and be seen; you know the ropes – and I want to recce another site for an experimental station, preferably with good underground water. I think we might try, on a small scale, coffee and tobacco. No matter how deep the water table is, a borehole's easier than a river pump. I've a few sites in mind.'

Hannington paused in the outer office to telephone the airline office, confirming his flights to Harare and onwards to Nairobi. As he hung the receiver up and prepared to re-dial for a taxi, Brian came out of the office, his coat draped over his shoulder, and offered to give him a lift to the Ridgeway Hotel where he kept a permanent reservation. The trouble-shooter readily accepted. Taxis were not plentiful and usually inefficient in answering a call, if indeed they did so at all.

They drove down Cairo Road and turned left into Church Road. The air conditioning in the Mercedes had the interior cooled before the junction at the Central Post Office and it was positively cold by the time they had covered the mile drive to the hotel.

'Coming in for a beer, Brian?' Hannington asked as they stopped at the main entrance.

'Give you a chance to show your gratitude for the lift,' Brian joked.

They entered the hotel, Hannington going to his room to lock away his briefcase and Brian finding a table by the pond in the central courtyard of the hotel. The water was muddy but had settled somewhat. By the reedbed in the middle of the

336

pool, which was surrounded by iron railings, floated the idle shape of the hotel's six-foot crocodile, only its eyes and a few pointed spinal scales projecting above the surface.

When Hannington joined him, Brian ordered two whiskies and they sat talking, avoiding the subjects of business and politics. It was not advisable to talk in public of matters that might be contentious. Instead, they spoke – as all expatriates do the world over – of 'home'. They discussed the restaurants in London or Washington, Hannington mentioning the Caprice and Brian the Tabard; they criticised the latest shows in the West End and on Broadway, the most recently released films, the advantages or disadvantages of flying with CPA or TWA, PanAm or Singapore Airlines or Thai International. Only once did Brian let the conversation stray towards politics and business, when he mentioned his worries about what might happen in Hong Kong in the light of the final agreement to return sovereignty to China.

'Will you pull out?' Hannington asked. 'There are those who are already seeking alternatives.'

'I already have, to a great extent,' Brian confided. 'Certainly reduced my shareholdings in Jardines, and I'll probably drop Hang Seng Bank B. I shall keep the Hongkong Bank stock, though. Knowing those fly buggers, they'll be running high street banks throughout China by 1997.'

As they parted, Brian wished Hannington well.

'Don't get lost if you go to Uganda. You don't want to be eaten and have a croquet pitch dedicated to your memory.'

It was a standing jest between them: Jim Hannington shared a surname with the first Bishop of East Africa who was murdered by his flock who had then, as ribald rumour had it, taken the act of communion to an ultimate conclusion. The chapel and grass lawn of Hannington Quad in Brian's Oxford college were named after Bishop James Hannington.

Driving back down Leopards Hill Road, the lowering sun cast the shadow of the Mercedes ahead of the vehicle and coloured the dry bush and the earth a golden, glowing brown.

19

The top of the dashboard, the recessed instruments, the air conditioner controls, the seats – everything was dusty with a fine brown talc of soil. Despite the fact that he had driven with the windows tightly shut and the air conditioning off – it was, in fact, inoperative due to a broken belt – the grit had still successfully infiltrated the Range Rover, seeping in through the door seals, the ventilator ducts, the tiny gaps where the wiring entered the interior from the engine compartment.

Brian was, like his vehicle, evenly coated. When he blew his nose, red earth stained his handkerchief and when he ground his teeth, the dust gritted on the enamel. His ears were sore.

The last twelve kilometres from the village had consisted of a bone-shaking path, little more than a game track on which he could manoeuvre only in second gear with the four-wheel-drive engaged. The vehicles which had gone ahead had not levelled the ground but merely blazed a trail he could follow.

At least, he thought with gratitude for the trail-blazers, he did not have to drive by the compass.

Finally, he reached the base-camp and drove the Range Rover into the shade of the trunk of a huge baobab in the scanty branches of which was roosting a solitary vulture. As he slammed the driver's door, the bird stretched its wings, ruffled its feathers but thought better of taking to the air. It was late afternoon, the thermals would be dying soon and, besides, the vulture obviously considered better pickings were to be had around the camp. To support its theory, a dead impala was hanging from a low bough of a nearby tree, being paunched by the camp cook.

'You got here, then,' Gary observed needlessly, Brian standing by his side as he tightened a nut on the rig. 'It's a sod of a drive, isn't it? That rocky escarpment was hell on the old Unimogs.'

'It was quite thrilling in the Range Rover,' Brian replied

338

taciturnly. 'We'll need to clear some rocks off for the return journey. Nose down it's a problem but driving back up that drop will be impossible.'

'I've sent a few of the boys off with that in mind. Did you see them?'

Brian shook his head and swatted his forearm hard. A tsetse fly fell onto the ground, its legs kicking and one wing buzzing futilely. He stomped on it with his boot.

'Many of those little sods about?'

'Crawling with them.'

'How's the drill?'

Brian gazed up at the top of the borehole drilling equipment where it poked through a clearing made in the branches overhead. From one sawn bough dripped a meagre ooze of sap.

'More or less ready. Took something of a pounding on that bloody escarpment but the chassis suffered more than the gear. Bent a member ...' He pointed to a shining crack in one of the struts of the rig frame. 'You've brought the necessary?'

Jerking his thumb in the direction of the Range Rover, Brian said, 'In the back.' Woodsmoke drifted across from the direction of the tent, temporarily removing the dry smell of dust from his nostrils. 'But I'll have a cup of tea first.'

While Brian rinsed his throat of dust, the tea acting as much as a cleaner as a quencher of thirst, Gary finished erecting the rig. It was a much larger unit of equipment than one would normally have seen being erected for the drilling of a simple borehole. This, however, was not just a borehole for a small settlement but one which Brian hoped would produce a very high rate of flow. The test station would require a bare minimum of five thousand gallons an hour and this site, seven kilometres from the station, was the best place for a test drilling. It would mean laying polythene pipes underground for that distance but this was not a disadvantage. When the test station ceased operating, Brian intended to turn over the water system to the local villagers. This action would improve his standing as a man of generosity and would additionally look good in the eyes of the funding agencies who would see a secondary end use for their grant.

With the help of two of the African camp staff, Brian unloaded the three blast-hole bits from the tailgate of the Range Rover. As the last was lifted clear, the shock-absorbers and suspension springs of the vehicle sighed with almost human relief.

The bits, in their wooden cases, were carried over to the rig, two men to a box, and lowered to the ground by the side of the generator.

'Here we are!' Brian exclaimed. 'Three M-51s. Reed Mining Tools of Grand Prairie, Texas, US of A; two hundred and twenty-nine millimetre, ideal for siltstones, mudstones, hard sandstone, limestone and shales.'

He unpacked the first bit. It weighed ninety-six pounds. Eighteen inches long and nine wide, it looked like a metal tulip painted scarlet, the cutting wheels fitted, as if for decoration as much as practicality, with rows of matching scarlet, conical-shaped tungsten carbide teeth. Gary regarded it with admiration.

'Lovely!' he remarked. 'Just the job. When did they get here?'

'Day before yesterday's Q Z flight from Frankfurt. Look after them, won't you?'

Gary grinned. 'Pricey?'

'Not much change from four thousand U S. Each . . .'

The rig began operating just after dark and, by floodlight, ran throughout the night. Gary and Brian took turns in the early hours to watch over it with the rigging crew, lengthening the shafts and recording progress.

It was not the way in which Brian enjoyed being in the wild. It was so noisy no sounds could be heard over the grinding of metal, the hiss of air, the thud of the drive motor and the thump of the generator and compressor. Any wildlife in the area would have been driven far away so there was no need for caution although Brian knew the area in which they were test drilling was well-populated by leopard as was most of the Zambian bush.

In the morning, the borehole being by now a thousand feet deep and the rig switched off for a few hours, the two men sat on camp chairs around a folding table in the shade of an awning stretched between three trees. The scrub bush around them echoed and sibilated with the call of birds and the scratch of insects but to both men it was like silence.

'All going well back at the centre?'

Gary broke into Brian's reverie; he was thinking of the American diplomat's daughter.

'Hmm, okay. Bit of trouble importing the bits. Nothing serious. Nothing a swift back-hander couldn't smooth.'

He took another slice of charcoal-toasted bread off the plate in the centre of the table and smeared it with white Zambian butter and guava jelly. 'Those anti-corruption posters all over the place are quite pointless.'

A dash of red flashed through the shade of the awning, a bird as brilliant as the paint on the second hole bit lying unused nearby. It alighted on a branch beside the one the awning was tethered to. It was about a foot long with a blue skullcap of feathers and a black streak along its eye line. It made a loud, bass 'cherk-cherk!' call, took to the wing and flew rapidly out of sight.

'*Merops nubicus*,' Brian announced as the bird disappeared. 'The Carmine Bee-eater.'

'I didn't know you were an authority on birds.'

Gary helped himself to the last piece of toast and ate it dry.

'I'm not. My father was a keen bird painter. When I was a boy, he introduced me to hundreds of species. And that particular bee-eater is one of the more memorable.'

Brian finished his toast, licked his fingers and returned to the conversation the bird had interrupted.

'Driving down here yesterday, I got stopped – as ever – at a road block. Middle of nowhere. The sponsored one. Know it?'

'A sponsored road block?' Gary retorted incredulously. 'You don't mean they've commercialized them! A touch of the Thatcherisms from UK? Privatize the para-military – now that would be a growth industry...'

He laughed and Brian shared the humour.

'Not exactly sponsored,' he explained. 'It's the road block half-way between Chongwe and Rufunsa. The para-militaries have built a sort of sentry-box-cum-bunker there out of gash metal. The side clearly states "Sponsored by Bata Shoes" – you must have seen it.'

'Don't recall it. But I'll watch out for it on the way back.'

'You only see it from the Lusaka side. Anyway, I pulled in there having been flagged down. Packet of ciggies on the dash, open, with one filter tip poking out. One of those French throw-away lighters next to it. The guard, finger on automatic trigger, saunters up and asks me where I'm going. I tell him. "Why?" I tell him. He and his chum insist on looking in the back. I open one of the bit crates. They fumble about in the packing. Then, "Open your briefcase," one of them orders. I do so, asking what they're looking for. "Why you want to know?" asks the one with corporal stripes on his sleeve. "Just being friendly," I reply. "Where is your passport?" I produce it; lived in Zambia long enough to know to carry one of them at all times. They thumb through the visas, see I'm British, check there's no R S A stamp on the pages. Of course, the one with South Africa and Israel in it's at home. Then comes the leading question. "You carrying any game meat?" asks the bloke shuffling through the papers in the briefcase. "In there?" I reply and risk a joke. "No buffalo in the briefcase." I grin as expansively as possible whereupon the bugger produces a half-eaten packet of biltong. There followed a ten minute explanation of the purchase of biltong from the Kabulonga supermarket during which time the biltong was confiscated, I was fined twenty kwacha – no receipt given – and the private had the gall to ask for the whole damn packet of J P Ss … Until that sort of graft gets snuffed out, nothing'll change.'

They lapsed into silence again and Brian watched a hornet exploring the underside of the awning, its needle-thin thorax with the bulbous abdomen bobbing up and down, its narrow wings swept back in rest like those of a jet fighter.

On his journey back, Brian pondered on the opportunity of dating the diplomat's daughter. She was a pretty girl and he could offer to show her a bit of Africa, take her to Vic. Falls or the Kafue National Park. Maybe take a few days off and fly up to Kasaba Bay on Lake Tanganyika, stop off at Lake Bangweulu on the way up. He could take the Cessna, just the two of them. Bill Athelrod at the airstrip at Mansa would lend him a jeep for a day or two for a visit to the lake. In the dry season they might get to see the elusive swamp deer.

Yet no sooner was the fantasy developing than he remembered it would not be possible, not for a while anyway. He had to be in Lusaka for a reception at the Russian embassy. Maybe, he considered, he could invite her to that as his escort. It might just appeal to her as an American. And her father was almost certain to be present which would make their meeting just a little more acceptable. She was, after all, less than half his age, and the embassy of the USSR was only just around the corner from the US consulate building, between United Nations Avenue and Haile Selassie Avenue.

The older he grew, he was discovering, the more difficult it was to persuade the parents of young women that he was not just a lecherous old expat., even if what he had in mind was, as Hannington termed it, a battering of the bedsprings. And yet, coincidentally, he was finding young women were increasingly attracted to him. His lifestyle, his wealth, his almost soldier-of-fortune type of existence appealed to their romantic natures. He was a change from boring fellow students or young men striving in stock-brokers' offices or lawyers' chambers in New York, London or Bonn with whom they were familiar for most of the year.

The disadvantage of such liaisons was that they could easily lead to his being tarred with a reputation and such reputations are the hardest to shift in expatriate communities. For this reason, he was choosey and careful about his partners. A reputation could – probably would – reduce his standing in the foreign aid funding circles to which most of his would-be conquests were connected by family or business. Competition was always fierce when there was free money for the asking and the filling-in of forms.

By the time Brian reached the rock-strewn escarpment, the labouring Africans had succeeded in clearing a way through the heaviest tumble of boulders. The Range Rover groaned and creaked and roared its way up the hillside but made the summit with comparative ease. He waved to the boys who were resting in the heat of the day beneath a lean-to of cut branches, throwing them three packets of cigarettes from the carton on the seat beside him: two packets remained to smooth the way through the road blocks. The Africans waved back and shouted their thanks.

20

In the capital cities of Third World countries foreign diplomats, like journalists, form their own enclaves. Not only are embassies often established within the same suburb or on the same street, but they tend to share the same social whirl – Brian remembered best a series of parties in the diplomatic enclave in New Delhi. Of course, nationals of the host country attend these functions, the receptions and balls and galas and cocktail parties celebrating treaties, national days or the birthdays of their respective heads of state, but they are the only injection of new blood. Within the consular circles, everyone knows everyone else. They may be representatives of nations at loggerheads in the corridors of the United Nations, who publicly berate and criticise each other, but unless war has actually been declared between their father- or motherlands there exists between them all a constant condition of *laissez-faire*, of live-and-let-live. Espionage – which each knows the other is busily and ardently engaged upon – and strictly national interests apart, diplomats are a fairly cohesive group of individuals living together and being obliged to work together for the common good. They share the pains and frustrations of their exile, their remoteness from the luxuries of home – be these an absence from vodka and caviar or Jack Daniels and hamburgers – and seek, within the parameters of their exclusive society, to make each other's lives at least tolerable if not enjoyable.

It was this loose-knit camaraderie which so amused Brian and fascinated Peta Cawflin.

For him, it was a source not only of humour but also of information which he could use to his advantage: a word here about potential funding becoming available in the new fiscal year, a snippet of information there about pressure group or lobby influence – the conservationists, the famine relief agencies, the medical charities – could give him an inkling of where cash might be up for grabs. He could then place an early application or know to whom he should extend an invitation to dine in Geneva, Paris or Boston. Failing that, he could telex Hannington to start oiling the wheels of contact.

For her, it was a miracle. The Russians – those of the S S 20 missiles against whom were aimed the Pershings and the Cruises – were, after all, just men; they spoke English like Polish immigrants or Eastern bloc tennis stars and they allowed women into high-ranking positions, much to her amazement. The Cubans were not all bearded and ageing brigands, the French not all romantic, the Italians not all Catholics. Indeed, the most devout Communist she had ever met, at an embassy reception in Guatemala, had been an Italian from Turin. And the Chinese were not all short and narrow-eyed, nor were all the Japanese obsequious and unyielding in trade negotiations, although they did all bow incessantly.

Brian drove the Mercedes in through the gates of the Cawflins' house, a US soldier closing them behind him. He was white with a rifle slung over his shoulder but Brian caught only a glimpse of him in the rear view mirror.

The girl was waiting for him on a patio to one side of the building, sitting on a swing settee beneath a jacaranda tree. From behind her came the sounds of children playing in a swimming pool.

'My father's not well,' Peta Cawflin told him as Brian walked towards her, 'and will not be present at the function. He's in bed with a high temperature and the embassy doctor has given him drugs to lower his fever.'

She continued to give details of the illness which was not, she assured him, either serious or contagious: she spoke as Americans do when they first meet a stranger, as if they feel at a disadvantage and need desperately to establish contact by imparting a resumé of family or personal history, going into the most intimate facts. Brian wondered if her father's illness had been brought on by a bacterium, a virus or a coded telex from Washington. Diplomatic diseases were as instant as they were debilitating.

'My mother is also not attending ...' she went on,

346

interrupted by Mrs Cawflin coming out of the house and crossing the patio. She was barefoot, wearing a pair of jeans and a loose blouse. She was, Brian guessed, in her mid-forties, and he fleetingly wondered if he ought to ditch the daughter and make a play for her mother.

'Mr Titchner,' she called as she approached, her voice going no quieter as she drew nearer. 'How good to see you! I don't think we've met since – when was that?'

'The UN visit,' Brian said.

'Why! That's right. In March ... No, April! When you agreed to give Peta part-time experience of your operation. I do think it's important for young people to experience, don't you?'

Brian agreed, wondering if there was a hidden motive in her words, an underlying message that he could, or could not, treat their daughter in the manner to which he was looking forward – if circumstances permitted.

'Well now, dear,' she addressed her daughter, 'you have a wonderful time. But remember what your father told you.'

Pondering on what advice her father might have given her, Brian led Peta to the Mercedes. The fresh-faced US Marine held the door for her.

'The gate'll open automatically for you, sir,' he told Brian.

'What did your father tell you?' Brian enquired as they drove slowly along Independence Avenue. 'Beware of bachelor employers,' he added jokingly.

'No! Of course not. He warned me not to say too much at the party.'

'Who to?'

'To anyone.' She leaned nearer to him as if there were other people in the car who should not share her confidence. 'The arms agreement talks are at a tricky stage.'

So, Brian thought, her father was suffering a bout of diplomatic influenza. He was a little relieved and relaxed inwardly. The parents did not object to his taking their daughter out: they were cautious not of his behaviour but of her possible political indiscretion.

'I'll not say a word,' he promised.

A number of Zambian police constables were patrolling

the street outside the embassy building, walking up and down, observing the arriving vehicles. Brian parked his car within their sentry beat. One of the policemen approached him, recognised him and nodded acknowledgement. The Mercedes would be safe.

Gregori Belomestnykh, the Russian trade attaché, accosted Brian as soon as he entered the room in which the reception was being held. Beckoning to the waiter, he handed both Brian and his escort a glass of chilled vodka.

'How good to see you, Mister Brian Titchner. And your charming companion.' Brian introduced her by just her Christian name; Belomestnykh replied, 'Oh, yes! Miss Peta Cawflin, how do you do? How is your father? I understand he is not well and the doctor has been called. Nothing serious, I trust.'

'Nothing serious, thank you,' she answered.

Brian could tell she was instantly put on edge by the diplomat's inside knowledge.

'Spies out, Gregori?'

The attaché laughed.

'Ha! Brian, you are in a witty frame of mind tonight. But no! There are no spies in Lusaka. One does not need them.' He held his hands open with a show of frankness. 'In such a close community, word travels without help. Now,' he looked about the room which was rapidly filling up, 'I must be a good host and introduce you to some others. And, later, our ambassador would like to speak with you – and introduce you personally to one of his guests. Andrej!'

The military under-secretary joined them. He was a young staff officer, Zambia his first foreign posting. He bowed stiffly to Peta Cawflin and shook Brian's hand firmly. Belomestnykh left them, greeting another arrival.

'We are meeting again, Mr Titchner,' Andrej Yepanchin said. 'How are you keeping?'

'Busy. I'm sinking boreholes in the bush.'

Their conversation moved from the subject of boreholes to, improbably, the latest James Bond film and the Bolshoi; but before they left the subject of drilling the officer let slip the information that he knew something of a search for water north of Kabul. It was, he said, difficult to cut through the stone there to the water-bearing strata. Brian wondered how well-trained Peta was, if she had picked up and stored this detail for later encoding by her father's cipher clerk.

For three-quarters of an hour, Brian and his companion mingled with the drinkers. He spoke briefly with one of the overseas development officers from the British High Commission and at greater length with one of the trade officers from the High Commission for India from whom he needed a specific importation document still tied up in the inevitable wrangle of Indian government bureaucracy; otherwise, he talked genially to everyone. Always at his side was Peta Cawflin who, as the evening darkened and the lights came on, began to lose the inhibitions caused by being in the embassy of what she considered her country's enemy, and started to enjoy herself. The vodka cocktails helped.

It had been Brian's intention from the start to leave the reception at eight o'clock – it would end of its own accord by half past the hour – take her out to dinner at one of the hotel restaurants, perhaps at the Pamodzi or the Inter-Continental, then see how things developed.

If she was willing, they would return to his house at Leopards Hill Road. In the grounds of the house, in the copse of eucalyptus trees behind the swimming pool, Brian had refurbished a large A-frame house which he used as a den, an escape from the main house and the pressures of work. In the building, originally built for the previous owner's sons when they were in Zambia on holiday from their English boarding schools, he had installed a video recorder and a large screen television as well as a pool table. On the first floor was a comfortable bedroom where he slept naked in the hot summer nights. If he was unexpectedly inundated with friends or business acquaintances in transit, seeking a bed for the night, as quite frequently happened, the A-frame became overflow accommodation. At other times, he used the building as an ideal setting for seductions.

If Peta Cawflin was not of the mind to be one of the latest visitors to the A-frame, he would drop her off at her father's residence.

A hand rested on Brian's shoulder, the fingers pressing firmly inwards. It was Belomestnykh's.

'Brian, can I ask you to come away for a minute, please?' he requested, adding to the two Africans with whom he was speaking, 'Do excuse us. My ambassador wishes to have a quick word ... Miss Cawflin, please excuse us for a moment.'

The trade attaché led the way along a corridor on the walls of which hung photographs of various places of achievement in the USSR – a modern-looking coal mine in the Ukraine, an oil field above the Arctic Circle, ships alongside the docks in Archangel and a nuclear power station closely resembling Chernobyl, with a tall chimney painted in black and white bands. At a door at the end of the corridor the attaché knocked and turned the handle without being bidden to enter.

Brian, who had been to the embassy on a number of occasions before and had met the ambassador twice there, knew this room was not his office and, for a moment, he was apprehensive.

'Come in, Brian,' Belomestnykh invited, holding the door back against a sprung hinge. 'I have someone I'd like you to meet...'

Behind a table strewn with copies of *Pravda* and the English language journals the Russians published for free distribution in the West, stood two Africans. They were outlined against a french window opening onto a lawn lit in blocks by the lights from the reception-room windows.

One was a very beautiful, tall woman in her early thirties dressed simply in an emerald green robe which enhanced her figure and gave a glow to her black skin. Her cheekbones were high, almost oriental in shape. Brian realised she was not a Zambian or central African but probably from northern Zaire or perhaps Sudan, where the Bantu peoples had Arab blood mixed with their own. On the table in front of her, lying at a tilt on the piles of magazines, was a grey Samsonite briefcase and a package the size of a hardback book sealed with parcel tape.

Beside her stood an African in his late forties. He was smartly dressed in a well-tailored beige tropical suit, a blue shirt and a navy-blue tie. His tightly-curled hair was greying slightly and the skin at the corner of his eyes was beginning to line.

'Hello, Brian,' the African said, stepping from beyond the table and offering his hand.

As the man moved, Brian saw simultaneously the Oxford University crest on the tie and the man's left sleeve tucked into his jacket pocket.

'Matthew?' Brian was perplexed, unsure of the identity of this man about his own age. 'Matthew Nchembe?'

'The same. One-time visitor to the domain of the Imps of Rhydisel.'

They shook hands. When Brian tried to release his, Nchembe retained it, holding it strongly.

'You look well, Brian,' Nchembe remarked. 'They said you were prospering and they were right. Africa agrees with you, my old friend. I always knew it would.'

The door closed behind Brian who noticed Belomestnykh had left them. This was not, Brian knew, to say he was not listening to their conversation by some other means.

'Let me introduce you to my friend,' Nchembe said. 'This is Miss Nkana. Juliet – this is Mr Brian Titchner.'

'How do you do, Mr Titchner.' She spoke coolly, remaining behind the table and her briefcase. 'I have heard much about you.'

'What stories have you been spinning?' Brian looked at Nchembe, who now let go of his hand and leaned on the edge of the table.

'I do not mean necessarily from Mr Nchembe,' she said curtly before the question could be answered. 'You are well-known to us and we have known of your work for many years.'

A chill crept through Brian. This was not a social meeting and he guessed it had been arranged some time before in collaboration with the Russians.

'Please, Brian, sit down,' Nchembe suggested, indicating chairs tucked in against the table.

Once they were seated, the magazines and papers pushed aside, Miss Nkana opened her briefcase and produced a clean manila folder, placing it on the table in front of Brian.

'We have only a little time to talk,' Nchembe said, 'and so we must do away with pleasantries. Maybe another day ... We shall discuss this later. But Juliet has to leave, and very soon.'

'Open the folder, please, Mr Titchner,' Miss Nkana ordered and Brian did as he was told.

Inside were a sheaf of pages neatly cut from the trade catalogues of a number of tractor manufacturers. Beside each glossy picture was written, in ball-pen, the price of each vehicle in either US dollars, sterling or German marks. Attached to each picture by a steel clip was a sheet of paper outlining the main points in favour of the machine. Brian leafed through the pages, noticing every vehicle chosen was near the top of the range for the respective manufacturer.

'These tractors are the best of their make and type,' Miss Nkana confirmed Brian's observation. 'We require to obtain six of them.'

'Indeed, they are the best of their sort. But I don't see how this is relevant to me ...'

'You are an agricultural expert,' she interrupted, 'an importer of agricultural machinery into Zambia, the proprietor of an international agricultural development corporation with many branches – Afriground (Zambia) Ltd, Groundswell (USA) Inc, ADC, Ltd of London, to name but a few – and a man with many contacts and friends. We wish you to obtain six of the machines you consider to be the best.'

'For what?'

'For use in the tropics, Brian.'

Whereas Miss Nkana spoke brusquely, as if she had as little patience as she apparently had time, Nchembe spoke quietly, calmly, rationally.

'Where in the tropics? There are many different environments. And how do you intend to use the tractors? To plough, to use as PTO sources, to tow?'

'In Tanzania,' Nchembe replied, 'to plough and for general agricultural work. Spraying manure, towing a seed-drill, cutting and baling perhaps. Just ordinary farm work such as on any mechanized farm you might see in Zambia.'

'Where in Tanzania? Soils vary.' Brian was casting for

more information. This might well be an enquiry originating from one of his competitors. 'And at what altitude?'

'You need not know where.' Nchembe was reading Brian's worries. 'This is nothing to do with any of your opposition. And the tractor does not need to change for the soils, only the ploughshare or the drill. All you need to know is that it is for general farm use at, say, 1500 metres altitude and on ordinary soils. No black cotton, no riverine areas. Just,' he smiled genially, 'ordinary Africa.'

'We need your expertise to evaluate the machines,' Miss Nkana went on. 'We do not have this kind of knowledge or experience. You do, Mr Titchner.'

Brian decided to try the question on them which was burning in his mind.

'Who are *we*?' he asked.

She glanced at Nchembe who spoke quietly, saying, 'The A N C. The African National Congress. We are seventy-five years old this year. And we require these tractors for use in our new agricultural school to be established in Tanzania where we already have school facilities for the children and young people of our cause, dispossessed of their own lands ... But I need not preach to you, Brian. I am sure you are already converted. I am sure you are as strongly against the apartheid system as we are.'

'I am.'

It was the truth. Brian saw the iniquities of the system in the Republic of South Africa, saw the moral and spiritual corruption of the Botha regime, knew of the inhuman cruelties perpetrated by the so-called 'state of emergency'. He was only too familiar, both from first-hand experience and from reports of those whose word he could trust, with what was going on under the cover of press and media censorship. Soweto, Sharpeville, Stellenbosch were not merely names to him: they were sites of inhumanity and injustice.

'Then you will help us,' declared Miss Nkana. It was a statement, not a question: almost a command.

'If I can. How can I contact you?'

'I will get in touch,' Nchembe assured him. 'We shall meet. Will the day after tomorrow be all right?'

353

Brian knew it would have to be and agreed.

'I'll have my opinion for you by then.'

'How soon could you purchase the tractors?' The woman closed her briefcase. 'We require them to be delivered in Dar es Salaam, not here in Zambia.'

'That depends,' Brian told her, 'on delivery dates from the manufacturer, though I'm sure virtually immediate release from stocks will be possible. There is no shortage of tractors. Shipping would take a while, of course, depending on where the tractors come from. And the method of payment will, to some extent, affect the purchase.'

'What do you mean?' She snapped shut the catches on the case.

'Well, if you are paying in roubles it will take time. Sterling or US dollars – the currency you have marked the file with – will be quick. Deutschmarks okay – maybe a little slower. I can arrange letters of credit for you,' he offered.

'The payment is up to you ...' she began, but Nchembe raised his hand from the table and she was instantly silent. Until now Brian had believed her to be the leader of the two: now he realised it was not so, that Nchembe was her superior.

'I don't think you quite understand, Brian. We want you – or your company – to buy these for us. That is, we also want you to pay for them. We are not rich. All our finances are put into fighting the struggle in South Africa ...'

Brian sat back. It took him only a second or two to assess approximately how much six tractors would cost.

'You want me to pay for them as well as deliver them?' he asked slowly.

'Yes. It will be for a good cause.'

Nchembe sounded as if he was asking for a small coin to be dropped into a collecting tin, not requesting a gift of tens of thousands of dollars.

'I'm not sure I can do this,' Brian hedged. 'It's not as easy as just buying a car.'

'What you drive around Lusaka in could be used to feed many mouths,' said Miss Nkana acidly.

'There is no need for acrimony,' Nchembe softly rebuked

her. 'Mr Titchner is not unreasonable, Juliet. He has our good at heart. That is why he does so much for Africa.'

Brian searched Nchembe's words for irony but found none. It was to come in his next sentence.

'After all,' the African finished, 'I am certain he gives as much to Africa as he receives from her.'

Nchembe looked hard into Brian's eyes and the white man knew he was being held over a barrel. Nchembe must know, he thought, of at least one fiddle – perhaps the source of the Mercedes Benz 300E – and a rumour of it was all it would take to set him and his company on a course to ruin.

'I'll see what I can do,' he said, rising. 'We'll discuss it further when we meet the day after tomorrow. You'll come out to my house? Perhaps you will both be my guests to lunch?'

'Miss Nkana has to leave Zambia tonight. But I gladly accept.' Nchembe stood and shook Brian's hand again, adding, 'I shall look forward to talking over old times. I assume the young lady with you this evening is not your wife?'

'No, she is not.'

Nchembe picked up the package from the table, winked at him and said, 'Goodnight, Brian.'

They did not leave by the door but by the french window. Brian was not surprised. They clearly knew their way around not only the Russian embassy but also its officials.

Rebecca conveniently had a number of errands to run as well as a few hours of work waiting for her in the office in Chachacha Road. It was not that Brian wanted her out of the house for the sake of preventing her eavesdropping on business conversations. Apart from himself, she was the only other person who knew of and understood all the twists and turns of his business, all the tricks, wrangles, bribes and double-dealings so necessary to keep ahead of rivals and avoid cash-flow crises. He had gradually given her this power so she was now, like him, implicated in the activities of the firm. He paid her a high salary, fifty per cent of it in kwacha, the remainder in Swiss francs and sterling, but he was well aware that this was not the price of silence or loyalty. If the balloon burst, she would go down with him and she knew it. It was in her interests to do all she could to see nothing went awry.

He trusted Rebecca and, before she went out, leaving her set of safe keys in their shared hiding place – it was policy for neither of them ever to leave the house with the full set of keys – he told her of his intended meeting that day with Nchembe.

'Matthew Nchembe?' She showed a moment's surprise.

'You know him?'

Brian was astonished. He knew Rebecca, like most of the continent's population, had an in-built sympathy for the ANC and a natural antipathy towards South Africa which swelled to hatred over their racial policies, but he had no idea she was *au fait* with the personnel of the movement.

'I know of him,' she corrected her employer. 'He's an ANC big-shot. Not one of the front runners like Oliver Tambo, but one of the back-room boys. He keeps a low political profile. He's an international lawyer ...'

'I knew he had studied law,' Brian replied, 'but I had no idea he had gone into practice. How did you hear of him?'

'He was brought in to represent someone in Pretoria when I was living there. He got them off. Scot-free. Everyone was amazed because it was, underneath, a political trial. It was to do with a journalist who – I forget now. It was years ago. But ever since, his name has cropped up here and there. I think he's a member of their policy committee or something like that. He doesn't have an actual law practice ...'

For a moment, Brian had the doubt cross his mind that perhaps Rebecca had tipped Nchembe off about the shady aspect of some deal; but as soon as this worry formed, he dismissed it. She would not. He was certain he could trust her.

'I think he's a very clever man ...' She paused and picked up her handbag with the keys of one of the Toyotas parked under the trees on the drive. 'But I'd not want to get involved with him. He is very ... important.'

She had no sooner left the house than Nchembe arrived in a taxi, the car rattling up the dirt road from the tarmac, a cloud of dust billowing behind it, thickening the plume caused by the Toyota pick-up. The cab driver held the door open for him, an act rarely seen in Lusaka. As Brian walked across the scorched lawn to meet Nchembe, he saw him speak to the driver. The taxi then reversed into the shaded space left by the pick-up and the motor was switched off.

'Hello, Brian,' Nchembe greeted him, taking the initiative, his hand outstretched.

'It's good of you to come,' Brian said, accepting the offered hand, at the same time knowing full well the meeting had been arranged at Nchembe's behest, not his own. 'I'll arrange for your driver to have a drink and a meal with my ...' he was about to say 'boys' but changed it in time, '... staff here.'

'That would be kind. He has been driving me about all over Lusaka all morning.'

A table for two had been set on the verandah, well back in the shade. A bottle of wine leaned in an ice bucket on the bar next to the tray of glasses, sliced lemons and limes.

'Will you have a drink?'

Nchembe lifted an expensive pocket watch from inside his jacket and said, 'Yes. It's after eleven. My doctors tell me to go easy but – what the hell! – one lives only once. What have you?'

'Whatever you like.'

'A gin and tonic, then, to keep in the same line as yourself.' He had seen Brian's own glass on the low table between the cushioned chairs, the bubbles rising around the circle of lemon.

Pouring the drink, Brian observed Nchembe as he sat on one of the padded seats and stretched his feet before him. And, as he looked at the man, the antagonism returned, the memory of the fury which had erupted that night twenty years before when he had struck the African and had been knocked to the ground by the man's one remaining arm. Yet the anger was now only a dull ache, an emptiness in him that had not been filled by a new rage or dislike.

Watching the lemon slice drop into Nchembe's glass, Brian saw himself reflected in the polished silver plating of the drinks tray. He was older now, middle-aged; it was true he had kept his figure, had not gone to flab like so many of his men friends, but he was ageing. His hair was thinner, his skin a little coarser, his eyes a little weaker. He did not require spectacles but he found the sun more glaring in the African summer than he had before and he wore sunglasses a good deal. And the skin by his eyes was lining just as Nchembe's was. At least his hair was not greying as was the African's.

'We are getting old – like *mzee*,' Nchembe commented, sharing Brian's thoughts. 'We shall soon be the elders of the village, sitting under the trees all day long and talking nonsense.'

'Not if I can help it.'

'Nor I, if the truth be told. There is so much to do.'

Brian handed him the glass, rang the bell by the bar and asked Tom, when he appeared, to take a drink to the driver and arrange a meal for him.

'Let us talk of business first,' Nchembe suggested as Brian sat opposite him. 'Get that out of the way and then we can feel more free.'

Brian agreed, rose, went into the office and returned with Miss Nkana's manila file.

'So what are your thoughts? Wait,' Nchembe reached inside his jacket and brought out a Polaroid photograph, 'and see what you are going to replace.'

The photo showed a young African in his early twenties, wearing only a pair of shorts, standing jauntily in front of a thirty-five-year-old Ford tractor. It was clearly at the end of its useful life.

'Think how proud he will be to drive one of your new machines.'

Over the past few days, Brian had made a number of international calls from the office, sent a number of telexes, contacted Jim Hannington. Between them, they had arrived at a decision.

'Frankly, tractors are much of a muchness,' Brian began. 'They are all good, all expensive and many capable of the task you have set for them. The deciding factors from your point of view – in Tanzania – are reliability, ease of maintenance, availability of spares —'

'And simplicity of operation,' Nchembe butted in. 'Few of our farmers for the future are well educated or trained.'

'No modern tractor's easy to operate. They are sophisticated, elaborate, technological tools of the earth – not just a petrol-driven *ngombe* with a forged-steel plough. What I have come up with is one of these[...'

He slid across the table to Nchembe a picture of a tractor painted in bright green.

'I know nothing of these matters. Tell me about it.'

'This is a Deutz-Fahr DX6.30. It is manufactured in West Germany and is one of the best in the world, in my opinion. It was not on your list of choices but I think it would be better than they were.'

'I shall have to convince Miss Nkana and her team so you must convince me.'

Sipping his drink, Brian thought sarcastically that this was one for the record books. He was buying them six of the latest tractors and they were dictating the terms. Nchembe's stance convinced him the African had a suitable blackmail upon which to fall back if all else failed.

'Right!' Brian put his glass down, the new ring of condensation linking with the old on the table top. 'I'll spell it out. This tractor is diesel operated so fuel supply is easier; it is powerful with a B S A U 141a output of 117 hp; 540 ground clearance to the diff, so good for rough ground; 6 gears through five ranges and, of course, four-wheel-drive; servicing is easy – the disc pads can be replaced as readily as on an ordinary car; the cab is dustproof and air-conditioned as standard; it has a rear P T O and hydraulic trailer brakes. The only extras you'd need are a weight carrier and, perhaps, a rear linkage control. You can change gear without clutch operation – there's synchro throughout.'

Brian stopped. Nchembe was looking him straight in the face.

'Don't you need to note this down?' Brian asked.

'I am a lawyer,' Nchembe answered. 'I can remember salient details. Do go on.'

'Not a lot else. Delivery is quick, spares not hard to get. I think it's the best around.'

'Why not the DX7?' Nchembe asked.

'Too fancy,' Brian replied, struggling to hide both his amazement and annoyance. Nchembe plainly did have more than a passing knowledge on the subject of tractors. It was no wonder, Brian considered, he was a good lawyer.

'And very expensive?'

'That, too.'

Nchembe laughed and said, 'I am sure you are able to get a fair deal on six Deutzes. But why are you not buying us the cheapest you can get?'

'Yes.' Brian decided to admit it. 'I have got a deal in line for the six. And it will cost me more than, say, six John Deere or a Japanese make. But you asked me for a good, appropriate tractor and this is, in my professional opinion, the one best suited to your needs.'

'What is the list price?' Nchembe asked bluntly.

Removing a telex read-out from the folder and running his finger down the columns of print, Brian read, 'DX6.30, pounds sterling 31,621 ex. tax and delivery. Plus two hundred for extras. Plus shipping.' He folded the telex. 'I'm buying them for 22,000 each, flat. I'll not see change from 160,000 at the end of the day.'

'So you are being generous.'

'No. I'm being practical. If they break down or prove worthless I'll get the blame. It's better to buy wisely than artfully.'

Again Nchembe laughed.

'We are grateful. Of that you can be assured. And I – I am more so. For you are helping Africa. Just as I said you must.'

'And what if I had refused to buy, turned you down?' Brian ventured.

'We should have gone elsewhere. But you were our first and most obvious choice. You have the expertise ...'

'And you the leverage?'

'Perhaps,' Nchembe smiled, 'but we would not have used it. There is no room for vindictiveness amongst our allies. We are all in the fight together, regardless of our colour or even, at this stage, our politics. The fight is for freedom, for a black Africa. You have done – you are doing – your part. If you are making a profit by the way, so be it. That is the nature of trade. So long as no one suffers.'

'That was not what your Miss Nkana thought.'

'Juliet is young. An idealist. She will see the way of men in due course. She sees your Mercedes as being half of a tractor, not half of a job bringing food to Africa. Or perhaps, under the circumstances, a whole tractor?'

It was Brian's turn to laugh. The list price in Britain on a 300E was within hundreds of the price he was paying for each tractor from a distributor in Italy.

Tom knocked on the door to the verandah, stepping out with a tray upon which were two plates of smoked salmon surrounded by watercress.

'Hors d'oeuvres,' Brian announced.

'Where did you get smoked salmon?' Nchembe exclaimed. 'This is Zambia.'

'Out of the freezer. It seemed appropriate.'

'Like the Deutz,' Nchembe mused as he moved to the table.

Over the meal, their conversation drifted away from tractors and the one-upmanship of their dealings. Brian now knew where he stood with Nchembe and felt more relaxed. The African had not exercised the power he quite obviously controlled and seemed not to be intent on doing so. Gradually, as they spoke of the current situation in South Africa, of the role of the church and the intransigence of the British cabinet towards making a positive move against the Botha regime, Brian began to wonder if he had not been unfair to Nchembe all those years before in Oxford. Twenty years was a long time to harbour a hatred, no matter how deep-rooted it might be.

'Tell me,' Brian took advantage of a lull in their conversation, 'did you marry Lucy?'

'Marry her! My god, no! She and I broke our relationship before the Christmas of that year. It did not last long, did it? She went off with the Indian gentleman whom you met on the night ...'

'I apologize for that,' Brian said.

'There is no need. You were upset. So was I. I had stolen

361

your woman and you had called me many things. It was but the rashness of youth.'

'We were in our late twenties,' Brian pointed out.

'We were still young.'

Tom served a side salad and two fat T-bone steaks with thin potato chips as crisp as brittle twigs. Brian took the bottle of wine from the ice bucket, the half-melted cubes ringing on the metal.

'Not the right wine for a red meat, but I thought you'd prefer it. I would.'

Nchembe twisted the bottle in Brian's hands.

'Chablis! Wonderful! I don't see much good French wine living in ...'

'Where do you stay?' Brian phrased it as a joke. 'A *dacha* outside Moscow?'

'Just because we met in the Russian embassy does not mean I am affiliated to the Communists. No. I use whomever I can. A man in exile must.'

'You've not been thrown out of Kenya, have you?' Brian retorted.

'I am not a Kenyan. Nor a Zambian, nor a Zimbabwean nor a Nigerian. I am an African. Africa is my country. And, as an ANC member, I am without a state. This is how I regard myself. In the part of my Africa which I consider to be my spiritual home now, I am banned. I travel the world on business but I have no land in which to reside.'

'You must be unique. To have dropped your tribe would have been bad enough, but your country ...'

'As long as my spiritual leader, Nelson Mandela, is in jail – the limbo of imprisonment – and Africans oppressed, I am without a home,' Nchembe said with finality.

'But you're Kikuyu, not Ndebele or Xhosa ...'

'That is by the way – South Africa is my natural home. It must be so now for all Africans. It is our last battlefield.'

Brian poured the Chablis into their wine glasses and cut into his steak. Blood oozed from the meat and collected by the rim of the plate.

As he had instructed Tom what to serve, there had lingered in Brian a perverse desire to gain any revenge he could for

Nchembe's cuckolding him. The thought of putting Nchembe at a disadvantage at their lunch, causing him embarrassment, had prompted Brian to order steak: cutting steak one-handed was difficult. However Tom, noticing the guest's handicap, had placed sharp kitchen knives on the table. And the beef, from a cattle farm owned by a friend of Brian's south of Lusaka, was tender. Watching Nchembe slice the meat from the bone made Brian ashamed of his churlishness.

'Are you married now?' Brian asked.

'Not any longer. I was married to a Kikuyu lady,' Nchembe responded, 'and we had two *toto*s. But they are dead.'

Nchembe did not elaborate on their deaths and Brian did not enquire further, saying simply, 'I'm sorry.' There seemed nothing else to say.

'It was a long time ago. Fourteen, maybe fifteen years. I forget.' He finished cutting his meat into manageable cubes and said, 'What about you? Did you marry that pretty girl you were with at the dance?'

'Judy. Yes, we were married, but it didn't last. I suppose I was on the rebound from Lucy. She left me two years later. It was a mutual parting.'

'Have you,' Nchembe lowered his fork and raised his glass, 'still that fine house in the country? I remember it well. I was very happy there with you. I think, now, that that was what I most missed after we fought. Oxford was good, but it was in the peace of your place that I was alive in a different way. Nowhere have I since found a place like it. Not even in Africa. Often have I thought of those days.'

'It went in the settlement,' Brian replied with a hint of melancholy. 'It was a good house.'

'She has it now?'

'I have no idea.'

Nchembe reached over the table, holding out his glass.

'Let us drink to those days,' he suggested. 'They were fine times.'

Brian sipped the Chablis. It was so cold it stung his gums.

'Let us also drink to the leopard in the fire. Maybe it was reborn in the bush as we hoped.'

'We were very drunk that night,' Nchembe observed nostalgically. 'Yes, let us hope the leopard did return to Africa.'

As he lowered his glass, Brian said, 'I was very angry with you. I...'

'Leave it now, Brian. It is the past. No apology is needed for the emotions are over. I, too, was bitter. And angry. I was encouraged by her, flattered by her attention. She – her fault was in her fickleness and, perhaps, she was curious to know a black man. Yet it was also my fault. It was vanity and ... Enough!'

He fell silent and Brian, deciding to remain quiet, helped himself to the salad, crisp and lightly tossed in vinaigrette dressing. It left a tart taste in his mouth after the Chablis.

'Lucy actually married an African,' Nchembe remarked suddenly. 'He is a Malawani.'

'Are they still married?'

'He is her latest husband. She has had four. The first was the Indian at the ball, the second was an Englishman she met in Mexico, the third was an American – he lasted the longest and was a banker – and the latest is a Malawian. He's a very rich man, too.'

'I think I owe you thanks more than an apology,' Brian said.

'And I owe the Indian a similar debt of gratitude! As for the Malawian – well, you know how pious they can be. If she seeks to annul yet another marriage ... It was a surprise to me the marriage happened in the first place.'

'How do you know all of this?'

'After Oxford, I kept tabs – that's an expression I learnt from my little book ... Do you remember my little book?'

From the dim recesses of his mind, Brian recalled Nchembe's hut in Wamumu, the dark interior smelling of people, Nchembe at the door, skilfully stropping the razor one-handed.

'Yes. I remember.'

'I kept tabs,' Nchembe repeated, 'on all those whom I

considered my friends – or potential friends to the struggle. Or of use to it. Many have helped us, just as you have.'

Tom cleared the plates away and served the dessert, a compote of peaches in red Italian wine. The sun was creeping across the house and the border of the shadow was edging towards the table.

'I still have the tooth,' Brian admitted suddenly. 'It was that which made me most ashamed, tearing it off you and throwing it away.'

He fumbled inside his shirt and, undoing one button, held the chain free of the material. The canine tooth swung like a shard of old ivory against the tanned skin of his chest.

'I, too.' Nchembe pulled his tie to one side and imitated Brian's actions. 'After you had gone, I returned to the fellows' garden and found it on the grass. I could not leave it.' Tucking the tooth back inside his shirt, Nchembe said again, 'We are growing old, my friend.' There were tears in the African's eyes. 'And there is too much animosity in the world. It will be many generations before it is ended, stamped out forever. The dream I had as a young man, of an Africa at peace, is not in sight. All we can do is nag at these diseases of mankind – worry them as a dog a rat, or a mongoose a cobra. Hope to weaken them. We must do this with our ideologies, with natural justice on our side and, though I once hoped it would never come to it again, maybe also with the gun and the bomb.

'As for you and me. Let us be a part of peace after all these years. Let us re-forge our friendship, as the old rusty iron can enter the charcoal and come out a new and shining spear. Take my hand, Brian, and shake it. Not as two men meeting for business but as two companions joining their strengths.'

Brian could say nothing. He felt the sadness of the years they had spent parted, the long rift caused by a woman who was evidently an unscrupulous manipulator of people. He grasped Nchembe's hand across the table, the two men's fists tightening about each other.

After they had eaten, while Tom percolated coffee in the kitchen, Brian and Nchembe walked slowly around the grounds of the house. They did not speak much to each other, commenting upon the dry air and the promise of the rains, watching a lizard scuttle across the dry, dead, sickle-shaped leaves of the eucalyptus. The leaves of the frangipani trees agitated in a warm breeze blowing from the low, distant hills. Crickets chirped and sawed in the grass.

Behind the swimming pool, Nchembe stood for a moment, surveyed the view and the guest-house-cum-den.

'I lived in an A-frame once.'

'Not as luxurious as this one.'

'No. Not as luxurious,' he agreed.

By the time they returned to the verandah, the sun had invaded more of it. They pulled two of the easy chairs out of the glare and sat down, the coffee between them.

'You are doing good for Africa.' Nchembe was returning to the theme of their earlier conversation. 'Do not think this is going unnoticed.'

'By whom is my work noticed?' Brian queried. He could guess the answer but wanted it confirmed.

'By the ANC. By the government here, President Kaunda's office. But also by the South Africans, both parties ... The pro-black lobby, the liberal whites and democrats know of you, admire you. One day, when South Africa is a free land, there will be a place there for you. Of course, the government there knows of you as well. They see what you are doing. For them, anyone advancing the cause of the black, even in pacific ways like agricultural development, poses a threat of some sort.'

Nchembe stopped speaking. On the parched lawn, a heavy-duty commercial sprinkler came into action, flicking bursts of water in a high arc over the grass. Within a moment of it coming into operation, birds appeared to bathe in or drink from the temporary puddles. Others strutted or darted about on the ground, pecking at insects the water disturbed.

'Are you staying in Zambia for long?' Brian enquired.

'I may be. Why do you ask?'

'I was thinking.' Brian shifted in his seat. 'I'm going up to the Luangwa Valley in a week or so. A bit of a holiday. I've taken to photographing game. It's only a hobby, really. Yet I do sell some of the pictures – had three of crocodile in the National Geographic a few years ago.'

'You no longer shoot?'

'No, not really. I still eat game – biltong, guinea fowl for the table – but I don't hunt.'

'Why did you stop?'

'I suppose I saw the error of my ways.' He cast his mind back. 'Do you remember Inspector Broomhall? At Wamumu?'

Nchembe nodded.

'Yes. He interrogated me. He was a fair man.'

'His wife,' Brian continued, 'set me thinking. We – the human species, that is – are killing the bush with our farming methods, deforestation, mining, poaching. There's no room for sport hunting now, not as there used to be. A few shooting safaris are not wrong. They cull as much as kill and can be a boon. They earn much-needed foreign exchange. But the old ways are gone.'

'Perhaps,' Nchembe said shrewdly, 'your farming ideas are doing the killing for you.'

'Perhaps. But I'm working on ways of preserving the bush and farming it. Game farming, game management controls, intensive crop growing. I've a few theories ... Farmers can live alongside big game – even elephants – if there is an understanding between the two. I believe that's possible.'

'Some places are doing this.' Nchembe thought for a moment. 'In Zimbabwe. In Botswana and Malawi.'

'Game does not only earn foreign currency through tourism,' Brian declared. 'It is a vital food source to the African, just as it has always been. But now, with the increased population, it must be husbanded ...' He paused, wondering how what he was about to ask would be received. 'Why don't you take a break and come to the valley with me?'

The telex clicked in the office off the verandah. After a few moments it stopped and there was a tiny beeping sound like a monotonous, high-pitched bird. Brian excused himself and opened the office door. The beeping grew instantly louder. He loaded a new cartridge of paper into the telex, forwarding the first sheet onto the feeder cogs. When he returned to the verandah, his shirt cooled by the air conditioning in the office, Nchembe was standing by the steps.

'I must be going,' he said. 'My driver will be wanting to return to his home soon and I have to see someone this evening. At Kapiri Mposhi. It is a long drive.'

'Another tractor deal?'

'No,' Nchembe replied simply. 'Guns.'

'I though you renounced violence long ago...'

'I did. And you know why, Brian – for you are the only white I've ever told, and I've told no black. The gun is not the best weapon of persuasion. But if your enemy will not talk and uses force, what other option have you? One has to fight fire with fire.'

Nchembe walked down the steps to the lawn and set off for the taxi parked under the trees, Brian at his side. The driver's feet projected through the passenger door window: his light coloured soles were grey with dust. He was asleep.

'What about Luangwa?'

Nchembe made no immediate reply but carried on walking to the car. The driver heard them coming and woke up. He swung his legs in and got out of the car to hold the door open for his client.

'Yes,' Nchembe said. 'I'd like that. I'll be in touch in a day or two to arrange to meet you. I have no address I can give you. Not at this time.' The Americanism was strange coming from him. 'I'll look forward to it.'

'I'll get it fixed up for us both.'

'Fine! And do let me know, when I phone you in a day or two, of the expected delivery dates of the Deutzes.'

The taxi engine was in dire need of tuning. As it started dense, acrid clouds of diesel belched from the exhaust, sending two scratching hens on an ungainly dash for cover in the direction of the servants' quarters.

Brian waved briefly, watching the vehicle go down the drive, turn at the gate and head in the direction of the tarmacked surface of Leopards Hill Road. He remained standing until the dust cloud had drifted away to settle on the roadside bushes.

21

'Boss! Boss!'

Brian reached out from under the sheet, fumbling for his watch on the bedside table. The cotton sheet, sticking to his skin with sweat, tugged across his chest and pulled painfully at the hairs on his forearm.

'Boss! Boss!' came the insistent voice again.

By the faint dawn light entering the room through the slats in the venetian blind, Brian could just see the face of his watch. It was six-fifteen.

'What is it?' he called sleepily. 'Do you know what time it is?'

He fought his brain, trying to remember what day of the week it was. There was no early flight he needed to meet at Lusaka airport. Yet there were jet engines in his half-waking stupor.

'Boss! Boss!' the voice reiterated a third time.

He recognised it as his houseboy's voice.

'Go back to bed, Tom. It's only just after six.'

The servant would not be put off, calling out even more imperatively.

'Come in then,' Brian said resignedly.

The door opened but Tom did not enter the room upright. He came in quickly, in a semi-crouched position, snapping the door shut behind him. His unusual entrance instantly jerked Brian awake. He sat up, the sheet still adhering to him.

'What's the matter, Tom?'

'Airplanes, boss. Guns, boss.'

In the half-light of the room, Brian could see the whites of the African's eyes. He was terrified. Outside the door to the bedroom there was a scuffling.

'What's that noise outside?'

'My family, boss.'

By now, Brian was fully awake. He swung his legs over the

369

edge of the bed, stood up and pulled on a pair of blue Y-front underpants. Tom did not avert his eyes but Brian had the feeling the servant wasn't so much looking at him as through him.

'What is your family doing in the house?'

'We are afraid. Listen ...'

Brian listened. He could hear nothing at first but then there was a far-off whistle which grew to a roar of jet engines. He separated the slats of the window blind in time to see a black jet fighter wheel by between the house and the hill. He guessed from its size it was flying along Leopards Hill Road at an altitude of not more than a hundred feet. No sooner had he seen it than it was gone, leaving only a searing noise and a faint grey vapour-trail against the dawn sky.

'What is going on?' Brian asked, nonplussed.

He was answered not by the houseboy but by an explosion.

He thrust his legs into a pair of khaki jeans, zipped up the fly and quickly ran from the room, stepping over Tom's wife and four children who were lying in the passage outside his room. In the lounge, in similar positions of hiding, were the gardener and his wife, one of the drivers and his girlfriend and the laundrywoman with her three children. They were huddling against the furniture, gazing fearfully at the window.

From the verandah, Brian could see a plume of smoke beginning to rise from the bush about a mile down Leopards Hill Road towards Lusaka. The smoke was lifting then flattening in the cool morning air. He had seen smoke behaving in just this manner on a thousand occasions over the rondavels of villages in as many locations of sub-Saharan Africa. The difference was that this was not the fine wisp of woodsmoke but the denser billows of burning oil, rubber or plastics.

'What the hell is going on?'

There was nobody to answer him.

'Jacob!' he shouted.

By the lounge window appeared a head.

'Where are the keys to the Range Rover?'

'Inside, boss.'

'Inside what?'

'Inside the car, boss,' came the scared reply.

For once thankful that his orders had been disobeyed, Brian ran to the vehicle and jerked the door open. The vehicle started at the first twist of the key and Brian, rather than reverse it, drove forwards over the kerbing of the drive, across the lawn, around one of the bougainvillaea bushes and on towards the gate. As he bounced over the flower borders, he checked the first-aid box was in its mounting on the rear panelling.

At the gate, he jumped out, pulled the bolt, shoved the gates open and drove through, the gears screaming in second. It was not until he tried to accelerate that he realized the vehicle was in four-wheel-drive. He jammed his foot on the brake, selected two-wheel-drive and thrust the accelerator to the floor.

Drawing nearer to the smoke, now a pillar of sooty blackness in the grey-washed sky, he discovered the scene of the fire was some way off the road. He stopped to get his bearings.

No sooner had the Range Rover halted than the jet fighter again howled overhead, not a hundred yards away. It was flying fast, but Brian could distinctly see the face of the pilot in the cockpit. It was a white face.

'Oh, Christ!' he said involuntarily.

He steered his vehicle off the road and under a leaning tree. The remains of a long-distance lorry chassis indicated why the tree was in such a position.

He switched off the engine. From the direction of the fire, which he could see burning with the dull orange flames of an oil blaze about half a mile away, came the chatter of small arms fire. This was interrupted by the louder, more staccato stutter of either a light machine-gun or, possibly, he thought, an S L R.

The firing ceased. A one-ton pick-up truck came racing along a dirt road from the fire, driving parallel with the main tarmac road beside which Brian had stopped. It was followed by another, similar vehicle on the back of which were men. They were firing into the blaze.

Brian started up the Range Rover, re-engaged four-wheel-drive and turned in the direction of the fire. He set off through the bush, flattening scrubby clumps of undergrowth, rocking from side to side. If he had not had the steering wheel to grip he would have been thrown mercilessly from door to door. As it was, it was extremely difficult to maintain an even pressure on the accelerator pedal.

He braked hard. One of the pick-ups was reversing down the track, the men in the back still shooting with automatic weapons. They were not a hundred yards away. Brian could see they – like the pilot – had white faces.

There was then a heavy return of fire from the direction of the conflagration. The pick-up spun its wheels.

One of the passengers aboard the truck must then have seen the Range Rover. Five shots hit it in rapid succession. Brian, somehow prepared by a sixth sense, flung himself across the front seats, the gear stick in the backward, second-gear position, catching him on the ribs. The windscreen crackled like an electric spark as two shots passed through it, hit the rear screen and shattered it. Another shot smashed the driver's door mirror and a fourth hit a tyre, exploded it then ricochetted away, whining as it struck and pierced the wheel-arch. The fifth, coming marginally later than the first four, blew out the nearside headlight.

There was another explosion. It was closer than the seat of the fire. It rocked the Range Rover. Brian risked looking up, through the laminated windscreen which now was cracked into a spider's-web pattern. Where the pick-up truck had been was a ball of fire. The other pick-up was nowhere in sight.

Sirens were sounding on the road and Brian realised that the Zambian Army was now arriving and he was in the wrong place. And he had the wrong coloured face. Despite the flat tyre, he reversed back the way he had come. As he drove, his left arm over the rear seat and his neck craned around, he broke into a cold sweat. At any minute, the Zambians would open fire on him.

Once on the road, he drove in the direction of Lusaka. Within a mile, he approached a hastily-constructed road

block manned by para-military troops in camouflage uniform, and police officers. He stopped, got out, raised his
hands where they could be seen and marched quickly towards
the roadblock. Several of the para-militaries levelled their
automatic rifles at him.

'I am a Zambian resident,' he shouted. 'I am Mr Titchner.
I live on Leopards Hill Road. Don't shoot. I have a first-aid
kit in my car.'

At that moment he prayed the driver hadn't been pilfering
the contents of it to sell. Elastoplast could fetch a handsome
sum in the Lusakan shanty towns.

'Your tyre is blown out,' challenged one of the para-
militaries. 'Why is that?'

'I was fired upon. Look at the windscreen and the
headlight.'

They had apparently not noticed the starred holes in the
laminated glass.

A police officer appeared from behind a bush.

'He is correct. He is a Zambian.'

The para-military guards lowered their weapons.

'Get the medical box,' Brian ordered one of them. 'It's in
the rear of my car.'

The African did as he was commanded. The contents had
fortunately not been disturbed.

Brian and the police officer ran towards the fire. The
flames were dying now but the smoke was not lessening.

By a burning car, the tyres aflame and the seats smouldering, Brian saw two bodies. One was a child, a boy of about ten.
He had only one leg: where the other should have been was a
ragged stump, the blood seeping into the dry earth like sump
oil. He was dead. A few yards off lay the body of a man. He
was lying on his front and twitching. The light brown soles of
his feet showed brightly in the growing morning light. It
would not be long to sun-up.

Brian grabbed the man's shoulder and tried to turn him
over. The body would not come. He dropped the box and
used both hands on the man. He rolled over suddenly. His
chest and belly had been skinned by the blast, the raw flesh
peppered with gravel from the earth. Where he had lain he

had left a mark on the ground like a grotesque shadow. He, too, was dead.

Beside him was a scarf in the black, green and gold colours of the A N C. It, like the car, was smouldering. Brian stamped on it, extinguished it and folded it loosely to cover the man's face.

As he lowered the scarf in place he thought how like this was to a military funeral, the man being honoured with his own flag. Then he saw the man was the one who had driven Nchembe to the house two days before.

A shallow *gully* ran along the side of what had been three buildings and several round huts. Brian went into it and vomited. Nothing came up but clear liquid, wrenching his gut and scouring his throat.

The policeman watched him.

'Can I have your medical box, sir?' he requested. 'Some of the people here are still alive.'

Brian nodded and croaked, 'I'll be with you in a moment.'

He wiped his mouth on a soiled handkerchief he found in the pocket of his jeans. This done, he discarded it and joined the police officer who was tending to the injured lying on the ground or leaning against vehicles which had not been destroyed.

As Brian bandaged a woman's head, he dreaded having to move to the next casualty. He was terrified of discovering Nchembe, dead or alive.

Smearing her scalp with Savlon, winding the lint around her brow, he tried to ignore the woman's whimpers and her grazed hand shaking violently on his arm. To take his mind from her pain and anguish, he forced his attention on to the sounds around him. The fires popped and crackled, orders were yelled and questions shouted; the wounded groaned – Brian could not escape the noises of injury and terror. Somewhere beyond the nearest ruined hut, which was now ablaze, a pi-dog was howling and yelping alternately.

The policeman's voice cut through the awful pandemonium and Brian listened to him speaking to one of the survivors yet did not really take in what he was saying.

'Speak slowly!' the policeman commanded in English, his voice high-pitched with tension. 'Speak more slowly!'

'White men ... Soldiers.' The survivor, his bare shoulder gleaming with unclotted blood, was still jabbering. 'They have guns and they was firing on us. We don't know them ...'

Some of the hut roof-timbers crashed down in a welter of sparks. Brian jumped, his hand jerking the bandage and causing the woman to wince and grunt.

'What else? You see their uniforms? What else you see? Speak more slowly!'

'Nothing ... All the time they shouting. Jan ... Peat ... Jan ... Peat ... Sta din! Sta din!'

It was gibberish. Brian tied a knot in the bandage and the woman struggled to her feet, her cheeks glistening with tears.

Another voice interrupted, calming the hysterical report. It was deep, unemotional, accepted the chaos as a sort of normality.

'We take it from here, officer.'

Brian glanced over his shoulder. A young Zambian army captain stood by the policeman's side, his automatic weapon nonchalantly hanging from his hand.

'One of them was hit ...' the policeman began.

'That is so. We know of it.'

When the sun rose, half an hour later, clearing the low clouds on the horizon, it shone a bloody orange through the pall of smoke.

22

Brian reached across the fascia of the Range Rover, switching on the radio and pressing one of the pre-tuned station buttons. The blast of cold morning air from the vent gave the skin on his wrist goose-pimples. The digital clock incorporated into the radio showed it to be just before seven a.m. – between the blue numbers a colon flashed the seconds. He absent-mindedly prodded the rubber windscreen surround with his finger. The mechanic replacing the bullet-smashed glass had left an inch of the rubber curled in on itself.

'This is London ...' announced a disembodied voice from the door panel. There followed the stirring tones of 'Lillibullero' followed by the familiar, strangely comforting sound of the pips. 'It is six a.m., Greenwich Mean Time. BBC World Service. The news, read by John Wing.'

Brian increased the volume. A bird hovered over the front of the vehicle then flew off, thinking better of landing on the shining metal.

'... A government spokesman in Lusaka has confirmed that part of the unit of the South African army which escaped after a gun battle at an alleged African National Congress training camp on the outskirts of the city yesterday is still on the run and in Zambia. Meanwhile Mr Pik Botha, the South African foreign minister, has reiterated his country's intention of fighting any source of terrorism which threatens to undermine further the stability of South Africa. Our Africa correspondent, James Fish, reports from Lusaka ...'

The first rays of the sun glittered through the lower branches of the trees surrounding the house. Brian stretched, the news broadcast reminding him of his waking hours on the previous day. They seemed already to be fading in the mists of his memory.

'... in the suburbs of the capital, Lusaka. The Zambian Army, previously found to be ill-prepared for such incursions by similar attacks in 1986, were already on the alert. In a heavy exchange of gunfire just after dawn, the South African unit, which had mounted its attack with air support, was routed. Five of its number are reported dead. At a press conference yesterday afternoon, a general of the Zambian Army announced no casualties in his ranks but seven civilians were reported killed. A diplomatic row has now developed between Lusaka and Pretoria, President Kaunda demanding an "unequivocal apology" from the South African prime minister for the slaughter of innocent Zambian nationals, and an acknowledgement of the illegality of the raid before he will return the bodies of the dead South Africans, all reported to be white, to Pretoria.' There was a pause in the broadcast followed by the announcer's voice. 'In Seoul, South Korea, a further day of rioting has forced President Chun Doo Hwan ...'

Brian's Mercedes Benz appeared on the dirt road. The gardener unlatched the gate and the saloon car came slowly through and up the drive to halt beside the Range Rover. The driver stopped and, as the taxi driver had done, stepped out and opened the rear passenger door.

Nchembe waved to Brian as the driver opened the boot lid of the Mercedes and removed two stylish canvas-and-leather holdalls.

'Good morning, Brian!' he called, raising his hand to the trees above his head. 'It is a good day for a safari.'

'Morning, Matthew!' Brian responded and, leaving the front seat of the Range Rover, opened the rear tailgate, the repaired rear window going up, the panelling lowering. The early sunlight, catching the glass, flashed into the branches.

'Put the cases next to mine, Jacob,' Brian ordered the driver. 'And can you find a length of rope to secure the jerry cans?'

'Yes, boss,' Jacob answered, placing the holdalls next to Brian's much-travelled, battered Antler case and removing a coil of rope from a nearby pick-up.

'How long will it take to drive to Luangwa?' Nchembe enquired as Jacob tied the rope to hooks and threaded them through the three-bar handles on the large, ex-army petrol cans.

'Eleven hours. Twelve if we're unlucky at the road blocks. With the alert on, I'd say twelve plus. A white face like mine in a bush vehicle isn't going to be overly welcome. Even with Zambian plates. I've got my passport – British, which won't inspire confidence ...'

'But you'll have a black face with you. That should make a better balance.'

Nchembe touched the paintwork on the vehicle, running his finger along the hinge of the lower half of the tailgate. Small splinters of glass stuck to his skin: he scraped them off against the orange plastic lens of the indicator light.

'The slugs passed right through.' Brian raised the tailgate and secured it. 'I'm sorry about your taxi driver.'

'I was told it was you who found him.'

'Yes.' He closed the rear screen down and aimlessly kicked the tyre on the rear wheel. 'He was already dead. There was nothing I could do.'

Brian climbed in behind the steering wheel as Nchembe opened the front passenger door. He started the engine and they reversed away from the Mercedes. The digital clock showed 7:15.

'You did much,' Nchembe said as they bumped along the dirt road. 'To him you gave dignity in death, covering his face with his scarf. To the others, you gave life, bandaging deep cuts until the medical staff arrived, holding water to sore lips, giving hope. Just as your agricultural research work gives hope.'

The wheels hummed on the tarmac. In the bush to their right lay the remains of the burnt-out buildings, still surrounded needlessly by military vehicles, as if another hope existed, that the killers might return to the scene of their kill, as predators do, to finish off the scraps.

'I wanted to do more. I felt so useless. There were dead piccanins ...'

'They were all children – the piccanins, the men, the women – children of their race, of their continent. They died for history.'

'Was it really an ANC terrorist training camp?' Brian asked tentatively.

'In truth, no. Such places exist – I do not deny it: they are essential to the struggle – but so near a city? The buildings were occupied by only one family which was not Zambian. They came from Botswana. And, yes, they were members of the Congress, but not military people. The husband was a teacher and the mother a nurse. They were not killed although the man was wounded in the leg. You treated him.'

Brian did not remember.

'And their children?'

'They had no children ...'

Brian took a short cut through Kabulonga, around the outskirts of the University of Zambia campus and on to the Great East Road. As they drove, not talking, past the turn-off to Lusaka airport, a 747 flew overhead, banking for the approach to the final flight-path.

Once out of the city, the road became less busy. For some miles, they passed cyclists heading towards the suburbs and cars crowded with men making for the city centre but even this traffic soon disappeared.

The first hour and a half of their driving was through hilly countryside which, as they went on, became wooded and dense. They passed a few lorries juddering up the inclines, belching black smoke from their exhausts, and the stripped skeletons of chassis rusting away on the verges. There were few villages and little sign of local habitation. The sun rose hotter and, by the time they reached Rufunsa, the Range Rover was vibrant with heat.

Reluctant to put on the air conditioning as it caused the engine to use so much additional fuel, they drove with the windows open. As the road was tarmac-surfaced for three hundred and fifty miles, as far as Chipata, there was no fear of dust choking the car. After Chipata it would be different. In the meantime, the drumming of the wheels on the road, the hiss of the fan, the rush of the wind through the windows and the loud, constant hum of the engine did not make for conversation.

Beyond Rufunsa, the road began to drop in altitude. Ahead

lay the flat plain of the last of the Great Rift Valley. Twenty miles to the north they could just see the dull outline of the Muchinga Escarpment. The air gradually became hotter still, more tropical and drier.

'Here comes the first obstacle,' Brian said as the road wound down into a heavily wooded valley. 'You can bet your last kwacha this road block'll be a sod to get through.'

Nchembe opened the glove compartment and removed a packet of Peter Stuyvesant from the carton: he placed it on top of the fascia.

Brian laughed and asked, 'You know all the white man's tricks, then?'

'Most of them,' Nchembe answered. 'When in Rome ...'

The suspension bridge across the Luangwa River gorge shone steely in the sunlight. Over a hundred feet below ran the river, sand bars along one bank. The sides of the gorge were sheer. Being a vital road-link to the east and the only road to Lilongwe, the tiny capital of Malawi, and ultimately Mozambique, the bridge was of considerable economic as well as strategic importance. It was certain to be well guarded.

A sign by the side of the road proclaimed, 'Stop here: proceed at 5 mph.' There was not a single person in view.

Brian halted, let the engine idle, selected first gear and moved cautiously forward. There was a high shelf in the road between the tarmac and the bridge; the Range Rover jerked over it. As the vehicle edged along the bridge Brian could see, ahead of him in the centre, two para-military soldiers, guns slung over their shoulders, peering down into the gorge. At the other side of the bridge, several hundred yards long, stood two small figures.

As they drew level with the two troopers in the centre of the span, and just as Brian was about to greet them with a cheery wave, they turned, swung their guns off their shoulders and levelled them. Brian braked, the jerry cans banging dully against each other despite Jacob's efficient knots.

'Morning!' Brian tried the greeting in any case.

'Did you not read the notice?'

The guards looked squarely into Brian's face.

'Which notice?' He feigned ignorance.

'Back up.'

The guard waved his hand towards the western bank and Brian engaged reverse. He took the Range Rover back to the start of the bridge, nudged the wheels over the shelf and braked again. The guards, who had been walking abreast of the vehicle, stood on either side. Both cocked their stubby, automatic weapons. The metallic clicking was an ominous and unnerving noise but Brian was used to it. All road blocks, throughout Zambia, were manned by those equipped with such firearms, the Luangwa Bridge being one of the most sensitive places.

'Back more.'

Brian obeyed.

'Now you see the sign?'

'That sign!' Brian played stupid, removing his sunglasses. He was only too well aware that a man wearing dark glasses is more formidable than one who is not. He wanted to avoid appearing in any way threatening or superior. 'I saw it and I stopped then proceeded very slowly as it states.'

'You stop and wait. Engine off. Papers.'

Brian produced his passport and Nchembe took a wallet out of his jacket, removing a wad of papers from behind the folded kwacha notes. Brian gave their documents to the trooper who uncocked his weapon and slung it over his shoulder again.

'Where you going?' the guard demanded, opening Brian's passport and comparing the photo with the living being.

'Luangwa Valley. We are going on holiday to see the wild animals.'

'Where you coming from?'

'Lusaka.'

All the talking was being done by just one of the para-militaries. The other, meanwhile, walked slowly around the rear of the vehicle.

'You British. Where you live?'

'In Lusaka.'

He handed the passport back and unfolded Nchembe's papers, not reading them.

'You going too fast on the bridge.'

381

'I was going at under five miles an hour,' Brian argued, but not too forcefully.

'Over. This makes a fine of twenty kwacha. Not stopping also twenty kwacha.'

'That's outrageous,' Brian complained but not vociferously.

The para-military soldier was unmoved. His companion came to his side and muttered something which Brian, despite his knowledge of the language, found incomprehensible.

'What is in your cases? Open them, please.'

Brian put his fingers on the door handle, preparing to get out of the Range Rover and open the tailgate. The door catch rattled. Nchembe spoke to the trooper in Chinyanja.

'Read my papers.'

The para-military looked at the papers he had unfolded in his hands but disregarded. He studied them closely, his eyes darting from the papers to Nchembe's face and back again.

'Wait,' the soldier ordered.

Brian stopped and gently closed the door again, resting his arm on the window.

Beckoning to his comrade and showing him Nchembe's papers, the para-military spoke quietly. The documents shook slightly in his hand.

'Good,' the guard commented, refolding the papers and handing them to Brian with his British passport. 'Maybe you stopped, maybe no. I make a fine of just twenty kwacha. For speed.'

While Brian removed some five kwacha notes from his wallet, handing them to the soldier, Nchembe said in English, 'It must be very tiring at this roadblock. Always on the alert. Especially at the present time. Will you and your companion have a cigarette?'

Both of the para-militaries accepted a cigarette, asked for several more – 'for friends in the trees' – and were given them. The second man made safe his gun and hung it from his shoulder as he lit his cigarette, stuffing the extras into a tunic pocket. His comrade was having difficulty thrusting his cigarettes into the same pocket as that in which he had pushed the kwacha notes.

'Slow over the bridge,' warned the guard, puffing on his cigarette. Then he saw the bullet hole in the wing of the Range Rover and barked an order. Both men, simultaneously and with lightning speed, jumped their guns into the position for firing from the hip. Once again the cocking levers clicked.

Brian had not yet re-started the engine. One hand was on the steering wheel, the other on the ignition key.

'Hands up!' shouted the guard who had done all the talking. His words sounded like a line from a bad highwayman film, his voice tight with fear.

Two thoughts sped through Brian's mind: the first was, Christ! the man's going to fire and the second was to laugh at the incongruity of his order.

Slowly, Brian raised his hands and rested them on the plastic cover to the instruments. Nchembe put his one hand on the fascia above the radio. The second para-military ran around the front of the Range Rover and levelled his gun at Nchembe's head.

'Other hand!' he yelled.

Nchembe raised his stump.

This action defused the situation somewhat. The guard lowered his gun. A shamefaced smile crept onto his lips.

'This man,' Nchembe said, nodding in Brian's direction, 'saved the lives of our brothers. That hole was not made by a Zambian . . .'

For a moment, neither soldier moved. Then, once again, they lowered their guns.

'You go. Slowly.'

Brian started the engine, put his sunglasses on with artificial laziness – for it was diplomatic, even important, not to show a haste to get away, no matter what the mind dictated – and they drove so slowly over the bridge that the speedometer registered zero the whole way. On the far bank, the guards at the second sentry post merely waved them through.

As they drove up the hill from the bridge, Brian making sure he did not exceed thirty miles per hour – if they saw him accelerate, they might still open fire, or have others hiding in the trees do so – Nchembe laughed.

'What's so funny?'

Brian was shaken by their treatment. The demand to see their papers and the fine he had anticipated. The second cocking of the weapons had upset him.

'My arm!' Nchembe exclaimed. 'No one can harm a one-armed man. It has saved me from a mugging in New York, a beating-up in London, a particularly nasty body search in Tel Aviv. It has thrown many a prosecuting counsel, even in South Africa. It may not hold a fork or a glass of beer, but sure as hell it has saved my skin a few times.'

'Certainly your face didn't do all that much,' Brian retorted, thinking of Nchembe's remark as they had set off from the house in Leopards Hill Road.

'Maybe not ...' Nchembe admitted.

They drove on, through Kachalola to Nyimba where the petrol pump was unlocked for them after a fifteen-minute search for the key-holder who was, reputedly, absent at a funeral – a well-worn metaphor for hungover after a night in the nearest beer hall. From Nyimba, the road continued through Petauke and Katete, past rocky kopjes and outcrops, villages of rondavels and churches of mudbricks with hollow, gothic-shaped windows, beer halls and shops; it also ran through a number of road blocks but at none was the procedure as rigorous or as stubborn as at the Luangwa Bridge.

Eventually, after three hundred and sixty miles of driving from Lusaka, they reached Chipata, turning left a hundred yards short of the road block at the town boundary.

As he swung into the curve at the junction, Brian cast a quick look at the digital clock.

'Five to three. Not bad going considering. I've never done it quicker.'

The sun was scorching now and, as soon as the vehicle slowed, the reduction in the flow of air through the windows made it seem hotter. The needle on the temperature gauge rested on the last white mark before the red warning zone.

'Another three hours or so,' Nchembe speculated.

'About that,' Brian confirmed. 'We should get there at about six.'

Ahead of them lay the last one hundred miles of their journey, but it was the most uncomfortable sector of the whole drive. Within a few miles of Chipata the road changed from metalling to earth, the surface corrugated and strewn, whenever they came to a hill, with stones some of which were as large as tennis balls.

Twenty miles out of Chipata the road wound down an escarpment from the top of which Brian and Nchembe could see out across the expanse of scrub jungle through which they were to drive.

'Time for a quick break?' Brian suggested, and Nchembe readily agreed.

With the droning engine silent and the monotonous thunder of the wheels and suspension coping with the corrugations and ruts cut off, the sounds of the bush impinged upon them as they left the Range Rover. A mournful-sounding bird sang in the dry cover, the insects hissed and the exhaust pinged and dinged as it cooled.

From a crate behind the front seats, Brian pulled out two bottles of beer, breaking the crown caps off by striking them against the front wheel rim.

'Cheers!'

Nchembe raised the bottle to his lips after wiping the mouth on his shirt.

'You can tell Africa is poor whenever you drink a bottle of beer,' he said. 'From the state of the bottle. This one,' he held it before his face, 'has been used a hundred times.'

'How can you tell?'

'The side is so rubbed it is grey now and, for certain, there will be splinters of glass in the bottom.'

'The old law,' Brian said. 'Never pour or drink the last inch.'

They did not stop again for the remainder of their journey except at a tsetse control barrier where an old man, armed with a ragged muslin butterfly net, inspected the inside of the vehicle for the presence of flies and squirted a burst of insecticide into the back. Because the windows had been shut against the dust perpetually rising from the wheels and because the air conditioning had been switched on since they stopped on the escarpment, there was little chance of any tsetse flies entering. One, however, was sitting obligingly upon the windscreen wiper where it had been lodged, half-stunned by the buffeting of the wind. The old man trapped it in his net, releasing it into a gauze cage like a ramshackle aviary by the side of the barrier.

Suddenly, after eighty miles or so, the road became a tarmac strip again. On either side, tall, bamboo-like grasses leaned over the uneven verges and the road crossed a series of concrete bridges.

'Ten miles,' Brian announced as the tone of their journey changed from the din of earth road to the comparatively silent hum of the tarmac.

At a junction, a signpost indicated Mfuwe to the right and 'A-R P O-T' to the left and, twenty minutes later, another sign pointed the way to Chinzombo. They arrived at the camp as the sun was just above the horizon, to be greeted by the scent of woodsmoke.

The camp, four hundred miles upstream from the bridge where the roadblock was situated, was a centre for tourists, but not for the usual swimming-pool nightlife trippers, clad in bikinis and brightly-coloured shorts. Only dedicated wildlife enthusiasts, the photographers, film-makers and modern-day adventurers stayed in the Luangwa Valley.

Unusually, the camp was empty. A group of American biology students were booked in but were absent on a walking safari thirty miles north, at Big Lagoon. This allowed Brian and Nchembe three days in which to stay in the otherwise unused accommodation. The resident guide, Brian had been informed, was with the students and the camp was left in the charge of the African staff and a young English schoolmaster, earning his stay as a general factotum while indulging in his hobby of herpetology.

Brian had visited Chinzombo before. Operated by a trust dedicated to saving the rhino, almost poached out in the area, and the elephant, which was being heavily poached despite the small tusk-size of the local animals, it accepted overseas bookings and provided a very good service for up to two dozen clients at a time, all profits being ploughed back into the fight to protect the huge mammals and their environment.

A tall and handsome Englishman, Philip Terry was the camp guide, a long-standing friend of Brian's. They had first met at a party in Lusaka when Afriground was beginning to establish itself in the country. Terry had tried to involve Brian in the funding of the trust but he had not been interested.

Afriground was intended to make a profit: parting with a percentage of it to a charity was not in Brian's scheme. He had the shareholder to consider, he had explained, not mentioning that his use of the singular was deliberate – he was the only shareholder, the sole investor. Africa would benefit from the research he was embarking upon: he was, he argued, doing his bit.

Despite his refusal to support the trust, he and Terry had struck up a friendship and, when Brian gave himself a fortnight's holiday after a year of solid work setting up the Zambian subsidiary of the company, Terry offered him a trip to 'the valley', as the Zambians called it. In that fortnight, Brian had allowed himself to become re-acquainted with the bush and the ways of the animals.

Over the years since he had left Kenya for his first stay in Oxford, Brian had given little thought to the practicalities of living in the bush, of tracking the spoor of animals, minding the wind, minding one's step. Yet, no sooner was he in the bush once more, than all the tricks and techniques returned to him within a few days.

'It's like riding a bicycle,' Terry had assured him as they set off on the first morning. 'Once you know how, the skill never leaves you even if you don't keep practising.'

By the end of his fortnight in the valley, Brian was once more familiar with living in the bush. He automatically noted the wind, instantly knew if a lion's pugmark was fresh or stale, could immediately assess the proximity of an elephant from the heat and moistness of its dung pile, the time of the day and the direction and cover in which the animal was moving. He knew as if by instinct not to walk barefoot for fear of jiggers, to shake his shoes before putting them on in the morning, to avoid low branches with plentiful leaf-cover for fear of boomslangs. He recognized the difference between kudu and waterbuck hoofprints in soft sand, the various calls of the birds and the alarm whistling of puku antelope.

The Range Rover stopped under a huge shady tree behind the camp, close to the kitchens. A haze of woodsmoke from the fires for cooking and the hot water tank drifted lazily into the branches, picking out the late sunbeams in blue-grey. Beside an ancient Jeep, two children were playing with a pile of sticks.

Their arrival was expected and, no sooner had Brian halted and pulled on the handbrake against the ratchet, than a white man appeared through a wall of thatch matting, an African at his heels.

'Mr Titchner?' the European enquired. 'And Mr Nchembe?'

Brian got out of the driving seat, easing his back. His arms ached with the vibrating of the steering wheel and his eyes were sore with the sunlight despite his dark glasses. Nchembe opened the passenger door, lowering his feet to the ground and stood gingerly.

'We are getting frail in our middle age, Brian,' he remarked. 'We are too used to club-class seats and Mercedes Benz limousines.'

Brian grinned and said, 'That's us!' in reply both to Nchembe's comment and the European's welcoming question.

'Keith Macklor. I'm the snakeman.' They shook hands. Behind them, the fan under the bonnet was still spinning. 'I'll get a cup of tea on.'

They were shown across the camp compound, a group of thatched huts in a sylvan glade, painted white with deep verandahs. Brian's was at one end of the compound, Nchembe's next to it. Before them stood a huge, old acacia, the orange fruit looking like peeled apple rings, twisted and hard. In the centre of the compound was the thatched bar and, ten yards beyond it, an open thatch-roofed shelter above a circle of chairs, and the steep river bank.

'Dinner's at seven-thirty,' Macklor said. 'If you need me, I'm easy to find – my quarters're over there.' He pointed to a building across the far side of the compound. On the verandah of his hut he had a row of cages which he noticed Brian had seen. 'A number of lizards and three snakes. One's a spitting cobra but he's all right as he's behind glass.'

As Brian unpacked his case, he heard a splash. Looking out through the mosquito-proof mesh of the window, he saw the ripples ringing out from mid-river, where a hippo had just surfaced to announce its presence with a threating display. The last of the sunlight caught the interior of the hippo's gaping jaw, exaggerating the pinkness of its maw.

'Much poacher activity in the area?' Brian asked as they sat outside the bar after dinner. The food had been excellent – roast guinea fowl with bacon and sweet potatoes – and he felt satisfied.

'Some,' Macklor answered. 'We heard shots a week ago when we were taking an early morning game-viewing drive out. The patrol went out immediately – they'd only just arrived back from a fortnight in the bush – and they found an elephant. Tusks hacked out, of course. Followed the trail but lost it . . .'

'Rhino?'

'Again, some. One – what was left of it – was found at the end of the rains but it had been dead some weeks. There're not a lot about now. Maybe not more than one hundred in the whole valley. Many say far fewer. I've only seen a rhino on two occasions in the nine weeks I've been here. Once near the Mushilashi *dambo* and once here. They say there are two this side of the Luangwa in the GMA – Game Management Area.'

'It was near the camp?' Nchembe raised his eyebrows.

'In it! We were sitting here mid-morning. The viewing-drive was back and everyone was having breakfast. Suddenly, one of the tourists says, "What's that?" Well, nobody was quick to look. They were either eating or – well, you know how it is. They say "Look! Look!" at every butterfly. Anyway, I glanced up and there it was. A female rhino.

Standing under the acacia and grazing as if this was virgin bush. Fortunately, nobody moved. If they had ... I don't need to tell you, Brian. After five minutes, it gave up on the short grass and went out through the campsite like a tame cow.

'Then, of course, there was a frantic rushing for cameras and videos. But it was gone. We drove out to find it but it had just disappeared into thick scrub beyond the lagoon out the back there. Luckily, I had my camera with me at the table. Of course, I shan't get the film processed until I return to the UK ...'

Their conversation shifted to Macklor's snakes and his biology teaching post in a school in the suburbs of Liverpool which, he maintained, was more of a jungle than anything Africa could offer.

The fire around which they sat, burning in a shallow depression in the ground lined with baked mud, died down until only the embers glowed. From across the river came the sounds of nocturnal animals going about their business.

'Many lion about?' Brian asked, returning to quizzing Macklor about the whereabouts of the big game. He and Nchembe only had a few days to stay. They had been slotted in to the camp while the Americans were away: otherwise there was no accommodation available for them. The camp was booked up for the whole of the dry season.

'There're several prides about, plus some lone males. Their territory's quite small at this time of year, what with the water in the bush drying up and the game concentrating in the riverine areas. Lot of hippos are dying of some disease – no results from post mortems as yet – so there's an abundance of scavenging for them, too. Elephants are plentiful, as you know – probably the greatest concentration left in Africa. Having said that, there're not as many as last year. Thornicroft's giraffe: big family group half-way to Lion Camp last week. Zebra, kudu, impala, water- and bush-buck. Live hippos a-plenty and crocs by the dozen. Some of the crocodiles are massive – old Idi ...'

Nchembe's immediate guffaw echoed across the river. A creature on the far side returned the call.

'I can guess how he acquired his name ...' Nchembe began.

'I'm sure you can! A tourist who thought he'd take a dip in the river. The awful thing, I'm told, is Idi also took the African who dived in to save him. Why people won't take advice –it's not exactly the Thames, is it?'

'Leopard?' Brian enquired.

'Yes. One lives in the thickets on the bank opposite. We see him sometimes, even in the middle of the day. Patrols the bank or has a drink. All hell breaks loose when he's about in the day. As ever, there're a lot of leopard in the area. They are the last predator to leave a place when the ecological balance starts to go. They're almost common ...'

Brian slept deeply that night, woken only once by an elephant in the compound. It was shaking the acacia tree, eating the dislodged fruit.

The number-plate read AAG7469; on the driver's door was emblazoned the logo of the Save the Rhino Trust, a green circle with a black rhino head in silhouette over-printed with a rifle cross-sight. The Toyota was painted a creamy buff with heightened suspension and heavy-duty tyres. It had head-lights and rear lights but in most other respects it was as unlike an ordinary Toyota as it could be. It had no roof and no windows. The windscreen folded forwards onto the bonnet. There were two front seats, one each for the driver and a passenger, but the flat-bed rear was raised in two tiers of forward-facing benches upholstered with vinyl covers. In the post-dawn light, it looked more like military transport than a civilian truck.

'Are we ready?'

Macklor appeared through the archway which was the main entrance to the camp compound.

Brian and Nchembe were standing by the game-viewing vehicle watching two distant crown storks in the shallow lagoon across the track.

'I think so.' Brian climbed up, his foot on the rear wheel, swinging himself onto the rear bench. 'It's good of you to

391

offer to drive us. I could as easily have taken my Range Rover.'

'You don't see so much with a roof over your head. And, if you're intent on driving, you miss a lot.'

Leaning over, Brian grasped Nchembe's wrist and helped him onto the Toyota.

They drove around the rim of the shallow lagoon, through a clump of trees and along the dirt road leading to Mfuwe. It was cold once the vehicle was moving and Brian was grateful for his bush jacket over his shirt. He pressed his hands into his pockets. Nchembe had put on a pair of brown trousers and a military-style pullover. At the junction on the tarmac road, they went left, soon arriving at a concrete bridge over the river. Macklor slowed for the grid-iron gate, bringing the Toyota to a standstill by a notice reminding drivers to stay on the main roads and that animals had the right of way.

'Morning!' he called out as the lodge house door opened.

A Game Department guard came out, raised the bolt and pushed open the rusting gate. He waved a sort of salute as they drove through, down the bump between concrete and earth and on towards the trees. The road was on an embankment at this point and, in the brush on the right, they could see four or five elephants browsing on the undergrowth.

For two hours, Keith Macklor drove them through the South Luangwa National Park, as the valley was officially designated. They encountered more elephants, in both large herds and small family units with calves. Hippos, returning now it was first light, to the river after a night's feeding in the scrub forest, crossed their path. Impala leapt out of their way or ran gracefully through the long grass. Waterbuck and kudu stood in the cover and, just before they reached the farthest point of their drive, much to the surprise of all three of them, they saw a porcupine.

'He's late!' Macklor exclaimed but, no sooner had he spoken than the porcupine, its spines swept back like a thirties' bandleader's oiled hair, ran towards the base of a chipuwe tree to vanish down a burrow.

In the dust of the vehicle tracks and in the sand of a dried-out riverbed, they discovered the spoor of lion but none were less than two or three hours old. They returned to Chinzombo without sighting a single predator larger than a civet cat.

'It is good to be in the bush together,' Nchembe declared quietly as he and Brian sat in the shade of the thatched umbrella roof on the bank of the river, cups of coffee on a low table between them.

The sun was high, the shadows short, what shade there was dark and cooling. The buffet lunch was over and the afternoon stretched idly ahead.

Brian, studying the far bank through a pair of binoculars, said, 'Yes, it is.'

A fish eagle soared down from a sausage tree, dipped near the surface of the water and rose again to alight in a low kaonga tree.

'Do you know what the local tribes call the sausage tree?' Nchembe asked.

His companion shook his head.

'The Virgins' Hope.'

Brian shifted his arc of vision to study the pendulous fruit hanging from the boughs and laughed quietly. Then he lowered his binoculars to suspend them by their strap around his neck and refilled his coffee cup from a pot on the ground under the table.

'Do you remember the foxes and the badgers at Powerstock?'

'Do you remember the hyenas which used to come to the dump outside Wamumu?' Nchembe rejoined, adding, '*Fisi*!' with disgust.

The eagle took to the wing once more and flew away from the river. The outrunners of a troop of baboon appeared on the bank to the right, sauntering along the sandy, steeply-sloping shore. In the shallows lay Idi, all sixteen feet of him, motionless. The baboons eyed the crocodile and gave it a wide berth as did a kudu buck drinking at the water's edge.

'We should have met again in Oxford. After ...' Brian paused. 'Long ago. It was all so very foolish.'

'Only now we have the hindsight of experience,' Nchembe

replied. 'At the time, it was important. I had let you down, been a bad friend. I accept it.'

Nchembe squinted at the baboon troop. A squabble had broken out, two big dogs snarling and screeching at each other, pummelling each other with their fists and slapping each other's heads. They advanced, fought, retreated, advanced again. The other members of the troop, which numbered over fifty animals, ignored the combatants.

'Look at them.' Nchembe nodded his head in the direction of the fight. 'They are quarrelling over a woman. One of the females will be in season and they are fighting for dominance. The winner hopes to mate with her. He will not. The leader of the troop will be in her first, planting his seed. It keeps them strong. Some fate, some design, some natural law controls them. It is the same law as rules us ...'

'The difference is,' Brian said regretfully, 'in fifteen minutes, after the leading male has had his way, those two will be friends again, members of the troop sharing guard duty, watching out for snakes or leopards. We were not so civilised.'

Nchembe smiled.

'It is strange to hear of a baboon being considered civilised.'

'I remember,' Brian went on, 'in Kenya, when I was a boy, one of the insults Europeans used to throw at Africans was to called them *nugu* – monkey: they're just down from the trees, just lost their tails, they'd say. It seems to me that might have been an unintentional compliment. Animals generally behave better than we do ...'

A high-pitched bark echoed across the river. Immediately, the baboon troop was in uproar. Females ran for open ground, infants rushed to leap onto their mothers' backs, clinging to the hackles, riding jockey-fashion. Juvenile males congregated with the leaders to face the cover and gesture. They barked in a cacophony of rage and anguish.

'It must be the leopard Keith told us about last night ...'

The kudu galloped along the shore; a small herd of puku faced the way the male baboons were gesticulating and started to whistle their alarm. Several impala stood their ground, nerves taut.

394

The baboons fell silent. A big dog baboon, the magnificent ruff of fur at his neck bristling, climbed onto a fallen tree to obtain a better view of the scrub. He balanced on his hind legs, standing erect, then lowered himself to all fours once again. His movement momentarily calmed not only his followers but also a band of vervet monkeys.

Suddenly, the baboons commenced barking and screaming again, the males running at the undergrowth, stopping short of it, retreating with their teeth bared, snarling and yelping. Some tried to taunt the leopard – if leopard it was – out into the open, but it would not be so easily led.

Gradually, the troop settled down once more to gleaning seeds from the shore.

'The threat is passed,' Nchembe said. 'Their life will return to normal for a few hours.'

'They could teach us, those baboons, the antelope.' Brian, who had watched the upheaval through his binoculars, removed them from around his neck and laid them on the table. 'They see danger and pull together. One species, one race helping another ...'

'Is that not what we are doing? You are helping me through the tractor deal, helping Africa. We are fighting the oppression of apartheid in our own ways.'

When the baboons were lost to sight, Nchembe left his seat, going to rest in his hut. One of the camp servants removed the cups and coffee pot. The sun grew hotter. Brian dozed in his chair. The world of business and agricultural development grants, politics and strife seemed far away. The present and the past were the Luangwa river running sluggishly by ten feet from him.

23

Some miles upriver from the Mfuwe bridge, the Luangwa had, over the years, changed its course. Being a slow-moving river in the dry season, when the rains came it was a deceptively fast, muddy torrent which flooded the surrounding countryside, swamping and drowning tens of thousands of acres of bush. The floods and currents ate at the banks, demolished sand bars, built others, washed and scoured and worked away at the shores, cutting off corners, establishing lagoons, islands, new stretches of river. Where the course had tried to straighten itself, where trees or other obstacles had turned the currents and forced new courses, ox-bow lakes had formed, their entrances then silting up, resulting in huge lagoons.

Such a place of ponds and lakes once part of the river was Luangwa Wafua – the dead Luangwa. Yet these lakes were far from dead. Some no bigger than waterholes or English village duckponds, some many acres in extent, they were rich in fish and crocodiles, birds and frogs and large pods of hippos. To these lagoons and lakes many creatures came to drink, others to prey upon the drinkers and yet others to feed upon the spoils of the kills. The sandy slopes, eroded by sun and hooves, were tapestries of spoor – impala, puku, kudu, waterbuck, elephant, giraffe, warthog, hippo and crocodile, lion and leopard. Each left its distinctive trail which even the untrained eye could read to a degree – the flat, round plates of the elephant, the stub-toed prints of the hippopotamus, the zig-zag sweeps of a crocodile tail, the round pugs of the lion.

In the evenings, the lagoons were places of wonder. As the sun started to reach for the horizon and the air cooled, the herds of elephant made for the lagoons or skirted through them, on their way to their favourite river-crossings. The hippos in the water would start to venture on land, heading for the bush to feed through the night, their backs festooned with brilliant green bouquets of Nile cabbage beneath which they had wallowed all day. If an evening breeze rippled the clear water, the fish would rise to insects and larvae and the fish eagles would patrol the lagoons with lazy sweeps of their wings.

On the evening of their second day at Chinzombo, Brian suggested they take the game-viewing Toyota out in the evening. Keith Macklor agreed and offered to drive them, but Brian declined his offer.

'Don't think I'm not grateful. But we'd like to be alone,' he explained. 'There was a time as teenagers when we were out in the bush ...'

'Old codgers reliving their youth,' Macklor joked. 'It's the same world over.'

'That's enough from you, young whipper-snapper!' Nchembe entered into the spirit of the humour. 'Time you children showed a bit of respect for your elders and betters.'

'Yes, sir,' Macklor replied, emphasising the second word with mock insolence. 'I wouldn't want to be thought insubordinate, sir.'

They travelled at speed until they reached the Mfuwe bridge; from there, Brian drove more slowly, turning right at the junction past the tourist lodge. They took the track following an old course of the river and were soon in the area of lagoons.

The sun was low yet still bright. Brian disengaged the gears and allowed the Toyota to drift to a halt by what appeared to be a shallow lagoon, the surface almost entirely carpeted with Nile cabbage. Only a small patch of water in the centre of the lagoon, thirty yards out, was free of the floating plant.

At first, the only sound to be heard was the quietly idling Toyota but suddenly a coot-like cry echoed from the far bank; then, from overhead, came a strange rattling scream, husky yet penetrating.

'Look!' Nchembe said softly.

A brown and white bird flew down, its legs trailing behind it, until it was close to the covering of water-plants when it lowered them like a framework of stilts to settle on the greenery, raising its wings above its head. It was quite close to the vehicle and both men could see its creamy-yellow breast, blue-grey bill and blue shield on top of the beak. No sooner had it landed than, in response to another call, it set off running over the dense Nile cabbage. Its toes were almost as long as its entire body.

'Jacana,' Brian identified the bird. 'The lily-trotter.'

Half-way across the lagoon, the bird faltered, veering away from a thinner patch of water-plant.

'Crocodile?' Nchembe wondered aloud.

His query was immediately answered. From beneath the covering of cabbage rose the bulky head of a hippo. Beside it rose two more. Their heads behind their raised eyes were decorated with bunches of Nile cabbage like traceries of lace. The three hippos surveyed the Toyota, snuffled water and air through their nostrils and gently submerged again as if aware of their ridiculous appearance.

Brian drove on, disturbing several herds of impala and seeing, fleetingly, a small herd of zebra hiding in an area of loose cover. At one place, where there was tall grass right up to the road, they startled a lone buffalo, an old bull cast out from his herd, living his last months as a sad, solitary beast. The bull trundled away from them, stopped and faced them, his broad forehead of horn lower than his shoulder. His ears were nicked, his flanks lined by scars. His nostrils flared with annoyance. He made no effort to charge, though; he was past fighting for territory or a favoured cow.

They swerved on to a lesser and hardly discernible track, Brian almost missing the junction, so insignificant was it. He knew it led to a bluff overlooking a long stretch of the river where there was a common fording point for elephants.

It was just after six o' clock when they arrived at the bluff, thirty-five feet above the river. They parked the Toyota side-on to the bank so that, if need be, they could easily drive away should danger threaten. The elephant would not begin arriving for another half hour: they were still a mile or so away in thicker forest.

'We can stretch our legs,' Brian suggested.

He left the Toyota, walking the few feet to the top of the bank. As he looked over, a small crocodile thrashed across a narrow sandbar under the bank and slid into the water, only its eye-bulges and a few of the scales on its spine visible above the muddy swirl it had made with its tail in the already murky water. Far out, on a sand bank, a huge crocodile was lying in the late sun, its mouth gaping.

'*Mamba!*' Nchembe exclaimed from some yards off.

He had gone to a bush to relieve himself and Brian had heard the sound of him urinating onto the dead leaves.

Brian spun round.

'Don't move!' he whispered loudly.

Nchembe, who had been gazing over his shoulder at the river, zipped up his fly and shuffled his feet through the leaves.

'What did you say?'

'Where's the *mamba*?' Brian asked, puzzled that Nchembe – of all people – should tell him of a snake and then, contrary to the code, move.

'In the river.' Nchembe laughed, but not too loudly. 'In the middle of the river. *Mamba*. You've forgotten your Swahili. *Mamba* is a crocodile.'

Brian grinned self-consciously.

'I had forgotten! And when you said *mamba* … it was automatic association – you and the *nyoka*!'

'You won't need to save me from a snake again.' Nchembe smiled and winked. 'I look where I step now. Both in the bush and in the jungle of politics … I learnt an important lesson or two that day!'

They settled into the Toyota, Brian in the driver's seat, Nchembe higher on one of the tiers. The sun went down and orange blocks of light, filtering through the gaps in the scrub forest, hit the far bank, sixty yards away. They appeared almost artificial, as if the far shore was a stage-set arranged for a drama soon to follow.

As the sun had been setting, both men had heard the distant trumpeting of an elephant. This was soon followed by the sounds of motion several hundred yards away. Within minutes of the amber light beginning to fade, the first of the elephants edged down the bank and entered the river. For such huge creatures, the elephants moved with care and grace. They did not stamp or clomp down the banks but stepped steadily, carefully, almost thoughtfully. A few drank before striding gradually into the current. The bulls moved stolidly forward, the nursing cows guided their calves, some of them only just big enough to make the crossing: one very young calf completely submerged in the centre of the river, only its trunk above the surface. Unattached females with no infant charges followed the bulls. On the far side, they walked slowly up the bank to disappear into the trees.

'One hundred and eight.' Brian had been counting. He spoke very softly, for the sound of his words could travel far on such a still evening and a human voice would alarm all the animals, both great and small. 'There can be few places left in Africa now where such a sight can be seen.'

'Sadly, you are right.' Nchembe also kept his voice down. 'And we are lucky. But we may be the last generation to see this and know it was – for aeons of time – the norm ...'

As Brian re-started the Toyota, bumping over the track now virtually invisible in the growing twilight, he asked, 'Fancy a walk?'

'If there are no *tembo*.'

'*Ndovu* is also elephant,' Brian replied. 'I've not forgotten everything. And I know an area where there will be no elephant by the time we get there.'

The headlights, as soon as Brian switched them on, started to catch the glitter of eyes in the deeper cover: the silver orbs of antelopes' eyes shone like tiny yet catoptric lamps.

For thirty minutes, they jolted, lurched and tossed through the bush, following a vehicle route but one, like that to the bluff, obviously not often frequented. Eventually, they arrived at the edge of a wide plain of about fifty hectares of sparse grass clumps, sandy earth and scattered bushes. Brian stopped their transport, playing the Toyota's hand-held spotlight cursorily over the entire area. Satisfied there were no elephants in view, he switched off the lights, removed a rubber torch from beneath the driver's seat and, having tested it, slipped it in his jacket pocket. For some minutes they sat, their eyes adjusting to the night.

As the engine cooled and the suspension creaked with the

release from movement, so Brian's consciousness of the bush developed.

It was always the same. No matter how long he had been away, attending conferences or government meetings in London or New York, visiting factories or laboratories in Hong Kong or Madrid, discussing funding or finance with aid agencies or bankers in Rome or Zurich, as soon as he stepped out of the aircraft in Lusaka or Nairobi the mantle of Africa would begin to envelope him again. By the time he had reached his house on Leopards Hill Road, or his room in the Norfolk Hotel, he would have reassimilated into his subconscious the smell of flowers and dust, the call of birds, the commonality of women carrying loads upon their heads or men cycling with their heels on the pedals rather than their toes. They were insignificant details, yet gave him a deep sense of place: if he had seen a bicycle messenger in New York or a secretary in a hot, London summer street riding a machine in such a way, the sight would have jarred.

There was no moon. The sky was dotted with clouds but there was sufficient starlight by which to see and, with their eyes accustomed to the night and ears tuned to the noises around them, Brian and Nchembe left the Toyota to set off along the track ahead of the vehicle.

From the grass came the rustle of the small nocturnal creatures, rodents and insects, birds momentarily disturbed by their passing. An owl called briefly half a kilometre off.

It was Brian's plan to cross the plain to the tree-line, turn and return to the Toyota. This was not as adventurous as he would have liked but there was no knowing if there were elephant or buffalo in the trees, where the track wound southwest – not to mention grazing hippo which could be very dangerous, especially if one inadvertently stepped between them and the river. He was not certain at this point in which direction the Luangwa lay.

Walking in the starlit darkness brought back to Brian the thrill of anticipated, reasoned danger which he had so craved and relished as a boy. He remembered the fear he had so often self-indulgently enjoyed when following a *donga* without knowing what might be beyond the next corner, skirting a thick clump of thorn bushes or creeping to the edge of an overhanging rock.

Neither of them spoke. To do so would be to drive away any creature.

The track bent slightly by a tall stand of kasense grass. As they walked silently around this, a small herd of impala started at them and trotted off in the direction of a thicket. They did not flee for neither of the men presented a threat.

After another hundred metres or so, Brian and Nchembe stopped simultaneously, both spying at the same moment a movement ahead. Together, they cautiously advanced.

The track at this point reached a shallow depression in which the earth was dusty. There, rolling on the dry earth, was a full-grown female leopard. Even by starlight, the spots and rosettes of her coat showed up clearly against the light background of her fur and the dark, dry ground.

She sensed the men had arrived and stilled. She was facing away from them but studying them over her shoulder. She spread her front legs out and drew her back legs in, assessing the humans in the way wild animals have when they are not afraid. Then, with graceful ease, she stood and turned side-on.

Brian held his breath. This was the danger he loved. They had no gun. The Toyota was a kilometre away.

The leopard, after surveying them for a minute or so, padded off to the right, disappearing behind some dense bushes.

Carefully but not stealthily, the men stepped forwards to the point where the leopard had been rolling. The surface of the dust was smooth, the marks of her pugs showing clearly in the starlight.

There was a movement behind them. Slowly, the two men looked over their shoulders to discover the leopard standing where they had halted. Their positions were reversed and Brian momentarily wondered if she was expecting them now to frolic in the dirt.

For several minutes, the leopard watched them as they slowly turned around to face her. Bored with this, she then sauntered off into another thicket.

No sooner was she out of sight than Brian signalled with his hands that they should follow her, going around the cover she had entered. There was – his fingers made horn prongs – the small impala herd on the far side and, as soon as they scented her, they would be up and off. There were few sights in the world of the bush as beautiful as alarmed impala. They would, he knew, break into organized panic, run in every direction to confuse their enemy, prance and leap through the air like dancers, the white and black markings below their tails flashing an added confusion.

Nchembe understood his signals and they set off to walk around the bushes, keeping some yards out from them. They knew the leopard was in the undergrowth but there was not a single tell-tale sign of her presence.

As Brian had assessed, in a large patch of grass beyond the cover the impala were grazing. They looked up at the arrival of the men, unsure of what to do. They ceased their grazing and stood motionless. Perplexed, the impala gave the men all their attention. Their ears fanned, their noses tested the air. The lead buck tossed his head.

Any moment now, Brian thought: at any moment, one of them would smell the leopard, sense it near. His heart pounded with expectancy.

The bushes twitched. It was no more than that. The leopard burst from the cover. Brian spun his head. In three bounds, faster than the eye could follow, the leopard was amongst the impala. The antelope were already running, jiving, leaping, weaving.

The leopard was not confused. It had its target set, a doe in the centre of the group.

The doe knew. It tried to spring. The leopard curved through the air, landing on the antelope's back, its forepaws on either side of its neck, its head round and under the throat, its teeth fastened on the gullet. The leopard and its prey fell into a welter of swaying grass.

Then there was silence. No night birds called. The insects and rodents were silent.

The leopard stood in the grass, the impala under her belly, its neck in her mouth. The antelope kicked its spindly legs but the leopard was positioned so that the sharp hooves could do no harm. For ten minutes, until it was certain the impala was throttled, the leopard stood stock-still.

Brian and Nchembe did likewise. During the kill, both of their minds had been blank. There had been no time, no necessity for thought. Now, with their brains working once more, they realised they had been a part of the leopard's plan, that they had aided in her kill. They had distracted the impala, had given the leopard the advantage.

The antelope dead, the leopard commenced to drag it off, walking with her legs astride the length of the carcass, pulling the kill beneath her. Brian had seen leopard carry their prey either in this fashion, as the lion did, or by lifting it in their jaws. A full-grown leopard could easily carry a man in its mouth, holding the body high enough off the ground so that the arms and legs dangling on either side did not touch the ground to leave a drag mark.

They followed. The leopard took twenty minutes to reach the perimeter of the scrub forest. There, beneath an m'njel-enjete tree, she relinquished the kill, the impala's head dropping limply to the ground, one of the horns gouging the earth. Climbing on to a fallen tree trunk, the leopard lay down and began to clean herself, licking her paws and wiping her whiskers, bending her head downwards to remove a few traces of blood from her frontal fur.

Cautiously, the two men approached the leopard until they were about twenty feet from her. She twice stopped her toilet to watch them and it was only when she snarled tentatively that they stopped.

The moon had risen as the leopard was dragging her kill. It was in its last quarter yet sufficiently powerful to illuminate the bush with a grey, flat light.

Although his senses were pricked for whatever might be in the night around them, Brian's main attention was taken by the leopard. Now the moon had risen, he could see her patterning, the thick base and the white underside of her tail, her rounded ears with their inner tufts of hair, her long white whiskers one of which had a bar of black half-way along it, her flat paws and the pink T of the front of her nose. When she moved her head, the muscles of her shoulders bunched and flexed.

Again, the leopard looked at the men and snarled, her lips drawing back and up. Her teeth showed in the moonlight. She rose from her haunches and faced them.

Suddenly, Brian became aware of something standing by him. He moved his head. Not five feet from his side stood a male leopard.

Very slowly, he touched Nchembe with his elbow, warning him.

The male leopard ignored the two men. It growled. The sound was so deep, so resonant, that Brian could feel it as well as hear it.

The female snarled again, moaned her anger and bounded across her kill. This was a sign of defiance the male would not accept. It charged the female. She swirled about, backed off then attacked. The two spat and scratched at each other, growling and hissing. Then, his patience at an end, the male went for her, chasing the female away into the darkness.

Brian and Nchembe stepped backwards, away from the scene. The male would be wary now, would tolerate no intruders as he fed.

When they were well on their way back to the Toyota, Brian switched on the torch. The batteries were new and the beam cut through the moonlight, flashing in the eyes of creatures otherwise unseen. They reached the Toyota, hoisted themselves into the front seats, Brian starting the engine. The crude racket of machinery, of metal upon metal, eradicated the natural music of the darkness.

Just as Brian was about to put the vehicle into gear, Nchembe spoke.

'That leopard.' His words were filled with such confidence. 'That was the leopard I skinned and we saw drifting in the smoke.'

Brian nodded.

'I think it may well have been,' he answered.

24

Keith Macklor left them at ten o'clock when the generator was powered down for the night.

'Your last day tomorrow,' he remarked as he emptied the dregs of his beer glass on to the bare earth where, in the morning, butterflies would gather in the early sunlight to sip at the damp stain. 'It's a pity you can't stay longer. After the leopard anything might hapen. You should go all out for a rhino tomorrow. The way your luck's running, you'll see two – mating!'

'Any reports?' Brian enquired.

The anti-poaching units usually knew where the rhino were and would give word to the staff at Chinzombo so the clients could head towards the appropriate cover. Usually, they drove out filled with expectation, returning five hours later having seen nothing but a rhino's midden with, if fortune was smiling on them and their Nikons and Canons, recent dung spread upon it.

'There's rumour of a rhino cow and a calf around Chichele Lodge, south of here. Down river. Though she's very wary, not only because of the youngster but also because there's been poacher activity in the vicinity. Mostly, they've been taking elephant but one rhino – a male, possibly her mate for this calf – has disappeared and the odds are he's been killed. You could try down that way. She keeps quite close to the river as a general rule but you'll need to track her. She's certainly shy of vehicles for no one driving has set eyes on her. A walking safari seven or eight weeks ago spotted her, briefly. And an APU saw her last about a fortnight back.'

Brian looked to Nchembe for his opinion.

'Yes,' the African agreed, 'let's go and find a rhino. I have not seen one since ...'

Macklor put two opened bottles of beer on the counter then went behind the bar to check the storeroom was locked.

'If you do go out that way, lighten your load: there's a lot of sandy *dambo*s to cross – you'll need four-wheel-drive for some of them,' he advised, pocketing the store keys. 'And don't stay sitting here too long. The locals don't wait long after the electricity's out before they move in. That winter thorn's fruiting heavily and the elephants love it. Not to mention the ebony. I heard a few branches snapping out beyond the lagoon an hour ago. The old female we get around here'll be waiting to come in. These camp elephants can be a bit of a nuisance – the big tusker they call Mr Mfuwe chases people at the lodge over the bridge. Nasty experience, bumping into a hungry elephant in the pitch dark.'

'Don't worry,' Brian assured him, 'we know the ropes.'

'Helps to know the lianas, too,' was Macklor's quick-witted answer.

They did not speak until they heard the door shut on Macklor's hut across the compound.

'When did you last see a rhino?' Brian asked, pouring the beer into their glasses.

'When I was in the forest. I was going through a big *shamba* near Naivasha and suddenly came face to face with it. I don't know which of us was the more surprised, the more afraid. I thought it was going to charge. It was only thirty paces away. Perhaps less. I didn't measure it.'

'What did you do?'

'Put my gun to my shoulder. I was ready to fire but had no idea what might be the result. It was the same ramshackle *bundooki* ...' He raised the stump of his arm. 'The rhino did not charge, however. It veered around – so fast, I was amazed – and rushed off through the tall mealies.'

'In view of subsequent events, it's as well you didn't fire.'

'Yes,' Nchembe said thoughtfully, 'it was.'

Beside Chinzombo, on the river bank, was a plot of land where those who wished could pitch a tent. They were forbidden the use of the facilities of the camp but were provided with a lavatory hut – of thatched walls and roof – a few standpipes and a *boma* of sorts made of thorn bushes and stakes. There were no visitors on the plot and, being empty, it provided a way in for the elephants entering the compound to feed on the trees and their bounty.

When Nchembe ceased talking, they heard the first sounds of an approaching elephant.

'If we go across to my hut,' Brian suggested, 'we can sit outside and be relatively safe. And, unless the elephant's between our huts, you can safely get to your door without going near it.'

They picked up their beers and walked smartly across the sparse grass, the moonlight casting their shadows firmly on the sandy soil. On the verandah of Brian's hut was a bench and they sat on it, looking out over the compound. Behind Brian's hut was a very small swimming pool of the variety found more usually in suburban gardens in England than in the middle of the African bush. The water it contained was brilliant green with a curtain of algae clinging to the sides. It was not long before they heard the elephant test the water and blow it out in a short, gaseous burst. It disliked the tang of chlorine.

'You know,' Brian said, his voice low, 'I have spent my life stealing from Africa.'

Nchembe turned and looked at him in the shadow of the verandah roof. The moonlight reflecting from the ground just lit his face.

'When I was a boy, I shot and hunted avidly. Collected butterflies, kept chameleons in cages, lifted cowries by the score from the reefs at Malindi – in what was subsequently designated a marine reserve to stop the predations of people like me. Sometimes, I shot without even the trophy in mind, or the biltong. Just did it for the sheer pleasure of handing down death.

'That changed, in time, as you know. I only photograph animals now, rarely pick up a gun and only fish to eat the catch. I don't chloroform butterflies or gather sea-shells as one might pebbles. And yet, Matthew, I'm not changed.'

'I do not agree,' Nchembe said. 'You have ...'

'Let me finish,' Brian interrupted. 'When we were up at Oxford – and when I was reading for my bachelor's degree – I was fired with the idea of saving the world. Feeding the starving masses. India, West Africa … You were largely the source of my inspiration. I saw in you, in your hopes and dreams, what might just be possible if we all pulled together.

'Even jacking in my job and going back to read for my doctorate was a part of the process. I was wealthy enough to support myself. It seemed the best way to do things, to achieve something. When we met again in Oxford, it was an added spur in a way. Our friendship returned and it was valuable to me because of what I was doing. Then, with the Lucy business – well, I thought, fuck it!' He laughed quietly at the inappropriate pun. 'I had the expertise and I could use it.'

'And so you do! Look at what you have achieved, Brian.'

A dark bulk cut off some of the moonshine from the river. The elephant, hearing their low voices and scenting them, had gone the other side of the bar and was circling round the compound trying to assess the danger they might pose, and how it might get to the peeled-apple-like fruit of the acacia.

'It's not what I've achieved,' Brian remonstrated, 'it's why. I've used my expertise not for Africa but for myself. Your Miss Nkana is right. How many seed-drills or tractors or miles of irrigation piping might the Merc buy? And where did the Merc come from? It came from aid funding from the First World. The house, the well-stocked bar, the club-class rather than economy-class air tickets, the Hilton Hotel rooms … Paid for, ultimately, by aid funding. Whatever I do, achieve, succeed at – it's all for selfish motives. Even the tractor deal for your people will have its spin-offs, its perks, its freebies.

'I fiddle the figures. They call it creative accounting. Laundering the columns, cleaning the money. I'm economic with the truth, as the British government would put it. And I feel ashamed.'

From the thatch over their heads a gecko started to click loudly, ceased, rustled in the straw. The elephant was feeding on a stunted tree halfway between the two men and the dining shelter.

'You are not the only one,' Nchembe admitted, 'whose

ideals have altered. So have mine. You remember in Wamumu I renounced violence ...'

'It was one of the most important things you said to sway me ...'

'... and why was this? It was a compromise. Of the soul, perhaps. A compromise forced upon me by reality. A load of ill-trained youths in the forest was no match for the British. There had to be other ways. I tried them. I still try them. And yes, before you ask it, I had the dream of Communism once but realized it, too, was unrealistic.

'I became a lawyer because I thought I could do good in that profession. And I could. And did. I suppose I still can. But have you ever seen a poor lawyer? There were my own motives at work, too, you know. All men are basically selfish. What they must do is realize this and remain so, but do something worthy as well as look after their own interests. That is you. And that is me. To a point ...'

Their glasses of beer remained untouched on the concrete step at their feet.

'To a point!' Brian exclaimed. 'You live in Africa, running schools and agricultural training places. You work for an organization seeking racial equality, natural justice. You exist in the bush, with the people you are trying to raise from their present lot. I do not. I live in a fine house in Lusaka, have an apartment in Paris. I have the very best. I make no sacrifices as you do.'

Nchembe laughed.

'I make few sacrifices, Brian. I have good suits, a house in another country. Maybe not as good as yours but far superior to what most blacks have the world over. And I have the power. It is that which provides me with my comparative wealth. I am not the saint you seem to think I am. Nor ever was.

'You see, Brian, I have renounced my early renunciation. I gave up violence because of ...' He paused before uttering the word, '... Lari. I have shame, too. And my shame is based not upon obtaining a Mercedes Benz by creaming off money. It is to do with my having killed Africans and now, again, I kill Africans. They are not of my tribe but they are of my people.

410

The "necklaces" of burning tyres in the townships of South Africa, the deaths of innocent Zambians only a few days ago, the killing by the Afrikaners of blacks who are merely throwing stones at automatic rifles ... The old futility, that! They die because of me, my dream, my politics and those of others like me. I do not face the tear gas and the sjamboks. I do not tread the prison cell and exercise yard. I am the coward who runs the war, I do not run with it.

'Of course, the struggle is just. It is essential. One cannot have a dialogue with those who will not answer, will not even listen. Where there are no words, there must be fists. But that does not mean I am right, am good, am brave.'

The gecko clicked metallicaly again like a Christmas-cracker toy frog-snapper.

'Yet you are fighting for Africa. There are bound to be casualties. Every cause must have its martyrs. I am just a common criminal ...'

'That's rubbish, Brian! You are not a criminal. You are a man being a man. If anything, I am the immoral one. All you have is a Mercedes to feel guilty about. I have blood ...'

'We adapt, change our colours like that gecko can. Or a chameleon. Yes! We are like the chameleon, changing our colours when we need. Mottled or bright, green or black ... Whatever the situation dictates, the chameleon follows. Yet we are always still what we are beneath the skin. That cannot alter.'

There was a splintering of wood as the elephant cracked a bough.

'Even the chameleon,' Brian said, 'cannot manage all colours. It cannot turn black despite all the evil the legends claim it holds. I am white yet there is a blackness in me.'

Nchembe laughed softly and said, 'You are white but I *am* black. Perhaps I am the only black chameleon!'

There was a tiny rustle over their heads and the gecko clicked once from a new position in the darkness of the thatch. Across the compound, the elephant was snuffling, stripping the bough of its leaves and cramming them into its mouth. They could hear it chewing.

'We are on the only road, Brian,' Nchembe said quietly,

411

'travelling with our guilts and secrets, our fears and hopes. Moments of joy light up the way – the beauty of a woman and, tonight, the beauty of a leopard – and moments of pain darken it. We can do nothing to alter the way it is. So ... Goodnight, Brian.' Nchembe rose to his feet. 'See you in the morning.'

He moved so swiftly and silently Brian hardly saw him go. One moment Nchembe was at his side, the next he was not.

Between the track and the river was a grassy plain criss-crossed by dried-up watercourses upon which grew a large number of nyamavuno palms interspersed with vegetable ivory palms. The former stood against the morning sky, the characteristic bulge two thirds of the way up each trunk giving the impression they were being inflated. In several of the latter perched kestrels with white heads, dark brown wings and greyish breasts. When they took to the wing at the approach of the Range Rover, they fanned their barred tails.

As Brian manoeuvred his vehicle round the trees, keeping to the sinuous track, he saw the signs of elephant feeding on the palm fruits. Dung heaps littered the two grooves cut by previous wheels and one tree, as they passed it, had been recently pushed over.

'Elephants are destructive buggers,' he remarked. 'What they can't reach they'll tear down. The small tree in the compound was demolished last night. Stripped bare of every trace of leaf.'

Nchembe grunted a reply, his hand grasping firmly the handle mounted on the dashboard.

The sun was becoming unbearable. The heat reverberated through the roof and Brian, despite the sweat pouring off him, was glad they had taken his own vehicle and not the Chinzombo Toyota. A whole day in the sun without a roof would be far more unpleasant, for they would be walking a fair distance as well as driving.

They were going about fifty miles, twenty there and twenty back – although where 'there' was was debatable – with a series of detours if necessary. The best speed they could maintain was ten miles an hour but only for short distances. Most of the while they were restricted to four or five.

In the heat of the day, the majority of the animals were hiding in the thick cover, sheltering from the sun. Only men ventured out in the harsh hours.

'Mad dogs and Englishmen,' Nchembe said, wiping his brow with a handkerchief already sodden with perspiration. 'And now Africans. You colonials make us do the damnedest things. Contrary to our natures.'

Brian laughed.

'You'll be wanting the air conditioning on next. And you a native, too. By all rights, you ought to be running ahead, picking up thorns. Or running behind with the provisions piled on your head. But that would be cruel . . .' He swung the steering wheel, trying to avoid a log half hidden in the track; the Range Rover lurched over it to the accompaniment of splintering, rotting wood. 'And I'm not such a cruel master as to make you suffer the exhaust fumes.'

'T'ank you, *bwana mkubwa*! Ah'm mos' grateful to you,' Nchembe retorted with a thick accent.

Shortly before midday, they stopped by the river and removed a packet of sandwiches and bottles of beer from a small cold box, spreading them out on the tailgate on a tea-cloth provided by the Chinzombo cook. Besides beef sandwiches in grainy bread there were hard-boiled eggs and discoloured grey salt in twists of paper, a lettuce which had remained crisp, and soft, sweet tomatoes.

'This is wrong,' Nchembe commented as he helped himself to a second sandwich.

'What is?' Brian asked, pouring the beer into two enamel mugs.

'This.' He moved his head to indicate the view of the river in front of them. On the opposite bank six hippos were lying on their sides on the sand, their bellies bright pink in the sun as if they were sunbathers on the first day of their holidays, unwisely staying too long in the glare. Two crocodiles lay motionless at the water's edge.

'I don't see anything wrong.'

'Well, look at us. Eating out of the back of a car like civilised folk. We should be at Henley watching the sculls, not Luangwa watching the crocs.'

413

'Henley's very hooray-ish,' Brian observed. 'I'd rather be by the Thames at Christ Church Meadows. Or the Cherwell watching the punts ...'

'What was his name?' Nchembe asked after a moment's silence.

'Whose?'

'Had a big motorbike and a girlfriend who castigated the louts. And what was the name of that pub?'

'The pub was the Victoria, wasn't it?' Brian squinted against the glare but he might have been trying to look back into his memory. 'We called it the Vicky ... No! The Victoria Arms. The Vicky Arms. And the motorbike was owned by Dash. Dashiell ...' Again, he screwed his eyes. 'His surname's gone.'

'That girl was a funny little thing, wasn't she?' Nchembe mused.

'Which girl?'

'Dash's girl. The day we had the fight on the punt. Don't you remember?'

'I remember but I don't recall a girl. I was with Lucy then and you were with – what's-her-name? – Lucy's flatmate ...'

'Angela?' Nchembe suggested.

'It was a good fight. Lucy holed their punt. It sank.'

One of the crocodiles thrashed its tail and slipped into the river. It dived immediately and Brian wanted to see where it would surface. Instead, a hippo rose from the river. It remained with the water up to its belly and defaecated, its short tail rapidly fanning the dung out over the surface.

'They were good days. The best of our lives,' Nchembe said, 'before we became real men. It was better then to be "unreal", as the slang had it. Real men are too worldly. Like we have become.'

The food finished and the beer drunk, Brian put the tin mugs back into the glove compartment, wedging them with cotton waste to prevent them knocking together. There was nothing more annoying to him than a deep-seated rattle under the fascia.

They drove on along the river until, an hour later,

414

descending the side of a sandy depression, they both saw simultaneously the fresh wet tracks of a rhino.

The creature had obviously been to the river for a drink or had crossed at that point from the far bank. The main stream was wide, silted-up and consequently shallow. The footprints were large, suggesting a male.

Brian steered the Range Rover towards a lilac jacaranda tree in partial blossom, parking it between the trunk and a nearby sausage tree. There was a thicket there which would afford more shade. They wound the windows up, leaving only a two-inch gap at the top which would allow the air to circulate but keep out the thieving, inquisitive paws of the vervet monkeys Brian knew would come along later in the day to drink the nectar from the huge maroon and yellow flowers of the sausage tree. They also locked the car, for some monkeys had discovered the means to open vehicle doors by yanking on the handles.

Together, they set off after the rhino.

Both men had dressed for a day's tracking in the bush. They were wearing safari-jackets with several deep side and breast pockets, shorts and long socks with stout, soft-soled shoes. Brian wore a buff-coloured T-shirt beneath his jacket, Nchembe a cream open-necked shirt. Neither carried a gun but Brian had in one of his pockets a compact Olympus camera. He was not intent on photographing what they might see – he had often photographed rhinos in the years when they were plentiful, and the camera was inappropriate without a telephoto lens – but he carried it on the off-chance that they might be presented with an unusual sight. He could not help thinking of Macklor's quip that his luck would give him rhinos copulating.

For an hour, they followed the rhino. It was staying in dense brush, holding to game paths and travelling from midden to midden, depositing fresh dung at each in much the same manner as the hippo, spreading it about. In two depressions the rhino had stopped to graze upon an area of chisonso plants, the hard, thorny, thistle-like herb favoured by the animal, but it had soon moved on. At no time were they more than ten minutes behind the rhino but it was either moving quickly or aware of them for they were unable to draw close to it.

Eventually, and with great reluctance, they decided to call off their pursuit. It was obvious the rhino would not allow them a sighting. It was getting late and Brian was anxious to have at least half the return journey covered by the time night fell.

The Range Rover was where they had left it but the roof was dotted with the delicate bell-like blooms of the lilac jacaranda.

'That's strange.'

Brian put his hand on Nchembe's arm, restraining him.

'What is?'

'No monkeys. When we parked there were monkey droppings all over the place. I was sure they'd be back by now.' He glanced at his watch. It was five minutes to five. 'Time they were feeding.'

'Leopard?' Nchembe said, his thoughts mimicking Brian's.

'Possibly. But it's a bit early ...'

'Perhaps the car has put them off?'

'I doubt it. They'd be curious rather than cautious, especially with no movement about.' He considered the situation. 'Let's just wait a few minutes. If it is a leopard, he'll move off now he's heard us.'

'Lion?'

'You keep your eyes sharp around us and I'll glue mine to the cover. Between us we should be able to see what's driven off the vervets.'

An abandoned anthill, much weathered by the last season's rains, afforded them a suitable vantage point. Together, they stood for quarter of an hour and surveyed their surroundings. Nothing which could be a threat seemed to be in the vicinity. No lions were in the grass, no movement in the trees or brush. A puku doe walked by the Range Rover without so much as a flap of the ear.

'It's gone,' Brian decided at last, stepping off the anthill. 'Whatever it was, the puku wasn't spooked. Let's be getting back.'

Still with their nerves alert, they walked towards the Range Rover. Brian unlocked the driver's door as Nchembe went around the bonnet to the passenger side. The twigs of the cover brushed against him and he peered into the branches but could see nothing. He put his fingers under the catch and, as he operated the handle, he heard a click. It was metallic but out of synchronization with his action.

'Right! Both of you keep absolutely still or we'll blow you both away.'

The voice did not seem to come from any one direction.

Brian was startled. He spun around but there was only the expanse of grass, two feet high, through which they had walked.

'Throw down the keys. On to the ground in front of the car.'

The accent was unmistakably South African, brusque and brutal.

Brian did not obey. He could not understand how this voice could address him, how its owner could see him. He had studied the area closely, a square metre at a time, for the past fifteen minutes.

'Do it!' The voice ordered, repeating, 'Throw the keys on to the earth in front of the car. Now!'

Brian obeyed.

'Now, both of you face the rear of the vehicle.'

Nchembe turned. Brian did not.

'Turn round!'

Brian did as the voice commanded.

'Walk to the rear.'

They did.

'Face the rear of the car, put your hands on the bottom of the window and move your legs back.'

Nchembe put only his one arm on the Range Rover, prompting the order, 'Both hands.'

'I've only got one,' Nchembe answered.

Brian wondered ironically if his friend's deformity would break the ice with these men as it had the guards at the Luangwa Bridge. No sooner had the thought occurred to him than he dismissed it.

'Okay. In your case, just the one. Put it in front of your eyes, not to one side. Legs back further. Further.'

That done, there was a scuffling in the grass. Brian moved his head slightly to see a white man in fawn-coloured battle fatigues rise from the grass not six feet from where he had walked. He could see the tracks he and Nchembe had made, the bent and leaning stalks.

'Legs apart. Spread them.'

They did as they were told.

'Right!' the man called. 'It's okay now. Gather on me.'

From the brush, from behind the jacaranda and from within the shade of the sausage tree, appeared six other men. They were all dressed in a similar uniform and were all white. Brian caught just a glimpse of them.

'Well done, Jan! Very well done indeed.'

'Thank you, sir.'

'Frisk them, corporal.'

Brian tried to look at the men.

'Face the car. Look down at the ground!'

Two of the men patted both Brian and Nchembe, feeling under their armpits, around their waists. The man searching Brian's pockets found the Olympus which he removed.

'They're clean,' the corporal reported.

Brian could hear the camera being opened and the film being spooled out.

'Where are your guns?'

Neither Brian nor Nchembe replied.

'You! The kaffir!' Nchembe was prodded in the small of his back. 'Where are your guns?'

'We haven't any,' Brian said.

'You mean to tell me you've been out trekking in the bush without a firearm? What kind of a fool do you think I am? How do you hunt without a gun, eh?'

'We aren't hunting. We were hoping to photograph a rhino.'

This reply was met with a moment's silence.

'You can stand up. Turn round. Keep your backs pressed to the car.'

Brian shifted his stance, straightening his back and flexing

418

his arms to release the pressure in his biceps caused by leaning at such an acute angle against the Range Rover, and faced their ambushers.

Before him, their automatic weapons held at the hip, were seven whites. They were unshaven, all but one of them in their twenties or early thirties. Their faces were tanned. One had his left hand wrapped in cloth with a wide strip of plastic bandage across the side of his forehead. Beneath it, through the gauze pad, Brian could see a brown clot of dried blood.

'So you're wondering who we are,' stated the older man.

'I think I can hazard a guess,' Brian replied. 'You are the commando unit of the Republic of South Africa army who attacked buildings outside Lusaka a few days back.'

'Perhaps.'

The older soldier's accent was almost Teutonic. As he spoke, he removed his buff, peaked cap and scratched at grey hair cut short in a close military crop. His eyes were narrowed against the glare but also, Brian thought, from the cruelty in his soul. His forehead was prominent, one of his ears folded by a long-healed wound.

'If you do exactly —' he continued, raising his finger in emphasis '— exactly as I say, you will be released once we get to the border with Mozambique. Our problem, as you can guess, is we've lost our vehicle. If we still had it, then we would not be here but already home and dry.'

'And you intend to take my Range Rover?' Brian asked needlessly.

'That's correct. I'm afraid you won't see it once we drop you off. Until then, for obvious reasons, we'll have to keep you captive. Both you and the kaffir with you. Is he your boy?'

He regarded Nchembe as almost beneath his notice.

'No,' Brian said, 'he is a friend of mine.'

As he spoke, a pride he had not felt before welled up in Brian: it was as if he was admitting to something great, something which had been in him for a long time, dormant but alive. It was akin to standing up at an evangelical meeting and shouting out, alone, 'I believe! I believe!'

The South African gave him a look of pained disdain and addressed his men.

'Tie them up. Not together. Arms behind their backs. Then sit them under the tree.'

'What about the native, sir?' The soldier was nonplussed. 'He's only got one arm.'

The older man, obviously the officer in command, gave a snorting short laugh.

'Rope round the wrist, round the body twice and then tied round the remaining elbow. That should hold him. The rest of you get this,' he banged his hand on the side of the vehicle, 'to the river bank. Theuns! Get the boat out and run a line across the river. Check it is as shallow as we recced. Jan! See if you can grease up the electrics and maybe run a pipe from the exhaust.'

Brian and Nchembe were trussed and seated on the ground five feet apart in the shade of the sausage tree.

It soon became clear what the South Africans intended to do. Brian watched as they inflated a small dingy and one of them paddled across the river where it was at its shallowest, where the rhino had either crossed or drunk its fill. Across the other side, he secured to a tree a nylon rope which he had taken with him. It was attached to the steel hawser on the front winch of the Range Rover which had been paid out to its fullest extent. The vehicle, its electrics smeared with oil and its exhaust pipe extended with a length of hose tied vertically to the rear window handle, was then revved up, driven down the steep bank, across the sandy beach and into the water. A third of the way across, the engine stalled but the driver succeeded in starting it again and, with its four-wheel-drive in operation as well as the winch, it forded the river, driving and pulling itself forward. At no time did the river come as high as the windows.

Hidden in the bush nearby was a surprising amount of equipment. Brian marvelled at how the seven of them, with one of their number wounded, had managed to transport so much through the bush.

After the attack, he reasoned, what was left of the raiding party must have headed out of the Lusaka area along the bush

420

roads on top of the Muchinga Escarpment. Or braved it on the main road to Tanzania.

Considering in his mind's eye a map of Zambia, Brian reckoned they had travelled forty to fifty miles across scrub bush. They must, he reasoned, have had to abandon their own vehicle somewhere near Musoro: perhaps, he thought, they were hoping to be picked up by air at the strip at Delkin – if it was still in operation.

The Range Rover and equipment across the river, Brian and Nchembe were walked to the inflatable, helped into it and transported to the far bank. The dingy was then deflated and stored in the vehicle. Brian and Nchembe were bundled into the rear with the equipment. It was a tight squeeze.

'How's the fuel?' enquired the officer.

'About three quarters, sir.'

'Good! We'll need a bit more though, so we'll stop a car on the main eastern road.' He turned, leaning his arm on the rear of the front seat. 'You got any spare fuel?'

'No,' Brian told him, glad he had taken Macklor's advice to lighten the load, removing the jerry cans, 'none.'

The officer shrugged.

'Och! Let's move out then.'

One of the soldiers started the Range Rover and they struck off through the bush arriving, after a few miles, at a disused road where the party stopped as the officer studied a map.

'This is it,' he declared. 'Fifty-five or sixty miles to Sinda. Should make it at about midnight. Couple of villages on the way but they'll be no problem. Go as fast as you can so long as it's light.' He lowered his head to look at the sky. The sun was already well down towards the horizon, behind the trees. 'Won't be long to nightfall.'

They drove at the best possible speed. Brian and Nchembe were shaken and knocked against the sides of the boot and each other. As night fell, the driver reduced his speed but not substantially. When they encountered the few villages or native subsistence farms along the ungraded road, the driver beeped the horn and waved cheerily to the shadowy people gathered around the fires; soon it was too late for villagers to be out of doors.

Not long after midnight, they reached a road over which a grader had been drawn, smoothing the surface somewhat. Driving by compass at any junctions they came to, they arrived at the main tarmac road down which Brian and Nchembe had driven a few days previously.

'The last chance of any fuel,' the officer announced as they pulled up at the edge of the road.

The moonlight was bright and illuminated the strip of metalling in either direction.

'According to intelligence,' he went on, standing by the passenger's door, 'the nearest pumps are at Petauke to the west and Katete to the east. We can't make for one of them. We'll need to stop a few cars. In the morning ... Get this off the road. Pieter, do a recce. See we're not near any villages or pathways. Everyone else get the vehicle camouflaged. You two,' he grabbed Brian's lapel and heaved him to the tailgate, 'out! I'm going to untie you one at a time so you can have a piss. Then it's under the car.'

Brian stroked his wrists and rubbed the circulation into his forearms. He relieved himself and had his hands re-tied in front of him; he and Nchembe were then pushed under the chassis.

The South Africans soon fell asleep except for the wounded soldier who kept first watch. He did not sit still but wandered about, listening to the night sounds of the bush. As soon as he was out of earshot, Brian and Nchembe carried out a whispered conversation, their heads twisted, their lips touching each other's ears.

'Will they let us go?' Nchembe wondered. 'They've no reason.'

'I doubt it. But they might, though.' Brian's emotions wavered from extreme optimism to the depths of pessimism. 'I'm white which might count for something. But you're black. And if they get to know ...'

The sentry returned, the thread of conversation was severed. When he had gone, Brian spoke again.

'We can't escape. That's for sure.'

Nchembe agreed, nodding his head in the darkness under the rear differential.

'The border's not far. Twenty miles, if that. They must intend to go a long way if they need a full tank.'

Again, Nchembe nodded.

At first light, Brian and Nchembe were gagged. The South Africans then left them and the vehicle in the charge of the wounded man and disappeared. Several vehicles raced by on the road a hundred yards away: from the sound of their motors, they were diesel lorries but, half an hour later, the six commandos returned in a much battered Peugeot 309 which they drove across the grass to where the Range Rover was disguised as a thorn bush.

'Syphon out the tank! Be quick about it!'

Brian noticed there were bloodstains on the bonnet, smears of blood on the driver's door.

'Any jerries in the back?'

A soldier jemmied the boot open with a tyre lever from the tool box in the Range Rover.

'Two, sir.' He tested their weight. 'Both full. Fifty litres each, sir.'

'Good. That should do us.'

The officer approached Brian and Nchembe, but ignored the latter as he spoke, keeping his voice low.

'Listen to me. We are going to drive from here to the border. When we get there, we'll let you go. I'm not in the fight to kill a fellow white. We've got to stick together or we'll be overrun by bloody niggers. If you don't see it that way – well, you will, in time.'

'What about him?' Brian tossed his head in Nchembe's direction.

'I won't kill your kaffir friend, either. Not this time.' He grinned. 'Next time, maybe. Anyhow, him aside, we still have a problem. We shall need a good twelve hours clear before you reach a telephone. So when we let you go, it will be in the bush and you'll still be tied. And we'll be tying your feet together. Not so you can't walk, but so you can't run. You'll be ten miles from the nearest village and it'll take you some hours to get there on a bush track. Evening, probably. That's plenty of time for us.'

One of the soldiers reported in a low voice, 'Fuel's done, sir.'

'Get these two into the back. Take their gags off. They know what'll happen if ...' He left the threat unspoken.

The officer drove while the soldier named Jan read the map. They skirted Sinda and the nearby settlement of Chassa. Ten miles further on, they similarly avoided Nyanje, going slowly through the bush, again driving by the compass. It was slow going and the interior of the Range Rover was baking hot. Grasshoppers and tsetse flies came in: the two captives were at the mercy of the flies, unable to swat them off. Brian was bitten painfully twice on his arms, Nchembe once on his ankle.

'Border's about three miles, sir,' the map-reader warned after they had regained the road beyond Nyanje. 'Intelligence was a bit sketchy about the military here.'

'We'll stop just now and scout ahead,' the officer announced and, half a mile further on, put the Range Rover behind a hillock of boulders overgrown with bushes.

'Three of you,' he pointed to the chosen trio, 'see what it's like. Don't engage the enemy. Just report back. Watch out for telephone lines. See if they have radios.'

When they had departed, the officer helped Brian over the tailgate. Nchembe he left in the vehicle.

'Have some water.'

He held a water bottle to Brian's lips. Most of the liquid dribbled down his chin.

'Could you untie me?' he requested. 'Tie my feet as you intend, if you like. I can't drink like this and it's wasting it.'

The officer acceded to Brian's request, releasing his hands and tightly binding his feet.

Taking the canteen, Brian thankfully drank from it. His throat was sore and dry. As he quenched his thirst and swilled out his mouth, the officer ignored him, sitting next to his wounded commando who was crouching against a boulder nursing his head with his unbandaged hand.

'How are you feeling?'

'A bit groggy, sir. It'll wear off. It's the driving ...'

'Do you mind if I give him some water?' Brian enquired.

424

'Who? The kaffir?' The officer glanced with unbridled disgust at Nchembe. 'Yes, all right. But not out of the water bottle. I don't want his thick kaffir lips touching it. Use your hands.'

'I've got a tin mug in the glove compartment,' Brian said. He had, he recalled on the spur of the moment, put the mugs there after drinking the beer the day before; it seemed weeks had passed since their Henley-on-the-Luangwa lunch.

'Very well. Get it.'

With difficulty, Brian hopped to the front of the Range Rover, rummaged for a mug, filled it and held it to Nchembe's lips.

'Thank you,' Nchembe muttered; then he glanced quickly around him.

The officer and the wounded man were by the boulder fifteen feet away. The other two commandos were out of sight, keeping watch on the road.

'In the seam of my jacket, Brian,' Nchembe hissed.

'What?'

'In my jacket. Under the right pocket. Feel there.'

Brian did as he was asked. There was something of unrecognizable shape tucked behind the folded seam.

'I have it,' he murmured.

'Take it out.'

It was a strangely shaped object the like of which Brian had never seen. It was about four inches long and shaped like a winged sycamore seed. Made of plastic, one end was flattened like a seed propeller and the other fatter, like the kernel. In the middle was a small aluminium disc. The whole thing was dirt brown in colour and could not weigh more than a few ounces.

'Hold it so I can touch it,' Nchembe whispered urgently. 'Quickly!' As soon as his fingers felt it, they twisted the disc. 'Put it under the passenger seat. Jam it between the seat frame and the floor. Anywhere it will get pressure put on it.'

'What is it?'

Brian refilled the mug to play for time but the officer was not paying him any attention.

'My last resort. Anti-personnel mine.'

Brian's face went white.

'Where did you get it?'

'Russians.' Nchembe winked, a momentary grin on his face. 'Now do it. Carefully . . .'

Brian returned the mug to the glove compartment, surveying all the while for a spot to plant the tiny mine.

The rear of the front seat tipped forward with the release of a black lever. It was not secured. Pushing the seat-back slightly forward, Brian saw behind the lever a silver metal hook which clamped on to the seat frame. Where the hook met a retaining bracket, he wedged the mine, cautiously resting the seat-back down on it.

This, he thought, was working for Africa. And it was easy. It seemed such a little thing. Without compromise, without an ulterior motive, without question, he was making a decision, taking an action which was so small and yet would have such far-reaching consequences. It took him two seconds yet it would make headlines in the newspapers. There would be a photo of the wrecked Range Rover and his body and Nchembe's body. An explosion here would probably set the bush alight, as well.

He was accepting Nchembe's premise that violence can only be met with violence, fire with fire: where there are no words, he thought, there must be fists. Africa can only be free with the blood of its people and he, like Nchembe, was one of them.

The irony did not evade him. He was, by deed as well as implication, a terrorist now. He was one of the feared, one of the dreaded international brotherhood. Like the Mau Mau had been. He was, he suddenly realised, actually fighting alongside a Mau Mau terrorist, and for essentially the same cause. He was no better than a skulking murderer, with a bomb instead of a *panga*, but he did not see it in such a light. He was a fighter for freedom and it was good.

It was only then, in the cold consideration of what he was doing, that Brian realised he was going to die. And, like any man who expects death, can almost time its arrival, can say with reasonable certainty that, in one hour – two at the outside – he will no longer be alive, he set about planning to avoid the inevitable.

'Here is your canteen.'

He returned the water bottle to its owner.

'You had your drink?' The officer didn't wait for an answer but accepted it and tossed it through the window on to the rear seat. 'The last you'll get from us.'

'Do you mind if we sit in the shade of that bush? It's unbearable in there.'

'Very well. You get your friend,' there was a hint of sarcasm in the officer's voice, 'out. I'll tie his feet and release his arm. Okay?'

'Thank you.'

Brian helped Nchembe out of the Range Rover and they sat in the shadow of a kaonga thicket, brushing the spiny twigs out from under them with a stick.

For an hour, they rested in the shade. Brian tried to force himself to sleep. He was tired, his every muscle aching: lying on the ground was a luxury, yet he could not even nap. Nchembe had closed his eyes but his hand, occasionally swatting a fly or ant, indicated he too was wide awake.

One of the two soldiers on sentry duty returned from his look-out on the boulder-strewn slope. He moved with the agility of an animal, not dislodging one stone.

'Patrol returning, sir.'

'Anything else?'

'No, sir. Not a sign.'

The scouting party appeared and the soldiers sat in a group around their wounded comrade who seemed to perk up at their arrival.

Brian strained his ears to catch their conversation.

'The border's about two miles off and the road ends there,' the corporal reported. 'There's no army post or any sign of troops but we think the road's maybe been mined.'

'What gave you that impression?'

'The surface is smoother. Just for a distance. And someone has cut down the bushes on either side. There are no tyre tracks either. No vehicles use this road.'

'How recently was the bush cut?'

'Not too lately. Six months ago, perhaps.'

'Any chance of a diversion?'

'It's possible, sir ...'

When the officer had considered the situation, he made his announcement. He spoke loudly so Brian and Nchembe could hear, too.

'We'll move out in an hour. Rest until then. Assess the chance of a minefield when we get there. You two,' he looked at the captives, 'will stay here. When we go, you get freed. You won't be likely to make it to the nearest settlement by dark so maybe you've a night in the bush. I reckon it won't do you any harm. Pieter, get some oil from the vehicle and smear the knots in their ropes. Really tighten them first. Soak it in well. We don't want them untying them.'

From the front of the Range Rover, one of the soldiers called to the officer who strolled around the vehicle.

'Have you seen this, sir?'

The officer bent and studied the metal of the wheel-arch.

'Now I wonder how that got there ...'

He pushed the first joint of his index finger into the bullet hole.

'I remember, sir, as we were getting away from the attack, the boys in the second truck had their fire diverted to a target at about nine o'clock to the road. It looked, now I come to think of it, sir, a lot like this ...'

Rubbing his stubble, the officer walked over to the two prisoners.

'You!' He kicked the sole of Brian's foot.

Brian, pretending to be asleep, pretended to wake up: but he had heard.

'Yes?' he murmured like a man being aroused from a deep sleep.

'What's your name?'

Brian made no answer. He continued to feign semi-consciousness.

The officer bent over him and felt the breast pockets of his jacket. Discovering something hard in one, he unbuttoned the flap and removed Brian's passport. He opened it.

'We've got a pongo here,' he remarked. He peered at the name written in the top window of the cover but the ink had faded almost to invisibility. 'N 544398 C', he read from the lower window then opened the passport. ' "Her Britannic Majesty's Principal Secretary of State for Foreign and Commonwealth Affairs Requests ..." – all printed with capital letters. "Name of bearer ..." '

He stopped, turned the page, studied the photograph without comparing it to Brian's face, thumbed over more of the pages and let the array of green, red, blue and black visas and stamps flick by.

'Well, Mr Brian Titchner ...'

Brian sat up.

The officer felt inside his own tunic pockets and produced a military identity pass. He tossed it to Brian who caught it.

It contained a photograph of the officer, his service number, name and rank; Brian read, 'Stadden. R.P.; Major.'

For a moment, Brian's pulse halted, his nerves quivering involuntarily, the hairs of his neck rising like hackles. In the shocked silent void within his head he saw a bare, black shoulder shiny with fresh blood, heard the snapping and crashing of the burning hut's roof-timbers and the injured interrogatee's gabbling voice saying, 'Jan. Peat. Jan. Peat. Sta din. Sta din.'

'It's been a very long time,' Stadden said quietly, 'but I knew it would come. Get him on his feet!' he ordered through clenched teeth.

The corporal, perplexed by this sudden turn of events, pulled the prisoner upright.

Brian looked hard at the major. His prominent forehead was not as bulging as Brian remembered it but, adding on thirty years of life and change to the image in his memory, he could now see before him Rudi Stadden.

'Let me tell you lads a cautionary tale,' Stadden began, looking from one of his soldiers to the other. 'Once upon a time, there was a white boy who thought he was better than his fellows. He thought he was clever, educated. Nobody liked him, but they put up with him because he was one of them. He was white. Then, one day, he turned against his fellows and befriended their enemy. He was still white but he mixed with blacks and soon he became a white kaffir. When he was accused of his treachery, he ignored his accusers and

429

when they tried to teach him a lesson, he ran. And I expect he's been running ever since. Until now.'

The younger soldiers exchanged puzzled glances.

'You have before you, gentlemen, a white kaffir. Not just a white man who lives in Zambia but a white kaffir. And I will tell you how I know – because I went to school in Nairobi and this white kaffir was a pupil there with me. We've known each other from way back, haven't we?' He made a sudden movement at Brian who instinctively flinched. 'See! He's scared shitless. And something else has just occurred to me.' He grinned, showing yellowed teeth unbrushed for days, and commanded, 'Get that black kaffir up!'

Nchembe was manhandled to his feet and pushed to Brian's side.

'By incredibly good luck, gentlemen, we have not only the white kaffir but the black kaffir whom he befriended. And how do I know for sure? Because he only had one arm. Can't be too many crippled kaffirs like that. What's more, he's not just any kaffir. He's one of the big boys from the ANC.'

He paused to let the fact sink in and Brian, as plainly as if the intervening years did not exist, heard Stadden's phrase again: he could see the cross-country runners passing by and Stadden saying – 'This crippled kaffir of yours ...'

'How do you know, sir?'

'How do I know, corporal? Intelligence service. I should have seen it from the start but I didn't. This man,' he prodded Nchembe in the chest, 'is a hedgumacated kaffir. He's not a bush bunny. Och, no man! He's a lawyer,' he gave the word a mock dignity, 'hedgumacated at the University of Oxford as well as at a Rusky one. He is a senior ANC man and his name's Doctor Matthew Nchembe.'

He turned as rapidly as a cobra and spat in Nchembe's face. Fine flecks of spittle spattered the African's cheek.

'You're Matthew Nchembe,' he wagged his finger in his prisoner's face then redirected his attention at Brian, 'and you're Brian Titchner, the white kaffir. Also hedgumacated at Oxford. We've got ourselves two professors here.'

He moved away then, as if to spit again, he spun round but

430

instead struck Brian across the side of his head with his fist. Brian tasted the gush of blood in his mouth.

'No need to oil the knots, Pieter. They're not walking anywhere. Tie their hands again.'

Brian and Nchembe were tightly bound and thrust back against the kaonga bush. The wounded soldier was set guard over them while the others made ready to leave. All the while they were repacking equipment and stowing it, Stadden whipped up animosity amongst his men, directed at the captives.

'Bloody traitors to their race,' he was saying, and, 'Nothing worse than a white kaffir ... deserve all they get ... ought to be dosed with AIDS like the black bastards: it was a monkey's disease in the first place ... ought to be castrated ... imagine a white man shagging a kaffir woman or, worse, a black screwing a white woman – that's what all this anti-apartheid crap is heading towards ...'

Skilfully, with a psychological manipulation both Brian and Nchembe watched with mounting alarm and fascination, Stadden prepared his men for the cold-blooded killing of a white man. The African they'd kill without thinking twice about it but a white was different, even if he was a liberal, an enemy of the state.

At last, the equipment inside the Range Rover was re-arranged for maximum space.

'If you survive,' Nchembe said in quiet voice, 'tell my people of this.'

'I shall,' Brian assured him.

'I mean, tell them of the names, of this escape route. Let the press know.'

'A last few words, eh, white kaffir?'

Stadden had come across to them without their noticing. As he had before, he made to strike, but this time Brian did not flinch: he had sworn to himself that he would not. Not a second time.

'Getting brave, eh? We'll soon see.'

'You don't really think this will work, do you?' Brian's voice was flat and soft.

'Sure. We're as good as in Pretoria.'

'So there is a covert agreement between you and the Mozambique government?' Nchembe hinted.

'I don't know about that,' Stadden answered. 'I'm not a politician.'

'You are very confident of getting back across a hostile Africa. The blacks will have your guts if they catch you,' Brian commented, making his statement deliberately provoking.

'They won't. We give the rebel kaffirs a hand so they'll look after us.'

The corporal, who had come to stand next to his major, said, 'We're not going through Mozambique. We're going round it.'

'Tell them, corporal.'

'Down to the Zambezi, then down to the coast. We'll get picked up there. Two hundred and fifty miles of river. No sweat!'

'Why didn't you go down the Luangwa in your dingy?' Brian asked. 'It would have been a lot easier.'

'And go under that guarded bridge? Along the border for fifty miles? Guard posts everywhere? Not a bloody chance. This way's the best route. It's only a fall-back, anyway.'

'So your attack was a failure,' Nchembe suggested.

Stadden glared at Nchembe and growled, 'How many of your black bastards were killed, eh?'

'None,' Nchembe answered. 'You killed some Zambians who happened to live there, unaffiliated to us, but you didn't hit a single A N C member. How many of your men died?'

With deliberate slowness, Stadden positioned himself and kicked Nchembe in the kidneys. Like his fellow prisoner, he did not flinch, just bent under the force of the blow.

'We're ready, sir.'

'Good!' Stadden faced the two prisoners. 'Now it's your turn, kaffirs. Are you ready to die?'

Neither Brian nor Nchembe replied but they exchanged brief looks.

'I've a surprise for you. You're not going to. Yet, anyway. Doctor Matthew Nchembe, lawyer and Number Two kaffir in the A N C, is coming with us. He'll make a fine parade in

432

Pretoria. What the politicians will call a propaganda coup. A real live saboteur. A real nice present for Mr Terre Blanche. Maybe they'll throw you in the next cell to Mandela.' He looked at one of his men, 'Reserve this kaffir a room on Robben Island, Pieter,' then back to Nchembe. 'You can tell him all about your struggle – and how it's still a struggle, eh?'

The corporal helped the wounded soldier over to the vehicle and returned. The others followed, gathering round.

'Undo their hands.'

One of the soldiers cut the ropes around their wrists.

'Now, white kaffir, your time has arrived to be like your black monkey chum here. Grab him!'

Two of the soldiers jumped on Brian, but he made no attempt to resist.

'Hold his left arm out.'

Before they could obey the order, Brian raised his arm in front of him, holding it there as would a man feeling his way in the dark.

Stadden pulled his pistol from its holster.

'You call my people barbaric!' Nchembe shouted.

With the barrel, Stadden struck Nchembe on the neck. The blow knocked him off balance. Two of the soldiers grabbed him.

'Remember our last day at school, Titchner?'

Brian had nothing to lose now.

'Yes, I remember it. It was the day I last beat the shit out of you. And I've been running,' he cast a meaningful glance from one soldier to the next, 'ever since.'

Stadden ignored the taunt.

'I can't change the colour of your skin, Titchner, but I can make you like your nigger friend.'

He pressed the barrel of his automatic pistol into the crook of Brian's elbow and pulled the trigger. Brian's legs collapsed but the soldiers held him up. His forearm was loose, streaming with blood.

'One more. Hold his arm out.'

The corporal obeyed. Stadden put the muzzle of his pistol to the elbow and fired again. The chipped end of the bones showed ragged through the remnants of flesh. Nchembe turned his face away as Brian passed out.

'*Vir vryheid en vir reg*,' Stadden remarked then ordered, 'Now get the first-aid box.'

With a length of gauze bandage and a thick wad of cotton-wool, Stadden crudely dressed the smashed elbow, tying a tight tourniquet around the bicep. Already, Brian's hand and forearm were pale and blue-ish. With a length of wood cut from a nearby shrub, the South African fashioned a crude splint and lashed Brian's arm to it.

'Take him to the track and leave him facing the way back. If he makes it, he's lucky.'

As Brian was carried between the corporal and one of the others, he regained consciousness. His arm ached but curiously did not hurt. He looked down at it as if it were another entity, surprised to find it heavily bandaged. His legs were still weak and, on reaching the road, the soldiers tried to make him stand but he could not. They sat him on the ground, his useless hand trailing in the dust and, while one held him up, the other rolled a log out from under a clump of bushes. He picked it up and dropped it several times to dislodge the termites which had built their mud-roofed tunnels on the wood, then both men propped Brian against it.

'That's the way to Nyanje. About five miles.'

They left him then and, a few minutes later, Brian heard the Range Rover start up and move towards him. He struggled to get a look over his shoulder, his shattered arm trailing uselessly over his body.

As the vehicle broke from the cover, Brian could see Nchembe's face through the open window. He was smiling. The driver halted. Stadden walked over to Brian.

'Have a good stroll, Titchner. If you don't get going soon, the vultures'll have you.'

He pointed overhead. High on a thermal one bird was spiralling, two thousand feet up.

Brian thought then, through the haze of the dull ache, of the mine under the seat frame.

'You'll not make it,' he prophesied, his voice so weak it was barely audible.

Stadden smirked, nudging Brian with his foot much as he would the corpse of an animal run over in the road. He said nothing and, stepping over the log, returned to the Range Rover.

Brian craned his neck. Nchembe nodded just once to him.

Brian scrabbled with his hand to get a purchase on the log. He had to stand. Instead, he slipped lower, his head jerking back and his neck punching the hard, dead wood.

The vulture had been joined by another. Both were circling inexorably in clockwise circles.

Stadden climbed in to the front passenger seat and sat back heavily.

From behind Brian came a roar. It sounded like a jet aircraft approaching fast and low, the sound building to a crescendo. It did not fade, however, but stopped abruptly. A warm wind washed over him and he was peppered with grit and twigs.

Again, he fought to stand, managed to get into a kneeling position. He shuffled round like a penitent paying masochistic homage.

The Range Rover was fiercely burning. Dark, orange flames licked from the driver's side windows and the tailgate had fallen open. Black, dense smoke billowed out of all the windows. Already, the bushes on either side were alight. The soil under the chassis was flaring with spilt oil and petrol. Stones cracked loudly in the inferno.

As Brian watched, the nearside door opened and two figures fell out. He saw them hit the ground below the door sill. The clothes of one were smouldering, the other's were alright.

Fighting to stay conscious, the skin on his bare knees ripping, Brian moved towards the Range Rover. It took him nearly ten minutes to cover the twenty yards. During that time, several minor explosions occurred in the vehicle but the petrol tank had already ruptured, bursting into flames in the initial blast.

Nchembe was lying on his front thirty feet from the vehicle. His face was raw, his head bent to one side and one of his legs was askew.

Brian summoned all his strength and rolled the African on to his side against some tussocks of grass.

'Get him,' Nchembe whispered through his bloody lips.

Brian could not understand.

'What? Wait!' he exclaimed hoarsely. 'The smoke'll draw attention. They'll see it. Wait! Hang on!'

'Get him,' Nchembe repeated. He rolled his eyes in the direction of the bush.

Some yards off lay Stadden. His body was badly charred, his fingers blackened and crisp, his short hair singed off. Brian made his way to the South African's side.

'Dead?' Nchembe questioned hesitantly when Brian returned.

'Yes.'

'Are you sure?'

Nchembe's words did not falter. He seemed to be gaining strength.

'Yes,' Brian said, and, 'Hold on, Matthew.'

'Good. Africa is free ...'

The African tried to close his eyes but the lids were too badly scorched.

'Keep alive,' Brian begged, touching Nchembe's hand which was remarkably unharmed.

'Brian – the earth is burning.'

Brian wanted to touch Nchembe's face, to stroke him, cool his burns, give him some comfort but he dared not lean forward. Nchembe's skin, where it was visible through the remnants of his jacket and shirt, looked as if it had been japanned.

'No. It's just the oil.'

The African said nothing.

'They'll see the smoke,' Brian repeated. 'Someone'll be here. Soon. Smoke in a border area.'

Nchembe's hand was limp.

'Keep alive,' Brian shouted.

Nchembe's eyes were glazed but his lips moved.

'Brian!' His voice was strong. 'Don't forget. The leopard...'

'What leopard?'

436

Brian's arm jarred with pain as Nchembe fell against it. He screamed. A staccato chatter from the heart of the fire signalled ammunition exploding. Pieces of shrapnel whined off the ground, spat chips of dust over Nchembe's face.

'What leopard?' Brian demanded again. He could feel himself going light-headed.

Nchembe made no reply yet Brian heard him say, from somewhere in the fog gathering in his brain, 'The leopard in the fire.'

25

Brian eased himself up on the lounger and scratched his left toes with his right heel. While he had been dozing, an insect had bitten his foot and the itch was irritating. The tissue under the nail of his big toe was mauve still from the removal, with a red hot needle, of the jiggers he had picked up after his shoes had come off.

The sun was high overhead but he was protected from it by an umbrella made of a new material which was said by its manufacturers to reject the harmful ultra-violet rays while letting the heat and tanning rays through.

From his half-lying position, he looked over his body as if it were a map. The hair on his legs was matting from perspiration and his stomach was slightly flabby from lack of exercise. A thin layer of fat ran along the elasticated waist of his swimming trunks. On his right wrist was a gold Rolex Oyster Perpetual. It was a tight and uncomfortable fit, for his wrist was not used to the heavy watch. On his chest rested two yellowing leopard's teeth attached to a thick, twenty-two carat gold chain.

He lifted the chain, the two teeth dangling in the air. They clicked together as he swung them idly to and fro. He did not drop them but lowered them slowly to his chest. The metal strap of the Rolex snagged in the hair on his chest and he winced.

'Boss!'

Brian moved his head an inch. Tom was trotting across the lawn towards the swimming pool. He was carrying a portable telephone, pulling out the aerial as he went.

'Who is it?'

'They not give a name,' Tom shrugged.

The houseboy pressed the receive button and handed the instrument to his employer. Brian sat up fully, pleased he could do this without the use of his arm: his stomach might be flabby but the muscles were toning up again.

'Hello,' he said into the mouthpiece. 'Titchner here.'

From the telephone he heard a raucous trumpet followed by two sung lines of music, and he recognized the musician as Hugh Masekela, the jazzman banned from his native South Africa:

Bring back Nelson Mandela, bring him back home to Soweto.
I want to see him walking down the streets of South Africa – tomorrow!

The telephone went dead and Brian hung up, putting the receiver on its back and pressing the receive switch to the off position.

'Thank you, Tom.' He held out the instrument. 'One more for lunch today. I think we'll eat out here by the pool. Is that all right?'

'Yes, boss.'

'The gardening boy can help you serve again. I think we'll make a good house-servant of him yet – you and I between us.'

Tom gave a broad grin.

Brian swung his legs over the side of the lounger. The water in the pool was blue and inviting. He balanced on the extremity of the short diving-board at the deep end, his toes over the edge, and raised his arms. Then he lowered the remains of his left arm to his side once more. He was still not used to diving with only one hand over his head.

He remembered how, at the hospital in Bonn where he had gone for specialist physiotherapy, the nurses had laughed with him at his first attempts to dive.

'Sere's no need to raise ze arms. You must learn, Herr Titchner, to dive into ze vater vis just your head.'

Brian's answer had been one of the turning points of his healing, not so much a physical watershed as a mental one.

'The hell with that!' he had retorted. 'I'm only one half of an arm short and normal apart from that. I'll dive as I bloody well like!'

The nurses had giggled, ribbing him for being a stubborn

Englishman, but they were well pleased at this development and the doctor was delighted when he was informed.

The insects in the eucalyptus trees were silent in the heat of the day. Beside the shallow end of the pool, the young gardener, a lad in his early twenties now proudly dressed in a white apron, was laying the table under the awning.

Brian dived, his body barely splashing the surface, the warm water soothing him as he went under.

By the time Jim Hannington arrived, driving the Mercedes Benz 300E, Brian had put on a short-sleeved shirt and a pair of khaki shorts over his swimming trunks. From the left sleeve of his shirt protruded the upper part of his arm, the stub end neatly rounded off with skin grafts which were now losing their pinkish ugliness and beginning to tan.

'How's my new Merc?' he greeted the visitor.

'Coming along. They'll have it done inside a week now. The parts came out yesterday on the QZ flight from Frankfurt.' Hannington sat on the second of the three loungers. 'Always fancied one of those two-seater open Mercs myself. Want to swap?'

'Not a chance!' Brian pointed with the stump of his arm to the drinks trolley. 'Fix your own. There's a bottle of tequila there – and salt and lemon.' He returned to the subject of the cars. 'Besides, the 300E's your company car now. Entered in the books. Can't readjust it without having it added as an asset ...'

Hannington crossed to the trolley, mixed himself a Margarita and stood on the edge of the twilight afforded by the umbrella. He flicked the plastic frill with his finger.

'This any good?'

'Could be. I'm tanning under it. Even the grafts are doing well. The ones on my back are hardly visible so there must be something to it.'

'Practicality?'

'Maybe. I've ordered a roll of the stuff and we'll try it out at the facility.' Brian raised his own glass. 'We'll have the best-tanned mealies in central Africa.'

Hannington sat down again. From the direction of the

servants' quarters came the incongruous and unlikely sound of a choir singing Christmas carols.

'Two weeks to the festive season,' Hannington remarked. 'Going home for it?'

'No. Staying here.'

'Rosy said for me to tell you you were welcome to spend Christmas with us. We're going to the Maldives and on to Hong Kong. Be a pleasant break for you.' He winked and shook his glass. 'Rosy's widowed younger sister's coming along: only thirty-eight, poor girl, and pretty as my share of her family.'

'No, thanks.' Brian smiled to show his appreciation of the gesture. 'And don't think I'm being self-pitying and morbid. But I've got to see something through here.' He paused. 'Tell you what! Seeing you're desperate to see me hitched to this damned sister-in-law of yours, I'll come on and meet you in Hong Kong. New Year's Day. Agreed?'

The sound of a car on the driveway was accompanied by a cloud of dust drifting over the lawn.

'Expecting guests?'

'One other,' Brian replied. 'You know who ...'

'Just as well we're ready,' Hannington observed.

Around the corner of the house appeared Miss Nkana. She was smartly dressed in a tight skirt and flower-printed blouse; she was carrying her briefcase.

'Juliet! There you are! Good morning.'

Brian got to his feet, followed by Hannington.

'Hello, Brian. Jim.' She nodded pleasantly to them. 'And before you ask, I'll have an American, please.'

'I suppose it's foolish to ask you if you've had a good journey as we've no idea where you've come from. And is there really a need to play code records over the phone?'

'Certainly,' she answered, her face serious. 'The South Africans will be watching you. Even here.' She took her drink. 'Cheers! Here's to the meeting in Dakar. May we finally find common ground with the liberal whites. It's a start, anyway.'

'Is that where you've just come from?'

'Perhaps!' She tossed her head coquettishly.

They fell silent. The low hills beyond the link fence shimmered in the heat.

'Shall we go up the back before lunch?' Brian suggested.

'Business before pleasure!' Hannington exclaimed, putting his now empty glass on the paving stones of the pool surround.

Walking in the glaring sunlight soon made them hotter but it was only a few hundred yards to the new storage sheds, glistening silver in the sunlight, almost too bright to look at. At the door to the biggest of the five sheds stood an African watchman armed with a shotgun.

From a pocket in his shorts, Brian produced a cruciform key and inserted it in the lock. Hannington did likewise with a similar key in an identical lock. The keys were twisted, and Brian punched a six-figure code into a security system.

Inside the shed it was cool. A large fan, set high in the roof, circulated the air and blowers sucked unseen in the walls.

'There you are, Juliet,' Brian said. 'Compliments of Afriground.'

The Deutz-Fahr tractors were parked side by side. The main bodywork on each was painted in the standard brilliant green of the German manufacturer. The cabs were painted standard black and the wide windows were tinted. The mudguards, however, had been oversprayed in bright yellow.

Juliet Nkana looked from the brochure she was holding to the nearest tractor and back again.

'The originals don't have yellow on them,' she commented. 'You have ...'

'It seemed a little thing to do,' Brian interrupted her. 'They're already in the other A N C colours.'

'We ordered six.' She cast a quick glance around the shed. 'There are only four here.'

'I've bought eight,' Brian said. 'And, before you ask, the other equipment you required is in those crates. For these four.'

'I was under the impression these were to be delivered direct to our farm.'

'Four are there already, with the add-ons,' Brian confirmed. 'We've brought these four here for a publicity event.'

442

'On Christmas Eve,' Hannington explained, 'we are going to have a big promotion. It will mention Afriground is making this donation – the first of a number – to the cause of the African National Congress, to further inter-racial harmony, to increase the well-being of Africa and as a direct show of our disgust at the South African government's flouting of international boundaries and other countries' sovereignty. We've put our P R people in London on to it and it's going to get wide, international media cover. Hopefully, it'll lead to more, similar donations.'

Walking to the nearest of the DX6.30s, Juliet Nkana put her hand on the huge front tyre. It was still shiny black from the factory.

'Soon, this will be biting into the scorched earth of Africa ...'

In the stillness of the shed, broken only by the wheeze of the ventilators and the gentle swish of the fan, Brian heard Matthew Nchembe's voice whispering in his memory, as if coming from the very coolness of the air, 'Brian, the earth is burning ...'

When Juliet Nkana turned away from the tractor, her eyes were moist with tears.

'There is something else,' Brian said, his voice quiet with emotion.

He took her hand in his and they walked to the back of the shed, past the tractors and the wooden boxes of supplementary fittings. Hannington followed.

In a corner of the shed, farthest from the door, stood three more crates. They were stencilled 'Machine Parts. Manfd U S A.' Below the black writing, soaked into the wood, were stapled customs papers and waybills in polythene wrappers.

One of the crates had been opened. Brian thrust the lid aside and reached in, removing a small wooden box the size of a lady's dressing-table jewel-case. Balancing it on the rim of the crate, he fingered the catches aside and, from the wrapping of greaseproof paper and oiled cotton waste, lifted a Walther PP 7.65 mm automatic.

Outside the shed again, Brian walked behind Hannington and Juliet Nkana. In the distance, the low hills were blue in the harsh sunlight. A lorry, crowded with people, sped along Leopards Hill Road.

In the eucalyptus trees, a red-eyed turtle dove was making its characteristic song, a melodious *coo-cook-kuk-coo* sound. Like women carrying loads on their heads or men pedalling their cycles with their heels, like the smell of the bush in the dry season, the sawing of crickets and the vastness of a dawn sky, the bird's song was, to Brian, an intrinsic part of Africa.

And underfoot, the red earth was parched and hot.